Adopted by
Leah McCool

The
Library

PETTICOAT DETECTIVE

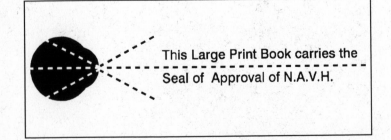

This Large Print Book carries the
Seal of Approval of N.A.V.H.

PETTICOAT DETECTIVE

MARGARET BROWNLEY

THORNDIKE PRESS
A part of Gale, Cengage Learning

GALE
CENGAGE Learning·

Farmington Hills, Mich • San Francisco • New York • Waterville, Maine
Meriden, Conn • Mason, Ohio • Chicago

GALE
CENGAGE Learning®

LIBRARY OF CONGRESS CATALOGING-IN-PUBLICATION DATA

Brownley, Margaret.
　　Petticoat detective / by Margaret Brownley. — Large print edition.
　　　　pages ; cm. — (Undercover ladies ; book 1) (Thorndike Press large print Christian mystery)
　　　　ISBN 978-1-4104-7648-7 (hardcover) — ISBN 1-4104-7648-0 (hardcover)
　　　　1. Large type books. I. Title.
　　PS3602.R745P48 2015
　　813'.6—dc23
　　　　　　　　　　　　　　　　　　　　　　　　　　　　　2014043999

Published in 2015 by arrangement with Barbour Publishing, Inc.

Printed in Mexico
1 2 3 4 5 6 7 19 18 17 16 15

For all the good men in my life,
George, Darin Keith, Daniel,
Warren, Danny, and Brian

Jacob awaked out of his sleep,
and he said,
Surely the LORD is in this place;
and I knew it not.
GENESIS 28:16

CHAPTER 1

1883

Goodman, Kansas

"Whoa!"

Former Texas Ranger Tom Colton reined in his horse and stared at the sign hanging from the roof of the two-story brick structure: MISS LILLIAN'S PARLOR HOUSE AND FINE BOOTS. In the faint glow of a full moon the building stood tall, solid, and proper as an old church. Only the red light shimmering in a downstairs window suggested otherwise.

He fingered the letter in his vest pocket. Addressed to his brother Dave and signed simply "Rose," the letter had brought him to this very address searching for answers.

The red light gave him pause. Perhaps coming here had been a mistake, but he'd traveled too far to turn back now. He hesitated for several moments before dismounting. Securing his horse to the hitching post, he stomped up the wooden steps to the porch. *For once, God, let me be wrong about my brother.*

The door opened to his knock, and a stout-figured woman peered at him from a painted face. Designed for a woman half her size, the bright blue gown and exaggerated bustle did her no favors, nor did hair piled on top of her head like frothy red frosting.

Her appearance quelled any doubt as to the nature of the establishment, and his spirits dropped yet another notch. *Dave, oh, Dave . . .*

"Are you going to stand there all night, cowboy? Or are you going to tell me what you want?" Her lilting Southern drawl seemed at odds with her sharp-eyed gaze.

He pulled off his wide-brim hat. "Sorry to bother you, ma'am. Name's Tom, Tom Colton. I came to see Rose."

Her eyes narrowed. "Don't believe I've seen you around these parts."

"I'm new in town."

The woman's gaze traveled the length of his six-foot frame like a worried mother scrutinizing a daughter's suitor. The gun belt sagging from his waist made her hesitate. She then glanced at his gelding tied out front next to one other.

Apparently his horse, Thunder, gave him a good recommendation because the woman stepped aside to let him in.

"Pleased to meet you, Mr. Colton. I'm Miss Lillian."

He wasn't especially pleased to meet *her,* but he gave a polite nod and glanced around the entry. Many were the times he'd stepped into a house of ill repute on official business back in his Ranger days. Even so, he'd never seen anything like this. Men's boots, women's boots, and boots that no rational person should ever have occasion to wear were arranged on every possible surface, from shelves to tables and even the floor. What's more, they were all for sale.

"You want to see Rose, eh?" The proprietor closed and locked the door, her taffeta skirt rustling like autumn leaves. "That'll be five dollars, but you'll have to wait."

He held his hat in his hand and shifted from one foot to the other. "I only want to talk to her."

"Then it'll cost you ten. More if you're a lawman."

He hoped she was simply stating the rules of the house and not making a guess based on appearances. He'd left the Texas Rangers three years ago but still thought like one, and some even said, talked like one — a blessing and curse on both accounts.

"That's a lot of money." He rubbed his chin. Whoever said talk was cheap hadn't met Miss Lillian.

She shrugged. "Jawing is a lot of work."

The woman showed no curiosity as to his business with Rose. If anything, she seemed more interested in his scuffed boots.

Slapping his hat on his head, he pulled his money clip from his vest pocket and peeled away a single bill. "She knew my brother. His name was Dave Colton."

The madam stuffed the banknote into the shiny cloth purse at her waist. If the number of bulges was an indication, the woman had enough greenbacks in her purse to burn a wet barn.

"Sorry, but we don't make allowances for family members. Everyone pays the same."

He raised his eyebrows. "I'm not asking for favors. I just want to ask her about my brother."

She tilted her head, and suspicion bled through her face paint. "Are you sure you're not a lawman?"

"I'm sure."

"Not that it matters, mind you. I run a respectable business here."

He glanced at a purple leather boot. "I can see that, ma'am."

10

"I also insist that my girls protect our guests' privacy. You won't get much information out of Rose." She sniffed. "Or anyone else for that matter."

He rubbed his chin. "I'll keep that in mind."

"See that you do." She lowered her gaze to his feet. "Got yourself some good-sized ant mashers there. Looks like you could use some new leather."

He followed her gaze downward. His dusty boots sure did look out of place on the red floral carpet. "I'm rather partial to the boots I'm wearing, ma'am."

"Partiality killed the cat."

"I'm pretty sure that was curiosity," he said.

She smiled. "So aren't you at least a little curious as to how your foot would feel in one of these?" She picked a brown leather boot off a nearby counter and thrust it into his hands. "It's amazing what a man with a hammer and a mouthful of wood pegs can do," she said. "Had the Southern army worn boots like that, they might have won the war."

"Now there's a thought." He turned the boot over. It had a wide square toe and well-angled heel. He found no fault with the construction; his objection was with the effeminate red rose hand-tooled on the crown. Folks back home in Texas didn't cotton to people walking around duded out like a fancy barbed-wire drummer.

He handed the boot back to her. "If I ever have occasion to go to war, I'll be sure to stop here first."

"You do that, Mr. Colton."

She set the boot upright on a shelf before leading him through the high-ceiling entry-way to the parlor. A log burned in the fireplace, and orange flames lazily climbed the chimney. An upright piano commanded one corner of the room, and a hand-printed sign on the instrument read SINGING LES-SONS, ONE FIFTY. He couldn't imagine anyone coming here for singing lessons, but then he wouldn't have thought to come here for footwear, either.

In the opposite corner stood a barber chair and a tray of shaving cream and brushes. A sign listed the cost of a shave and haircut. He pulled his hat down a notch to hide his collar-length hair. He didn't want Miss Lillian coming at him with scissors or razor.

He backed away from the barber chair and almost knocked a crystal ball off a small table in a darkened alcove. Not only was the room heavily furnished with upholstered hassocks, brocaded settees, and all manner of fuss and feathers, it was also booby-trapped.

Miss Lillian watched him set the glass sphere on its wooden stand. "Would you like me to read your fortune while you're waiting? I'll only charge you half price."

He drew his hand away. The woman was a regular jack-of-all-trades. "If it's all the same to you, ma'am, I prefer not to know what the future holds. I like to be surprised."

"Very well." She pointed to a red settee. With a sweep of her gown, she stooped to pick up a black-and-white cat curled on a red upholstered hammock. Stroking the cat as she carried him in her arms, she paused beneath the archway and stared over one bare shoulder. "Be careful, Mr. Colton. I see danger ahead for you."

"There goes my surprise," he said.

Accepting his sales resistance with good grace, she shrugged and left the room.

He sat and a sickly sweet whiff of perfume rose from the faded upholstery. At least Miss Lillian didn't charge him to sit — so far as he knew.

The clock on the marble mantel struck nine. It was a weeknight, which probably accounted for the quiet. He balanced his forearms on his knees and rubbed his hands together. Anxious to finish his business with Rose and return to his hotel room, he waited with growing impatience.

The crystal ball seemed to stare at him like a large, unblinking eye. Good thing he didn't believe in fortune-telling. Didn't worry much about danger, either.

Okay, maybe a little . . .

Someone was coming up the stairs.

Jennifer Layne, working undercover as Amy Gardner, glanced frantically at the row of closed doors and darted through the nearest one. She was in luck; the room was empty. Hands clutched to her chest to still her pounding heart, she pressed her back against the door, or at least as much as her bustle allowed. *God, what did I get myself into this time?*

Squeezing her eyes shut, she waited, praying that the person in the hall wasn't a john. The sound of a floorboard signaled someone outside the door. She held her breath until the footsteps faded away. Her shoulders slumped, and her breath escaped in a single gasp of relief. That was close. *Too* close.

She strained her ears. A man's laughter sounded from one of the other rooms, but otherwise all was quiet. For now.

She moved away from the door. Catching

sight of herself in the gilded framed mirror, her mouth dropped open. Frowning, she stuck out her tongue. It was her, all right, but with all that face paint it was hard to tell.

Turning, she viewed herself from all angles. *Ugh!* She looked worse than she'd thought. Her bustle forced the skirt almost horizontal from the waist. Sideways, she looked like the front part of a horse, but it was the top of her dress that caused the most alarm. Covering her exposed neckline with crossed hands, she glanced about the room for a shawl, a cape, a newspaper — anything with which to cover herself. Except for a brass bed, upholstered chair, desk, and more mirrors than a carnival, the room offered no help for modesty. She resisted the urge to pull a sheet off the bed and wrap herself in it.

As a Pinkerton operative, she'd worked undercover as a Southern belle, a heartbroken widow, a jilted schoolteacher, and even a secretary (though with terrible typing skills). But never before had she worked in a bordello or had to wear face paint. Her only hope was that she would get what she came for without having to defend her virtue.

She'd arrived at the brothel that afternoon, hoping to convince the proprietress that she was Rose's long-lost cousin. She never had a chance to share her well-rehearsed story. Thinking she was seeking work as a "fancy lady," Miss Lillian took one look at her plain skirt and prudish white shirtwaist and dragged her into the house.

"What do you think I'm running here? A nunnery?" the madam demanded.

Quick to see the advantage of approaching the woman named Rose as a colleague, Jennifer-slash-Amy decided to play along, indeed, considered it fortunate to have fallen into what at the time seemed like the perfect disguise.

She would conduct her business and leave posthaste; at least that was the plan. Not once did she consider what such a pretext would entail until Miss Lillian ordered two women in corsets and bloomers to "make her look decent."

Decent, indeed! Her boss, Mr. Pinkerton, should see her now. On second thought, no he shouldn't! She prayed that no man would.

Wringing her hands, she paced the floor. The horrid corset felt like steel around her middle, and she could hardly manage an honest breath. *Think, think.* She was almost certain the room directly across from this one was Rose's. She would simply knock on the door. With a little luck, Rose would be alone and, if all went as planned, tell what she knew.

She could do this, had to do it. After botching her last assignment, she couldn't afford another failure. The Pinkerton National Detective Agency wouldn't stand for it. Mr. William Pinkerton, head of the western division, had been very clear on that account.

This time she would get it right if it killed her. After months of investigation, the trail to one of the most notorious criminals in the West led to this establishment. Guilty of fraud, theft, and murder, the Gunnysack Bandit had a hefty price on his head. He also had a gift for evading every lawman, bounty hunter, and detective on his trail.

We'll see how good you are at dodging a female *detective, Mr. Gunny.* The thought made her smile. For once her gender worked for and not against her. The room was proof that a female operative could go where angels — and male counterparts — feared to tread.

She lifted a foot onto a trunk and gathered up miles of taffeta fabric to check the derringer holstered to her thigh. The voluptuous skirt would prevent anything resembling a fast draw, but unless she bumped into a persistent male, her chances of needing a weapon were low. Probably. Hopefully.

Certainly, the woman named Rose had no reason to pose a threat. Unless, of course, she was in cahoots with the bandit.

Amy tightened the buckle of her holster attached to a silk-stockinged thigh just as the door flew open. Much to her horror, she found herself face-to-face with a tall, square-jawed man in a wide-brim hat. If his height wasn't bad enough, the determined look on his face was worse. This was a man who wasn't about to take no for an answer.

CHAPTER 2

Tom Colton caught a glance of a shapely leg before the woman named Rose dropped her voluminous skirts. Rounded green eyes met his and her red-rouged lips formed a perfect O followed by an audible gasp.

He closed the door behind him. "I apologize for startling you." He should have knocked, but Miss Lillian told him that Rose was expecting him and to just walk in.

Rose crossed her arms in front, an act that surprised him. How odd that a woman in her profession would worry about bare shoulders. Her attempt at modesty — if that's what it was — couldn't have been more misplaced. No amount of cover could hide her appeal or the intriguing way her gown molded against her slim feminine form.

The scarlet gown would look garish on most women, but it gave Rose's complexion a pearly pink glow. Honey-blond hair cascaded down her back in a riot of ringlets and long dark lashes ringed the eyes staring back at him.

His brother had made more bad choices than could be found on a ruffled shirt, but he knew how to pick his women, that's for certain and sure, at least appearance-wise.

Rose's mouth closed but the dismay in her eyes remained. It didn't seem possible, but the lady looked downright . . . what? Scared? Terrified?

Of him?

He was tall and he was strong and many were the outlaws who had once feared him, but never had he known a woman to feel threatened by his presence. Perhaps she saw a family resemblance. She certainly looked like she saw a ghost. Except the only things he and Dave had in common were the same parents and similar height.

"Howdy-do, ma'am. My name is Tom. Tom Colton."

Not so much as a shadow of recognition flickered across her painted face at mention of his name, but her crossed arms stayed stubbornly in place. Maybe clients were expected to follow a certain protocol.

Having no knowledge of the etiquette that such an establishment required, he clarified.

"I'm Dave Colton's brother."

Still no response.

Considering the amorous tone of her letter to Dave, her lack of emotion struck him as odd. When the silence continued to stretch between them, he looked around. The only chair in the room was piled high with enough feminine under-riggings to make the most jaded man blush. That left only one place to sit.

She followed his gaze to the neatly made bed. "Oh!"

He frowned. She looked like she was having trouble breathing. Hand out, he stepped forward, but she backed away quicker than chain lightning. "Are you all right, ma'am?"

She gave a slow nod as if she couldn't make up her mind whether she was or wasn't. "It's just that I'm not working tonight, Mr. Colton." She looked like she was trying to put up a brave front. "If . . . if you would kindly leave . . . ?"

Not working? His gaze traveled down her shiny taffeta gown before he zeroed in on her red-rouged lips. She could have fooled him. "I'm afraid I can't do that, ma'am."

Her eyes narrowed, and he detected a spark of combat in their sea-green depths. "And why is that?"

"I paid Miss Lillian ten dollars, and I

21

mean to get my money's worth."

Her eyes widened. "There are other women —"

"But you're the one I came to see." The madam had assured him that Rose agreed to talk, if that's what he wanted, so why was she making it so difficult? What kind of game was she playing?

She glanced past him to the closed door as if measuring its distance. "I want you to leave." She dismissed him with a wave of her hand. "Now!"

"Not till you tell me what you know about the Gunnysack Bandit." Surprise crossed her face at mention of the outlaw, followed by a look of curiosity. Ah, now they were getting somewhere.

"I'm waiting," he said.

"I have no knowledge of the man."

An out-and-out lie if he'd ever heard one. Frustration built up inside, and he punched a fist into his palm to relieve it.

She shrank clear back to the mirrored wall. Much to his dismay, he realized how his thoughtless action could be misinterpreted. He began again, this time in a gentler tone.

"Forgive me. I didn't mean to alarm you."

She studied him much as a cat studied a mouse. "You didn't alarm me, Mr. Colton.

Now if you would be so kind as to let yourself out —"

He pulled off his Stetson and raked his fingers through his hair. Things weren't going as he hoped, but he'd come too far to give up. "I'm sorry. I can't do that." He replaced his hat and hung his thumbs from his holster. "Not till you tell me what you know."

The stubbornness on her face matched the hands placed firmly on the deep valley of her neckline. "I know nothing."

He narrowed his eyes. "You do know that my brother is dead."

She looked genuinely confused, or maybe that was an act, too. "I'm sorry about your brother, but —"

"Sorry? That's all you can say?" Anger erupted in him like a blown cork. His brother loved this woman, and she was as cold and heartless as a fish. "I'm not leaving, lady. Not till I get what I paid for."

Fury darkened her face. "I'm warning you, Mr. Colton. If you don't leave, you'll be sorry!"

Was that a threat? He stared at her, but she turned slightly sideways, and, keeping one hand firmly on her chest, she dropped the other hand to her side. Had it not been for the mirror on the wall behind her, he wouldn't have given her strange behavior another thought. But the reflection showed her bunching up the fabric of her skirt. A nervous habit?

He pretended not to notice — until the hem of her skirt raised high enough to reveal his second glimpse of her leg. Suddenly he had trouble recalling his purpose for being there.

He drew his gaze away from the mirror and cleared his throat. One moment she wanted him to leave. Now she was apparently trying to seduce him.

In no mood for such tactics, he decided to show her he meant business. "I'm not leaving until I get what I came for and paid for," he said, his voice gruff. "Now, either we do this civilly or not. Your choice." When she failed to respond he added, "Let me know when you're ready."

For a moment neither spoke, but the lady's skirt kept inching upward. "I'm ready," she replied.

He nodded. "Now we're getting somewhere."

The hem of her skirt fell to the floor, and suddenly he was on the serious side of a double-barrel derringer. Blast it all!

Berating himself for not suspecting she was armed, he drew in his breath. "You better put that toy away before someone gets hurt."

The corners of her mouth tipped upward in a half smile. "Make no mistake, Mr. Colton. I know how to use this gun, and I seldom miss."

It was amazing what a little iron in hand could do to one's self-confidence. All that remained of the reserved, modest woman he found when he walked in the room was the hand still strategically placed on her bodice.

There were perhaps a dozen ways to disarm someone with a gun. If Rose were a man, he wouldn't hesitate to use full force. Disarming a woman was a bit trickier because he didn't want to cause unnecessary harm or discomfort.

Still, he was in no mood to let the woman get the best of him — not when he'd traveled this far and had so much at stake. His mind made up, he stepped forward and grabbed her wrist. Her hand left her chest and caught him on the jaw so hard that his head snapped back.

For such a small package, she packed a good wallop. Still, she was no match for him. Okay, maybe a little.

Clenching her arm tight, he grabbed the barrel of the gun with his other hand. With a flick of his wrist, her derringer fell to the carpet. That alone might take the wind out of most people's sails, but not hers.

She dived for the gun, but he grabbed her around the waist and spun her in his arms. Fighting like a wildcat, she pounded on his chest with her fists.

"Hey! Stop that," he commanded. Never did he see a woman so fired up. "I don't want to hurt you."

A high-pitched scream filled the room. Rose stilled in his arms, and that was when he realized the scream hadn't come from her.

He released her, and in a flash, she scooped up her derringer and darted to the door. Together they ran into the hall where a couple of scantily clad women peered into a room. Nearby, a thin bald man hopped around, trying to put on his trousers. One woman slumped against a wall, sobbing.

Next to her, a comatose Miss Lillian sprawled on the floor like a marlin on a ship's deck. Two women were trying to revive her with smelling salts.

"What's wrong?" a redheaded woman clad in only a petticoat asked.

"It's . . . it's . . . Rose," a dark-skinned woman squeaked out.

Tom stared at her. Rose? Did he hear

right? He pushed past the female residents and into the room on the other side of the hall. A woman in a blue gown lay on the floor. He didn't have to look twice to know she was past saving.

If this was Rose, then who in the name of Sam Hill was the green-eyed beauty with the iron-like fist?

Ignoring the chaos around her, Amy dropped to her knees in full detective mode and studied Rose's body. One thing she'd learned from experience was to pay close attention at crime scenes. Even the most minor details could turn out to be significant in solving a case.

It was clear by the blood in her hair that Rose had been hit over the head. The bloodied candlestick holder on the floor next to the body was apparently the murder weapon.

Earlier, Amy had guessed Rose's age at thirty. Now she realized the woman was much younger, perhaps in her early twenties. How did such a pretty young woman end up in a place like this? How, for that matter, did any of them end up here?

She pushed the thought away and scanned the room from one end to the other. It was a mess. Clothes were strewn all over the floor, and a lamp lay on its side, kerosene dripping onto the carpet. Rose must have put up quite a fight during the last moments of her life.

Amy gave Rose's hands a cursory glance. Other than the wound on her head, no other marks were evident.

Mr. Colton hunkered down on the opposite side of the corpse, his face grim. "Now look what you've done." His low voice was meant for her ears only, along with the accusation in his eyes.

She lifted her chin. What an annoying man. "What *I've* done?"

"Had you told me from the start you weren't Rose —"

"You never asked me," she shot back.

He frowned in cold fury. "You must have known I mistook you for someone else. Now, thanks to you, she's dead."

Holding her gun by her side, she glared at him. "You have your nerve blaming me!"

He leaned over Rose's body, his nose practically in Amy's face. "What do you know about the Gunnysack Bandit?"

She seethed inwardly. The man was probably a bounty hunter or private detective interested in the reward. Amateur sleuths were the bane of professional detectives and always got in the way of an investigation.

"I told you I know nothing," she retorted. "What did you want to talk to Rose about?"

"It's none of your business," he said, his voice curt.

"Any time I'm accused of someone's death, it's my business," she sputtered.

"Excuse me?"

Both their heads swiveled toward the throaty voice.

Miss Lillian was on her feet, but just barely. It took three women to keep her from falling. Even with their help, she leaned back at a ninety degree angle with only the heels of her shoes on the floor. "Would someone please fetch ole Tin Star?" she said in a weak voice.

Amy shot her accuser a fiery glance. "I'm sure Mr. Colton would be happy to fetch the marshal for us." The sooner she got rid of him, the sooner she could concentrate on the crime scene. She also wanted to query the others while their memories were still fresh. Given the appearance of the room, someone must have heard something.

A muscle tightened at Colton's jaw, but he rose. "I'll be back." He made it sound like a threat, but before she could respond, he stomped from the room.

CHAPTER 3

The following morning, Amy slipped quietly down the hall and stopped in front of Rose's room. She tried the brass knob but the door held firm. Having gotten little sleep, she stifled a yawn and tried to decide her next move.

Stolen money from Gunnysack's last holdup had been deposited into Rose's account. Was Rose in cahoots with the bandit or merely an innocent bystander? How Rose fit into the grand scheme of things might never be known, and that sure did put a damper on Amy's investigation. The worst thing that could happen to a detective was for a suspect or witness to turn up dead.

Despite Amy's attempts to examine the crime scene the night before without arousing suspicion, she'd made little headway. The woman named Coral grew suspicious and, after chasing everyone out of Rose's room, stood guard waiting for the marshal.

The name of the guest seen in the hallway was Mr. Pepper, and his only interest had been making his escape. He was more interested in preserving his reputation than in helping solve a crime.

By the time Colton returned to the parlor house with the marshal and doctor in tow, Amy had still not uncovered any useful information. Marshal Flood immediately took over, forcing her to play the part of one of Miss Lillian's good-time girls. She answered the marshal's questions and looked appropriately saddened by Rose's demise. Ignoring Mr. Colton's icy glares was the hard part. The man had his nerve, blaming her for Rose's death.

In due order, the body was removed from the premises, and the marshal, doctor, and Colton departed. Since no one could sleep, Miss Lillian ordered one of her girls to make pots of hot tea.

While the women sat forlornly in the parlor, Amy managed to sneak in a few questions, but the answers were worthless at best. No one heard anything, saw anything, suspected anything.

The person who interested her most was Colton. Was he a bounty hunter? The Gunnysack Bandit was wanted dead or alive. With a ten-thousand-dollar bounty, every criminal chaser in the country was on his trail.

Still, Colton didn't seem to fit the part. The bounty hunters she'd had occasion to meet were rough and tough and often uncouth. Always in transit, they seldom worried about hygiene or appearances, and most sported long, shaggy beards and mustaches — none of which applied to Mr. Colton. Not only was he clean shaven, he looked and smelled like he'd just made friendly with a bathhouse.

So what is your business, Mr. Colton? What did you want with Rose? And what do you know about the Gunnysack Bandit? Somehow she had to find out. Recalling their angry exchange, it wasn't something she relished, but so far Colton was her best bet for information.

Pushing her thoughts aside, she stooped to examine the doorknob. She had never had any luck picking locks, but she could try. Just as she pulled a hairpin from the back of her head, an ear-piercing scream sent chills down her spine.

Reaching in the false pocket of her skirt, she pulled out her gun and darted down the hall. In her haste, she practically stumbled down the stairs. *Oh, God, please, not another body.*

The scream grew louder as her slippers hit the ground floor. Mr. Beavers, the cat, streaked past her as she dashed into the parlor.

She practically fell over the back of an upholstered settee in her haste. Miss Lillian looked up from the piano, curved fingers poised above the ivory keys. Next to her a tall man with a pencil-thin mustache sent a gargling shrill note into the stratosphere before falling silent.

Miss Lillian was the first to speak. "Good heavens, child. What are you doing with that gun?" She looked tired today, and even the thick coat of paint failed to hide her pallor. Amy wasn't the only one who got little or no sleep last night.

Amy hid the weapon behind the folds of her skirt. "I thought I heard a scream."

"A scream?" Miss Lillian's eyes widened. "I didn't hear a scream. Did you, Mr. Studebaker?"

"No ma'am," he said. Considering the high-pitched volume he'd managed moments earlier, his speaking voice sounded surprisingly normal.

"You must be hearing things," Miss Lillian said, turning back to the piano.

Studebaker stared down his long, thin nose at Amy, as if resenting the intrusion and straightened his bow tie. With his patent leather hair and carefully waxed mustache, he bore a striking resemblance to an embezzler she had recently helped put behind bars.

"My mistake," she said, backing up. No sooner had she left the room than a piano chord sounded, followed by what could only be described as a blaring foghorn.

The music abruptly stopped. "Stand up straight and breathe!" Miss Lillian ordered. "Okay, again, one, two, three . . ."

SCREEEEEEEEEEEEEEEEEEEEEEEEEE-EEEEEEECH!

Amy slipped her weapon through her false pocket and into the holster at her thigh. After the unfortunate incident with Mr. Colton the night before, she'd ripped open a seam in her skirt so she could more easily retrieve her weapon. She was still miffed for allowing the man to wrestle the gun from her hand. Something like that would never happen again. Not if she had anything to do about it.

But Mr. Colton wasn't the only reason she was riled. A murder had been committed beneath this very roof, and no one saw anything suspicious. The room was in terrible disarray, yet no one heard a thing. Either someone was lying or . . .

Somehow she had to get into Rose's room. Where did Miss Lillian keep the keys?

The volume of Mr. Studebaker's voice increased, and Amy clapped her hands over her ears and looked up. Prisms of the crystal chandelier rattled like a bunch of old bones. A man caught in a bear trap couldn't sound worse.

That morning over breakfast, Miss Lillian had announced that no "guests" would be allowed for three days out of respect for Rose. Too bad the woman's regard for the deceased didn't extend to singing lessons.

"Breathe, breathe!" Miss Lillian thundered.

SCREEEEEEEEEEEEEEEEEEEEEEEEEEEEEEEEEEEEEEEECH!

Fortunately, the man either ran out of breath or passed out, and blessed silence followed. With a sigh, Amy studied the door leading to Miss Lillian's office. Maybe the key to Rose's room was in there.

"Psst."

Amy whirled about. One of the girls — Coral — stood next to the staircase, motioning to her.

"I want to show you something," she said, her voice hushed. She was a tall, slender woman with a broad nose and full lips. As was the fashion for dark-skinned women, her black hair had been straightened with a hot metal comb and piled on top of her head.

Motioning with her hand, Coral led the way through the dining room and into the kitchen. A cookstove filled one wall and a tall icebox and baker's cabinet another.

Coral reached under the counter and pulled out a Peacemaker.

Amy slapped the barrel of the gun away. "You mustn't point a gun like that!"

Coral pushed her lips out like a petulant child. "You can't kill anyone with an unloaded weapon."

"Tell that to the man who was shot by one." The nonmusical assault began again in the next room, and Amy had to raise her voice to be heard. "Where did you get that?" It was obvious the woman didn't know beans about handling a firearm.

Coral laid the gun on the counter. "From Harry's Gun and Bakery Shoppe."

Amy's eyebrows shot up. *Guns and baked goods?* And she thought a parlor house selling boots was odd. "What do you plan to do with it?"

Coral looked about to burst into tears. "After what happened to Rose . . ." She pulled a white linen handkerchief out of a leg-of-mutton sleeve and dabbed at the

36

corners of her eyes. "A girl's got to protect herself." She tossed her head. "I noticed you had a gun."

Amy couldn't blame Coral for being scared, and she softened her voice. "You'd do better with one like mine." She pulled out her derringer.

Coral made a face. "But that's so small."

"Trust me, it gets the job done, and it's easy to hide." She slipped the weapon back in place. "I suggest you go back to Harry's baked gun store and exchange it for one you can handle."

Coral frowned. "If . . . if you think that's best."

"I do, but if you insist upon carrying a gun, you must learn to use it properly."

"Will you teach me?" Coral asked.

Amy hesitated. She had been sent to Kansas to do a job and didn't have time to give shooting lessons. Already she was behind in writing her report to headquarters. The principal wouldn't be happy that the Gunnysack Bandit investigation had come to a halt because of a funeral, but it wasn't her fault, and all might not be lost.

"Pleeeease?"

Amy didn't know how long she would be in town. Now that Rose was dead, there was no advantage in being a female detective.

Mr. Pinkerton might decide to use her elsewhere and replace her with a male operative.

Coral looked so upset Amy couldn't bring herself to say no. "All right. I'll teach you."

A look of relief fleeted across Coral's face. "Thank you."

Amy waited a beat before asking, "How long have you . . . uh . . . lived here, Coral?"

Coral tucked her handkerchief back into her sleeve and regarded Amy with soulful brown eyes. "Three years, two months, and twenty-one days."

Amy considered her answer. How could people do that? Be so precise? "And Rose?"

Mr. Studebaker had started singing again, and Coral cupped her ear. "What did you say?"

Amy lifted her voice to be heard above the racket coming from the parlor and the dishes rattling in the cabinet. "HOW LONG HAD ROSE WORKED HERE?"

Coral shrugged. "Longer than me." She sighed. "Too bad she didn't leave as she planned."

"ROSE PLANNED ON LEAVING?"

"Shh." Coral glanced at the doorway, and it was then that Amy realized the music had stopped. "I don't think she wanted anyone to know."

"I guess it doesn't matter now, does it?" Amy said softly.

"No, I guess it don't."

"Do you know why she was leaving?" Amy asked.

"She never said." Coral shrugged. "I guess she just didn't want to work here anymore."

Amy couldn't imagine anyone wanting to work here. "Do you know of anyone who wanted to harm her?"

"No, no one."

The exchange had a sobering effect. For a moment, she and Coral were lost in thought. Mercifully, no sounds came from the parlor.

Amy was the first to break the silence. "Last night . . . Rose's room was a terrible mess. But you told the marshal you didn't hear anything."

"My room's at the end of the hall. But . . . some of our guests tend to get noisy on occasion. Even if I'd heard something, I wouldn't have thought much about it."

"I see." She had been in the room directly across from Rose's and hadn't heard a thing, not until the screams. But then again, she'd been occupied at the time. Had Mr. Colton not commanded all her attention, might she have been able to save Rose? It was hard to know and depressing to consider.

Coral's eyes narrowed. "Why you asking all these questions?"

Amy tried to look apologetic. "I didn't mean to be nosy. I only met Rose the one time, and she struck me as a very nice person."

"She was okay, I guess."

Not wanting to sound overly interested in Rose, Amy changed the subject. "If you don't mind my asking . . . Have you thought about finding another line of work? Something safer?" Something more in keeping with God's commandments.

Coral laughed, but her painted face held no mirth. "It looks like you're in the same boat as me, honey. If a white girl like you can't find respectable work, how do you expect a darky like me to find it?"

CHAPTER 4

Long after the others had retired to their rooms that night, Amy fought with the dormer window in the attic. Gritting her teeth, she pushed up on the window frame with the heels of her hands, and at last it grumbled open. The sound made her stop to listen.

The walls groaned and the eaves sighed, but she heard no voices or footsteps. Confident that she and the mice scampering behind the attic walls were the only ones awake, she stuck her head outside.

Cool night air nipped at her cheeks like a playful puppy. A full moon illuminated the worrisome pitch of the porch roof slanting away from the window. She turned her head to study the distance between the window and the large gnarly oak tree at the side of the house.

No more than eight feet away, the tree appeared sturdy enough for her purposes. In her youth she could outrun, outclimb, and outride her brothers. It wasn't for nothing that she earned the name tomboy. Normally she would welcome the challenge of climbing down the tree's twisted limbs.

But there was nothing normal about her current situation. Not the fancy, bright-colored gowns she was forced to wear with their flyaway sleeves and Grand Canyon necklines. And certainly not Miss Lillian who, since Rose's death, kept the outer doors locked night and day so no one could enter the house or leave without her knowledge.

The window offered the only way to circumvent Miss Lillian's guard. Upon arriving in town, she'd checked into the Grande Hotel and Bath House, and her clothes were still there. She'd searched for the skirt and shirtwaist worn the day she arrived at the parlor house but was told that any clothes deemed unsuitable by Miss Lillian's standards were relegated to the ragman.

Amy had free use of the garments in her room, but some dresses started too late and others hardly started at all. Retrieving something more practical, not to mention more modest to wear, took top priority.

To allow free movement she was dressed

in only a white silk camisole and petticoat, under which she wore silk drawers. She dropped her bundle of clothes outside the window to be donned once she reached the ground.

She was willing to do a lot of crazy things, but climbing down a tree in a long skirt and saddlebag bustle was not one of them. The bundle also held her report to headquarters. The post office was closed, of course, but she hoped to find an outside box in which to deposit mail.

She glanced at the ground below. It had been many years since she'd last climbed a tree, and though she'd done her share of chasing outlaws, most had been on flat land. But she could do it. Had to do it. She desperately needed something decent to wear.

Lord, just don't let me break my neck. There were many honorable things worth dying for, but modesty wasn't one of them.

Careful preparation and planning were essential parts of undercover work, but since arriving in Goodman she'd been working on the fly, and that's how mistakes happened. But tonight she was ready for anything. More than ready.

With a bracing breath, she raised a leg over the windowsill, careful not to dislodge the gun holstered to her thigh. Ever so carefully, she stepped onto the shingled porch roof and worked her other leg free. Stars winked overhead as if daring her to proceed.

Palms flat against the rough brick wall, she shuffled slowly sideways to the edge of the roof, forcing the bundle along the roofline with her foot as she moved. Somewhere in the distance a dog barked, but otherwise all was quiet.

Reaching the edge, she pushed the bundle of clothes over and watched it fall to the ground. Lifting her arms, she grabbed hold of the nearest tree branch. Torso twisting, she wrapped her other hand around the limb as well. It seemed sturdy enough. She didn't look forward to climbing back up after completing her errands in town, but she'd face that problem later.

She counted: *One, two, three . . . Here goes nothing.*

She swung her body forward and her feet landed on a lower limb. The bough dipped and creaked beneath her weight but held. So far, so good.

Straddling the lower bough, she released the limb overhead and scooted toward the trunk where stronger limbs grew. The tree smelled old and dusty, and somewhere in the upper crown came the flutter of wings.

She adjusted the holster at her thigh.

A soft thump sounded from somewhere below. Stilling, she scanned the moon-dappled ground but saw nothing. Thinking it a rabbit or maybe even a fox, she worked her way down the gnarled branches. Leaves rustled and twigs snapped.

Her petticoat snagged. Grimacing, she tugged gently before giving it a hard yank. The fabric pulled free with a ripping sound, exposing the leg of her bloomer drawers. She hated ruining perfectly good clothes, however useless, but it couldn't be helped.

Hugging a limb, she scanned the ground below and smiled. She'd managed the hardest part; the rest she could do blindfolded. Not bad for a twenty-seven-year-old woman.

Holding on tight, she worked her body free until she dangled from both arms. The rough bark cut into the palms of her hands as she scrambled for a foothold.

One slipper fell off, followed by a muffled yelp from below. She held her breath. Someone stood beneath the tree — a dark figure — a man! Why was he sneaking around at night? Whoever he was, he could be dangerous. Could even be Rose's killer . . .

Since she was hanging from both arms, it

was impossible to reach for her weapon. A fine pickle! Before she could decide on a course of action, a cracking sound like gunfire rent the air. The branch snapped in two, and she dropped like a stone.

Hitting the ground with a jolt, she found herself entangled in legs and arms — not all of them hers. Ready to fight tooth and nail, she lifted her head. Much to her horror, the intruder was flat on the ground with her on top and he was —

"Mr. Colton!"

With his head lifted, his nose practically met hers, and his eyes sparkled in the moonlight. "We meet again."

They gazed at each other for a full moment before she regained her senses. Gasping, she pulled free from his arms and scrambled to her feet. A pain shot through her shoulder as she glared down at him.

"You near scared the life out of me!" she sputtered.

Sitting up, he reached for his hat and slapped it on his head before standing. "I have to say, ma'am, the feeling is mutual." His gaze shifted momentarily to the holstered gun showing beneath her torn petticoat. "Sorry to catch you at an inopportune moment."

Face blazing, she folded her arms across

the front of her thin camisole. Considering that she had just extracted herself from a compromising position, her effort at modesty was futile at best. She worked her fingers against her sore shoulder and tried to calm her racing heart.

"What are you doing here?" she snapped.

He tipped his hat back with a finger to the brim and hung his thumbs from his belt. "I was about to ask you the same thing."

Maintaining as much dignity as possible under the circumstances, she glared at him. "I have every right to be here." Thank God she had resisted the urge to scrub the annoying makeup off her face. It made it easier to play her part.

"Can't argue with you there, ma'am. I just hope that the next time you decide to go out on a limb, you issue a warning. Being attacked by a lady's shoe is one thing. But when it comes with the whole kit and caboodle, that's something else." He stooped to retrieve her slipper and handed it to her. His fingers brushing against hers made her quickly pull away.

"I thought I was being attacked by a wildcat," he added. "You're lucky I didn't shoot you."

Balancing on one foot, she slipped the shoe on the other. "It's late. I didn't think anyone was around."

His forehead creased. "I was under the impression you ladies kept late hours." He glanced at the dark windows. "My mistake."

"We're closed in memory of Rose." As much as she wanted to question him about the Gunnysack Bandit, she wasn't about to do it in her undergarments. "So if you would kindly leave —"

He crossed his arms and leaned against the tree trunk. He looked like he was enjoying himself at her expense.

"Not till you tell me what you were doing in that tree." His gaze flickered down the length of her. "Undressed."

"A gentleman wouldn't notice," she said primly. She glanced around. Fiddlesticks! Where was that bundle of clothes?

He laughed. "Only if he was dead." His eyebrows rose to half-mast. "So let me guess. You were on the way to meet a client. I didn't know you ladies made house calls."

"I dare say there's a lot you don't know," she huffed.

He thought for a moment. "Actually, it's fortunate that you . . . uh . . . dropped by. Perhaps you could answer a few questions."

"It's not a good time, and even if it was, I have nothing to say to you." Anxious to escape, she tried to sidestep him, but he blocked her way.

"What should I call you? Miss . . . ?"

She considered whether to tell him her assumed surname but decided against it. "Amy's fine." William Pinkerton assigned her the moniker. It was better than the name he gave her last time — Charley. The rumor was that he liked to name his undercover agents after his pets. She just hoped that Amy wasn't a reptile.

"Amy," he said as if testing it out. "I apologize for the other night." The amusement had left his eyes and his face was now serious. "I honestly thought you were Rose. I had no right to blame you for what happened. I'm afraid we got off to a bad start."

His apology surprised her, and she studied his face. He sounded sincere, but that could be an act. Thinking him a "guest" the first time they met, she'd hardly noticed what a fine-looking man he was, though the golden moonlight didn't do him justice. His rugged, square face was anchored by an intriguing cleft in his chin. Though his eyes looked dark now, she seemed to remember they were the color of a deep blue sea.

Nevertheless, one of Miss Lillian's girls had told her not to judge a man's character by his looks. "Handsome men often have the worst reputation," she'd said. Amy wouldn't know; most of the criminals she'd helped track down had faces that only a mother could love.

"I need to ask you about Rose," he said.

She studied him. Maybe the night wasn't a complete loss. If she played her cards right, he might reveal something useful. Of course, she'd feel a whole lot better if she wasn't standing in a torn petticoat and thin camisole, but it would be foolish to let an opportunity like this slip by. Having decided to put prudence before modesty, she nonetheless moved out of the moonlight and into the shadows.

"Why are you so interested in Rose?" she asked.

He hesitated as if trying to decide how little or how much to say. "I have my reasons."

And she intended to find out exactly what those reasons were. "It has something to do with your brother. You said his name was Dave, right? How did Rose know him?"

Just as he opened his mouth to say something, Miss Lillian came shooting around the corner. She wore a dressing gown tied at the waist, and her hair fell down her back in a single braid.

"What is the meaning of this?" Looking and sounding like every one of her fifty-some years, she addressed her question to Mr. Colton, but her sharp eyes bored into Amy. If her strident voice wasn't bad enough, the moon turned her face a sickly yellow.

Amy balled her hands by her side. Miss Lillian couldn't have picked a worse time to make an appearance. The night had gone from bad to worse.

Mr. Colton didn't seem the least bit intimidated by the woman. If anything, he looked more amused than perturbed. "Miss . . . Amy was just explaining that your establishment is closed."

The madam gave a self-righteous sniff. "As the sign on the door plainly states, we'll be closed until after the funeral."

Mr. Colton swept off his hat and held it to his chest. "A fitting tribute, indeed."

His comment failing to win any favors, he replaced his hat. "I won't keep you any longer. Good night, ladies."

Under his breath he added for Amy's ears alone, "I hope to see *more* of you soon."

Heat raced to her face. "Don't hold your breath," she shot back.

With a flash of his perfect white teeth, he turned to leave.

"Not so fast, young man." Miss Lillian held out her hand. "That'll be ten dollars."

He looked startled. "Why so much?"

"Off-hours," she said.

Amy opened her mouth to protest but decided against it. His presence had caused her to be caught and kept her from doing what she'd set out to do. He deserved what he got.

He paid Miss Lillian without complaint and sauntered down the path, whistling. He let himself out the front gate to his tethered horse.

Amy found her bundle of clothes in the bushes and hid them behind her back.

After making certain the unwanted guest was leaving, Miss Lillian spun around to face her. "Apparently you failed to read the rules of the house. Had you done so, you would know that meeting men outside is forbidden."

Since the rules were plastered on every wall, every door, and every tabletop, ignoring them was impossible. Amy kept her head bowed in what she hoped passed as remorse. Like it or not, without Miss Lillian's goodwill she would not be able to complete her investigation.

"I apologize. It won't happen again."

"See that it doesn't." Looking unbearably self-righteous, Miss Lillian continued. "I run a high-quality business that caters to the town's most discerning citizens. I won't have my girls flaunting their wares on the street like those horrid crib girls on Maple. Do you hear?"

"Yes, ma'am, no flaunting wares," she said demurely, though she couldn't imagine what the low-cut gowns were meant to do except flaunt.

Apparently satisfied that Amy had shown appropriate remorse, Miss Lillian softened her tone. "Since you're new, I'll let it pass this time. But nothing like this better happen again. Do I make myself clear?"

"Yes, Miss Lillian. Perfectly clear."

"Then go." The madam flapped her arms like a farmer chasing a chicken. "Hurry, hurry. We need our beauty rest."

Tom stood next to his horse and watched the madam usher the woman he knew only as Amy into the house. A vision of pretty green eyes came to mind. Eyes that changed from meadow green to shades of jade on a whim.

He still recalled how she felt in his arms, and his shirt still held a hint of her sweet lilac fragrance — a tangible reminder that played havoc with his senses.

God forgive me for thinking it, but she sure did look fetching in those fancy under-riggings.

With her tiny waist, rounded hips, and soft ivory shoulders, she curved in and out in all the right places. The weapon clearly outlined beneath her petticoat offered a startling, though no less intriguing, contrast to all that feminine softness.

It sickened him to think that a pretty young woman would choose such a life . . . that any woman would. What had driven her to Miss Lillian's? Desperation? Of course, nothing about her struck him as desperate. Fought him like a wildcat, she did, so she obviously could take care of herself.

So why, then, was she in such a place as this? A place where even God might be tempted to hang His head in shame . . .

He sucked in his breath. He'd spent most of his life trying to figure out why people made the choices they did. He and his brother had had the same opportunities. The same home life, the same religious upbringing, but they couldn't have been more different had they been born on opposite sides of the planet.

He took some of the blame for that. His father died when Dave was knee-high to a mustang, leaving the two of them in the care of an invalid mother. Tom, being the oldest by three years, looked after his then six-year-old brother. At least he'd tried.

They'd attended the same one-room schoolhouse. Tom was a model student and he did his best to tutor Dave. But Dave had no interest in book learning; he was more interested in creating mischief to the point that he was always in danger of being expelled. And would have been had his teachers not felt sorry for the family.

Tom took the blame for some of Dave's pranks to save his brother's skin. That only made Dave more sullen and difficult to handle. Eventually he quit school and left home, upsetting their mother and sending her to an early grave.

At twenty, Tom followed his dream and joined the Texas Rangers. A year later, he heard that Dave was married and he felt encouraged. Nothing tames a man like a wife. Perhaps the worst was over. For five years, he never heard a word from Dave, had no idea where he was or even if he was still alive.

Then one day, Tom tracked down a group of stage robbers who had terrorized the Panhandle for months, only to find the leader was his very own brother.

It nearly killed Tom to handcuff Dave and turn him over to local authorities. That's when he learned Dave's wife had died of smallpox, leaving him a widower with an infant son.

While his brother was incarcerated, Tom cared for the boy. He fully expected Dave to return for his son when he left prison. That didn't happen; Dave served his time, but Tom had no idea what happened to him afterward. Not wanting to be in a position of having to arrest his brother a second time, Tom left the Rangers and started a small cattle ranch in the San Antonio Valley, taking Dave's son with him.

That's when Tom discovered he had a knack with horses. A gift, some called it. Horses weren't like people. Treat a horse well and the animal generally returned the favor.

He never thought to hear from his brother again, never wanted to. Almost hadn't opened the letter addressed to him in his brother's hand, when it finally came. He feared Dave would be coming for his son. For more than ten years, Tom had cared for the boy — treated him like his own. He wasn't about to let the lad go without a fight.

The letter carried a Goodman, Kansas, postmark. When he finally cut through the wax seal, he read the letter with growing skepticism. His brother had written about finding God. Said he was ready to be a good father to Davey and wanted to make his boy proud. He was also engaged to be married to a woman named Rose. He asked if he could bring Rose to the ranch. Said his fiancée had information about the Gunny-sack Bandit and feared for her life.

It wasn't the first time his brother claimed to have turned over a new leaf. Nor was it the first time Dave had spun a cockamamie story about supposed danger.

Ignoring the letter was the easy part; learning about the single bullet to his brother's head nearly tore him in two. Having to tell eleven-year-old Davey his father was dead was about as close to torture as Tom ever hoped to get.

He felt responsible. Dave had reached out for help, and he had let him down. Some brother he was — some man.

His horse pawed the ground, bringing Tom out of his reverie.

"What's wrong, boy?" For answer, the gelding bobbed his head up and down and nickered.

After running his hand along his horse's slick neck, Tom untied the reins from the hitching post and jammed his foot into the stirrup. Astride the saddle, he glanced up at the windows of the tall brick house. The red lamp had been turned off, and in the dark of night the house gave no clue as to its real purpose.

The glass panes of the second floor glowed in the pale moonlight, and a curtain moved in an upstairs window. Someone was watching him. In the recesses of his mind came a vision of green eyes.

CHAPTER 5

It rained that early April morning of Rose's funeral. Somehow that seemed fitting.

It had rained the day they buried Amy's father, and her mother said it was heaven crying. Her pa had started drinking heavily after his three-year-old daughter, Cissy, had disappeared in the middle of the night, never to be heard from again. Some said he literally drank himself to death.

The thought of heaven crying comforted her then as it comforted her now. God really did care about His lost sheep.

The madam led the way to the cemetery like a general marching to war. Umbrella held high to accommodate her unwieldy hat standing three stories and a basement tall, she looked neither left nor right.

All five women, including Amy, followed behind like ducks in a row. All sported large feathered hats to match their colorful gowns. All held umbrellas over their heads and wore kid gloves.

The rain was a blessing as it allowed for modesty. Amy wore a tiered shoulder cape over her emerald-green dress. Miss Lillian insisted that her "girls" never leave the house unless properly attired, coiffed, and painted — a downright nuisance.

Obviously, Miss Lillian had never tried to climb through a window, run across a roof, and climb down a tree wearing such garments. Had she done so, she might have settled on a more conservative uniform.

Certainly, she would have insisted on more substantial footwear. Anything would be an improvement over the dainty slippers she insisted her girls wear. No decent woman would be caught dead showing her ankles, and Amy felt naked without her high-button boots.

The memory of one of her slippers falling on top of Mr. Colton brought an unbidden smile to her face and a scowl from the woman named Coral.

Reminded of the solemn occasion, Amy snapped her mouth shut and tried to look appropriately somber. Rose's death had complicated her investigation, which now had to be conducted with care and sensitivity. Miss Lillian's girls weren't particularly friendly to one another. If anything, they regarded each other with suspicion and maybe even jealousy.

Still, their grief for Rose seemed real, as did the fear for their own safety since her death.

The women paraded along the boardwalk in silence. Out of habit, Amy kept her gaze focused on the windows as they passed each establishment, not to admire the array of goods but to watch behind for followers. An operative could never be too careful.

Men stepped out of the way and pretended not to notice them. Mothers with small children detoured across the street or ducked into shops as if the women's mere presence would corrupt little minds.

Amy lowered her head in an effort to hide her blazing face. Posing as a strumpet at the parlor house was one thing, but here on the street she felt like a penny waiting for change. She sighed. Great guns! There had to be an easier way to make a living.

A carriage slowed as it drove by. Pulled by two large black horses, the carriage was fitted with bright, shiny carriage lamps and rubber-tired wheels fitted with inner brass rims. Amy never expected to see such a fine carriage in a small prairie town. She caught only a glimpse of the passenger, a man in a tall top hat.

"Who is that?" she asked Coral.

"That's Mr. Monahan." The dark look that crossed Coral's face made Amy shiver. "He's got the dimes. He's so rich, he practically owns the town." As an afterthought, she added, "He always asked for Rose."

This latest bit of news got Amy's attention. It also explained the way Coral glared at the carriage. "Do you think he'll be at the funeral?"

Coral gave her a sideways glance. "No respectable citizen would so much as admit to knowing Rose, let alone attend her funeral."

"Seems to me she should be pitied rather than censured. A young woman like that murdered . . ."

Coral's lip curled. "You really don't know how things work, do you?"

"I know how things work," Amy snapped. If growing up with a drunken father wasn't bad enough, her job as a Pinkerton required her to associate with society's worst criminals. Sometimes it was hard to remember that good, honest people actually did exist.

The group strolled pass Lloyd's Haberdashery and Insurance (we've got you covered) and Joe's Funeral Parlor and Lending Library (read where it's quiet). Despite the rain, a group of children circled the ice wagon parked in front of the hotel, clamoring for ice chips.

Amy cast a longing look at the hotel. If only she could find a way to sneak inside and retrieve her own clothes.

From the Grande Hotel and Bath House it was only a short distance to the church and the iron gates in back leading to the cemetery.

The rain had stopped, and a watery sun peeked from behind the clouds, touching the earth with fingers of golden light. But even with the change in weather, not one outsider attended the simple graveside service.

Rose was to be buried beyond the Christian area, behind a weathered fence reserved for criminals, vagrants, and other social undesirables. The young woman would be shunned even in death.

The stubble-bearded preacher who was probably in his mid- to late-fifties looked pleasant enough. He greeted Miss Lillian with a nod of his grizzled head.

"Are you going to give us a bad time, Reverend Matthews?" the madam asked.

"No more than usual," he replied. Tall black hat askew, he patted down both pockets of his frock coat before locating the *Book of Common Prayer.*

Out of habit, Amy scrutinized him as she mentally went down the Pinkerton checklist. Height: five foot eight. Eyes: hazel. Hair: mostly gray. He had the contented look of a married man, and if his generous girth was an indication, his wife knew her way around the kitchen.

The ridge on his nose meant he generally wore spectacles. Had he forgotten them? Lost them? Or were they broken?

Though the circumstances were definitely awkward, he seemed as perfectly at ease around a bunch of sinners as he no doubt was in the company of the choir.

He checked all his pockets again. He gave up the search with a shrug and opened the prayer book. Amy added *absentminded* to her mental list.

He adjusted his arms to and fro until he found a comfortable position in which to read.

After opening the ceremony with the reading of scripture and respectful prayer, he gave a short sermon sprinkled liberally with words like *forgiveness* and *redemption.*

His discourse had a sobering effect on the group, and they all stared at the plain pine coffin in silence.

As the preacher droned on, a movement on the Christian side of the fence caught

Amy's attention. She recognized Mr. Colton's tall, straight form at once. Arms folded, he leaned against a towering gray tombstone, watching her. He acknowledged her gaze with a finger to the brim of his hat. Recalling the last time they'd met, her cheeks flared, and she cast her gaze downward.

The man had made a perfect nuisance of himself. While most of Miss Lillian's "guests" had accepted the temporary closing of the bordello in memory of Rose with good grace, he had not. Instead, he had appeared on the doorstep with annoying regularity and insisted upon talking to her.

Though she longed to finish the conversation begun the night she fell out of the tree, Miss Lillian denied him entry. Amy didn't dare show her hand by going against the madam's wishes. Fortunately, he never gave up. Now here he was again. There had to be a reason he was so persistent. Her inquiries about him had mostly garnered blank looks from Miss Lillian's girls. *So what is your game, Mr. Colton? And what exactly is your interest in the Gunnysack Bandit?*

CHAPTER 6

The preacher returned the *Book of Common Prayer* to his pocket. "Would anyone like to say something on behalf of the deceased?"

No one knew Rose's last name or even if she had a family, but the other women appeared eager to talk about her.

The blond woman named Polly went first. She dabbed her eyes with a handkerchief and stuttered, "R–Rose was the k–kindest person I ever met. She was p–p–popular with everyone."

The preacher cleared his throat and kept his gaze focused downward, his blunt-fingered hands held in prayer.

Polly's eyes widened and she glanced around in a panic. "I — I meant she was p–p–popular with us girls."

Next to her, Coral shook the water off her closed umbrella. Today she wore a bright gold frock that complemented her dark complexion if not her critical expression.

"You don't have to apologize for Rose."

"I w–wasn't apologizing, Coral."

"Sounded like it to me."

A moment of strained silence followed the exchange, and finally the preacher asked, "Anyone else wish to say something?"

"She had dreams. Big dreams." The words were spoken by the woman who called herself Buttercup, a name that said more about her generous girth than her orange-red hair.

After a short pause Coral added, "And she didn't want to be here."

"None of us want to be here." This came from a stick-thin woman with raven hair named Georgia. "And I'm not talking about a cemetery." Her gaze flicked around the circle of mourners. "Though certainly no one wants to be here, either."

All eyes turned to Miss Lillian, but she was too busy staring at the minister's shabby boots to pay heed to the women's laments.

Silence followed as they watched two grave diggers lower the coffin and spade wet soil into the hole.

The service ended with a prayer and collective sigh. The minister asked if anyone needed his counsel, and when no one did, he bolted like a jackrabbit in tall grass.

Folded umbrella raised over her head, Miss Lillian chased after him, presumably to try and sell him a pair of new boots.

Instead of following Coral and the others out of the cemetery, Amy lingered in front of the newly dug grave, giving Mr. Colton ample time to catch up to her. She didn't want to appear obvious, but neither did she want to miss an opportunity to find out how he fit into the picture.

He tipped his hat in greeting. "We meet again."

Recalling their last encounter, warmth crept up her neck. "Yes, what a surprise."

He gave her a crooked smile, and once again she was reminded what a handsome man he was. "About the other night . . . I hope Miss Lillian didn't give you a bad time." He raised an eyebrow in query.

No, the bordello owner just watched her like a hawk, making it impossible to do much in the way of sleuthing. But she said none of this. Instead, she returned his smile with one in kind.

"I told her it was all *your* fault," she said.

He laughed. "And no doubt she believed you."

His laughter made her smile, and for some reason she felt a surge of guilt. "I'm sorry Miss Lillian made you pay."

"It was worth it just to see you fall out of that tree. I trust the man you planned on meeting wasn't too disappointed when you failed to show up."

She forced herself not to look away from his probing gaze. "I made it up to him," she said, and immediately the light went out of his eyes.

Disarmed by the disapproval on his face, she forced a deep breath. She didn't realize she'd allowed her hand to grow slack at her neckline until his gaze dropped to her open shoulder cape. She squeezed the closure so tight her fingers ached.

He pushed his hat back and studied her with quizzical eyes. "Excuse me for asking Miss . . . Amy, but have you worked for Miss Lillian long?"

Her professional training kicked in, and she considered her answer carefully before responding. "The night Rose died . . . that was my first time at Miss Lillian's," she said in a conspiratorial tone. Mr. Pinkerton insisted that the art of gaining information required skill and fortitude, but she often got better results by playing on a man's sympathy.

Her ploy worked, or at least softened his expression. "That explains it, then." He frowned. "You looked scared enough to make the hair of a buffalo robe stand up."

She couldn't help but smile at the image he invoked. "That bad, eh?" Her smile failed to coax one in return.

"Have you been in the . . . business long?" he asked.

"Awhile," she said, and the censure on his face couldn't be more pronounced. "Obviously you don't approve."

He narrowed his gaze. "There are other ways to make a living."

"Only if a woman wishes to live in poverty." She hated defending a profession she loathed, but she couldn't afford to blow her cover.

He cleared his throat and changed the subject. "Do all the ladies carry firearms?"

She frowned. "Why do you ask?"

He shrugged. "Just curious."

"Had Rose been armed, she might still be alive," she said.

"Maybe. Maybe not." He stared at the new grave in silence. Studying his profile, she tried thinking of a way to bring up the Gunnysack Bandit without rousing suspicion.

"I would like to make you a proposition," he said.

"A . . . proposition?" His disapproval of her profession apparently went only so far.

This time she pulled her cape so tight she practically cut off her own breathing.

"I want to hire you to do a little spying for me."

She stared at him. Did he say what she thought he'd said? "You want me to . . . spy?"

"I have it on good authority that the man known as the Gunnysack Bandit is no stranger to the parlor house."

He had done her a favor in mentioning the outlaw's name, but she was careful not to react. "You mentioned him previously." She gave herself a mental pat for showing only the slightest interest. Too bad she got so little credit for her acting abilities.

Colton's face darkened. "Yes, and I'm anxious to find him. He's a conniving thief and a cold-blooded killer."

His description of the man matched the one in the Pinkerton file almost word for word. Nevertheless, she stayed in character and opened her eyes wide to feign shock. "And you want me to spy on him? A thief and a killer?"

"Even if we knew his identity, which we don't, I'd prefer that you didn't go anywhere near him. He's dangerous, but I doubt that after what he did to Rose he'll show his face

71

at Miss Lillian's again. At least not for a while."

This time she didn't have to fake surprise. "You think *he* killed Rose?"

"I'll bet my boots on it."

His well-worn boots looked like they'd been trampled by a herd of cattle. Someone would have to be pretty desperate to take him up on his offer.

"As certain as that, Mr. Colton?" she asked, her tone wry.

"Yes ma'am." Apparently, he didn't see the humor in his comment, and the hoped-for smile failed to materialize.

"How do you know this man . . . is responsible?" There were only two guests at the house the night Rose died, and one of them was Mr. Colton. The other man was Mr. Pepper. Standing little more than five feet tall, he hardly fit the description of the Gunnysack Bandit.

"I have my ways." He glanced around and lowered his voice. "I want you to talk to the others and find out if Rose mentioned him to anyone at the house. Perhaps even revealed his name . . . I'll pay for any information you can give me."

She weighed the pros and cons of his proposal. If either of the two Pinkerton brothers got wind that she was working for another, she would be fired on the spot. William and Robert demanded complete loyalty from employees, just as their founding father had done when he was still in full charge of the company. On the other hand, if Mr. Colton *thought* she was working for him, he would be more likely to share whatever knowledge he had with her.

"So what do you say?" he prodded.

"If I decide to do this, how will I reach you?" she asked, stalling for time. She'd received a telegram from headquarters with orders to continue investigating. That meant she had to find a way to remain at Miss Lillian's without compromising her morals — a goal she hadn't the foggiest idea how to accomplish.

"I'm staying at the hotel." His brow furrowed. "So is that a yes?"

His staying at the hotel posed a complication. They could easily bump into each other whenever she went to her rented room. She moistened her rouged lips and immediately regretted drawing his attention to her mouth.

"I'll let you kn–know," she stammered.

His gaze met hers. "Fair enough." He seemed oblivious to the three matronly women standing a short distance away, watching them from the other side of the fence. "But I'll expect an answer by four tomorrow afternoon. Agreed?"

That didn't give her much time to figure out how to proceed with the investigation, but she nodded. "Is that the only reason you came to today? To talk me into spying?" she asked.

"That and" — he tossed a nod toward the fresh mound of dirt marking Rose's grave — "to pay my respects to my brother's fiancée."

He doffed his Stetson and walked away. She hardly had time to recover from the surprising new information when the three women stepped through the gate separating the two cemeteries and advanced toward her.

Their gray skirts and long dark capes were more suited for a funeral than the bright colors worn by Miss Lillian's girls, but none of the women so much as glanced at the new grave.

A barrel-shaped woman, whose size alone gave her the right to be the leader, moved closer. Her hips were so wide she looked like a carriage with the doors flung open, the bustle in back ready to receive passengers. Three neatly stacked chins competed with the ribbon holding her straw hat in place. Peering through spectacles that rested on the bridge of her pointed nose, she studied Amy like a surgeon about to cut open a patient.

"I'm Mrs. Givings, and we're from the church." She pointed toward the First Community Church that stood at the entrance of the cemetery. The other two women confirmed her statement with nods and stiff smiles.

"This is Mrs. Compton," she said, pointing to a tall, thin woman with jet-black hair and a pale white face. "And this is Mrs. Albright."

The third church member, with her drab dress and sallow complexion, hardly suited her name, nor did the swift bucktoothed smile that failed to reach her eyes.

"I'm Amy, and I'm pleased to meet you," she said as politely as she could without encouraging further conversation.

Mrs. Givings folded her gloved hands, and her drawstring bag dangled from her thick wrist. "I think you'll be happy to know that we've come to save you."

Amy didn't want to be rude, but she couldn't keep her gaze away from Mr. Colton striding across the cemetery. He let himself out of the church gate and grabbed his horse's reins. Before mounting, he spoke to the horse as if asking permission to ride.

Even in the saddle, he held his back straight and head high. Like a military man. Trained to be suspicious of everyone and everything, she couldn't help but wonder if his character matched his good looks.

A clearing of a throat reminded her that she wasn't alone, and she turned her gaze back to the churchwomen. "Excuse me, but did you say *save*?"

Three heads bobbed up and down like the springs of a wagon.

As if there could be any doubt as to her meaning, Mrs. Givings wagged a finger skyward. "Save!"

Amy felt a sinking feeling. The last thing she needed was another sermon, no matter how well meaning. Reverend Matthews's discourse had been enough for one day, thank you very much, and she had work to do.

Anxious to return to Miss Lillian's, she tried to think how to get rid of the pious-looking three without sounding rude or unkind. She needed to find out who knew of Rose's engagement and what, if anything, it had to do with the Gunnysack Bandit.

"Why, that's very thoughtful of you," she said, purposely pretending to misunderstand their meaning. "I've never had body-guards before. Do you all carry weapons?"

CHAPTER 7

Amy was anxious to talk to Miss Lillian in private, but the madam retired to her room upon returning home from the funeral and stayed there for the remainder of the day. No one else felt much like talking, which meant more wasted time. The only person downstairs was Beatrice, the housekeeper.

Amy followed the housekeeper into the parlor. A thin woman somewhere in her late twenties, Beatrice flicked her feather duster from table to lamp to piano to floorboard.

Amy cast a covetous glance at the maid's apparel. Had Miss Lillian mistaken her for a maid instead of a harlot she would now be wearing a plain gray dress with a starched white apron — a much more practical uniform for her purposes.

"How long have you worked here, Beatrice?"

The question seemed to surprise the woman, and her gaze darted around the room as if to check for eavesdroppers before answering. "Three years."

"That's a long time."

The woman merely shrugged.

Closemouthed people were a detective's bane, and this house was full of them. "Then you must have known Rose quite well."

Beatrice swiped the hand-painted glass lamp shade with her duster. "I keep pretty much to myself."

Encouraged that the woman could string more than two or three words together, Amy persisted. "I noticed that you and the cook don't live here."

"I stay overnight only when I'm asked to work late." She glanced at the doorway. "I have a room at Miss Trumble's Boarding House."

"But you must know the residents quite well." How could she not?

"Like I said, I keep to myself. What they do . . ." Beatrice made the sign of the cross and shuddered. "I clean the house. That's all."

Amy sympathized with the woman's obvious discomfort. Staying at Miss Lillian's for these past three days had taken an emotional toll. For the first time since working as a Pinkerton operative she'd been tempted to quit before completing an assignment. She couldn't imagine working at such a place for three years.

"Could you at least tell me what Rose was like?" Amy probed. It struck her as odd that neither the cook nor the housekeeper attended her funeral.

Beatrice flicked her feather duster over the piano keys a second time. "She was quiet but friendly."

"Did you know she was betrothed?"

Beatrice hesitated — a sure sign she would either not answer the question or lie.

Not wanting to give her a chance to do either, Amy quickly asked, "Who told you?"

"I don't know. One of the girls. I must have heard them talking or something."

If that was true, then the four women had lied when they claimed they didn't know Rose's plans. The question was, why? "Had you met her fiancé?"

Beatrice lowered her gaze. "I'm generally gone by the time most guests arrive."

Amy tried to think how best to phrase her next question and decided to come right out with it. "Can you think of anyone who might have wanted to cause Rose harm?"

Beatrice's brown eyes narrowed. "Why are you asking all these questions?"

"I don't mean to pry." That's exactly what

she meant to do. "I only met Rose the one time, and I just got back from her funeral. Naturally, I'm curious."

The answer seemed to satisfy Beatrice; at least she looked less suspicious. "I don't know anyone who wanted to hurt her. Like I said, she was friendly. Now if you'll excuse me . . ."

The woman seemed anxious to get on with her work. Amy let her go without further comment and watched her scamper away like a little mouse. The woman had secrets no doubt, but so, it seemed, did everyone else in that house.

The following morning after breakfast Amy dressed in the blue calico skirt and white shirtwaist collected from her hotel room on the way home from yesterday's funeral. Without the face paint and fancy clothes, she felt more like herself. Maybe now she could get some real work done.

She hurried downstairs, determined to gain Miss Lillian's attention, but never got a chance for the house was a beehive of activity.

A man by the name of Mr. Deering had delivered a wagonload of groceries. Three times a week he brought fresh fruits and vegetables to the house, along with steak, chicken, and cheese, but according to Polly, never without a battle. Today was no different, and a loud argument rose from the kitchen.

"I'm not paying that much for chicken!" the cook yelled. Her outburst was followed by the clang of pots and pans.

Mr. Deering sounded more indignant than angry. "Do you think I like charging this much?"

No sooner had Miss Lillian rescued the hapless grocer and restored order than Miss Paisley, the local dressmaker, arrived loaded down with a trunk full of colorful silks, satins, and lace. Sporting women were expected to keep up appearances, and that meant maintaining five or more fancy gowns at all times.

Miss Paisley's drab gray skirt and mousy-brown hair seemed at odds with the bold, outrageous gowns she designed. It was almost as if she purposely downplayed her own appearance so as not to compete with her colorful creations.

Holding up various pieces of fabric and lace, she kept up a running commentary about the pros and cons of each. With her thick French accent, Amy had a difficult time understanding her.

While the women all sat around the parlor,

poring over fabric samples, Miss Paisley's hawkeyed gaze zeroed in on Amy.

She said something in French before switching to thick-accented English. "What have ve here? Stand up, stand up."

Amy waved her hand from side to side. "No, that's all right. I'm just here to watch." She didn't know how long she would remain at the parlor house, and she doubted the Pinkerton brothers would relish paying for a ball gown.

"You're here to work," Miss Lillian said. "Don't worry about the cost. I'll take it out of your salary."

"Oh, but —"

Miss Lillian would hear none of what she tried to say, so Amy decided it was easier to play along than argue. At least until she had a chance to talk to the madam in private.

Miss Paisley gazed at Amy's attire and muttered something that sounded alarmingly like "Murder, murder."

"Amy is our newest resident," Miss Lillian explained with an apologetic air. Not only did the madam run a tight ship, she ran the language of iniquity through a moral sieve. Thus clients were called "guests," working girls "residents," and anything that happened behind closed doors, just plain old "hospitality."

"Not to worry," Miss Paisley said, hands all aflutter. "I have just the thing." She pulled a rose-colored swag of fabric from her trunk and draped it across Amy's chest. "*Parfait!* The color — how do you say — completes your skin."

She said something else, but Amy couldn't make out what it was. She also chose not to correct the dressmaker's use of the word *complete.* "She's asking what fabric you prefer," Georgia explained.

"She means other than calico," Coral added, staring at Amy's skirt with a roll of her eyes.

Buttercup laughed and Polly glared at her. "Th–there's nothing wrong with c–calico . . . in the r–right setting."

Sensing an argument about to follow, Amy hastily murmured, "Taffeta." She was anxious for Miss Paisley to leave so she could get back to work. One of the residents had to know something about Rose's death, the Gunnysack Bandit, or both.

Her choice earned Amy the first look of approval from the seamstress. "Ah, *oui.* I do believe you're more the taffeta type. Do you want it in wild rose or strawberry? Or would you prefer another color?"

"Uh . . . green."

Miss Paisley couldn't have looked more

appalled had Amy asked for zebra stripes. "Plain green is for pheasants!" she snapped.

"I think she means peasants," Georgia whispered.

"For Miss Lillian's ladies, only the most artful shades will do. With your coloring, I suggest jade or maybe even moss green."

Amy had no intention of staying at the bordello long enough to warrant a gown, but the woman obviously wasn't going to leave her alone until she had made a selection. She picked out meadow green, which everyone in the room agreed went with her eyes.

"Good choice." Miss Paisley then directed her attention to the others.

The array of colors and fabrics from which to choose didn't seem to faze anyone else. After staring at herself in the mirror, Buttercup settled on a cornflower-blue silk, and Coral went with a burnt-almond taffeta. Polly couldn't make up her mind between shell pink or crushed roses, and Miss Lillian insisted she take both.

While Polly, Georgia, and Buttercup had no objection to the type of necklines Miss Paisley suggested, Coral wanted hers lower.

"Give her an inch and she'll wear it," Georgia whispered.

Amy covered her mouth to hide a giggle.

Oddly enough, she and Georgia had developed an easy rapport. Under different circumstances they might have even become friends. But Amy couldn't afford the luxury of letting down her guard and getting close to anyone. Not while she was working.

Thinking Miss Paisley was done with her, Amy rose. This practically sent Miss Paisley into a tizzy. Rushing to her side, the dressmaker circled her waist with a measuring tape like a dog sniffing out a place to bury a bone. She examined Amy's plain shirtwaist and shook her head. The look on her face was one of pure horror.

"I think a cuirass bodice would suit you quite well. What do you think?"

"I —" Amy didn't know a cuirass from a catfish. Never one to kowtow to fashion, she'd paid little attention to the latest styles, except for when undercover work required it. No-nonsense skirts and tailored shirtwaists were more her style and more practical for chasing suspects.

Speaking in her native tongue, Miss Paisley fiddled with the back. "Do you want a butterfly or waterfall?"

"Uh . . ."

At last the ordeal was over, though Amy hadn't the slightest idea if she'd purchased a gown or a national park.

Miss Paisley wrote Amy's measurements in her notebook. "Your total is three hundred dollars."

Amy's mouth dropped open. "For . . . for one gown?"

The dressmaker stiffened. "You wanted a waterfall."

"Yes, but I didn't want to purchase Niagara." She could well imagine what William Pinkerton would say if she turned in a three-hundred-dollar bill for a dress. William already considered female operatives too expensive to maintain. This was part of the reason he wanted to do away with the women's detective division begun by his father. Father and son were still at loggerheads over the subject. Amy feared that if anything happened to the old man, her career would come to an end.

Miss Lillian made an impatient gesture with her hand. "I won't have us making all this fuss over money. People will think we're running a poorhouse."

It was two hours later before Miss Paisley finally packed up her samples and left. Amy tried to gain Miss Lillian's attention, but the madam waved her away.

"Georgia, take her upstairs and get her dressed properly. We can't have her insulting our guests with her plain clothes and dull appearance."

Amy gazed down at her modest attire. Insulting? "But I need to talk to you," she protested.

"First things first," Miss Lillian sniffed. "And for goodness' sakes, do something about your walk. You'll catch more fish by wiggling the bait."

To demonstrate, she walked away swaying her hips from side to side like a pendulum.

Amy dreaded the beauty sessions almost as much as she dreaded being called on the Pinkerton carpet. Every pimple, every patch of red skin, every imperfection no matter how small was attacked with liberal doses of castor oil, glycerin, or vinegar.

Raw potatoes were applied to eye bags and dark shadows. And though no one but Buttercup had even a hint of a double chin, all were required to sleep with chin straps.

Buttercup had been given the task of teaching Amy how to look and act like a proper lady of the night, while Coral, Georgia, and Polly watched from the sidelines.

"I've never known anyone with such green eyes," Buttercup said. She applied green paint to Amy's eyelids and stepped back. "See how that brings out the color?"

Amy stared at herself in the mirror, and the first thing that popped into her mind was Jezebel from the Bible. "It's rather . . . loud," she said. "Perhaps a little less." A *gallon* less.

"Nonsense," Buttercup said. "You look beautiful."

"Beauty is in the eye of the beholder," Georgia said, grinning. She had blackened her teeth with charcoal. "In the Labrador Islands, only women with black teeth are considered beautiful."

"Why not just paint her face blue like they do in Greenland?" Coral asked.

"Or b–bind her feet like those p–poor women in China do?" Polly hobbled around on tiptoes.

The women continued to make teasing comments. Ignoring them, Buttercup held up a porcelain container. "You're all wrong. Beauty comes from within . . . a jar."

Laughter followed her comment, but Amy was in no mood to join in. This was all a waste of time, and she needed to get to work.

"I don't know why we have to go through all this torture just for men," she muttered.

All four women stared at her. "Is that w–what you th–think?" Polly stammered.

Amy was confused. "What else would I think?"

Coral leaned so close Amy could smell the tobacco on her breath. "Paint is a mask. It's how we keep men from getting too close. He's not looking at you. He's looking at a woman who doesn't exist."

Georgia concurred with a nod of her head. "We don't paint for men. We paint to survive."

CHAPTER 8

By the time Amy left Buttercup's room, her face felt ten times heavier. She didn't think she could survive another day in this horrid place. Never had she prayed so hard or so much as she had these last five days. *God, please, let's get this job done fast, so I can leave.*

A steady stream of men followed Miss Paisley's departure, some to get haircuts and shaves, others to buy boots or to have fortunes read.

Mr. Studebaker was the only singing student, and for that Amy was grateful. Though the man's futile attempts to hit a high C made her head ache, she kept her expression immobile for fear the heavy coat of powder would crack if she so much as grimaced.

Dressed in a vibrant red gown and her hair caught up in a cluster of ringlets, she waited at the top of the stairs for the last man to leave. Mr. Studebaker stopped to inspect a black leather boot. Catching sight of her on the second-floor landing, he doffed his hat and left.

At last! How she longed to finish this assignment and sink her teeth into a case less nerve racking. After this, she'd gladly go undercover as a librarian or even a nun.

Just as Amy reached the ground floor, Miss Lillian emerged from the parlor and stopped to straighten the merchandise.

The madam gave her a once-over and nodded approval. "Much better." She moved a leather wader from one shelf to another.

"Why boots?" Amy asked. It seemed like an odd thing to sell at a place like this.

Miss Lillian pointed to the ROWDIES WILL BE BOOTED OUT sign on the wall. "When the railroad came to town, the workers gave us a heap of trouble. So I put up that sign next to a pair of men's boots to show I meant business and wouldn't stand for any nonsense." She laughed. "I sold that first pair and ordered another. Soon the boots were selling even before I got them out of the box."

"Sounds like someone's trying to tell you to give up the guest business," Amy said. *God, probably. Hopefully.*

"Then he or she would be telling me wrong. I couldn't keep up this place by boots alone. The taxes —" She rolled her eyes. "Saloons and brothels pay for law and order in this town. Our taxes also built the new school building." She straightened another boot. "People depend on the wages of sin more than they care to admit."

Knowing that was true, Amy couldn't argue the point. "How did you get into this . . . particular business?"

"I was born and raised in a bordello. Not as nice as this one, mind you. But since I was the only child, the residents all doted on me. I didn't even know who my real mother was until I turned nine." Miss Lillian's voice took on an oddly impersonal tone, as if talking about someone else's childhood.

Miss Lillian straightened a pair of hand-tooled boots. "I guess you can say I was born into the business." A strained look crossed her face, but just as quickly it was gone and a tight smile took its place.

But Amy saw and she knew; beneath the fixed smile and Southern good manners, shielded by a barrier of heavy paint and perfume, beat a heart full of sadness and maybe even regret.

Words of God's grace and mercy bubbled

up inside her, and it was all she could do not to voice them. It almost killed her to keep quiet. She felt like Peter denying his Lord. Not that she had a choice. Her job required her to act a part, and that meant keeping her faith to herself. *Just don't let me hear a rooster crow, God.*

Amy wasn't the only one acting a part; Miss Lillian was doing a pretty good job of it, herself. Hiding her main trade behind a myriad of respectable activities allowed her to pretend she was a successful and legitimate businesswoman.

People lied to themselves all the time rather than face a painful truth. Amy's own father denied his drinking habit, but he wasn't alone. She once captured a train robber who gave half his ill-gotten gains to a church widows' fund to pay penance for his dastardly deeds. Claiming to be a philanthropist, he was shocked by his arrest and insisted that transferring money from a train safe into a poor widow's hand didn't make him a thief.

Having arranged the boots to her satisfaction, Miss Lillian raked Amy over with a critical eye. "We're open for business tonight." With a swish of her gown, she headed for her office. "I trust you'll be ready."

Amy dashed after her. "Wait! There's a problem!"

Miss Lillian paused at the threshold. "Problem? Problem?" Motioning Amy inside, the madam sat behind her desk and thumbed through a stack of mail. "What are you talking about? What problem?"

Amy lowered herself onto the only other chair in the room, the bustle forcing her to perch on the edge of the seat. She chewed on her lip but stopped beneath the madam's critical stare.

With a flick of her wrist, Miss Lillian slit an envelope open. "Well, get on with it. I haven't got all day."

Despite the madam's impatience, Amy had good reason to hesitate. Mr. Pinkerton was adamant about operatives following the rules, which meant revealing her occupation was strictly forbidden. Entrusting even family members was grounds for dismissal. It made life difficult and long absences hard to explain. No beau willingly pursued a woman with the annoying habit of leaving town at a drop of a hat to bury yet another "relative."

But this was an emergency. Without enlisting Miss Lillian's help, she was doomed to failure. She only hoped that what she was about to do didn't come back to haunt her.

"What I'm about to tell you must be kept in the strictest confidence." As if that wasn't clear enough, she added, "No one else can know."

Miss Lillian lifted her gaze from the letter in hand "Good heavens, don't tell me you're a virgin."

Amy drew back. Miss Lillian made chastity sound like a disease. "It's worse than that," she said wryly. She reached over the back of the chair and nudged the door shut. Thus braced, she turned and lowered her voice.

"I'm a detective working undercover. I work for the Pinkerton National Detective Agency."

Miss Lillian dropped her letter opener and sat back. Her carmine-rouged lips formed a perfect O, and her eyes looked ready to pop out of her head. "But . . . but you're a woman!"

"Yes, so I've heard." That was generally the first thing out of an outlaw's mouth whenever she whipped out her Pinkerton badge. One had even made the mistake of laughing in her face. He was probably still laughing, but since he was behind prison bars, she tried not to take it personally.

Miss Lillian's startled expression faded. "Are you looking for Rose's killer?"

"Possibly," Amy said, though that wasn't her assignment. Her job was to track down the Gunnysack Bandit, but Miss Lillian would be more likely to help her if she thought it was about Rose.

"What else do you do? Don't tell me you track down philandering husbands?"

Amy shook her head. "Mr. Pinkerton refuses to take on cases that involve matters of the heart." To put the madam's mind further at rest she added, "Nor would he ever accept an assignment that would reflect poorly on a woman's reputation."

"How rare. A man with integrity."

Amy smiled. Not everyone would agree. In years past, the Pinkerton agency had been criticized for what some considered questionable tactics.

"I hope whoever killed Rose hangs," Miss Lillian said, then lowered her voice to a conspiratorial whisper. "Is there money in that sort of thing? Detecting, I mean."

It wasn't a question Amy had expected. "Why, yes, I do get paid." Compared to most jobs women held, she got paid rather handsomely, though nowhere near as much as her male counterparts.

"I didn't know that women could be detectives. Why didn't someone tell me this before?" She sounded peeved. "Detecting

96

sounds like a whole lot more fun than giving singing lessons."

"It's also easier on the ears," Amy said.

"On the voice, too, I imagine."

Seeing the cogs turn in Miss Lillian's head, Amy hastened to add, "Yes, but the job can be tedious at times and quite boring." Amateur detectives often hindered investigations. She didn't want the madam getting any ideas. "It's also dangerous."

"I imagine so. That's why you carry a gun, right?"

"Yes, but fortunately I've never had occasion to use it." She prayed she never would.

Miss Lillian pondered this a moment before asking, "So what else are you detecting? You couldn't possibly have known in advance that Rose would be killed. So why are you really here?"

Already having said more than she'd planned, Amy hesitated. "We have reason to believe that the man known as the Gunnysack Bandit is one of your" — she almost said *johns,* a word Miss Lillian had banned — "guests."

Miss Lillian gasped and her thin eyebrows practically disappeared into her frothy hairline. "That awful outlaw? Why, that's impossible. I run a respectable business here. Why would you think such a thing?"

"A few weeks back, Rose made a deposit at the bank that included stolen money."

Miss Lillian's eyes widened. "Are you saying that Rose had something to do with the Gunnysack Bandit?"

"It's possible she didn't even know it. We were hoping she could tell us where she got the stolen bills." After a pause, she added, "The truth is, I shouldn't even be telling you this."

"It's a good thing you did. Is that what you were doing outside the other night with Mr. Colton? Detecting?"

Blue eyes and a crooked smile flashed through Amy's mind and a warm, pleasant feeling crept up her neck. "Yes."

"My word. You don't think that he —"

"I honestly don't know." She didn't want to believe that Colton was the bandit, but neither could she discount it. At this point of the investigation, everyone was suspect. Thinking she heard a sound, she jumped up and tore open the door. Mr. Beavers the cat scooted into the room and disappeared under the desk.

She closed the door but kept her hand on the brass knob. "There were only two guests here the other night when Rose was killed — Mr. Colton and one other."

"Mr. Pepper, owner of the Pepper Hardware and Medical Dispensary," Miss Lillian said.

"Mr. Colton was with me." At least part of the time.

"And Mr. Pepper was with Buttercup."

Buttercup had said as much to the marshal. "Were the outside doors locked during this time? The back door, too?"

"Oh yes, I always keep the doors locked at night. You can't be too safe these days. I once hired a bouncer, but he kept falling asleep while on duty."

"Who else has a key?"

"Why, no one." She lifted the key chain from around her waist and jiggled it. "I keep them with me at all times."

"So no one can come or go without your knowledge. Is that correct?"

"Absolutely."

Amy hesitated. "When was the last time you saw Rose alive?"

"I didn't actually see her. I spoke to her through the door. Told her Mr. Colton wanted to talk to her. She said to send him up."

Prior to Mr. Colton entering the room, Amy remembered hearing someone in the hallway. She was fairly certain now that it had been Miss Lillian.

"Did Rose's voice sound normal?"

Miss Lillian was quiet a moment. "Far as I could tell."

"How much time passed between sending Mr. Colton upstairs and discovering Rose's body?"

"I don't know. Not long. A few minutes."

"Who found the body?"

"I did. I have strict rules about preserving guest privacy. When I noticed Rose's door ajar, I went to close it. That's when I saw her on the floor."

Amy chewed on her lip as a worrisome thought crossed her mind. Did Mr. Colton kill Rose? What if instead of entering the room across from Rose's in error as he claimed, he had been looking for a means of escape?

If he was Rose's killer, he could also be the Gunnysack Bandit. Standing more than six feet tall, he certainly fit the description physically, at least according to witness accounts.

As much as she hated to think Colton guilty of anything but an attractive smile, she couldn't ignore the possibility that he was the man she'd been sent to track down.

"Did you know that Rose planned on leaving?"

"I'm not surprised. They all buck at the halter eventually. But most come back. It's a hard world out there."

"There's talk that Rose planned to marry."

"Really?" Miss Lillian shrugged. "Like I said, a hard world."

"Some would say this life is hard," Amy said.

"Some people might say the same about being a woman detective."

Amy would be the first to admit her life *was* difficult. Her job made it impossible to marry or maintain a home of her own, but at least she could look God in the eye. She couldn't say this out loud, of course. She needed the madam's help. It wouldn't do to alienate her, so she abruptly changed the subject.

"I have a room at the hotel. If you would allow me to work here undercover, I'll be able to watch your guests. One of them could be the Gunnysack Bandit. I will, of course, need to come and go as I please."

Miss Lillian considered her request for all of a minute. "My girls might think it odd that you're not entertaining guests."

"That's why I need your help to cover for me. I also need access to your ledgers and client list." She indicated the key chain in Miss Lillian's hand. "I noticed Rose's room was locked. I need to do a more thorough search of the crime scene."

"You can count on me to help in any way I can." Miss Lillian pulled a key off her key ring and handed it to Amy.

Amy felt like a weight had lifted. Miss Lillian's willingness to help would make things a whole lot easier. "Thank you. I'll return it as soon as I'm finished."

Miss Lillian heaved a sigh. "Rose didn't deserve to die like that." Her shoulders fell as did the corners of her mouth. "To think it happened here under my very nose."

"No one blames you."

"I blame myself." Miss Lillian rubbed her forehead. "It's my job to keep my girls safe."

"The best thing we can do for Rose right now is to find her killer." If Colton was right about the Gunnysack Bandit killing Rose, then catching him would give Rose the justice she deserved.

Miss Lillian appeared cheered by the thought. "I can't believe I'm working with a real live detective." She afforded Amy a brilliant smile. "This is more exciting than reading a dime novel. Would I be entitled to the reward for the capture of the Gunnysack Bandit? I'll use it to do something in memory of Rose."

"We can discuss that with the marshal when the time comes," Amy said. "But of course, if you speak out of turn —"

"No need to worry. Men used to want my affection." She paused for a moment as if thinking back on lost youth. "Now all they want is my discretion. I reckon you could say I'm in the business of keeping secrets."

Amy stood. "I'm counting on it." Little did the madam know how much.

CHAPTER 9

Tom Colton sat in the hotel lobby and pulled out his watch. It was half past four. The lady — Amy — was late. Or maybe she wasn't coming. He tucked his watch back into his vest pocket and waited. Now that Rose was gone, the green-eyed beauty was his best bet for finding the information needed to track down his brother's killer.

Another twenty minutes passed before he spotted her. Pausing at the entryway, she glanced around, her trim figure outlined by the bright afternoon sun. She was tall for a woman — about five foot eight — yet she carried her height with easy grace. Despite the unseasonal warmth of the day, she wore a prim and proper shoulder cape that would have done justice to a schoolmarm.

Had the very idea of a woman selling her body not been so distasteful, he might have laughed. Some lady of the night. Obviously the woman was in the wrong profession.

Despite her show of modesty, men gazed at her with covetous eyes. One man approached her, but she gave him the cold shoulder. She turned toward a young blond woman with a small child. For a moment it looked like she knew the young mother, but then she turned away.

He stood to make his presence known. Acknowledging him with a nod, she walked toward him with stiff dignity. No exaggerated hip swing, no fluttering eyelashes. No flirtatious moves. Just a walk, plain and simple, yet no less fetching.

"I didn't think you were coming," he said. Half expecting Miss Lillian to pounce on him and demand payment, he glanced toward the hotel door. No sign of the madam. His pocketbook was safe — for now.

"Do you mind being seen in public with me?" she asked, apparently misreading his intent.

He never much worried about what people thought. Being seen with her wasn't the problem; working with her was. He'd arrested his share of shady ladies in the past, but never before had he done business with one. Could he trust her?

"I reckon we could go to my room. That is, if you'd feel more comfortable."

She shook her head. "If we go to your room, I'll have to charge you."

"I just want to talk," he said.

She shrugged. "Miss Lillian's rules."

"Then I'm all for sitting down here. If it's all the same to you, ma'am."

For answer, she lowered herself upon the upholstered chair across from him and occupied herself with what seemed like an excessive arranging of skirt and cape.

The memory of her tumbling out of a tree and into his arms flashed through his head. It was hard to reconcile this stiff, painted woman with the freewheeling, disheveled spirit seen that moonlit night.

He sat and waited until he had her full attention. "Now that we're working together —"

"Working?" She sat back. "I haven't given you my answer. It could be no."

"No is not an answer. It's a retreat." He rubbed his jaw. "I had you pegged as a fighter."

"I *am* a fighter, Mr. Colton. But I don't like fighting other people's battles."

He leaned forward. "The man who killed Rose . . . He's still out there. I need your help before he kills again."

She studied him with wary regard. "You said Rose was your brother's fiancée. Miss

Lillian was unable to confirm that."

"Perhaps Rose didn't want anyone to know."

"Or maybe you made it up."

"I've never been one for making up things." He arched his brows. "Don't know why I'd start now." He reached inside his vest and drew out the letter addressed to his brother and signed by Rose. "This was found on my brother's body."

Pulling off her gloves, she laid them across her lap all serious-like. Most painted ladies had little or no education, but Amy wasn't like most. Question was, could she read? He debated whether to read the letter aloud to prevent embarrassment, but she showed no hesitation in taking it from him. The thin paper crackled as she unfolded it.

While she read, he studied her face, feature by feature. The other women working for Miss Lillian had hard faces and cynical eyes, but Amy's features still held the softness of youth. Had it not been for the face paint, he would never have guessed her profession.

Pursing scarlet lips, she refolded the letter and handed it back. "The letter makes no mention of the Gunnysack Bandit."

He hadn't wanted to go into details, but obviously she wasn't going to work with him unless he came up with appropriate answers.

"My brother and I weren't close. In fact, I hadn't seen or heard from him in more than two years. Not since the day he left prison."

She raised her eyebrows. "Your brother was in prison?"

He gave a curt nod. "He led a gang of stagecoach robbers." Cooperating with authorities had earned him an early release, and he only served half his time. "He was lucky he didn't hang."

The searing pain in his chest took him by surprise. It still hurt, even now. "Then out of the blue he contacted me and asked for my help. Said that his fiancée, Rose, had accidentally discovered the identity of the Gunnysack Bandit and he lives here in Goodman. According to my brother, Rose feared for her life, and he wanted to bring her to the ranch. Guess he figured she'd be safe in Texas."

"Why didn't she go to the marshal?"

He scratched his head. The woman was ignorant of her profession in more ways than one. "Do you really think that the marshal would take a sporting lady seriously? Or even afford her protection?"

She fixed him with a stony gaze, allowing him to peer unfettered into the mesmerizing sea-green depths of her eyes. It wasn't

108

polite to stare, but he couldn't seem to help himself.

"He should. Part of his salary depends on the licensing fees and taxes Miss Lillian pays."

"The money assures that the marshal will leave the house alone and look the other way," he said evenly. "Nothing more."

She cleared her throat. "Is there any chance your brother misunderstood? About the Gunnysack Bandit living here in Goodman, I mean."

"Like Rose, he was murdered. No fuss, no bother, just a simple shot to the head. Been my experience that people shot that way either cheated at cards or knew too much. Where money was concerned, my brother liked a sure thing. That leaves cards out."

"Aren't you forgetting something, Mr. Colton?" She moistened her lips. "Rose was hit on the head." She didn't elaborate, but her meaning was clear; criminals seldom strayed from their method of operation. That wasn't exactly common knowledge. He stroked his chin. There was more to this woman than first met the eye, that was for sure and certain. Perhaps someone in her family was a lawman.

"A gunshot would have been heard by the other residents. Sometimes even creatures of habit have to improvise." When she didn't reply, he inclined his head. "So what do you say? Will you help me?"

"Help you how, exactly?"

"Talk to the other women. Find out what they know. If Rose was suspicious of one of the men, maybe the others are, too. A list of regulars would help."

She rearranged her gloves on her lap. "What's in it for me?"

He afforded a quick smile. Well, look a there. Not only could the lady read, she had a head for business. So what in blazes was she doing at Miss Lillian's?

"Like I said, I'll pay you. I'll even help you find another line of work, if that's what you want." Here he went again, out to save the world. When was he going to learn?

Her eyes flashed. "And what line of work would that be, Mr. Colton? Scullery work?"

"Honest work."

Her green-eyed gaze wasn't any more revealing than her expression. All that paint made it hard to know what went on in that pretty head of hers. Most women were a mystery to him, but never more so than this one.

She put on her gloves, working each finger into the right spot with utmost care before standing. "How do I reach you?"

"I take that to mean you're not retreating." It was a statement rather than a question.

The corners of her mouth curved upward in a half smile. "I discovered long ago that it never pays to turn one's back on either friend *or* foe."

"So what am I?" he asked.

"That's to be determined. Meanwhile, I'm sure you'll understand my need to be cautious."

He studied her. Cautious? That wasn't how he would describe someone in her profession.

"I'm in room fourteen," he said. "If I'm out, you can leave a message at the desk."

"I'll be in touch."

He watched her walk away with mixed feelings. The woman intrigued him and, yes, even puzzled him. Not in any sort of personal way, of course. Okay, maybe a little . . .

CHAPTER 10

Following the meeting with Colton, Amy returned to the parlor house, anxious to continue her investigation. She knew even before entering her room that someone had been there in her absence.

The intruder had no way of knowing about the lengths of thread she placed in the cracks of doors and drawers — a Pinkerton trick that had served her well in the past. Once it had even saved her life by alerting her to the presence of someone wishing to do her harm.

Weapon in hand, she cautiously entered her room. Coral and the others thought nothing of walking in unannounced to borrow facial creams or hair pomades, but the missing threads told a different story; every last one was missing, and that meant someone had done a methodical search but was careful to leave things intact.

Did someone suspect she wasn't who she

said she was? Fortunately, she kept nothing there that would reveal her identity. Still, she felt a sense of unease as she pulled off hat and gloves and reached in her pocket for the key to Rose's room.

Moments later she let herself into the room across the hall.

A stagnant smell greeted her, and a veil of death hung in the air like fine dust. It was a smell she'd become all too familiar with during her years as an operative.

The room hadn't been touched since the night Rose's body had been found. A dark stain marked the place where her corpse had lain. The kerosene had dried, but a faint odor lingered.

Stepping over the clothing strewn about the floor, she reached for the bureau and opened the drawers one by one. The top one was empty except for a scarf and a tintype of a man and woman — an older couple. Rose's parents? The back of the picture held no markings or even a studio name, so there was no way of checking.

She replaced the tintype and searched the other drawers but found nothing of interest. She studied the mirrored tray. Only God knew what poisons lurked in the jars of facial creams and powder boxes scattered across the top of the bureau. Or in the iron rust washes that darkened the hair. More than one prostitute had died from lead or mercury poisoning. Not only were the cosmetics dangerous, they dried the skin and made it feel itchy.

She examined a vial of glycerin and picked up a bottle of perfume and sniffed. It had a citrusy smell that was more delicate in fragrance than the norm at Miss Lillian's. She poked at the burnt cork used to darken eyebrows.

The bureau held all the necessary tools of the trade but nothing personal except for the tintype. No letters or diaries. Mr. Colton had shown her a letter Rose had written to his brother, but where were his letters to her?

Several books were scattered on the floor, all about birds. She stooped to pick one up and flipped through the dog-eared pages of illustrations and descriptions of every feathered species from the stately blue heron to the smallest hummingbird.

She set the book on the dresser and stared at the room with a sigh. No matter how much she tried to trust God, little doubts crept in on occasion, just as they were creeping now. What if she couldn't track down the Gunnysack Bandit? What if Pinkerton fired her? What would happen to her then?

Shaking her worrisome thoughts away, she turned slowly, surveying every nook and cranny. A detective was only as good as his or her observation skills. The firm's founder, Allan Pinkerton, believed this so strongly he chose for his logo an eye. The Pinkerton eye never slept, but neither did it merely "see": it observed and analyzed.

An open trunk caught her attention, and a closer look revealed that the lock was unbroken. It was almost identical to the one in Amy's room. Miss Lillian insisted that her girls keep personal belongings under lock and key at all times. Loose morals and sticky fingers went hand in hand.

The money box in the depths of the trunk was empty, as was the hand-carved jewelry case. Nothing of a personal nature was contained inside the trunk. Had Rose walked in on a robbery in progress? Was that why she was killed?

Amy lifted the window shade, and golden sunlight fell onto the sill and spilled across the plush red carpet.

Flocked scarlet wallpaper adorned the walls. The paper lay flat with no compromised seams to suggest hidden wall safes. A still painting of a green vase filled with pink roses hung slightly off center but revealed nothing behind.

After examining the walls, she lowered her gaze to the bed. The mattress was crooked with the pillow at the foot instead of the head.

Dropping down on hands and knees, she peered beneath the bed. A man's gold fob chain was coiled next to a single satin slipper, but there was no way of telling how long it had been there. She reached for it and examined it carefully. A 14-karat yellow-gold chain was not something the average man could afford. Standing, she slipped it into her dressing gown pocket.

At first it bothered her that no one heard Rose struggling with her assailant. Now she knew why. No struggle had occurred, which explained the lack of defense marks on Rose's hands. The room was in disarray because someone had done a hasty but thorough search. The same person who had searched her room earlier that day?

With that question came another: Had the killer sneaked up on Rose, catching her unawares? But that made no sense. The room offered no place in which to hide. That suggested that Rose knew her killer. Perhaps had even let her assailant in.

She turned a circle once again, her gaze

sweeping the room from top to bottom. One would expect a person to stop searching upon finding a lost or hidden object. Yet every portion of the room had been ransacked. Even the clothes in the tall wardrobe closet had been pulled from their hooks. Hats spilled from overturned band boxes; gloves, handkerchiefs, and stockings were scattered on the floor.

To catch a thief you had to think like one. What could the killer have been looking for? Anyone familiar with the bordello knew that anything personal or valuable was kept in the trunk. So the fact that the entire room had been ransacked was odd, unless the killer was a stranger. But that made no sense, either.

The killer had to have been someone Rose knew; *someone who may even live beneath this very roof.*

Back in his Ranger days, Tom Colton found hanging out at saloons a good way to get the lay of the land and learn about the locals. Nothing loosened the tongue like tonsil paint, providing one didn't overindulge. So timing was everything. Arrive at a saloon too early and everyone was tongue-tied, too late and a person might find flying fists instead of loose lips.

Each night that week, he'd visited a different saloon. So far his efforts had produced no useful information. Several people had known Dave — had even hired him to do odd jobs. Except for the fact that his brother drank too much, most had nothing but good things to say about him.

The Idle Hands Saloon and Dance Hall was in full swing when Tom arrived. Someone was playing a frenzied tune on the fiddle, and several men were playing faro.

Some saloons offered more than just alcohol. Some offered tea and coffee. If Tom was lucky, this one might even serve milk.

Tonight, luck smiled down on him. The poker-faced bartender slid a glass of cow juice across the bar without comment, and Tom let it sit. Milk offered two distinct advantages: it kept the mind clear and it got attention, usually from troublemakers. But then they were the ones with the most information.

The fiddler played a medley of frenzied tunes and voices grew louder. Tom stared at his milk, startled by the vision of green eyes that stared back. Drat! Now he was seeing things.

Tom's choice of a nonalcoholic drink caught the attention of various men, but none admitted to knowing Dave. He'd just about given up when a beefy man with tree-trunk legs and bulging arms bellied up to the bar. Two wings of greased black hair curled toward his ears. With his broken nose and flattened jaw, he looked meaner than a newly sheared sheep.

He set his glass next to Tom's and heaved a dusty boot on the brass-foot bar. "Your mama wean you too young, boy?"

Tom picked up his glass and took a sip. The milk was lukewarm and just this side of sour. "Could be."

"You new 'round here?"

"Yep," Tom said. "You?"

"Been here since the war. Name's Tanner, but everyone calls me Buckeye."

"Nice to meet you, Buckeye. You can call me Tom."

"What brings you to these parts, Tom?"

"Looking for someone. Name's Dave Colton."

Buckeye picked up his glass and tossed the liquid down his throat in a single gulp. He slammed the glass on the bar and wiped his hand across his mouth. "You can stop looking."

Tom kept his gaze straight out in front of him where he could watch the man in the mirror behind the bar. Some troublemakers took offense if you looked them square in

119

the eye. "Why's that?"

"Colton's dead. Took a piece of lead right here." He pointed to his temple. "What did you want him for?"

"Owed me money."

"Yeah, well, tough luck."

After a while, Tom asked, "How well did you know him?"

"Who? Colton?" Buckeye shrugged. "We spent the night in the hoosegow together, so I guess you could say we were iron bar buddies." He shook his head. "The man was knee-walkin' drunk that night. Babblin' like a newborn babe. Kept jawin' about the Gunnysack Bandit."

Tom raised his glass to his mouth and tried not to look overly interested. He took a sip and set the glass down with puckered lips. Next time he'd remember to ask the bartender how long the cow and milk had been divorced before placing his order.

"What did he say, exactly?"

"Nothing that made sense at the time. Makes me sick to think about it."

"Think about what?" Tom asked.

"The ten thousand dollars that slipped through my fingers."

Tom frowned. "You loaned this Colton fella ten thousand dollars?"

"Not me. Where do you think I'd get that

kind of money?" He lowered his voice. "I'm talking about the reward for the Gunnysack Bandit."

" 'Fraid you lost me, there," Tom said.

"What I'm saying is that I finally figured out what Colton was babbling about the night we spent in jail. What he said was that *he* was the Gunnysack Bandit."

CHAPTER 11

Amy knew she was in trouble the moment she stepped out of the mudroom door and into the backyard. Against her better judgment she'd agreed to meet Coral for a shooting lesson. Instead, all five women, including Miss Lillian, greeted her with firearms in hand.

She frowned. That's all she needed, a bunch of women running around with guns. Especially since one of them might very well be Rose's killer. "What are you all doing here?"

Miss Lillian held her weapon straight out in front with both hands. "Heard you were teaching Coral to shoot. Sounds like something we should all learn. So I had Harry Piker send over a weapon for each of us."

"Th—that w—way we'll be safe," Polly added, her hand shaking like a wet dog.

Amy knew not to discount anyone as a suspect so early in the game, but it was hard to imagine nervous Polly wielding a candle-stick holder. Coral with her snippy tongue and dark glances was still a consideration. Buttercup was certainly large enough to overpower Rose. Georgia was thin, but hardly a weakling. Then, of course, there was always Miss Lillian, but Amy doubted the madam would do anything that would harm her business.

"I can understand why you might want to protect yourselves." In light of Rose's death, Amy couldn't blame them for wanting to be armed. Still, she always thought firearm safety undervalued, but never more so than today.

"Of course we need to protect ourselves," Miss Lillian said. Little remained of the soft Southern drawl used on guests. Today, her voice had a steel-like edge. "Wasn't that long ago that a woman felt safe in her own home, but those days are long gone."

"It's the railroad," Coral said. "Nothing's been the same since the iron horse came to town."

Miss Lillian nodded. "Yes, but there's nothing we can do about it except learn to fend for ourselves. So let's get on with it, shall we? Before we all shoot each other."

Miss Lillian had every reason for concern. It was obvious that Buttercup and Polly had no experience with weapons, and the others didn't fare much better.

"I can't believe I'm doing this," Georgia said with an anxious giggle.

Amy blew a stray strand of hair away from her face. "That makes two of us."

Polly's gun dangled from her hand like it was a dead rat or something equally unpleasant. "I've always been af–fraid of g–guns."

Coral sneered. "You're afraid of your own shadow."

Polly tossed her head. "Am n–not." She glanced around as if looking for someone to agree with her and finding none, fell silent.

Taking charge, Amy placed her hands on her hips. "Muzzles down," she yelled, and all arms dropped to the side. "Now keep them down until I tell you to raise them."

Georgia's gun fell out of her hand and she stooped to pick it up. "It's so small," she said as if to apologize for her clumsiness.

"Don't let the size fool you." Amy walked back and forth in front of the women as she spoke. At nearly four inches long, derringers were stubby and lightweight. This made them the concealed weapon of choice. "Booth shot Lincoln with one of these. Just don't try to shoot farther than ten feet away."

"How come you know so much about guns?" Buttercup asked.

Coral's eyes narrowed. "I was wondering the same thing myself."

"My brothers taught me," Amy replied. At least that part was true. She wasn't about to tell them that she also graduated from the Pinkerton detective school at the top of her class.

Changing the subject, she lectured them on gun safety. Eventually, their eyes glazed over, and she ran out of ways to postpone the inevitable.

Now she would have to show them how to load and fire their weapons. *God help them all.*

She reached into her pocket and pulled her derringer from her thigh holster. Clouds hovered overhead, but the air was calm. Perfect for shooting.

"All right, men . . . uh . . . ladies. This is how you hold a weapon." She explained how the two-shot over-under pistol worked and showed them how to open the breach to load their weapons. "Keep your finger off the trigger until ready to fire."

Earlier, she'd salvaged three empty tin cans from the kitchen. Now she arranged them on the woodpile and walked back several paces. Raising her arm, she aimed, fired, and missed. Adjusting her aim, she fired again, and this time a can flew off the stack of wood.

"All right, on the count of three I want you all to aim at the woodpile. Keep your finger off the trigger. Don't shoot till I tell you."

She then stepped out of the line of fire — or at least she hoped she did. "Aim!"

The women lifted their arms and pointed their guns directly at the target. "The weapons are small but the kickback is —"

Just then Tom Colton barreled around the corner of the house, shooting iron in hand. Before she could issue a warning, a startled Polly cried out and fired. The shot triggered a chain reaction, and the other four guns went off in rapid succession. Birds rose from the treetops with loud squawks and a flutter of frantic wings.

For a moment, none of the women moved. When the smoke cleared, the only sign of Colton was his hat on the ground.

Snapping out of her shocked state, Amy ran to the woodpile with dread. "Mr. Colton!"

Tom had hit the ground hard and now lay spread eagle facedown. His hat had flown in one direction, his firearm in another.

Raising himself on his arms, he spit the dirt from his mouth. Miraculously, he was still in one piece.

Amy was the first to reach his side. She fell next to him in a cloud of shiny blue skirts, a horrified look on her face. "Are you all right?"

At sight of the gun in her hands, he raised his hands shoulder high. "Yes, but only if you don't shoot."

Eyes rounded, she slipped her shooting iron into her pocket and was all over him like a mother hen. She brushed off his vest and, taking his handkerchief, wiped the dirt from his face.

"What are you doing here?" she asked, her voice barely above a whisper.

"I heard gunfire and I thought you ladies were in trouble."

Her hand stilled, and their gazes locked. "You could have been killed."

"That's for sure and certain." Fearing he was about to be drawn into the depth of her eyes, he pulled his gaze away and glanced over the stack of wood. Five women peered back. "What in the name of Sam Hill are they doing with guns?"

"They're scared. They fear that whoever killed Rose might kill them."

"The way you ladies shoot, he needn't

bother. You'll save him the trouble." Since it appeared he was in no imminent danger, he pushed to his feet.

Miss Lillian glared at him as if he was the one in the wrong. "You can't say you weren't warned, Mr. Colton." She sniffed. "I told you danger lay ahead."

"Can't argue with you there, ma'am." He reached down for his hat and brushed it off. He then picked up his Peacemaker and jammed it into his holster.

"W–we're learning to sh–shoot," one woman stammered. The recoil had evidently hurt her hand. Holding her arm by the wrist, she shook it.

The woman in the bright yellow dress gave a nervous giggle. "I feel so much safer now."

Tom slapped the hat on his head. "Wish I could say the feeling was mutual."

"That's enough for today," Amy called. "We'll practice more tomorrow."

One by one, the women headed for the house.

Miss Lillian followed at the rear and paused by the back door. "Would you care for some refreshment, Mr. Colton? Or perhaps you would allow me to read your fortune? On the house, of course. It's the least I can do for your . . . inconvenience."

He scratched his temple. The woman had

an interesting way with words. "No inconvenience, ma'am. I like being ambushed by a bunch of gun-toting women."

Amy's laughter rippled through the air. Momentarily caught off guard by the musical sound, his gaze met hers, and he wondered not for the first time how she ended up in such a place. All too soon the laughter faded away, but the memory remained.

"Very well," Miss Lillian called. "Coming, Amy?"

"In a minute." In a softer voice, she asked, "So what are you doing here?"

"I waited for you at the hotel." He tilted his head. "Thought you might have information for me by now. Perhaps the names of Rose's clients."

"Guests."

"What?"

"They're called guests."

He pushed his hat back with a finger to his brim. "If we're gonna work together, there's something you should know about me. I'm not much for beating around the bush. I'm what you might call a simple man. I like keeping things plain and uncomplicated, and that includes language."

"Does that go for women, too?" she asked. "The plain and uncomplicated part?"

"It's been my experience that them's the

best kind." He hung his thumbs from his gun belt. Not that Amy was in any way plain. Complicated, yes. Plain, no. "So if it's all the same to you, ma'am, I'd appreciate it if you'd be straightforward with me. It'll make things a whole lot simpler."

"I'll get you the list you want. Is that straightforward enough?"

"It'll do. For now."

Her eyes met his. Today they were the color of freshly mowed grass. "I really am sorry for what happened," she said. "The guns — that wasn't my idea."

He rubbed the back of his neck. "Thank God for bad aims."

She smiled. "And quick cowboys."

Every time she smiled it was as if some unseen signal passed between them, and today was no different. "Why do I get the feeling that you don't belong here?"

The smile vanished, and the light in her eyes seemed to dim. He wished he hadn't said anything, but he couldn't seem to help himself. She was throwing her life away. There had to be something he could say or do to make her see that.

"I'll be in touch." She started for the house, but he stopped her with a hand to her wrist.

"I'll be mighty obliged for any help you

give me." The encounter with the man named Buckeye had shaken him more than he wanted to admit. If what he said about Dave was true, he didn't know how he would live with that. How he would break the news to Dave's son waiting back at the ranch.

Aware, suddenly, that the madam was still watching and looked like she was about to charge him good money, he released Amy's arm.

"I'll help you the best I can," she said in a hushed voice. "Just as long as we keep it simple between us."

"In other words, keep my nose out of your business."

She gave him a half smile, but even that was a treat. "We understand each other."

"I doubt it'll ever come to that, ma'am. The understanding part, I mean." Never in a million years would he understand a woman in her profession.

"Probably not. But it'll be fun trying."

"Now there's a thought," he said.

She walked away and, with a quick glance in his direction, vanished into the house.

A noticeable chill filled the air and the trees began to sway. It was as if the sun had vanished with her. Sudden wind kicked up the musty smell of rain.

Annoyed with himself for letting the lady get to him, he made a dash for his horse tethered in front of the house. With a little luck, he'd make it back to his hotel before the storm.

Peering down at the street from her bedroom window, Amy had mixed emotions as Tom Colton rode away on his shiny black horse. No sooner had he vanished from sight than a flash of lightning zigzagged across the sky followed by a sudden downpour.

Streams of water raced down the windowpane as if to chase away her unbridled thoughts. . . .

Was Tom Colton the Gunnysack Bandit? The question had been very much on her mind these last couple of days. If the answer was yes, then perhaps the real reason he wanted her to spy was to find out what, if anything, the other women knew about him.

That business about his brother sounded true, but that could have been a ruse and the letter a forgery. The outlaw had terrorized Kansas for the past four years and had outwitted the country's smartest detectives and lawmen. Obviously he was no fool, and neither was Mr. Colton. The man could charm the gold out of a rock.

So was he or was he not the Gunnysack Bandit?

She didn't have the answer yet, but one thing was clear: she hoped to God he wasn't.

CHAPTER 12

The next day Amy sat in her room at the Grande Hotel and Bath House. Maintaining a hotel room was a luxury, but it afforded her much-needed privacy.

The Pinkerton brothers would complain about the added expense, of course, but it couldn't be helped. Her chameleon-like ability to adapt to her surroundings generally served her well. But this . . . this was altogether something different. No other assignment had required her to stay in character around the clock, seven days a week. No other case had challenged her on so many levels. Perhaps the hardest part of all was the necessity of keeping her faith in God under wraps and not let it slip out in general conversation as it tended to do.

She also had a practical reason for maintaining a hotel room. As the new girl, she was given the least desirable room at the parlor house. That didn't bother her; the broken lock on her door did.

Coral and the others thought nothing of walking in without knocking. She was in constant danger of being caught going over Miss Lillian's ledgers or writing her reports.

Hand on the back of her neck, she rolled her head to work out the kinks. Her report to headquarters was still missing the names of Miss Lillian's guests, so she opened the ledger.

The madam kept perfect records, and every transaction, whether for entertainment, singing lessons, boots, haircuts, or fortune-telling, was recorded in clear, precise handwriting.

A total of forty-two transactions were recorded the week prior to Rose depositing stolen money into her bank deposit. Amy felt a surge of excitement as she studied the names of the men who had done business at Miss Lillian's, including the marshal who, according to the ledger, purchased a pair of leather boots.

Miss Lillian paid her girls by check, but Polly explained that sometimes the men gave them a little something extra on the side. That meant Rose could have gotten the stolen banknotes directly from one of the guests. But which one? Not Tom Colton. He wasn't even at the bordello on the week in question. In fact, his name showed up only once, on the day of Rose's death.

The marshal's name posed a problem. Pinkerton operatives were required to introduce themselves to local lawmen, and she had planned to do so that very day. Not only was it a matter of courtesy but also of necessity. Obtaining the marshal's co-operation was part of the job.

But what if *he* was the Gunnysack Bandit? It wouldn't be the first time a lawman had turned to a life of crime. Politicians, lawyers, and doctors were also known to participate in illegal activities. And only last fall, a minister had robbed a train to build a church. A detective couldn't afford to discount anyone.

She copied the names onto her writing tablet to include with her report to head-quarters. Reports were required to be ac-curate to the last detail and any dialogue recorded verbatim. Though she had to think hard to accurately record her conversations with Miss Lillian — and that of the four working women — Amy had no trouble recalling every word exchanged with Tom Colton.

"Does that go for women, too? The plain and uncomplicated part?"

"It's been my experience that them's the

136

best kind."

The memory of his voice was so clear it was almost as if he were in the room with her. She shook her head to clear her mind. Somehow she had to conquer whatever hold he had over her. She had a job to do. That meant she had no time for silly schoolgirl fantasies.

Forcing herself to concentrate on her report, she wrote until her fingers ached from gripping the pen.

The Pinkerton National Detective Agency had the world's largest collection of mug shots in its criminal database. So the first order of business was to see if any of the forty-two men had a criminal record. This required detailed descriptions, and Miss Lillian had been a big help in this regard.

Amy reread what she had written and frowned. She may have gotten a bit carried away in describing Mr. Colton's eyes as peacock blue with flecks of gold. The French dressmaker's influence, no doubt.

Satisfied that at last she was making headway, she wrote a separate list of the men for herself and one for Colton, though she had yet to decide whether to give it to him. Completing her tasks, she drew the draperies shut. She then pulled a dress, two skirts, and matching shirtwaists from her valise and tucked them into the carpetbag borrowed from Miss Lillian. Last, she added the ledger.

She cracked open the door and peered cautiously down the hall before stepping outside and turning the key. *His* room, number fourteen, was several doors away, and the very thought quickened her pulse. Attributing the sudden warmth rushing to her cheeks to a sudden bout of anxiety, she headed for the stairs.

No one would be surprised to see a woman of easy virtue at the hotel, but the last thing she needed was to bump into Mr. Colton. If he really was the Gunnysack Bandit, he might have hired her just to keep her under surveillance. She'd best watch her step around him until he had been thoroughly checked against the agency's vast file of known criminals.

The second-story landing was empty, but people milled around the lobby below.

She was halfway down the stairs before noticing Mr. Colton seated in the sitting area, reading a newspaper.

Ducking her head beneath the banister, she turned and raced up the stairs to the top landing. Was there another way out of the hotel? Perhaps a second set of stairs for domestic help?

"Bless my soul. Fancy meeting you here."

She glanced over her shoulder and her heart nearly stopped. The three church ladies stood beaming at her. Pushing her spectacles up her nose, Mrs. Givings was the first to speak.

"We are putting a Good Book in each of the empty rooms," she explained, pointing to a box filled to the brim with Bibles. "We thought weary travelers might appreciate a comforting word."

"Yes, I'm sure they would," Amy said. She peered over the railing just as Mr. Colton rose and headed for the staircase. "Let me help you."

Holding her valise in one hand, she scooped several leather-bound Bibles from the cardboard box with the other. The three women's mouths dropped open.

"Oh, but that won't be necess—"

Not giving Mrs. Givings a chance to finish, Amy sprinted down the hall, dropping a Bible as she fled. "I'll go this way," she called.

Spotting the top of Mr. Colton's wide-brim hat as he ascended the stairs, she panicked and ran through the first open door. An older man with a white mustache and beard was emptying his suitcase.

He took one look at her and licked his

chops. "Now that's what I call room service."

CHAPTER 13

The next day, Amy sat in her room and stared at the calendar. She couldn't believe she'd been at Miss Lillian's Parlor House for a week. The worst part was that she had precious little to show for it. She'd questioned the others at length, but no one had anything useful to say. Never had she met more closemouthed women. Her frustration grew with each passing hour.

Living at Miss Lillian's was an odd experience that clawed at Amy's conscience. It sickened her to see women spend so much time primping, flirting, and kowtowing to men. Most everything of an immoral nature was kept behind closed doors, of course, but that didn't make it any easier to bear. For her own peace of mind, she constantly reminded herself that she was there for the greater good. Her job was to catch a criminal, not to judge the way others lived their lives.

Isn't that what the Bible said? *"Judge not."* Easier said than done. Never before had she struggled so hard to be charitable. Harder still was holding her tongue.

It was all she could do not to shake Polly and the other women and make them see what they were doing was wrong and destructive. God had a better plan, if only they would put their trust in Him. She couldn't say that, of course, couldn't take a chance on blowing her cover. But it nearly killed her to keep quiet. It surely did feel like God was testing her.

She also felt guilty for enjoying the luxurious living conditions at Miss Lillian's. That she couldn't deny.

The madam had spared no expense in creating a pleasant environment for her "girls." The flocked red wallpaper was from France, the ornate carpets from the Orient, and the crystal chandeliers had been shipped directly from Italy.

Indoor plumbing was an extravagance that Amy had only heard about but had never personally experienced except in hotels. It was something she imagined that only kings and the very rich could afford. The highlight of her day was sinking into the footed porcelain tub with its gold-plated faucets and letting her cares float away. The hot, soapy water provided a soothing salve for the soul and cleared her mind.

During nonworking hours, the atmosphere at the house became notably more relaxed. At times it seemed more like a women's school dormitory than a bordello. The low, smoky voices trained to capture a man's ear grew more natural and therefore more high pitched. Without layers of face paint, expressions appeared softer, but no less sad.

Each woman was expected to keep her own room tidy and to attend to any necessary mending, but the wash was sent out to Soo's Chinese Laundry and Fine Tea on Third Street.

When they weren't working, the women enjoyed parlor games. Only Polly and Georgia could read. Polly devoured dime novels like candy, but Georgia's reading tastes were more refined. Once, Amy caught her reading a book of love poems, which she hid behind her back. Sometimes Miss Lillian played the piano and Buttercup and Georgia joined her in song.

One afternoon Amy offered to play the piano for them, and though she was sorely out of practice, her command of the yellowed ivory keys brought oohs and aahs from the women.

"I had no idea you were so talented," Miss

Lillian said. "You must play for our guests."

Amy shook her head. "I haven't played in years." She was amazed that she still had the music memorized. Her old music teacher, Mrs. Jeremy, had been tough on her, and it had paid off.

"What's the name of the piece you played?" Buttercup asked, pulling her gaze away from the wall mirror.

" 'Für Elise.' It's by Beethoven. I'm afraid I hardly did it justice." Between the tuneless piano and wrong notes, the poor composer was probably turning over in his grave. She could almost hear Mrs. Jeremy's voice now. *"A cow could play with more grace!"*

"Some people think the real title is 'Für Theresa,' but Beethoven had such poor handwriting no one can be certain."

"M–maybe he c–couldn't s–say T–T–T–," Polly stammered.

"Beethoven was deaf, not dumb," Coral said. To her credit, a look of horror crossed her face the moment the words left her mouth. "I didn't mean that how it sounded."

Georgia broke the stiff silence that followed with a wistful sigh. "He must have loved her very much to name a song after her."

Amy expected Coral to make some disparaging comment about love or men or both, but she said nothing. Apparently she really did feel bad about her careless remark to Polly.

Georgia's sentiment did, however, have a sobering effect on the little group, and no one said much after that. It was times like this when the masks slipped off, giving a hint of the women behind them, a hint of the broken dreams and disillusionments that brought them here.

Amy turned back to the piano and started playing again. From the deep recesses of her mind came a memory, came a voice. *"Pay Do-dah, Tenfer."*

Her little sister, Cissy, couldn't pronounce "Jennifer," so she called her "Tenfer" instead. Do-dah was her name for the "Camptown Races." Cissy had never learned to say Jennifer correctly because she disappeared at the age of three and was never heard from again.

The memory stabbed through Amy like a knife, and grief the size of a whale rose up and threatened to swallow her. Her hands crashed to the keys and the discordant tone resonated through the room.

Shaken by the feeling of loss and despair that suddenly overwhelmed her, she spun around on the piano stool to apologize. But the ringing dinner bell had everyone on their feet and heading for the dining room.

The noon meal was a grand occasion at Miss Lillian's. The table was set with fine damask linen, sterling silver cutlery, and bone china plates. Fresh flowers decorated the center of the table, their dainty, sweet fragrance a pleasant change from the heavy perfume that usually tainted the air.

The laughter and easy chatter that greeted Amy on her first day had, since Rose's death, been replaced with mostly sullen looks and reserved exchanges.

Now that the women had firearms, they toted their reticules with them everywhere. Even Miss Lillian had grown attached to her drawstring bag and was never seen without it.

The madam sat at her usual place at the head of the table, but it was the empty chair that continued to draw sideways glances.

This didn't escape Miss Lillian's notice. "I need to find someone to replace Rose," she announced while daintily cutting her meat.

This brought an outcry from Polly. "H—how could you even think of rep–placing her. After she w–w–was —"

"The world doesn't stop because someone

146

died," Coral said.

Buttercup gazed at her reflection in the silver serving spoon before helping herself to mashed potatoes. "And it's been what? A little over a week," she said, her voice thick with sarcasm.

Coral glared at her. "Life goes on."

Polly jumped to her feet and tossed her napkin at Coral. "I don't know how you can b–b–be so h–heartless." She grabbed her reticule and ran from the room.

Silence thick as fog followed her departure. One by one, the women left the table. Amy purposely lingered over her meal until even Miss Lillian gave up and left the room.

Amy then picked up her empty plate and carried it into the kitchen.

The cook's name was Coffey. She was a large woman with doe-like eyes and black frizzy hair. A former slave, she took great pride in her cooking skills and had no patience for picky eaters like Georgia. Seemingly unaware of Amy's presence, she muttered to herself.

"I'm a'tellin' you, that girl is gonna waste away to nothing. Mark my words. She'll be so skinny we won't even be able to find her body to bury her."

Amy set her plate on the counter next to the sink. Coffey glanced at her, but her complaints continued uninterrupted: Buttercup took more than her fair share of helpings, Coral put salt on her food. . . .

"Lawdy, you'd think the girl would taste the food first."

Amy waited for Coffey to finish her diatribe. "I need to ask you something, Coffey."

Coffey shook her head. "I'm not giving away my recipes, if that's what you have in mind."

"Actually, it has to do with Rose. Did you know that she was engaged to be married?"

Coffey's eyes narrowed. "Who told you that?"

"Her fiancé's brother. Does the name Dave Colton ring a bell?"

Coffey made a face. "I remember him. He always stuffed his pockets with my macaroons. Had himself a healthy appetite but never looked you square in the eye. Know what I mean?"

"I think so," Amy said. Tom Colton certainly didn't have any trouble looking people in the eye — looking *her* in the eye.

Coffey scoffed. "A man who can't look you in the eyes ain't to be trusted, and I told Rose as much. Now you're telling me she was gonna marry him!"

"Did you notice anything different about

her before she died?"

"Whatcha talkin' about, girl?" Coffey scrunched up her face. "How, different?"

"Did she seem nervous or worried or act strange in some way?"

"Only in the morning." Coffey smacked her lips together. "She was always the first one downstairs. Looked bright and shiny as a new penny, she did. Then one day she walked into the kitchen, took one smell of the coffee, and turned three shades of green."

Amy stared at her. "Rose was with child?"

Coffey frowned. "Well, it sure wasn't my coffee making her sick."

Rose's pregnancy was a twist Amy hadn't counted on. "Did you tell anyone about her condition?"

"Now why would I go and do that? It was nobody's business but hers."

That was true only if it was Dave Colton's child. But what if it had been someone else's? Would that have provided a motivation for murder? "Do you think the man she planned to wed was the father?"

"Now how am I supposed to know that? Don't even know how she knew who the father was herself." Her features darkened beneath a veil of suspicion. "Why you asking all these questions?"

149

"No reason. I was just curious."

"Seems to me that nobody's business is everyone's curiosity. Now, scat. I've got work to do." Waving a flour-sack towel, she chased Amy out of the kitchen.

CHAPTER 14

Amy was still mulling over her conversation with Coffey moments later when she climbed the stairs to the second floor. Muffled sobs made her stop in front of Polly's room. The poor girl sounded like she was crying her heart out.

Amy knocked twice before entering the room.

Polly lay facedown on the bed, nose buried in the pillow. Sobs shuddered through her body, and it sure did look like her heart was broken.

Amy sat on the edge of the mattress, knocking a dime novel to the floor. "Talk to me." When Polly made no response, Amy's mind suddenly flicked back in time, and she was sitting on her sister's bed. She blinked, but the vision of a young child refused to budge. She never knew what would transport her back to that terrible time when it seemed as if her private world had come to an end.

Sometimes it took no more than a certain word or sound for the memories to return. The other day it was walking into the hotel to meet Colton and seeing a woman with a young child. Now, it was the simple act of comforting a distraught woman — a blond like her sister, Cissy.

Tracking down outlaws was now her job, but secretly it was Cissy for whom her heart searched. If her sister was still alive, she would now be eighteen, only a few years younger than Polly. *But God, please, don't let her end up in a place like this.*

A movement on the bed chased her thoughts away, but she knew the reprieve was only temporary. The memories of Cissy and the night she disappeared were never gone for long.

Amy pulled her hand away. Polly turned over and stared at her with watery red eyes.

"Where can I find a handkerchief?" Amy asked.

"In the drawer."

Amy crossed to the bureau and chose one from the neatly stacked pile in the top drawer and returned to the bed. Polly took it from her and dabbed at her paint-smeared cheeks.

"Anything I can do?" Amy asked.

Polly blew her nose. "Not unless you can bring Rose b–b–back."

Amy heaved a sigh. "That would take a miracle." She'd stopped believing in miracles the night Cissy disappeared.

"I'm not expecting a miracle. I just w–want to know wh–who did it."

"I do, too." Amy knew from painful experience that nothing was worse than lingering questions. *Why did this happen? What could I have done different? What happened to Cissy?* Not knowing was sometimes worse than the actual loss.

"Everyone seems to agree that Rose had no enemies," Amy said gently. She didn't want to upset Polly any further, but in her current vulnerable state, she might be less reticent and more willing to answer questions.

Polly started to say something but couldn't get past the first consonant *b*. She paused for a moment and tried again, this time choosing her words carefully. "I c–can't imagine anyone w–wanting to harm her."

"You said you didn't know that she was engaged to be married."

Polly sniffled. "I didn't."

"Are you sure?"

"I kn–know th–there was a man she liked.

Whenever he left t–town, she was m–miserable until she received a l–letter from him. His name was D–Dan or Dave — s–something like th–that. I met him a c–couple of times."

So Colton did write to her. So what happened to the letters? Why were they not in her room? Had her killer taken them?

"Did he leave town often?" Amy asked.

"T–twice that I know of."

"Do you know why?"

Polly shook her head. "R–Rose never said."

"Did you know she was expecting a child?"

Polly's eyes widened. "Are . . . are you s–sure?"

"Fairly sure." Though there didn't seem to be any doubt in Coffey's mind. "Someone told me that one of Rose's clients was the Gunnysack Bandit. Did she ever mention that to you?"

Polly's hand flew to her mouth. "Th–that awful outlaw?"

"It's what I heard. Did Rose ever say anything about being afraid of one of the johns?"

Polly shook her head. "W–we're not allowed to t–t–t– . . . gossip about guests."

It was hard to believe that a group of

women who lived and worked under the same roof adhered to such strict rules, but something was keeping them from talking.

"Can you think of anything that might help the marshal find Rose's killer?"

"N–no, nothing."

Amy tried not to show her frustration. Never had she met a more reticent group of women. Prying information out of them was like chiseling rock.

"Did you notice a difference in Rose's behavior in recent weeks?"

"Only that she was s–sick." She glanced past Amy's shoulder at the closed door. "We thought she was f–f–faking."

Amy frowned. "Why would you think that?"

"She d–didn't want to work here any-more."

"Why didn't she just leave?" She had two good reasons to do so: one, she was getting married, and two, she was with child.

"I d–don't know why."

Amy let the words hang in the air for a moment before asking, "Polly, what . . . brought you here?"

Polly's forehead creased like a folded fan. "To G–Goodman?"

"To Miss Lillian's?"

"N–n–no one else w–would hire me."

Amy frowned. "Because you stutter?"

Polly nodded. "Some p–people think I'm dumb b–because I can't always g–get the words out."

"You're not dumb, Polly. My . . ." Amy almost said *minister.* "My friend told me that Moses had the same problem and yet he became a great leader."

"Women can't be l–l–leaders," Polly said. "We c–can't be anything."

"You're wrong," Amy said. "God gave us the same abilities and talents as men."

"If th–that's true, then why do men have all the p–power?"

"Because we gave it to them," Amy said.

After leaving Polly's room, Amy walked to town, careful to steer clear of the hotel. She didn't want to bump into Colton and have to make excuses for not having the list he requested. Several times she thought she saw him and once even dashed into Adam's Barbershop and Tailor to avoid him. Peering out the window, she soon realized her error. Not only was the man in question *not* Mr. Colton, he didn't even look like him.

The barbershop owner lifted his gaze from his lathered client and waved his straight-edged razor at her. "Get out," he bellowed. "I'll not have you plying your trade in here."

He said a lot more, but Amy didn't stay around long enough to listen.

So far that morning she'd crossed eight names off the list, including Mr. Baxter's, who ran the livery and blacksmith shop. An older man, probably in his sixties, he walked with a limp. Witnesses had consistently described the Gunnysack Bandit as moving like a younger man with no obvious physical defects.

The outlaw performed his dastardly deeds with a sack over his head and only two small holes for eyes. No one could describe his face, but neither could anyone agree on his voice, except that it was male and sounded muffled.

According to Miss Lillian, only fifteen of the forty-two men who had done business at the parlor house the week Rose deposited stolen money were similar in height to the Gunnysack Bandit. Still, Amy had to check each suspect herself. It never paid to leave anything to chance.

So far the only one matching the bandit's physical description was the rich man, Monahan, who lived outside of town in a sprawling two-story house with an iron deer in front.

The banker, Mr. Bennington, was short with a rounded belly that practically popped the buttons on his vest. But it wasn't just appearances that made a man suspect; witnesses were notoriously bad at descriptions. Other things had to be taken into consideration, other questions answered. Did the man live beyond his means? Travel abroad? Did he drink only the finest whiskey or smoke only the best Cuban cigars? How often did he gamble, and how high were the stakes? What about his livestock? Were his horses thoroughbred or mixed?

Then there was his wife or mistress to consider. Did she sew her own clothes or favor French fashions? Did she do her own cooking and cleaning or depend on hired help? Even church tithing could provide clues. Some outlaws had been known to pay penance by giving vast sums to churches or charities.

Amy stared at the list of names still to investigate and sighed. It didn't look like her work would be done anytime soon. That meant she was stuck at the parlor house for only God knew how long.

Later that afternoon, Amy scurried downstairs anxious to speak to Miss Lillian. Having whittled the original forty-two suspects down to twenty-five, she still had questions she hoped the madam could answer.

The house was oddly quiet, but that was only because Georgia and the others had decided to visit Rose's grave. However, voices greeted her as she crossed from the stairs to the parlor.

Seeing that Miss Lillian had a guest, she paused beneath the archway. "I'm sorry. I didn't know you had a visitor."

"It's all right." Holding a teapot in one hand, Miss Lillian waved her into the room with the other. "You remember Reverend Matthews, don't you? From the funeral?"

The reverend stood. Today, he wore his spectacles, but his fob chain dangled, so either he'd misplaced or forgotten his watch. "Ah, yes, you're the new girl."

Amy didn't know what to say. A man of God having tea with a madam?

He chuckled as if enjoying a private joke. "I know what you're thinking. But I can assure you, I'm here on the Lord's business."

"He's here to pick up his new boots," Miss Lillian said.

The reverend held out his foot to show off his new brown leather footwear.

"Very nice," Amy said.

He grinned like a schoolboy with a new slingshot. "Did you know that God used shoes and feet in the Bible to show acceptance, humility, and deliverance?" His

159

eyes twinkled. "So Miss Lillian is doing the Lord's work, too. Only she doesn't know it."

Miss Lillian set the teapot down. "Don't make me out to be a saint, Reverend. The last time I looked, the saints were all dead."

"You'll be happy to know you have little danger of receiving sainthood. I am, however, obliged to point out the dangers that lurk in the garden of evil. So many people fail to see the connection between pleasure and sin."

"Sit and finish your tea, Reverend," Miss Lillian said. "Sermons and tea should never mix."

He bowed. "Very well." He glanced at Amy. "Would you care to join us?"

Amy's mind scrambled for an excuse. "No, thank you. I —"

A loud crash came from another part of the house, and Amy jumped. Mr. Beavers hopped off a hammock and vanished beneath a settee.

"What on earth . . . ?" Miss Lillian shot to her feet, and the three of them rushed from the room to investigate.

A gaping hole was centered in the middle of the dining room window. Someone had thrown a brick. Amy flew to the window to peer outside, glass crunching beneath the soles of her shoes.

Seeing no one, she pulled away. "Quick, the key!"

Miss Lillian wasted precious moments unfastening the key from her waist. By the time Amy worked the complicated lock and dashed out the front door, the street was empty and the perpetuator nowhere in sight.

Just to make certain, she raced to the gate and glanced as far as she could see in all directions. Whoever had thrown the brick was probably young. Certainly young enough to run fast.

Pocketing her gun, she returned to the house. The housekeeper, Beatrice, was already sweeping up the glass in the dining room, her thin mouth as tight as her bun.

"Did you see anyone?" Miss Lillian asked.

Amy shook her head and handed over the key. "Have you any idea who would do such a thing?"

Miss Lillian shrugged. "Roughly half the population of this town. There's not a woman out there who wouldn't like to see this place burn down."

Amy doubted the brick thrower was a woman. No one wearing a skirt could run that fast.

Reverend Matthews held the brick up to the light as if it contained some secret message from God. "Let's finish our tea," he said amicably. "And I'll tell you what the Bible says about fallen bricks."

CHAPTER 15

"Thared, Tenfer. Monster tay me."

Amy twisted and turned until her bedding tied up in knots. She flopped over on her back and stared at the ceiling. The house seemed especially restless tonight. Its studs groaned and joints creaked. Was it possible for a house to absorb the fears and worries of inhabitants? Or was it simply the ghosts of the past having a bad night?

The half moon peered through the open window, and lace curtains fluttered in the gentle breeze. Shadows danced across the room much like Cissy's last words danced in her head.

The sheriff believed that Cissy had wandered from the house in the middle of the night. "Children do that all the time," he'd said.

Now as then, she questioned his theory. Cissy woke up crying on that long-ago night and claimed a monster had tried to take her.

Amy calmed her down and told her that it was just a bad dream. "There's no such thing as a monster." But what if it hadn't been a nightmare? What if someone really had tried to snatch her sister out of her bed? The questions persisted now as they had done for years with no answers in sight.

Though Amy was only twelve at the time, she blamed herself for not taking her sister seriously and investigating. Why hadn't she? And why, after all this time, did the memories still haunt her?

Turning her back on the past, she glanced at the mechanical clock. Unable to read the face, she slid out of bed and carried the clock to the window. The silvery light of the half moon bathed the street, and the trees swayed gently. It was only after midnight, but she felt as if she'd been twisting and turning all night. A movement caught her eye. Another brick thrower?

She pressed her head against the glass pane and squinted. A stick-thin figure hurried through the gate. Unless her eyes were playing tricks on her, it sure did look like Georgia.

The woman vanished into the folds of the night. Where was she going at such a late hour? Did she have a lover?

Amy grabbed a dressing gown and shoved

164

her arms into the sleeves. It was filmy and, like all the parlor house garments, offered little in the way of modesty. It would have to do. She shoved her handgun into the pocket.

Opening her door quietly, she stuck her head through the crack and peered into the hall. A gaslight on the wall hissed and sputtered, but otherwise all was quiet. Pulling the door shut behind her, she tiptoed past the other rooms to the stairs. Padding barefoot down the edge closest to the railing where the stairs were less likely to creak, she crossed the entry hall to the door. It was still bolted and locked on the inside.

Feeling her way through the dark hall, she reached the kitchen. She ran her hand along the kitchen counter until she found the lantern. After lighting the wick, she searched the pantry and pushed against the well-stocked shelves in search of a hidden door. Nothing. She checked the windows in the mudroom, but all were locked and looked as if they hadn't been opened in years. The back door, too, was locked from the inside.

So how did Georgia escape?

She returned to the kitchen and decided to wait. Sooner or later Georgia would return. *Please, God, let it be sooner.* She was cold and in desperate need of sleep.

It wasn't more than twenty minutes later that footsteps alerted her. She turned off the light and ducked behind the counter in front of the icebox.

A sudden movement by her side startled her. Mr. Beavers!

The cat rubbed against her with loud, rumbling purrs — a fine time to be friendly. "Go away," she whispered. She pushed against him, but that only made him purr louder.

The cellar door creaked open, and Amy held her breath. Mr. Beavers made enough noise for a choir.

Amy peered around the counter. Georgia's dark form emerged, and the cellar door closed behind her with a muffled thud. She stood perfectly still, her raven hair gleaming in the light of the half moon.

Amy debated whether to confront Georgia now or later and decided to wait. She was more likely to get the truth out of Georgia if she had more information.

Mr. Beavers's purrs now sounded like a chugging train. Georgia moved toward the counter. Amy gave the cat a good shove with both hands. Mr. Beavers protested with a loud meow before streaking away.

Georgia gasped as the cat ran past her. "Dumb cat," she muttered. She pulled off her slippers and ever so quietly tiptoed away on stocking feet.

Amy sat on the cold kitchen floor and leaned her back against a cupboard until the squeaking floorboards overhead told her Georgia was now upstairs.

She stood and walked to the cellar door. She had checked the cellar earlier in the week and found nothing of interest. Obviously, she'd missed something.

The dark hole of the underground room gaped before her, and her mouth went dry. She liked cellars almost as much as she liked rattlers — especially in the still of night.

Turning back to the kitchen, she relit the kerosene lantern and, holding it over her head, started down the stairs.

The cellar smelled musty, and dust tickled her nose. Cobwebs hung from raftered ceilings. Along the length of one wall stood a row of narrow windows. They were too high to reach and probably hadn't been opened since the house was built.

She moved the light across the rough brick walls. Old furniture was piled in one corner. A couple of trunks and a rocking chair clamored for space with a glass-paneled secretary and, inexplicably, a child's rocking horse. A folding screen stood in one corner, each panel painted with scenes of nature.

She stepped over a wicker basket and moved a panel. This time she saw something she had previously missed. The screen hid an alcove and stairs. At the top of the stairs a trapdoor opened to the back of the house.

So there *was* a way in and out of the old house without going through Miss Lillian. This could explain how Rose's killer managed to enter and leave without being seen. Georgia obviously was familiar with the hidden door, but how many of the other women knew about it? How many in town?

The next morning after breakfast a horse-drawn wagon with CUBBY'S WINDOWS AND FINE LAMPS painted on the sides pulled in front of the house.

While the man known only as Cubby replaced the broken dining room window, Amy walked out to the backyard to check the trapdoor from the outside.

It really did feel like spring. The temperature was somewhere in the low seventies, and fluffy clouds floated across an azure sky. Rays of golden sunlight filtered through the trees, and the warmth was a welcome change from the cool interior of the house.

Overgrown bushes against the back of the house hid the cellar trapdoor. Unless someone was specifically looking for the entrance, it was almost impossible to find.

She walked the width and breadth of the yard. Old wizened trees prevented all but the most stubborn flowers from surviving. A rambling rosebush climbed up a leaning fence in an effort to reach the sun.

The house lacked neighbors but not wildlife. A jaybird squawked loudly as it chased a squirrel down a tree. A rabbit ran across her path and dived into a hole. From somewhere up above came the tap-tap-tapping of a woodpecker, but she couldn't locate it.

Buttercup walked into the yard, and her presence caused a sudden twitter of birds. It soon became apparent why when she dumped a pan of table scraps into a bird feeder.

Amy joined her. Already, yellow-winged birds fluttered down to peck at pieces of suet. "I've never seen so many different types of birds."

"That's because Rose put food out for them every day," Buttercup said. "Now I do it in her memory."

"I noticed several bird books in Rose's room." Amy knew very little about birds and could only identify a few.

"She loved birds and sat for hours watching them. She even left little pieces of yarn outside for their nests."

Buttercup nudged Amy with an elbow and pointed upward. A large black-and-white bird sat on a window ledge, preening in front of a second-story window.

"He comes every morning to primp in front of the glass. Rose said he was a magpie."

The way the bird turned first one way and then the other made Amy laugh. "He's a regular Beau Brummell."

Buttercup pulled her gaze away from the windowsill. "A bow what?"

"Brummell. He was a very fashionable man." Buttercup couldn't read and had little education. Regretting having mentioned someone known mostly through literature, Amy quickly changed the subject. "It sounds like you really miss Rose."

Buttercup heaved a sigh and looked about to burst into tears. "The others . . . they make fun of my weight. Rose never did. She was kind to me."

Amy had so many questions she wanted to ask, but Buttercup suddenly pointed to the fence. "Oh, look at the hummingbird," she said, smiling.

Amy's gaze followed her pointed finger. Like a jeweled ball being tossed in a game of catch, the tiny bird flitted from blossom to blossom. It hovered in the air for a moment, its green wings but a blur, then darted away.

The smile vanished from Buttercup's face. Amy hated to return to such a depressing subject, but she so seldom had a chance to speak to any of the women alone.

"I need to ask you something. Did you know that Rose was with child?"

Buttercup's eyes widened. "No, but she wouldn't be the first who got herself in a family way."

"I suppose not. I heard she was seeing someone and it was serious. Dave or Dan somebody."

"Dave. I met him a couple of times. He wasn't like the others."

"How do you mean?"

"I think he really cared for Rose. Brought her flowers and books and stuff." Buttercup sighed. "It's too bad what happened."

"You mean when he was shot?"

"That, too. But I'm talking about the argument they had just before he died. Right here in this yard."

"Do you know what they argued about?" Amy asked.

"Something about him wanting her to go to Texas, but she said she wouldn't go without him. That's all I heard."

So the part about Dave asking for his brother's help was true. "Rose must have been heartbroken when he died."

"She was heartbroken all right." Buttercup tossed a small piece of suet to a noisy blue jay perched on the woodpile. "She didn't get out of bed for a week. Miss Lillian called the doctor, but it didn't help much. After a while, she did try to eat, but she wasn't the same."

"Do you know of anyone who might have wanted to hurt her?"

Buttercup glanced at the house as if to make certain they were still alone. "I think she was scared of someone. One of the guests."

"What makes you say that?" Amy asked. Everyone else she'd questioned insisted that Rose had no enemies.

"The week before she died, she wouldn't sleep alone. She slept on the floor in my room."

"Did she tell you who she was afraid of?"

"No, but . . ." Buttercup gave the house another quick glance. "I got the feeling it was Mr. Monahan."

Since Monahan was at the top of her list of suspects, Amy wasn't surprised to hear his name. Coral said he was the richest man in town, and from what little Amy had been able to turn up on him, it appeared to be true. His house alone had cost more money than what most people in town saw in a lifetime.

"Why would she be afraid of him?"

"I don't know, but one night I heard them arguing. The next day she stayed in her room."

"Did you hear what they were arguing about?"

Buttercup shook her head. As if suddenly remembering the rule forbidding gossip, she backed away, pail in hand. "I better go."

Amy made no move to stop her. She needed time to think. She could understand why Rose might argue with her fiancé. But Mr. Monahan? Why would she argue with a guest?

Unless . . . She considered a new theory: What if Monahan was the father of Rose's baby? Maybe Rose threatened to go public and Monahan refused to let that happen.

It made sense but was still only speculation. Even if she was right, solving Rose's murder wouldn't necessarily bring her any closer to tracking down the Gunnysack Bandit, and that's what she was paid to do.

One by one, the birds took flight until at last the bird feeder was deserted. She started toward the house, but something stopped her. A strange sensation came over her, and she shivered.

She glanced about the yard, but all was quiet. Even the magpie had taken flight. She scanned the widows. The draperies and shades were drawn shut.

Still, unable to shake the feeling that someone was watching, she hurried to the house and banged on the back door until the cook let her in.

CHAPTER 16

Her conversation with Buttercup still very much on her mind, Amy hurried into town later that morning to mail her report to Pinkerton headquarters.

She walked quickly along the boardwalk, looking neither left nor right. She didn't want to see the disapproving stares or judgmental looks. It was bad enough having to feel their gazes.

Though the sun was warm, her shoulder cape was securely fastened. Her bright purple gown set her apart from the "respectable" women whose modesty and morality were properly stated with drab gray or stoic black dresses. Amy would have had a better chance of blending in had she worn a pickle barrel.

It was now the middle of April. It didn't seem possible that she'd been living at Miss Lillian's Parlor House and Fine Boots for more than a week. She had precious little to show for her efforts. But then again, Rose's death caused the loss of valuable time. She had to move slowly so as not to rouse suspicion.

A telegram waited for her. As always, it was coded and signed "Octavo at Napthia," cipher for the Pinkerton principal. It was too soon to expect a report back on the list of suspects she'd sent. Nevertheless, the tersely worded dispatch telling her to keep investigating was disappointing. How was she supposed to do that without information?

She folded the telegram and slipped it into her cloth pocketbook. She then headed for Harry's Gun and Bakery Shoppe. The owner, Harry Piker, was a regular at Miss Lillian's. He was also one of the men on Amy's list of suspects.

An odd, though no less pleasant, smell greeted her as she entered the tiny shop. It was a combination of baked bread and pastry with just a hint of molten steel. An impressive assortment of rifles and shotguns was displayed on polished wood wall racks.

At the sound of jingling door bells, a stout man hobbled from the back room. Wiping his hands on a grimy apron, he grimaced with each step he took.

A fringe of gray hair circled a glaring bald

spot. Somewhere in his early fifties, his excessive weight and flaring gout suggested an insatiable sweet tooth. His age, shape, and thin hair reminded her of Sallie Wiseman, the notorious female bank robber. Amy had shadowed her for a month before they had enough evidence to put her behind bars.

Standing behind the counter, Piker tossed an anxious glance at the door before shifting his gaze in her direction. "What can I do for you?"

Guns were scattered on top of the glass counter in no particular order. She moved a Colt aside to get a better view of the pastries displayed on the shelves below.

"Are you the baker?" she asked, perusing the variety of cakes, pies, and cookies.

"No, I'm the gunsmith. The wife handles the bakery. She stepped out for a moment."

"I'll take one of those," she said, pointing to a cherry-filled tart.

He slid the glass door open on his side of the counter and reached between the glass shelves. "You new around here?" he asked.

"Yes. I work for Miss Lillian." When he failed to meet her gaze she added, "I understand you're a regular client." She found him disgusting. He availed himself of Miss Lillian's "hospitality" and sold her five weapons but couldn't look Amy in the eye.

His jaw hardened and a vein stood out in his neck. "Don't know whatcha talking about."

"My mistake." The man was a liar, but his appearance and poor health exonerated him; clearly he wasn't the Gunnysack Bandit.

He placed the pastry in a small box. "That will be fifteen cents."

Anxious to take her leave, she counted out the correct change, thanked him, and turned, package in hand. She reached the door just as it flew open, revealing a matronly woman wearing a shapeless floral dress.

She took one look at Amy and her face contorted into a hateful expression. She had a long, thin face with thick black eyebrows — just like the outlaw known as Horse Face Freddie.

"What are you doing here?" She addressed Amy but glared at Harry. "I warned you to stay away from those horrible women!" She made no effort to lower her voice, and passersby stopped to stare through the open doorway.

His face drained of color, Harry's mouth flapped open and shut like a dying fish before he was able to get his words out.

"She . . . she was only buying pastries, my love."

Amy glared at him. He deserved his wife's wrath but, not wanting to make matters worse, she held up her purchase. "That's all I was doing."

Harry's wife snatched the box out of her hand and tossed it to the floor. "Get out!"

The woman shoved her on the shoulder and pushed her out the door. "I won't have the likes of you eating my pastries!" The small crowd gathered in front stepped back to let Amy pass.

Face flaring, Amy hurried away, but this only seemed to incite the woman more. A string of obscenities followed her up the street. Amy had done nothing wrong, but her face burned in embarrassment.

A beggar pawed her arm as she raced past him. Ignoring him, she hurried along the boardwalk, weaving around a baby carriage and barely avoiding the crates stacked in front of Max's General Mercantile and Flower Shoppe.

Spotting the three church ladies passing out handbills ahead, she ducked into the hotel lobby and ran straight into a wall. It was only when the wall moved that she realized her mistake.

"Whoa!" Colton steadied her with hands to her shoulders. "Where you goin' in such a hurry? You came barreling in here like a cat with his tail afire."

She lifted her gaze upward, and his compelling eyes riveted her to the spot.

"I'm sorry . . . I . . ." Surprised to find herself shaking, she glanced back, but no one had followed. She stepped away to gain her composure and put up her guard.

He dropped his hands to his sides and studied her with a look of concern. "Are you all right, Amy?"

"I'm fine," she said. His worried frown remained, and so she smiled. "Just trying to dodge a bullet."

The corner of his mouth quirked upward. "There seems to be a lot of that going around lately." He glanced over her head at the door. "Come and sit for a spell. Looks like you might could use some refreshment." Ignoring the disapproving glance from the desk clerk, he took her by the arm and led her into the dining room.

He released her arm to pull out a chair for her. Pretending not to notice the polite gesture, she chose the opposite one. Even in public a detective couldn't afford to let his or her guard down. That meant sitting where she could keep an eye on the entrance.

He sat on the chair originally meant for her without comment but tossed a glance over his shoulder before picking up the bill of fare. Was he, too, worried about the proximity of the door to his back? If so, that made him either a criminal or lawman, although he didn't seem to fit in either shoe.

Why was that?

It was too early for the noon meal, but several tables were already occupied. Amy never sat in a public place without analyzing the people around her. Today, it took every bit of willpower she possessed to pull her gaze from Colton and focus on the other diners.

Two older men were having a serious conversation at a corner table. Judging by the way one stabbed the air with his fork, they were either discussing politics or religion. Few other subjects elicited such passion.

At another table, a young couple appeared to be having a lover's quarrel. The man looked cornered and on the defensive. That could only mean one thing: the woman was the wronged party.

A man in an unfortunate checkered suit had followed them inside and was now seated at a corner table, facing the door. He obviously didn't belong in these parts; he was probably a salesman, but she hoped for his sake he wasn't selling men's suits.

"What would you like?" Colton asked.

She met his gaze and tried to ignore her quickening pulse. "I'm not hungry," she said.

He closed his menu and studied her. "There's always room for ice cream. Let me guess . . . coffee, right?"

"What?"

"That's your favorite ice cream. Coffee."

She leaned back and regarded him with curiosity. "How did you know?" She loved coffee ice cream, but not every restaurant or ice cream parlor carried it.

He rubbed his jaw. "I figured a woman with an iron-fist punch like yours wasn't the vanilla or strawberry type."

She couldn't help but laugh. "You figured right," she said, though she didn't know whether to be flattered or alarmed by his ability to discern her preference in ice cream. "Most men might have guessed chocolate."

He shook his head. "Too conventional."

She was still trying to decide if he meant

182

that as a compliment when a waiter appeared at their table. Colton ordered two dishes of coffee ice cream.

He then removed his hat and set it on an empty chair. A strand of brown hair fell across his forehead, giving him a boyish look. Wondering how it would feel to push the wayward strand back in place — and run her fingers through his hair — she twisted her fingers around the napkin on her lap.

Elbow on the table, Colton studied her over clasped hands. Feeling certain he could see through her disguise, she drew her gaze away from the intriguing cleft on his chin and rearranged the silverware.

"Do you always get it right?" Head lowered, she peered at him through the fringe of her lashes. "About the ice cream, I mean."

"Most times." He inclined his head toward a pinched-face woman complaining to the waiter in a loud voice. "Lemon," he said. "Definitely lemon."

Amy covered her mouth to hide a giggle. "What about him over there?" She indicated the man in the checkered suit.

"Neapolitan," Colton said without hesitation.

This time she laughed out loud. She couldn't help it. He laughed, too, a deep chuckle that lit up his face with warm humor.

All too soon the light moment faded away, and his expression turned serious. "What brings you to town?" he asked.

"I needed to make a few purchases."

"And?"

She hesitated. *God, please don't let him be the Gunnysack Bandit.* A man who loves coffee ice cream and has such an attractive smile has to be one of the good guys.

"I have information that Rose . . . was with child."

He arched an eyebrow and sat back. Clearly that was news to him.

She gave him a moment to digest this before asking, "Do you think your brother was the father?"

He rubbed his chin. "I don't know. Maybe."

"How did he meet Rose?" she asked.

"Probably the same way most men meet . . . ladies like you."

Ladies like you. Normally, she would have been flattered by his remark. It meant she played her role if not perfect at least well enough to get the job done. Today, however, the words stabbed at her heart, as did the disapproval in his voice. She bit her lip to keep from telling him who she really was.

Why it mattered what he thought of her she didn't know. She only knew that it did.

"What about the list of Miss Lillian's clients?" he asked. "Any luck there?"

"I'm working on it." She wasn't about to turn anything over to him until headquarters either confirmed or denied his story. "Tell me about your brother," she said, breaking the sudden strained silence.

A shadow fleeted across his face, but after a moment he began. "Dave was what you might call a maverick. His wild ways got worse after Pa died."

Dave's troubles started early with petty crime and that didn't surprise her. The Pinkerton detective agency found that most criminals started on the road to crime early in life, some as young as eight or nine.

Nothing, it seemed, was safe from Dave's pilfering hand, even the offering plate at church. Colton's disapproval of his brother's illegal activities alleviated her fears that he was the Gunnysack Bandit, and though questions remained, she felt profound relief.

"He gradually progressed to more lucrative hauls." He fell silent for a moment before adding, "He was mad at the world. Nothing anyone said or did could get through to him."

Knowing all too well how it felt to fail a

sibling, she sympathized. "It must have been difficult for you."

"Yes, it was, but nowhere near as difficult as the day I learned of his death. I arranged to have his body returned home by train, but my grandpappy refused to let me bury him in the family plot because of his criminal activities. Said Dave brought shame to the family name."

Commiserating with a nod, she thought of Rose buried with society's outcasts.

"There's another reason why I want to prove Dave had changed his ways." He heaved a sigh. "Dave has a son. He's eleven now, and I don't want him growing up thinking ill of his pa."

"I see." She tried to think of something to say that would ease his pained expression, something comforting, but God's words, not hers, came to mind. Voicing them would only blow her cover.

As if to guess her thoughts, he continued. "He said he'd found the Lord. I prayed it wasn't just another one of his lies to get me to help him. Looks like maybe it was." After a moment he added, "Nothing I hate worse than lies."

He was talking about his brother, of course, but a surge of guilt rushed through her. She was only doing her job, and lying

186

was part of it. So why did it suddenly feel so wrong?

The waiter appeared and placed two bowls of ice cream on the table. During the interruption, she noticed the man in the checkered suit peering at them from behind his newspaper. His interest meant he probably wasn't a salesman.

Then who? Another Pinkerton operative? None of the communications from headquarters mentioned reinforcements. If Mr. Pinkerton thought there was something to be gained, however, he wouldn't hesitate to send another detective or two.

Only one way to find out. Operatives had been taught to communicate with one another nonverbally. She pulled a handkerchief from her sleeve, kept for just such a purpose. She waited for the man's head to pop out from behind his newspaper again. With a flip of her left wrist, she waved the handkerchief and waited. No answering signal.

He wasn't a Pinkerton operative, that much was certain. Perhaps he was just curious as to why a man would choose to entertain a harlot in public. That was a good question, and she swung her gaze back to her table companion.

"After you," he said.

She smiled, tucked her handkerchief back in her sleeve, and picked up her spoon. The last ice cream she'd tasted was in New Orleans. Unfortunately, hay used to insulate the ice had found its way into the frozen dessert, making it unpalatable. She proceeded with caution as she dug her spoon into the smooth round mound in her bowl and lifted it to her mouth. The sweet cool cream melted in her mouth with no bits of hay to spoil the flavor.

"Mmm. This is soooooo good."

Looking pleased, Colton picked up his own spoon. They ate in silence for a few moments before he asked, "Have any siblings?"

"Several," she said in a tone she hoped would discourage further questions.

He studied her a moment but, apparently taking the hint, he returned to the subject of Dave. "One of the hardest days of my life was the day I arrested him. My own brother . . ."

Her hand froze and she nearly dropped her spoon. "*You* arrested him?"

"As a Texas Ranger, I had no choice."

Her eyes widened. "You're a Texas Ranger?"

"Was," he said, his voice taut.

That explained his military bearing. "I

pegged you as a rancher."

"Actually, you hit the peg on the head." He sat back and studied her. "I left the Rangers and started my own ranch. A small one by Texas standards."

"A horse ranch," she said.

"Cattle."

"Really? I would have sworn you were into horses."

His eyebrows rose. "What makes you say that?"

The way he handled his horse was one clue, but she didn't want to let on that she had watched him from her bedroom window, not just once but twice. "Your hands," she said.

He opened his hands and stared at his palms. They were large hands, strong, each finger long and tapered.

"Cowhands have rough hands," she explained. "Horse wranglers wear gloves, which leave hands callus-free."

He gave her a crooked grin. "You have me there. I got me some pretty good cattlemen to do the heavy lifting. Me? You're right. I'm more of a horse guy." He dropped his hands. "Very observant. You should be a detective."

Her bowl now empty, she set her spoon down. Now look what she'd done, almost given herself away. Just being around him made her want to be more like herself and less like someone else, and that was a worry.

"I don't imagine being a detective pays as well as my current job," she said. Her ploy worked; his face grew tight and his eyes flat. As if suddenly reminded of who she was, he seemed anxious to distance himself. He reached into his vest pocket for his money clip to pay the tab.

She slipped her cloth bag over her wrist. Oddly, she hated to see their time together come to an end. "Thank you for the ice cream."

Colton nodded but failed to meet her gaze. "My pleasure."

She sighed. Always the gentleman, even in the company of a woman he considered to be anything but a lady.

He pulled out his money clip. "If you learn anything —"

Standing, she nodded. "Hotel, room fourteen."

He lifted his gaze and she smiled, but it was halfhearted at best. His "ladies like you" comment still stung.

He failed to return her smile, and her spirits dropped yet another notch. Puzzled by the way he affected her, she walked away, but with no less vigilance.

She ventured a quick glance at the man in the checkered suit. Surprise, surprise, his ice cream of choice was Neapolitan.

CHAPTER 17

That Sunday morning Amy sat alone in her room. She'd hardly slept the night before, and exhaustion hung heavy in her limbs. Strange sounds woke her, and once she even thought she heard someone crying.

She rubbed her pounding temples. Of all the assignments she'd had through the years, this one was the toughest, and the strain was playing havoc with her nerves.

Not only was she expected to act and dress in a way that went against her Christian beliefs, living at the bordello posed an endless set of challenges with no time off for church.

Most criminals worked at night and slept late. So even on shadow duty she could usually sneak away for an hour or two to attend Sunday morning worship. But with Coral watching her every move, she couldn't take the chance. Then, too, there was always the possibility that even dressed in her own clothes someone in church would recognize her.

Sighing, she reached for her Bible and thumbed through the dog-eared pages. No sooner had she settled down to read than the door flew open. She hid the Bible in the folds of her skirt.

It was Buttercup. "I'm out of hair pomade. May I use yours?"

Amy nodded and pointed to the dresser.

Buttercup glided into the room, dressed only in bloomers and laced corset. Her orange-red hair, normally twisted into an elaborate coronet with a fluff of bangs, hung down her back in tangled wet strands.

She stopped in front of Amy's chair, hands at her waist. "What are you hiding?"

"It's none of your business."

Buttercup reached for Amy's lap and the Bible flew to the floor. "Now look what you've done," Amy snapped.

Buttercup stared at her like one might stare at a coiled rattler. "Do you still believe in that?" After a moment, she added, "Believe in God?"

Amy picked the Bible off the floor and set it on the bedside table. She could deny who she was and from where she'd come. She could deny that the sun was yellow and the grass green. But when asked outright she suddenly realized she couldn't deny belief in her heavenly Father.

"Yes, I do." If admitting belief jeopardized the case, William Pinkerton would kill her. That is, if his brother Robert didn't do it first.

With an intake of breath, Buttercup lowered herself onto the edge of the bed. "I used to believe in God." She shrugged as if it no longer mattered what she believed. The wretched look on her face said otherwise. "That was a long time ago."

Amy leaned forward. "What happened to you?" And when she got no response she prodded. "What brought you to this place?"

Buttercup's lids fluttered shut, covering her eyes with painted blue half circles.

"You can trust me," Amy urged. "I won't say a word to the others. I promise."

For the longest while Buttercup didn't speak. At last she opened her eyes. "When I was twelve, a gang of boys . . ." Overcome with emotion, she could no longer get the words out. Tears mixed with black charcoal from her lashes trickled down her rounded cheeks.

Amy handed her a clean handkerchief and sat on the bed next to her. "You don't have to say any more." It seemed that all of life could be narrowed down to a single incident or memory. It was as if everyone had an inner compass, all pointing to one unforgettable moment in time and everything started and ended there — a personal north.

Amy's inner needle pointed to the disappearance of her sister. No matter how much time passed, the needle never moved away from that one traumatic loss, at least not permanently.

Buttercup dabbed her eyes. "After what happened I was shunned, and no decent man would have me. No one wanted me." She paused for a moment before adding in a hushed voice, "Not even my family."

"You're wrong about that. God still wants you." She pointed to the Bible. "I was just reading about Rahab. Even though she was a prostitute, God used her to save two of His servants. So you see? Everyone has value in the Lord's eyes. That includes you, me, and everyone in this house."

Buttercup made a face. "You think He's so great? Where was He when they . . . Where has He been since?"

"He's been here," Amy whispered with meaning. Though God hadn't seen fit to answer her prayers about Cissy, she never doubted His existence. He was, in truth, the only constant in her life. She picked up the Bible and held it out to her. "He's here.

We just have to reach out to Him."

Buttercup pushed the Bible away, and her eyes flared with angry sparks. "It hasn't done you any good. You're here, just like me. Just like the others. Where's your God now?" Seeming to forget her reason for coming, she stormed out of the room.

First thing Monday morning, Tom stormed into the marshal's office. He didn't think much of Marshal Flood. Judging by the lawman's dark frown when Tom entered, the feeling was mutual. Even Flood's black mustache seemed to droop when Tom entered, but his garish cowhide boots with the tooled red roses remained planted firmly on top of the desk.

"I stopped by to see how the investigation is going," Tom said, keeping his tone civil.

The marshal indicated the stack of papers on his desk with a wave of his hand. "Which one?"

Tom took a seething breath. "Have you even tried finding my brother's killer? Or Rose's?"

He didn't like what went on at Miss Lillian's parlor, but those women deserved justice, and he hoped to God they got it.

"I'm a busy man." Flood dropped his feet to the floor and tossed a thumb toward the jail cells. "Last night I made four arrests. This morning I got two reports of missing horses, plus a family altercation and a knife fight to deal with. I still haven't had a chance to check Reverend Matthews's report of vandalism at Miss Lillian's bed house and —"

Tom stiffened. "They were vandalized?" Amy hadn't mentioned trouble at the parlor house.

Flood shrugged. "No big deal. Someone threw a brick through the window is all. Not for the first time, I might add. If I didn't know better, I'd think that Miss Lillian owned stock in Cubby's Windows and Fine Lamps." He spread his hands. "Like I said, I'm a busy man."

It was all Tom could do to hold his temper. "And a prostitute's death is of small importance."

"Don't go putting words in my mouth. I'm doing all I can."

"Just as you're doing everything you can to find my brother's killer? You find his killer, you find Rose's. You'll also find the Gunnysack Bandit."

The mustache twitched, but the beady eyes didn't move. "There's no proof of that."

Tom patted the pocket where he kept Rose's letter. The letter had been found on

Dave's body, so Flood knew about it. Evidently it hadn't carried much weight. "I have all the proof I need."

The marshal's eyes glittered. "Yeah, well, you have your theory, boy. And I got mine."

"What is that supposed to mean?"

"A list of robberies credited to the Gunnysack Bandit was found clutched in your brother's hand."

Tom stilled. This was news to him. He had been led to believe that everything found on Dave's body had been sent to the family. "Go on."

"Makes me wonder what it was doing there."

Tom didn't like the implication. Didn't like it one bit. "If you were doing your job, you wouldn't have to wonder."

"If you think you can do better . . ."

Tom planted his hands on the desk and leaned forward. "A grasshopper could do better!" He turned and left the office, but once outside, his bravado deserted him.

What *was* that list of robberies credited to the Gunnysack Bandit doing in Dave's hand? A knot tightened in Tom's chest. At first, he had discounted Buckeye's contention that Dave was the bandit, but things were starting to add up. Fortunately, his Ranger days had taught him to keep a clear and open mind and not go jumping to conclusions.

Things looked bad, but his brother's name would be cleared once all the facts were known — of that he had no doubt. Okay, maybe a little . . .

CHAPTER 18

It was almost midnight by the time Amy ducked behind Miss Lillian's carriage house. Every night after the last "guest" had been sent home Georgia left the parlor house like clockwork. Maybe it had something to do with Rose or even the Gunnysack Bandit, maybe not. Either way, Amy intended to find out where the woman went and for what reason.

The glow of a thin crescent moon bleached the redbrick house white and turned the trees and bushes into soft sculptures. It's what Cissy used to call a fingernail moon. A rabbit sat perfectly still, its long ears pointed up like two arrows.

The air was cool, and Amy shivered beneath the knitted shawl. One by one, the upstairs lights turned off. Miss Lillian's room was the last to grow dark.

A squeak of the cellar door signaled Georgia's presence, and the rabbit hopped away. Hidden behind tall bushes, the door would be easy to miss if a person didn't know where to look.

Amy waited for Georgia to circle the house to the front before leaving her hiding place. She didn't want to lose her, but neither did she want to chance being caught following her.

Though there were private residences farther down the block, some offering room and board, Miss Lillian's Parlor House stood alone, surrounded by empty fields and groves of trees, like a shunned child.

At first it looked like Georgia was heading for town, but then she made a sharp right onto Madison, a narrow dirt road lined with modest one-story brick residences. By the time Amy reached the corner, Georgia had already let herself into a fenced yard. Amy waited until Georgia reached the front porch and vanished inside before drawing near.

It was too dark to see much, but the broken gate and untrimmed bushes suggested the house was in ill repair.

Georgia was never gone for more than fifteen or twenty minutes. That was hardly time enough for a romantic rendezvous. So what was she doing here? Amy could think of only one way to find out.

Not wanting to confront Georgia on the deserted street in the middle of the night — especially since she now carried a gun — Amy hurried back to Miss Lillian's. After letting herself into the house through the cellar door, she sat on the old rocking chair and waited. Since the cellar was her least favorite place in the house, she also prayed there were no spiders or mice or other creepy things waiting to attack.

Fortunately, she didn't have to wait long. The squeak of door hinges was followed by a muffled thud. Soft footsteps echoed from the wooden stairs.

Amy waited for her to round the screen. "Georgia?" she whispered. "It's me, Amy."

Georgia's dark form froze, and for a moment, she didn't speak. "What . . . what are you doing here?"

Amy stood so as to be seen in the soft glow of the crescent moon shining through the narrow cellar windows. "I was about to ask you the same thing."

"You can't say anything about this." Panic edged Georgia's voice. "Please promise you won't tell Miss Lillian."

"I won't say a word." After a pause, Amy asked, "Are you seeing someone? A man?"

"It's not a man." Georgia's voice sound resigned.

"Then who?"

A whoosh of breath preceded Georgia's answer. "My children."

"You have children?" Amy had conjured up all kinds of possible explanations for Georgia's midnight wanderings, but never that.

"Two. A boy, nearly six, and a girl, four." Georgia paused for a moment before adding, "My mother lives a couple of blocks away, and every night I stand by my children's beds and watch them sleep. I can't fall asleep myself until I've seen and touched them. They think an angel comes to visit each night." She gave a throaty laugh that held no mirth. "Can you imagine? Me, an angel?"

Amy's heart went out to her. "I had no idea, Georgia."

"I was once a respectable, married woman. Hard to imagine, isn't it? My husband was a gambler. He was caught cheating, and someone shot him."

"I'm so sorry, Georgia. It must have been awful for you."

"I can't begin to tell you." She took a ragged breath. "He left me heavily in debt. I lost the house — everything. My children, mother, and I were destitute. I took in wash, but no matter how hard I worked I could barely pay the rent, let alone put food on the table. One day I found my son eating the paper off the wall. He said he was hungry." She paused as if reliving the moment before adding, "That was the day I knocked on Miss Lillian's door."

Amy felt a surge of guilt for judging these women. For judging Georgia. Her own family hadn't been rich, but living on a farm they had never wanted for food. "It must be hard to be away from your children."

"You have no idea. I can't bear for them to see me during daylight hours. To see the paint on my face and the horrid clothes I wear. That's why I only visit late at night when they're in bed and it's dark."

"Does anyone else know?" Amy asked.

"No, only you."

Amy didn't know what to say. She couldn't blame Georgia for wanting to care for her children. Her mistake had been that she knocked on the wrong door.

The last thought made Amy think of something. "What about the cellar entrance? Does anyone else know about it? The guests?"

"I don't know." Georgia fell silent for a moment. "You're thinking that's how Rose's killer got in, aren't you?"

That was exactly what she was thinking.

Because either the killer came in through the cellar door or was already in the house. That would make the female residents suspects, or even Mr. Pepper.

"Come on, we better get some sleep," Amy said.

Georgia hesitated. "You won't tell anyone. . . ."

"Not a soul. Your secret's safe."

The next morning, Amy took a chance on traveling to town dressed in a ladylike blue skirt and white shirtwaist, her face scrubbed clean and hair tucked beneath a plain bonnet. After what happened at the Gun and Bakery Shoppe, she realized her disguise worked both for and against her. Today she sought to be anonymous.

Ducking out of the parlor house unseen had been a challenge, but the effort was well worth it. She could now conduct her business without the usual stares. She prayed her luck would continue and she wouldn't meet up with anyone who knew her.

That turned out to be a futile hope. Much to her dismay, she bumped into Mr. Crocker, a regular parlor house guest, at the post office. He'd seen her at Miss Lillian's on numerous occasions, but today he appeared not to recognize her.

He tipped his hat politely and held the door open for her. "Ma'am."

"Thank you."

He might have been less gallant had he known his mop of brown curls and oily smile reminded her of Deadeye Pete, a man now on trial for murder.

She planned to drop her letter in the mailbox but at the last minute decided to hand it to the postmaster directly to see his reaction.

He didn't recognize her, either. Neither did Mr. Piker at the Gun and Bakery Shoppe. Nor did his wife. Not only did Mrs. Piker sell her a cherry tart, but she engaged her in a pleasant conversation about the weather.

People apparently didn't look at prostitutes that closely, or maybe they just didn't see the person beneath the paint and fancy clothes. It was an extraordinary discovery, one she intended to use to full advantage.

Confident now that she could conduct her business in town without the bother of having to dress in a way she abhorred, she hurried along the boardwalk toward the leather and candle shop, its owner on the suspect list.

Suddenly, a body shot out of the Idle Hands Saloon and Dance Hall and sprawled facedown at her feet. Amy immediately recognized the checkered suit of the man in the hotel dining room.

She bent to shake him on the shoulder, wrinkling her nose against the strong smell of alcohol. "Are you all right, sir?"

For answer the man merely groaned. He then raised his torso off the wooden walk and squinted through unfocused red eyes. Climbing to his feet, he rubbed his jaw and spouted a slurred curse as he staggered away.

She was so intent in watching him she failed to notice Mr. Colton until he was only a few feet in front of her. He stopped; their eyes met and she heard his intake of breath.

"Amy?"

Startled, she shook her head and stepped off the boardwalk onto the dirt-packed road. No one else had recognized her. Why had he?

Dodging a horse and wagon, she hurried across the street, her heart beating as fast as her racing feet.

CHAPTER 19

Amy was still running by the time she reached Miss Lillian's. Hoping no one would see her, she rushed around back and lifted the cellar trapdoor. Closing it after her, she walked down the steps and stopped to catch her breath before moving through the dim underground room to the stairs leading to the kitchen.

She was in luck; Coffey hadn't started the noon meal yet and was nowhere to be seen.

Tiptoeing down the hall, she glanced in the parlor. The draperies were shut tight, and the candles were lit. A man Amy didn't recognize sat at a small round table opposite Miss Lillian. Both were staring into the crystal ball.

The man's pointy chin whiskers and hooked nose reminded her of the notorious outlaw J. C. Bitterman, who robbed thirty-seven stages before she'd trailed him to his boardinghouse where he was arrested.

"I see something," Miss Lillian said in a hushed tone. "I see the letter *M.*"

The man sat forward. "*M* for money?"

Shaking her head, Amy hurried up the stairs. How could anyone believe in such nonsense? Only God knew what the future held.

She didn't see Coral until she reached the second-floor landing.

Coral looked her up and down, her chocolate-brown eyes narrowed in suspicion. "Where have you been? And why are you dressed like a poor farmer's wife?"

"I wasn't feeling well so I stepped outside for some air." She moved away from the stairs, but Coral blocked her way.

"Seems like you've been doing a lot of that lately."

"I don't see that it's any of your business what I do." She tried to dodge around her, but Coral refused to let her pass.

"I think it is."

A door opened and Buttercup stepped into the hall. "What's going on?"

Coral folded her arms. "That's what I'd like to know."

Polly's head popped out of her room. "L–leave her alone, C–C–Coral. She's still new."

"Yes, she *is* new." Coral's eyes narrowed. "And, in fact, started work the very same day Rose was murdered."

"So what are you saying, Coral?" Amy kept her voice deceptively calm. It was the same voice used to pacify union rioters. She sensed Coral could be a formidable foe, and that was the last thing she needed.

"I'm saying that it seems like a strange coincidence."

Buttercup's gaze swung from Coral to Amy. "It does seem like that. And why are you dressed in those clothes?"

All three women stared at her.

"As I told Coral, I wasn't feeling well and stepped outside to get some fresh air. And I did not kill Rose. I didn't even know her." Did they believe her? It was hard to tell. "Now if you'll excuse me."

She walked past Coral. Moments later she stood in her room staring at herself in the mirror. Tom Colton had recognized her when no one else in town did. What a nuisance. From now on, she'd have to dress like a proper scarlet lady — or risk having him guess the truth.

Tom sat in the hotel lobby. Tapping the arm of the chair, he watched the door. It was the third day straight he'd waited for Amy. If that wasn't bad enough, she had the annoying habit of popping up in his thoughts at the most inopportune times. He even imagined seeing her in town on occasion. One poor woman he'd mistaken for Amy had run from him like a scared rabbit without giving him a chance to apologize.

He grimaced and rubbed his forehead. He didn't even know Amy's full name. Not that it mattered; his only interest was business. He could never fall for such a woman. Not like his brother . . .

Dave, oh, Dave. He'd been in town for nearly three weeks, and what did he have to show for his efforts? Nothing! He was no closer to finding his brother's killer than he was when he first arrived. No closer to finding out if his brother really had turned over a new leaf. If anything, the opposite seemed to be true, and he had more questions than answers. That was the reason he wanted to see Amy. The *only* reason.

Was she avoiding him on purpose? Or did she simply have nothing to report? Frustrated with his own lack of progress, he decided it was time for action. If Amy wouldn't come to him, he would go to her.

Only this time, he'd keep his eye out for bullets. Better make that both eyes.

It was just after dark when he arrived at Miss Lillian's Parlor House and Fine Boots.

211

A thin crescent moon seemingly mocked his presence as he tethered his horse and walked up the pathway to the porch. A new sign had been tacked onto the front door. SHOOTING LESSONS, TWO FIFTY.

His eyebrows shot up. Miss Lillian was at it again. The way these women wielded their firearms, she'd be advertising a funeral home next.

He rang the bell, and a tall dark-skinned woman, whose name he couldn't remember, opened the door.

She gave him a once-over before letting him in. A strange screech-owl sound greeted him as he followed her past the rampant display of boots for sale and into the parlor. Miss Lillian played the piano as she sang. The woman couldn't carry a tune in a corked jug, but that didn't stop her none. "If you can't sing well, sing loud" seemed to be her motto.

All the working women were present and seated upon ottomans amid clouds of colorful silk and taffeta skirts. The upholstered chairs was reserved for johns or, as Miss Lillian liked to call them, guests.

Several men were scattered about the room holding glasses of alcohol and puffing on cigars or pipes. Some Tom recognized from town, but not all. One he even remembered seeing in church on Sunday. Trying not to let his dislike for the place show, his gaze lit on Amy.

For some reason, she stood out from the rest. Her eyes widened at the sight of him. Tonight she wore a dazzling green gown. Though the room was cool, she held a fan in such a way as to allow a tantalizing peek at a creamy white shoulder, while keeping the valley of her neckline hidden.

Compared to the others, she looked as prim and proper as a preacher's wife at a prayer meeting. Given her attire, that was saying something.

Clearly, she was surprised to see him, but she looked away when he took the seat next to her.

The men came in various sizes and shapes and ranged in age from late twenties to early fifties. They all had one thing in common; they all sported shiny new boots, putting his old leather dogs to shame.

Miss Lillian finished her song and scooted around on the piano bench to face them. Though her singing voice gave her much to be modest about, she accepted the thin applause with an air of entitlement.

With a wave of a jeweled hand, she brushed aside a red curl and pressed her hands together. "Tonight, gentlemen, I have a treat for you. Amy has agreed to play 'For Eloise' by Mr. Lewd Wig Bay-toven."

Amy rose amid a round of clapping hands. "That's 'Für Elise.' " She smiled before adding, "By Mr. Ludwig van Beethoven."

It was all Tom could do not to laugh out loud at Miss Lillian's gaffe. Instead, he cleared his throat and tried to look appropriately at ease.

Amy seated herself on the piano stool and raised her hands to the keys. She looked perfectly composed and comfortable, as if the piano were but a mere extension of her.

Almost instantly, the lilting tune filled the air, and he listened with rapt attention.

It didn't seem possible that this was the same tuneless piano that moments earlier had sounded like a dying cow. Even the occasional wrong note didn't spoil the pleasing musical sound.

There were four other men in the room, and they all sat forward. Amy's playing seemed to draw them in like a magnet.

All too soon, she completed the piece. She stood and accepted the applause with a modest bow.

"Bravo!" called out a bearded man who saluted her with his whiskey glass.

"Well done!" cried another.

The bald-headed man directly across from

Amy gave her a broad wink and patted the seat next to him. His complexion was as lumpy and pitted as a bad road, and his eyes bulged out like a toad's.

Tom felt a strange and totally unexpected protective surge rush through him. Where it came from, he had no idea. It was all he could do not to drag Amy away from the leering glances of the other men.

He balled his hands into fists to keep from acting on the impulse. What went on between these walls was none of his business. He wasn't out to save the world. All he wanted was to find his brother's killer.

Either Amy didn't notice the gesturing man or chose to ignore him. Instead, she let Colton catch her eye. For a split second it seemed as if he and Amy were the only two in the room, but the feeling passed when she took her seat.

"Gentlemen, it's time to choose your partners," Miss Lillian announced.

Tom shot to his feet. "I choose Amy."

The silence that followed suggested he'd acted out of turn. He glanced down at Amy, but she offered neither help nor encouragement. The guests weren't quite so neutral, and the bald-headed man's expression was downright hostile. If looks could kill, Tom would be gasping for his last breath. As it was, he felt compelled to loosen the bolo tie donned specially for the occasion.

Miss Lillian's hands fluttered around all nervous-like. "Amy is already spoken for."

"I believe this will speak louder." Tom reached into his vest pocket and slapped two bills on the low table. If he didn't watch out, Miss Lillian would send him to the poorhouse.

Just as he thought, the madam wasn't about to turn down such a generous amount of money. She exchanged a meaningful and maybe even an apologetic glance with Amy before shrugging to signal the matter closed.

He frowned. Amy and the madam were evidently in cahoots. He wouldn't put it past them to have a plan to wring him dry.

The toad-eyed man protested, but Miss Lillian hooked an arm around his. "Would you care to have your fortune told, Mr. Newhall, on the house?"

While the madam pacified him, the other women sprang into action and one by one led the other guests away with flirtatious chatter.

Tom expected at the least a little friendly banter from Amy. He did, after all, save her from toad man. What he got was an angry glare before she stomped out of the room and up the stairs ahead of him.

He had to hurry to keep up. Something told him he was in for a good tongue-lashing. Not that it worried him. Okay, maybe a little . . .

CHAPTER 20

Slamming the bedroom door shut, Amy whirled around to face him. "Why are you stalking me?"

He drew back, but his innocent act didn't fool her one whit. "Is that what you think I'm doing?"

"Every time I turn around, you're there." She paced back and forth. Two of tonight's guests were on the suspect list. She and Miss Lillian had devised a plan that would have allowed her to engage each of them in conversation. Now, thanks to Colton, she'd missed her chance.

"You had no right to drag me away from the other guests!"

"Is this the thanks I get for trying to save your virtue?" He bit the words out between clenched teeth. "Or rather, what's left of it?"

"I don't need your help," she sputtered. It wasn't just his interference that worried her;

it was the way his mere presence played havoc with her senses. She felt all at once disturbed and excited and, more than anything, confused. Whatever happened to the levelheaded woman who had helped put away some of the country's worst criminals?

"Ah, that's right. I forgot. The lady is armed." He availed himself of the only chair in the room and tossed his hat on the bed. "Relax. All I want is information. We have a deal. Remember?"

"I told you I'd be in touch if anything turned up."

"It's been three days," he said. "The guilty look on your face when I walked in tonight tells me there's a cat in the bag, somewhere. So let's have it."

She was just about to order him out of her room when she decided against it. Maybe tonight wasn't entirely a lost cause. She stopped in front of him and forced herself to think like a proper detective.

"How do I know *you* didn't kill Rose?"

His eyebrows shot up. "Me?" He shook his head in disbelief. "I was with you, remember?"

"You could have killed her before entering my room."

He pursed his lips. "What motive would I have?"

"Revenge. Perhaps you blame her for your brother's death."

"Makes sense." He nodded. "Makes perfect sense. Only it's not true. I never set eyes on Rose until I saw her on the floor, dead. That's why I mistook you for her."

"That could have been an act."

"Or it could be true," he said. "Ask Miss Lillian what time she sent me upstairs. Less than thirty seconds later I walked into your room."

Miss Lillian had more or less confirmed the time line, but she wasn't ready to let him off the hook just yet. "There's another way in and out of the house."

"Oh, you mean the cellar door?"

She blinked. "So you know about that."

"The night you were playing . . . kitty in a tree . . . I had just finished searching the grounds. That's when I found the trapdoor."

Recalling how she had fallen into his arms that night, she blushed. Hoping he wouldn't notice her reddening cheeks, she practically barked out the next question. "What were you searching for?"

"Another way in and out of the house. There were only eight of us here the night Rose died, including Miss Lillian and one other . . . what do you call 'em . . . guests? I know I didn't do it, and I'm pretty sure you didn't, so that leaves six possible suspects."

"Mr. Pepper was with Buttercup."

He rubbed his upper lip. "That still leaves four suspects."

"None of whom had a motive for killing her."

He shrugged. "That remains to be seen. But I doubt that any of the ladies or even Mr. Pepper had the strength to do the deed. She put up quite a fight, and if you recall, I was unruffled when I walked into your room. So that leaves the possibility that an outsider entered the house through the trapdoor."

"There was no fight."

He frowned. "What do you mean?"

"Rose probably never knew what hit her. Someone snuck up from behind and hit her over the head. Her killer then searched the room. Does any of this sound familiar to you?"

A dark cloud fleeted across his face. "I'm here for one thing and one thing alone — to find my brother's killer! You can think what you want, but that's the unbridled truth."

She lowered herself onto the bed. "The whole truth?" she asked. For all she knew, he was still a Texas Ranger tracking down the Gunnysack Bandit. That would make him a competitor.

His eyes brimmed with emotion. "I don't expect you to understand what it's like to lose a sibling."

Her breath caught. "I know very well what it's like," she snapped. *Why do others assume theirs is the only pain?*

The lines faded from his face. "Amy?" Before she knew it, he was on the bed next to her. "What is it? Talk to me."

Maybe it was his gentle tone. Or perhaps the way his gaze seemed to reach into her very soul. Whatever it was, she suddenly found herself telling him about her sister's disappearance. It was wrong to mention anything so personal, to reveal telling details about her past, but she couldn't help herself. It was as if an emotional volcano had erupted inside and she couldn't stop the flow.

He listened closely, intently, holding her gaze in the blue depths of his.

"I was twelve at the time, and Cissy was three." That fateful night had happened fifteen years ago, yet she remembered the details as if it was only yesterday.

"She and I shared a room. One night she cried out in her sleep, and when I went to her she told me that a monster was trying to take her." *"There's no such thing as a*

222

monster," she'd assured her. *"Hush, now. I won't let anything bad happen to you."*

"I waited for her to fall asleep again before tiptoeing back to my own bed. The next morning she was gone and . . . was nowhere to be found." She'd cried an ocean for her lost sister and thought she had no more tears to shed, but her burning eyes told her otherwise.

"Some people believed she might have wandered outside. Bears and wolves had been known to carry away small animals in the area. No one said as much, but I knew the dangers. A child wouldn't have a chance against such a predator." Wouldn't have a chance against a monster, either.

"Do *you* think that's what happened?" he asked.

"I don't know what to believe." She dabbed at her eyes. "Eventually, everyone stopped looking." But not her. She kept track of Cissy's age and imagined what she would look like as she got older. To this day Amy scrutinized every blond she met, each woman's face studied to the point that some people had accused her of staring.

"And you never heard from her again?" he asked, breaking the sudden silence.

"Not a word."

He studied her. "But you don't think she's dead."

She'd never really thought about it in those exact terms. Now that she did, she knew he was right. "It's just a feeling I have. I can't explain it."

It was crazy. Everyone else believed Cissy was dead, even her own parents. People back home said Amy was foolish to live in the past. Her mother had been convinced it was the reason Amy hadn't married and feared she was doomed to spinsterhood. Her father had simply refused to mention his missing daughter's name, even on his deathbed. If only she could get Cissy's last words out of her mind, perhaps she could let the past go.

Colton's hand on hers stunned her out of her reverie. The gentle touch of his strong fingers surprised her.

She looked up at him, and the tenderness in his eyes nearly tore away the last of her defenses. Battling for control, she pulled her hand away, but nothing could be done for the tears.

"The worst part is not knowing what happened to her," she said. With death came a sense of closure, but there was no closure with Cissy. It was like living with an empty tomb.

He nodded. "As a Texas Ranger, I saw firsthand what a missing person could do to a family."

Cupping her face tenderly, he brushed away her tears with his thumbs. No touch had ever affected her on such a deep level. It felt as if he'd reached into her heart and removed part of the pain.

"Thank you," she whispered. No gaze had ever made her feel more understood.

He released her physically, but his gaze never left her face. Sitting together on the bed they talked — he about his brother, she about her sister.

He leaned against the headboard and stretched out his long legs, letting his feet hang off the edge of the mattress. She sat next to him, hugging her knees. Her taffeta skirt nestled against a trouser leg, forming an intimacy between them she didn't want to break.

Despite their close proximity, she felt no threat — at least not from him. But the niggling inside cautioned against the dangers of forming a bond, a warning she feared might have come too late.

"Aren't we a fine couple," she said, after he'd shared a humorous story about his brother; not all his memories were sad.

He flashed a crooked smile before his face

grew serious. "Have you thought about hiring a private detective to search for your sister?" he asked. "The Pinkerton agency might be a good place to start."

Hearing the name of her employer startled her, but she managed to keep from reacting. She'd already availed herself of the Pinkerton resources, of course, but he had no way of knowing that.

"I heard they're expensive," she said, hoping that would end the discussion.

"I'd be willing to help with expenses."

She stared at him, shocked. "Why would you do such a thing?"

"Maybe if you found your sister —" He grimaced. "Amy, I hate seeing you in this place. This isn't what God wants for you. For anyone."

It was all she could do to breathe. It had been a long time since anyone had shown honest interest in her welfare, and she was touched beyond words.

"I should go," he said, apparently mistaking her silence for censure. He hesitated. "You look like you could use some shut-eye."

She didn't want to sleep; she wanted him to stay. "Wait," she said. Slipping off the bed, she dashed across the room and reached into the top bureau drawer for the

226

handwritten list she'd made.

"Here're the names you wanted." He had no way of knowing it, but handing him that list was a sign of trust; any suspicion that he had something to do with Rose's death had been completely put to rest.

Standing, he took the list from her. After a quick glance, he folded the paper in fours and tucked it into his pocket. "Thank you. That's a big help."

She smiled. Only then did she realize how much lighter her cares seemed. She hadn't talked to anyone about her sister for years, and it had done her heart good to open up to him. If only she could share the rest and tell him the truth about her residence at Miss Lillian's.

He reached for his hat, and she felt an odd sense of disappointment. She didn't want the evening to end.

"You can't go yet," she said. It was all she could do not to bar the door to keep him there. Already she felt loneliness creeping into the room and sensed the ghosts of the past waiting to pounce.

He donned his hat and tugged on the brim. "It's late."

"Not that late," she said. "Miss Lillian will think I . . . didn't treat you right." It was actually the other girls who worried her.

Coral was already suspicious.

He gazed at her for a long moment before slipping a hand around her waist and drawing her so close it was as if their hearts beat as one. He brushed his lips against hers, and when she offered no objection, he covered her mouth in a full but tender kiss.

Melting next to him, she slipped her hands up the front of him and wrapped her arms around his neck. Thrilling to the sensations that rippled through her, she willingly returned his kiss, surprising herself by how much pleasure it gave her.

All too soon he let her go, and she felt like something vital had been ripped away, the part of her that was real, perhaps. The part of her that was most vulnerable. It took every bit of willpower she possessed to slip back into her role.

He looked equally shaken by what had transpired between them. Puzzled even. He stared at her for a long moment as if he sensed that the woman in front of him wasn't the one that he'd kissed.

"I'll tell Miss Lillian you treated me just fine," he said, his voice hoarse. With that he slipped out of the room.

She grabbed the back of a chair to steady herself. Now she'd done it. Told him about her personal life, told him about the loss of her sister. He had enough information to uncover her real identity if he bothered to check. If either William or Robert Pinkerton found out what she'd done, she would be fired on the spot.

What was it about this house that brought back the past in such vivid detail? Was it that nothing about Miss Lillian's Parlor House was genuine? Certainly not the people who lived there. Even their smiles were false. It was as if this strange, phony world forced her to search within for something real, bringing long-forgotten memories of Cissy and the night she disappeared to the forefront.

As for Tom Colton . . .

Forcing herself to breathe, she turned and caught sight of her painted face in the mirror.

The reflection staring back looked nothing like her. The eye makeup was intact, as were the rouged cheeks and powdered nose. All she was willing to claim as her own were her lips, bare except for the burning memory of his.

It pained her to think that the woman he'd kissed — or thought he'd kissed — didn't even exist.

Pained her even more to wish that she did. For such a woman was likely to take such a kiss in stride and probably not give it a second thought.

Instead of heading back to his hotel, Colton rode his horse clear though town. He rode past the church and cemetery, past the train station and empty stockades, to the wide-open Kansas plains. It wasn't Texas. Didn't smell like Texas, didn't feel like Texas. Only the stars blazing overhead seemed familiar.

Many were the times he'd ridden beneath the starry Lone Star sky, but never before had he felt like this. Like his whole insides were on fire.

He needed to think. Or maybe he just needed to get his head on straight. Maybe then he could put the memory of her tear-filled eyes and sweet tender lips to rest.

He shouldn't have kissed her. Big mistake. He had no right to criticize his brother's choice of women, not after tonight. Not after the way he felt when he took her in his arms. He'd meant to comfort her, that's all. Instead, his heart had pounded like a blacksmith's hammer against his anvil ribs.

His hands tightened around Thunder's reins, and he sucked in his breath.

He'd practically drowned in those big green eyes of hers. The concern in their depths when he spoke of his brother had filled a hole inside that he hadn't even known existed. Of course, none of it meant a thing. Not her sympathy and certainly not anything that fell from her lips. Services paid for, services rendered. Though heaven knows, he believed it was all real at the time. In the name of Sam Hill, what had he been thinking?

Maybe he was just lonely. A strange town and all . . . He missed his ranch. Missed Davey, now more of a son than a nephew. He missed his cattle, his horses. But lately . . .

Maybe it was time to settle down, get himself a wife. If he had someone waiting for him at home, he sure in blazes wouldn't be longing after a woman of easy virtue, no matter how pretty her eyes or soft her lips or sorrowful her tale.

With a sigh, he tugged on the reins and turned back to town. Sleep, he needed sleep. He'd been in town for nearly three weeks and had nothing to show for it. He'd hoped and prayed he would find his brother's killer. More than that, he'd hoped to prove to his grandpappy that Dave really had turned over a new leaf and deserved to be buried in the family plot. For young Davey's sake.

But his chances of finding out anything

that would exonerate his brother looked about as promising as a summer drought.

He'd give himself one more week. Seven days. If he didn't find any new clues by then, he was out of there. *Seven days, God. Surely You can keep me away from temptation's clutches for seven more days.*

CHAPTER 21

Long after Tom Colton had left her room, long after he'd mounted his horse and ridden away, long after her heart finally stopped pounding, Amy sat staring out of her bedroom window. He was a complication she hadn't counted on. A complication she didn't need.

She no longer thought him guilty of anything except good looks and charm, but that didn't let her off the hook. Not only had she broken the number one rule of an undercover agent by revealing personal information, but she'd also allowed herself to become distracted.

It had to be this house. Never had she felt so out of place, so utterly alone. Sometimes she wondered if even God dared to tread between the wanton walls.

She was so deep in thought she almost missed the man in the checkered suit lurking outside. Pressing her forehead against the glass pane, she followed his progress until he disappeared by the side of the house.

She dropped the curtain. It was time that she and Mr. Checkers got to know each other.

Moments later, she let herself ever so quietly out of the cellar trapdoor. Earlier, a zephyr had blown across the Kansas plains, but tonight the air was still, and stars glittered like diamonds upon a black velvet sky. From the distance came the sound of a fiddle and what sounded like the baying of a wolf, but nothing from nearby.

Gun held by her side, she moved silently through the backyard and peered around the corner of the house.

She spotted Checkers before he saw her. Actually, it was the shadow of his hat that gave his location away behind the bushes. He appeared to be trying to look into one of the first-floor windows.

Gripping her gun, she moved in close. "Who are you and what do you want?"

The bushes rustled and his head popped out. She couldn't see much of his face save the whites of his eyes. "Blimey! Is that a gun?" he asked in a nasally British accent.

"Yes, and I know how to use it."

He lifted his hands shoulder high. "Don't shoot."

"Give me one good reason why I shouldn't."

He sniffled. "You'll mess up my suit."

"That would do you a favor." She lowered the gun to her side, and he dropped his hands.

He stepped out of the bushes and into the stream of light shining from the window. "You near scared the living daylights out of me." He brushed himself off. "You could have given me heart failure."

"That's what you get for sneaking around."

"I wasn't sneaking around. I'll have you know I'm working."

"Working?"

He cleared his throat. "I'm Winston Walker the third. I work for the Pinkerton National Detective Agency."

Not only was the man a sneak, he was as shy of the truth as a goat was feathers. "Try again."

He looked insulted. "You don't believe me?"

"Mr. Pinkerton strictly forbids operatives from using alcohol and foul language. I happen to know that you're guilty of both. He also frowns on peeping Toms."

235

"All right, all right. You got me. I don't work for the old bloke, and I don't much care for his sons. But I *am* a private detective."

She sighed. That's all she needed. Private sleuthhounds were as welcome as a swarm of bees. Most didn't have the slightest idea what they were doing and often had a negative impact on Pinkerton investigations. Shadowing was an art, requiring a person to be present but not noticed. Not only did his checkered suit stand out like a red flag, the clumsy use of a newspaper that day in the hotel pegged him as an amateur.

"What makes you such an expert on Pinkerton?" he asked.

She fell back on the stock reply kept for such occasions. "I have an uncle who works there."

"Talk about hard cheese." He made a face. "Lately all I have is bad luck. Last year, I was this close" — he held his thumb and index finger a sliver apart — "to catching Jesse James and claiming the five-thousand-dollar reward. And what happens? He gets himself shot by one of his own men. The year before that, I was hot on Billy the Kid's trail when he was gunned down by a sheriff. . . ." On and on he went about lost rewards and glory. He was like an old fisherman grousing about the catches that got away.

"So what are you detecting now?" she asked the moment she could get a word in edgewise.

He lifted his pointed nose and lowered his voice. "I have it on good authority that the man known as the Gunnysack Bandit is from these parts."

"Who told you that?"

"I'm not at liberty to reveal my sources, but I have reason to believe that the Pinkerton agency dispatched an operative here."

She stiffened. "How do you know that?" The only way he *could* know was if he bribed a Pinkerton employee. Unfortunately, it wouldn't be the first time that some blabbermouth clerk or secretary had betrayed the company's trust. *Just wait till the principal hears about this!*

"Like I told you, I'm a detective." He lowered his voice. "And I know who it is. I can pick out a fellow sleuth a mile away, and I'm telling you, it's that Colton chap."

It was all Amy could do to keep from laughing out loud. "You think *he's* a Pinkerton detective?"

"Shh. He doesn't want anyone to know, of course. I shouldn't even be telling you. All that business about looking for his

237

brother's killer is rubbish."

The man was dead wrong, but she decided to play along. "So what are you doing here?" Something suddenly occurred to her. "Are you following me?"

"Of course not." He threw up his hands. "All right, I was following you. I need to ask you some questions."

She slipped her hand into her fake pocket and holstered her gun. The man was annoying but didn't strike her as dangerous. "All right, but it will cost you."

He made a face. "No one does anything for free anymore," he grumbled. In a louder voice, he said, "Why would a Pink be interested in a . . . soiled dove such as yourself?"

She folded her arms. His holier-than-thou attitude was more offensive than the derogatory term. "I would think the reason was obvious."

"You're winding me up, right? Since when does a man ask a" — he cleared his voice — "a woman of easy virtue to dine?"

Okay, maybe he wasn't as inept as she thought. A good question deserves a good answer, but at the moment she would settle for a mediocre response — if only she could think of one.

"You tell me. You're the detective."

"I believe he thinks you know something about the Gunnysack Bandit, and I aim to find out what it is."

"And how do you propose to do that?"

Before he could answer, Miss Lillian came barreling around the corner like a runaway horse.

"Ha! I thought I heard voices." The madam stuck her hand out in front of the startled man. "That'll be ten dollars."

Mr. Walker's-slash-Checkers's mouth dropped open.

Amy couldn't help but smile; where money was concerned, Miss Lillian's timing was impeccable. "I told you it would cost you," she said. "Say one more word and the price will double."

Max's General Mercantile and Flower Shoppe was crowded when Amy walked in the following morning. An odd combination of cinnamon, tobacco, and coffee tickled her nose. Tin cans were stacked neatly on shelves. Clusters of onions hung from the rafters, and reams of calico were piled high on a counter ready to be cut. A potbellied stove stood in the center of the store surrounded by barrels of pickles, molasses, and kerosene.

The store owner shoveled coffee beans

into the red coffee grinder and turned the wheel. After grinding the beans, he scooped the grounds into a paper bag and handed it over the counter to a matronly woman with a walking cane.

Amy was immediately drawn to the display of cut flowers. She picked up a bouquet of pink carnations wrapped in green paper. Raising the feathery blossoms to her nose, she watched the store owner behind the counter.

Mr. Maxwell was a frequent guest of Miss Lillian's and number ten on her suspect list.

The stolen banknote had been folded only twice when Rose deposited it, making it unlikely that it had passed through a third or fourth person. It was possible, of course, that a store customer had made a purchase with the bill and Mr. Maxwell had innocently passed it along. Possible, but given the almost pristine condition of the note, highly improbable.

He seemed friendly enough and greeted each customer with a smile and a joke. With his thick blond hair, parted in the middle and worn shoulder length, he reminded her of Hans Bergman, the notorious embezzler she'd tracked all the way to Canada.

Standing nearly six feet tall, Maxwell fit the Gunnysack Bandit's description in height, but a thick German accent made it unlikely he was the right man. Not one robbery victim had mentioned an accent.

Still, she was required to provide a complete description to headquarters on every possible suspect, so a closer look wouldn't hurt.

"Why, Mrs. Monahan. How nice to see you."

The female voice drew Amy's attention to two women standing next to a cracker barrel. It took no special talent to identify which one was married to the town's richest man.

A willowy blond, Mrs. Monahan was younger than Amy expected, probably in her late twenties, early thirties. She wore a stylish brown walking suit that probably cost more than Amy's waterfall evening gown. The bodice was paneled with brown satin, and the collar and cuffs were edged with gold-beaded tulle. Her peaked crown hat was tastefully decorated with a nosegay of yellow flowers and tied beneath her chin with brown satin ribbons.

Without warning, Mrs. Monahan's gaze met hers, and Amy was struck by the look on her face. The woman's expression darkened with the shifting emotions of anger, hatred, and despair, but most prevalent was sadness, and Amy felt sorry for her. She was married to the richest, most powerful man in town and had everything money could buy . . . but not a faithful husband. No amount of money could buy that.

Unable to meet the woman's gaze a moment longer, Amy turned and took her place in front of the counter behind a young mother with a small child. The little boy, dressed in a sailor suit, stared up at her. He had a round face, a fetching smile, and big brown eyes. She smiled back at him. She guessed he was around three, the same age as Cissy when she disappeared.

He tugged on his mother's skirt. "I wike that pretty wady," he said, and Amy felt a pang. Cissy hadn't been able to pronounce the *w* sound either.

Her smile widened. What he no doubt liked was her bright scarlet dress and ruby-red lips. Children were drawn to bright colors. "I like you, too."

His mother turned and her face practically crumbled in horror. "No, you don't, Jimmy. You don't like her. She's not a nice person." Leaving the items she intended to purchase on the counter, the woman yanked her son by the arm and practically dragged him out of the store.

The other customers in line stared at Amy.

Odd as it seemed, the silence was deafening.

"May I help you?" the store owner asked in a thick German accent. He held out his hand for her money with an impatient gesture, as if he was anxious to get rid of her.

Face flaring, she paid for the flowers and left the shop without waiting for change.

Chapter 22

Walking along Main Street, Amy couldn't get Mrs. Monahan out of her mind. Not only was her husband a regular parlor house guest, but he appeared to have had some sort of relationship with Rose, as well. It was the most obvious explanation for the argument overheard by Buttercup. Had it been a lover's quarrel? Or something more sinister?

Perhaps Rose confronted him with her suspicions about his being the Gunnysack Bandit. If so, that would make him a suspect in her death.

Though it was a warm spring day, her dark thoughts chased gooseflesh up and down her spine. It wasn't just Mrs. Monahan that had upset her. She was still shaken by the encounter with the woman and her little boy. Did one ever get used to being shunned? Probably not.

Her steps faltered as she passed the

Grande Hotel and Bath House. Crazy as it seemed, the essence of Mr. Colton's kiss still lingered. Not wanting to relive, yet again, the memory of being in his arms, she quickened her pace. It didn't mean a thing, that kiss. Not a thing.

Little that happened between the walls of Miss Lillian's Parlor House meant anything. The only things that seemed genuine were the sobs sometimes heard coming from the other rooms in the still of night and the nightmares that plagued her sleep.

No, his kiss hadn't been real, no matter how much she wished otherwise. It had cost him dearly to be with her, moneywise. So who could blame him for simply demanding a service he'd paid for? He would have been within his right to expect more. Thank God he didn't. He probably hadn't given the kiss a second thought, so why should she?

Someone touched her arm, and she jumped. It was the beggar who'd tried to gain her attention a time or two before. Recoiling at his unpleasant odor, she pulled away and walked past him. Several feet away, she stopped and turned, shocked by the realization that she had treated him much like the little boy's mother had treated her. Shunned him, more like it, as the town had shunned her.

This time she looked him square in the eyes.

His face was weathered, not by years, for he was still relatively young, perhaps in his late thirties, but by sadness. The hair framing his gaunt face fell to his shoulders in tangled strands. How many times had she passed him without noticing that he was a veteran of that awful war? How many times had she failed to see the man inside the weary shell?

Even a person trained to be a private eye didn't always see what was right in front, clear as day. What else did she not see? *God, what else?*

Clutching the flowers in the circle of her arm, she pulled a banknote out of her purse. She held it outward as she walked toward him. He took it from her, his fingers curling around her offering like a man grabbing a lifeline.

"God bless you, ma'am," he said, and even his voice sounded old.

She smiled. "You don't know how much I needed to hear that." Now more than ever she needed God's blessings.

"I know," he said, and he gave her a gap-toothed smile. "I've been watching you, and I know."

Surprised that he knew that about her —
and maybe even a little ashamed that a beggar had given her the respect she'd failed to
give him, she thanked him and hurried away.

The church cemetery was located at the
edge of town. At times, Miss Lillian's Parlor
House seemed stifling, and Amy was happy
to escape, if only for a short while.

She reached the church and followed a
gravel path to the cemetery in back, entering through the ornate wrought iron gate.
Mentally, she ran through the remaining
names on her list. She'd hoped to have
something tangible to write in her report to
headquarters by now, but so far she had
more questions than answers.

She was so deep in thought that she failed
to notice the woman hunched over a grave
until she almost stumbled over her.

The woman looked up, and Amy's heart
sank. It was the churchwoman, Mrs. Givings.

"Forgive me." Not only had she almost
caused the woman physical harm, she had
also interrupted a private moment, made
obvious by the woman's red eyes.

Mrs. Givings struggled to her feet and
pushed her spectacles up her nose. "That's
quite all right."

Amy lowered her gaze to the inscription engraved on the tombstone.

"My daughter," Mrs. Givings explained. "Smallpox."

Amy's breath caught in her lungs. The little girl was only six years old when she died. "I'm so sorry."

"Yes, so am I," Mrs. Givings replied.

Amy's greatest fear was finding Cissy's name on a grave somewhere. "How . . . how do you live with losing a daughter?" It was hard enough living with the loss of a sister.

The question seemed to surprise the woman. Did she not think a harlot capable of feelings? Capable of compassion?

"It's not like I have a choice."

"I know, but it must be . . . difficult."

Mrs. Givings dabbed at her eye with a handkerchief. "Only when I focus on the loss of my daughter. It doesn't hurt so much when I think about the glory of God's love and grace."

Amy felt a surge of guilt. Not only had her sister's disappearance made her question God at times, but her job required her to make snap judgments about people, too, and she had judged Mrs. Givings a bit harsher than most. Today she realized her mistake. The woman wasn't the annoying Bible thumper she'd originally thought. She was simply a grieving mother holding on to God with both hands.

"You lost someone, too," Mrs. Givings said. It was a statement, not a question.

"Someone close. A family member."

Such an observation wasn't all that surprising. Sometimes Amy sensed loss in others, and had she bothered to look, she might have spotted it in Mrs. Givings. She often wondered if grief-stricken people sent out covert messages that could only be received by those going through similar losses.

"My sister."

"I'm sorry."

They stared down at the little grave, a "fallen" woman and a "pillar of society" standing side by side, bonded by grief and loss.

Amy leaned over and laid the flowers in front of the gravestone.

Mrs. Givings looked surprised. "That's very kind of you, but I'm sure that you meant them for your friend."

"That's all right. I'm sure my . . . friend would understand."

Someone called from a distance. It was one of the other churchwomen waving from afar. It looked like Mrs. Compton. Mrs. Givings waved back.

"I have to go. It's almost time for the

church quilting bee." Sounding vaguely apologetic, she hesitated as if wanting to say more. Instead, she gave her daughter's grave one last glance before hurrying away.

Amy watched until the two women vanished through the back door. The church with its tall steeple and stained glass windows seemed to beckon, and she was tempted to answer the call. She wouldn't, of course. Couldn't. Not dressed the way she was.

Never had she felt like such an outsider. The social barrier that separated her from Mrs. Givings had lifted, but only for a moment. Now it was firmly back in place, making even the church off-limits.

As a tomboy growing up, she'd always felt different. She would much rather chase her brothers than play with dolls or learn domestic skills. The feeling of isolation grew worse through her teens. While her friends were down by the swimming hole or enjoying wild carriage rides, she was at the sheriff's office inquiring about her sister.

By the time she was twenty, most of her friends were already married, and some even had children. She was clearly regarded as unusual, if not altogether strange. But never had she felt like such an outsider as she did at that moment. Never had she felt so far away from God.

Though it was only a little after the noon hour by the time she returned to the parlor house, already two horses were tied up in front. Amy recognized the brown gelding as belonging to Mr. Tully, a married man. Disgust turned her stomach, and she felt nauseous. People accused prostitutes of having no moral integrity, but what about the men who sought their services? Why weren't they held to the same standards? After living here she wondered if she could ever again trust a man — any man — even Tom Colton.

Amy had hardly reached for the bell when the door flew open.

"You're back at last," Miss Lillian exclaimed. "Come quickly." She motioned Amy inside and locked the door. "Hurry, hurry." She led the way into her office with a swish of her purple silk gown.

Bracing herself for yet another lecture on how she walked or chewed off her lip rouge, Amy reluctantly followed.

Miss Lillian reached across her desk for a brown leather book.

"Rose's diary," she announced with a triumphant gesture.

Amy's mouth dropped open. "Where did

251

you find it?" She had searched Rose's room and found nothing.

"Beatrice and I were getting the room ready for Rose's replacement, and we found it beneath a loose floorboard." She handed Amy the diary and tapped the leather cover with a jeweled finger. "There's not much there of a personal nature, but perhaps you'll see something I missed."

Heart leaping with excitement, Amy turned the book over. Had this been what Rose's killer had been looking for? Maybe this was the break for which she'd been praying.

Amy started to leave then thought of something. "You keep the front and back doors locked, but what about the cellar door?"

Miss Lillian looked confused. "The cell— ? Oh, you mean the trapdoor. That's padlocked and hasn't been opened in years. Why do you ask?"

"No reason." Thanking her, Amy left the parlor and hurried upstairs. She paused outside her closed door, hand on the brass knob. The threads placed in the cracks for security purposes were still there, but that's not what caused her to pause. She could no longer enter her room without thinking of Colton's kiss. The memory of being in his arms was so vivid she had to blink to make sure he was only a figment of her imagination.

Shaking away the vision, she flung the door open. For perhaps the hundredth time that day she reminded herself that his kiss was meaningless. She meant nothing to him, and certainly he meant nothing to her.

Her job didn't allow for romance, a fact she found out the hard way from a Chicago businessman named Paul Devereux. She might have married him except for one thing: he had no patience for her habit of disappearing on a case for several weeks at a time. Eventually he found what he called a "stay-at-home" girl. It hurt. It hurt a lot.

In retrospect, it seemed like a small price to pay for the profession she loved. Her job provided everything she ever wanted: independence, a chance to travel, thrills, and adventure. Solving crimes also gave her a sense of closure that had been sorely missing from her life since Cissy's disappearance.

She didn't need a man. If anything, it would only complicate her life. Complicate his.

Still, she couldn't help but wonder how it would feel to be kissed by Tom Colton under very different circumstances. To be

kissed by him as if it really *did* mean something.

CHAPTER 23

Reading Rose's journal was like reading the scattered thoughts of a twelve-year-old. Ink smears and crossed-out words dotted the pages.

Poor spelling and lack of punctuation made the writing hard to read, at first, until she grew accustomed to Rose's style. But even then some words and even entire sentences remained a mystery.

Poor handwriting could not be read; it had to be deciphered. A Pinkerton detective named Curt Cullins was considered an expert in the science of graphology, and she had learned much from him. He'd studied the penmanship of people from all walks of life. According to Cullins, physicians, politicians, and singers had the worst handwriting, ministers and lawyers the best.

Rose's sentences crowded together, suggesting she probably grew up poor. Such a person was inclined to use resources carefully, and that included paper.

Nothing of a sexual nature had found its way among the pages and almost nothing personal. She wrote about the terrible dust storms that had plagued the area and *"took the starch out of everything."* She described the wind being so strong that visitors arrived *"hatless and with coattails over their heads."*

Dave Colton was mentioned only once. *"D.C. asked me to marry him,"* she wrote, but oddly enough that was all.

Several pages were missing, and only the ragged edges remained. Amy ran her fingers along the seam holding the diary together. Pieces of Rose's life torn away? If only a person could pick and choose which memories to keep and which to discard as easily as ripping pages from a diary.

Months passed between entries until about midway when accounts appeared weekly and sometimes even daily, but were even less personal. It wasn't a diary, after all; it was a record of birds, and one sentence stood out from all the rest: *"Birds fly because they have perfect faith."*

A harlot writing about faith? Rose, it seemed, was full of surprises.

Hummingbirds, sparrows, wrens, and owls filled the pages, along with rudimentary

256

sketches.

Stuck between the pages was a piece of blank paper. Amy held it up to the light. It was straw paper, the kind favored by butchers. It was also similar to the paper used to disguise money at the First National Bank in St. Louis. Packets of currency had been replaced with straw paper that had been cut and packaged like the real thing. No one was the wiser until several days later, and by then the thief had probably fled the state.

She reached for her cloth purse and pulled out a dollar bill. The bill matched the size and shape of the straw paper exactly, and that couldn't be by chance. Was the Gunnysack Bandit behind the St. Louis Bank theft? As far as she knew, even Robert Pinkerton, who was very astute at such things, had not suspected the Gunnysack Bandit of that particular crime.

She put the paper aside to be included in her next report to headquarters and continued reading. The entry dated December read simply, *"Spotted Hummingbird and Waxwing in garden."*

At the end of January Rose had written: *"D.C. promised we would leave as soon as he returned. Don't want him to go. Saw Waxwing."*

How odd. Birds got equal billing with a

planned trip.

The last entry in the journal was written on February 6. The rest of the pages were blank.

Why would Rose go to all the trouble to hide a journal mostly of birds beneath the floorboards? Even more puzzling, why did she stop journaling on that particular day, nearly two months before her death?

Unless . . . She raced across the room and lifted her mattress. Flipping through the pages of the notebook hidden there, she found what she was looking for. There it was: February 6, the day Tom's brother's body was found. The empty pages of Rose's journal marked the day her world came to an end.

Amy mailed a detailed report to Pinkerton the following morning, addressing the envelope to Aunt Carolyn at the prescribed post office box assigned to her. She also included the straw paper and described where and how she found it.

A letter from "Aunt Carolyn" waited in her box. According to Mr. Pinkerton, Marshal Flood's record was clean, and she was to make contact. One problem solved.

None of the other names on her suspect list had criminal records, but the one name that commanded full attention was Tom Colton's. According to the Pinkerton report, he had, indeed, been a Texas Ranger until three years ago. The day his brother walked out of prison was the day Tom Colton resigned.

So far everything Colton had told her was true. Somehow she knew that, of course, but it was still a relief to have it confirmed by headquarters.

She folded the letter and stuffed it into her fabric drawstring purse to be destroyed later. Everything was written in cipher, but a Pinkerton operative could never be too careful.

Leaving the post office, she turned toward the marshal's office. Without warning, Tom Colton suddenly appeared out of nowhere and fell in step by her side.

"Looking for me?" he asked.

"Absolutely not." She slowed her pace, but only because his presence made her pulse skitter. It was annoying — more than that, distracting — the way his nearness affected her. "I'm on my way to the marshal's."

"Why?" The question popped out of him with the force of a bullet.

She had a ready answer. "Miss Lillian is anxious to know if there's been any progress made into Rose's death."

"I can save you the trouble. There hasn't been."

"Thank you, but I think she'd prefer I hear it out of the horse's mouth."

"Have it your way, but I get first dibs on any new information you might have."

She stopped midstep, forcing him to swing around to face her. "Why is that?"

"I'm paying you. The marshal is not."

She lifted her chin in open defiance. "I wouldn't be so certain of that." She hated having to throw her role as a loose woman in his face, but she needed to put a barrier between them. Maybe then she could free herself of the hold he had over her.

He stared at her long and hard. "Why, Amy? Why are you working for that . . . that woman? You're bright and smart and pretty and. . . . Blast it all!" He leaned over her. "Why are you throwing yourself away on a bunch of worthless men?"

She gazed up at him, her body rigid. She'd asked each of Miss Lillian's girls that very same question; now it was asked of her. "Why do you care what I do?"

He reared back and a puzzled frown fleeted across his face. "I don't know why," he said quietly. The words hung between them for a moment before he turned and walked away.

You don't care for me, she wanted to shout. *You don't even know me!* Instead, she called, "We found Rose's journal." It wasn't much, the journal. It was nothing, really. But she needed to remind him that it was business between them — nothing more. It could never be anything more.

It worked. At least he stopped walking. Holding his back to her for a moment as if bracing himself to face her, he then turned. "Did you say journal?" The remoteness in his eyes remained, but his voice held a note of hope.

She nodded. "It was in her room beneath a floorboard."

"Does it . . . mention my brother?"

"Yes, but it doesn't say much. I'm not sure you'll find it useful, but if you'd like to read it —"

"I would." He rubbed his chin as if trying to make a decision. "I'll meet you at Miss Lillian's."

"No!" The last place she wanted to meet him was in her room. Not after what happened the other night. Not after what passed between them today. "I mean . . ."

They locked gazes.

He was the first to break the silence. "Just so you know, what happened the other night was a mistake. It won't happen again."

It *was* a mistake, as much for her as it was for him. Still, his words hurt. She didn't want them to. She didn't want to feel anything for him.

"You're right, it won't," she snapped. Her breath caught. "Meet me at the house at three." She hurried away, but it felt as if she'd left a piece of her heart behind.

Tom watched Amy walk away. He was tempted to trail the "follow-me-lad" streamers that floated enticingly from her feathered hat.

Even from the back, her occupation defined her. The bright green dress practically screamed for attention, and men and women alike gave her a wide berth. She stood for everything he loathed, but it was sadness he felt. Sadness for her, sadness for women like her who sold their souls along with their bodies.

And yet . . .

"Why do you care what I do?"

"I don't know why."

All he did know was that when her eyes filled with tears she'd practically broken his heart. He also knew that when she kissed him it was like being kissed by an angel. She stirred something inside him that was new and exciting and, more than anything, worrisome. She was the kind of woman Dave would fall for, not him. *God, please don't let me do anything so foolish.*

CHAPTER 24

Marshal Flood looked up from his desk and greeted Amy with a bland expression.

"If you came here to inquire about Rose, I'll tell you what I told Colton. There's nothing yet, and when there is, I'll let you know."

Not a good start to what she had hoped would be a productive meeting. She gave her fan a coquettish flick. A little flattery generally went a long way.

"I don't doubt that for a moment, Marshal. Mr. Colton said you didn't care about solving a little old harlot's murder, but he doesn't know what he's talking about. The way you handled the investigation on the night we found her body was . . ." Adequate at most. "Brilliant."

"Well now." He rose from his seat, his face all red. Grabbing a spare chair from the corner, he set it in front of his desk. "Why don't you sit for a spell?"

She smiled. "Why, thank you, Marshal." She seated herself with great aplomb and waited for him to return to his own chair.

"Could you at least tell me if you have any leads as to who killed Rose? I'd sleep a lot better knowing you were . . . hot on someone's trail."

"Sorry, ma'am. I don't have any good news to report yet." He hastened to add, "But that don't mean I won't."

"Do you think it was the Gunnysack Bandit who killed her?"

His hesitation was a sign he knew more than he was saying. "Absolutely not, but . . ." He pointed to a telegram on his desk. "Pinkerton is sending an operative to town. Soon as he arrives I'll find out more."

He. She smiled. This was the fun part. She leaned over his desk so the prisoner behind the bars couldn't hear. "That would be me," she said in a hushed voice. "I'm that operative."

Flood blinked and his eyes grew round as wagon wheels. "You?" He frowned. "But you're . . ." He cleared his voice. "You're a woman."

She sat back. "Yes, that has been brought to my attention." She went on to explain how she happened to be staying at Miss Lillian's Parlor House.

He shook his head. "I never would have guessed. Why didn't you tell me before now?"

"I had to wait for approval from headquarters." She smiled so he wouldn't take offense.

"In other words, you had to make sure I was one of the good guys."

She straightened the fabric of her skirt. "One can never be too careful."

"I know what you mean." He lifted a wooden box, pulled out a cigar, and hesitated. "Normally, I would offer a detective a cigar."

"Normally, a detective would take one," she said. "But I'll pass."

He shut the lid and grunted. "So what have you uncovered so far?"

"Not much," she admitted. She wasn't ready to reveal her suspicions about Monahan. "If the Gunnysack Bandit didn't kill Rose, who do you think did? Do you have any other suspects?"

He bit off the end of his cigar and spat it into a brass spittoon. "Like I told you, I don't have much. Lots of people in town don't approve of . . . uh . . . gentlemen's clubs. I guess you might say they were once a necessary evil. That was back when women were in short supply. But thanks in part to the railroad, those days are long gone."

He lit his cigar and took a puff before continuing. "So, suspects? Yeah, I've got suspects. I'd say that half the women in this town would like to see harm come to Miss Lillian and her ilk. Why, just last year, I arrested an irate wife trying to burn the place down. You're living proof that it never pays to underestimate a woman."

She smiled. "I heartily agree." It was her turn to hesitate. "What about Mr. Colton? Do you trust him?"

"I have no reason not to. His brother, now . . ." He shook his head. "That's a different story."

"You knew his brother?"

"David Colton? Yeah, I knew him." He tossed a nod toward the row of jail cells. "He spent many a night here, mostly for disturbing the peace."

Given Dave Colton's history, she supposed that wasn't all too surprising. Still, she knew how much Tom wanted to think his brother had changed his ways.

"But no real criminal activity?" she asked

Flood narrowed his eyes. "I have my suspicions."

Elbows on the arms of her chair, she folded her hands in front. "What does that mean, exactly?"

He clamped his cigar between his teeth and shuffled through a stack of folders on his desk. He opened one and pulled out a sheet of wrinkled paper. "Found this clutched in Colton's hand." He handed it to her.

She unfolded the paper and immediately recognized the list of banks and express offices held up by the Gunnysack Bandit. It even included the St. Louis Bank. The list was typed, and judging by the lack of errors and cross outs, it was typed by someone familiar with a writing machine.

She looked up. "What was Dave Colton doing with a list like this?"

"My question, exactly."

She studied the list again. Under the right circumstances it was possible to determine if a letter had been typed on a specific typewriter. Every machine had its own peculiarities, and irregularities of type and word spacing often provided important clues. Allan Pinkerton once testified in court that a ransom note had been written on a defendant's writing machine. The demand for money clearly showed on the ribbon.

In this particular case, there was a slight defect in the letter *m* and the top of the *e* was furred. Both imperfections were the result of normal wear. Matching the letters with the type bars would be an easy task, providing the correct typewriter could be found.

She handed the paper back. It probably hadn't even occurred to the marshal to check the typewriters in town. Allan Pinkerton was way ahead of local authorities in his crime-solving ways, and no small-town marshal was likely to catch up anytime soon.

"Where do you suppose he got that list?" she asked.

"I'll give you three guesses, and the first two don't count."

"You think *he* typed up the list. But that would mean —"

"Dave Colton was the Gunnysack Bandit."

She stared at him. Nothing received from headquarters suggested such a thing. Could the marshal be right? She didn't want to believe it. *God, please no! Not Dave. It would kill Tom!*

The thought made her cringe, and she immediately pushed it away. She was a professional, and by George, she would act like one if it killed her. That meant keeping a clear and objective mind.

"Dave Colton could have found the list." Or maybe Rose stole it from one of the guests and gave it to him.

"If it was just the list, I would agree."

She stiffened. "There's more?"

The marshal took a puff of his cigar. "Colton's been dead for nearly three months, and there hasn't been a single crime attributed to the Gunnysack Bandit since. He never went that long between robberies. A month maybe, but not three or even two."

The marshal was right about the timing. "He killed a man during the last fiasco and was almost caught," she said. "Maybe he's just laying low for a while."

"Oh, he's low all right." The marshal blew out a puff of smoke. "Six feet under, to be exact."

The marshal's theory was not only surprising but disturbing. She tried keeping an open mind, but thoughts of Tom kept getting in the way.

"It makes no sense," she managed at last. "Why would Dave Colton keep a list that placed him at the scene of the crimes?"

"Some people like to keep track of their deeds. Kind of like notches on a gun or bedpost, if you know what I mean."

As much as she hated to admit it, the marshal had a point. Still, his theory contained holes.

"That doesn't explain who killed him *or* Rose."

The marshal discounted her comment with a wave of his hand. "A man like David Colton makes a lot of enemies. As for Rose . . ." He shrugged. "I have no reason to think the two deaths are related. Her money box was empty, her jewelry gone. If it smells like robbery and looks like robbery, in my book it is a robbery. Her killer could be in Timbuktu for all I know. Case closed."

She glared at him. The cavalier way he dismissed Rose's killer infuriated her. All that business about looking into her death had meant nothing, and it was all she could do to control her anger.

"What about David Colton? Is that case closed, too?"

"Not yet, but it will be. Just as soon as I send my report to your boss."

She leaned forward. "If he really was the Gunnysack Bandit, why would he turn to his brother for help when he thought Rose's life was in danger?"

"Who knows? Maybe he was trying to cover his tracks."

"Or maybe you're wrong about him."

"I wish that was true. 'Cause I sure don't want to break the news to Tom Colton." He took a puff of his cigar before removing it from his mouth with his thumb and forefinger. "No sir, don't want to do that."

She left the marshal's office, shaken. David Colton, the Gunnysack Bandit? She couldn't believe it. Didn't want to believe it.

"Why do you care what I do?"

"I don't know why."

The memory filled her with despair. Operatives had been warned against letting personal feelings compromise an investigation. Crime solving must be based on evidence, not emotions. She'd always prided herself on the ability to remain professional at all costs. So why would this time be any different?

Not wanting to risk bumping into Tom Colton again, she headed for the parlor house. She'd already gone over Miss Lillian's ledgers, but it had never occurred to her to check Dave Colton's visits against the dates of the Gunnysack Bandit's crimes. He couldn't be in two places at once. If he was with Rose, that would surely disprove the marshal's theory.

She turned the corner and spotted a group of about a dozen women gathered in front of the parlor house, several of them holding up signs. The word *Repent* was written in big bold letters on one sign, but that was one of the least offensive suggestions.

The Pinkerton agency had worked with various unions, and she'd learned from experience that the best way to deal with angry picketers was to remain calm. As she drew near, the chanting grew louder and fists pumped the air.

Someone called her an ugly name. A young woman cradling an infant in her arms yelled, "Sinner!"

The groups began closing ranks, and Amy reached for the latch on the gate. A matronly woman rammed into her, her walking cane raised high over her head. Amy managed to duck just in time, but the reprieve didn't last. Rough hands grabbed her by the waist and pulled her away from the gate.

Hate-filled faces pressed close, and dozens of hands pawed at her. She tried reaching for her gun, but someone pinned back her arms. Panic threatened. Even angry union picketers had not attacked her, at least not physically. These women looked like they were out for blood.

"Let me go," she cried. "Please!"

The mob ripped off her dress. Someone yanked her hat off her head and trampled it.

One woman slapped her across the face. "That's for my Charlie!"

"Stop, please, stop!" she cried, but her pleas went unheeded. A fist to her stomach was followed by a punch in the eye. Tears blurred her vision.

Then all at once her tormentors backed away. Her torn gown and petticoat were on the ground, but her holster was still attached to her bloomers. She pulled out her gun, but it was no longer needed.

Mrs. Givings stood a short distance away, glaring at Amy's attackers, hands at her waist. "What's the matter with you?" Trembling with righteous indignation, the churchwoman shook like a quaking aspen. "Is this how good Christians behave?" she sputtered. "You should be ashamed of yourselves. All of you!"

"She's one of *them*," someone shouted, and a couple of women joined in to defend their actions, but Mrs. Givings would have none of it.

"This is a sad day for our church," she said, her voice breaking. "A very sad day."

The picketers hung their heads in shame, and one by one they left until only Mrs. Givings remained.

Amy picked a piece of fabric off the ground and held it to her bosom. "Thank you," she whispered.

The churchwoman dropped her hands to

her side. "I . . . never meant you any harm. I'm so sorry. Would . . . would you forgive us?"

The woman looked so distressed that Amy felt sorry for her. "I do," she whispered.

Mrs. Givings looked about to say more but the sharp report of a gun made her jump.

"Oh dear," she cried and quickly hobbled down the street, leaving a trail of hat feathers in her wake.

Amy's gaze flew to the house. Miss Lillian stood on the porch, brandishing her weapon and looking unbearably pleased with herself. "Not bad for an amateur, wouldn't you say?" she called.

Amy managed a wan smile. Hands on her sore stomach, she limped toward the porch. "Not bad at all."

Miss Lillian led Amy into her office and ordered her to sit. Fussing over her mother hen–style, she issued orders like a general ready for battle.

"Polly, fetch my medical supplies. Georgia, tell Coffey to bring a pot of tea. And Buttercup . . . Land o'goshen, where's that girl?"

Buttercup stuck her head into the office. "I'm here."

"Well, don't just stand there. Get Amy a dressing gown."

No sooner had Polly returned with a basket of bandages and other supplies than Miss Lillian attacked Amy's wounds with a wet sponge and salve. Buttercup returned with a blue silk dressing gown, which she draped around Amy's shoulders.

The women stood around gaping until Miss Lillian chased them out of the office and slammed the door shut. "Mercy, you'd think they never saw a black eye before."

Never had Amy known such attention, not even when she had measles and chickenpox as a child. Back on the farm, time and attention were devoted out of necessity to animals and crops, not children.

"You were lucky," Miss Lillian said. "This group wasn't as bad as most."

Amy didn't particularly feel lucky. She felt sore and miserable and more than a little humiliated. She had misjudged the situation and fallen into a trap. She should have been better prepared.

"And I thought *my* job was dangerous," she muttered.

"You don't know the least of it." Miss Lillian clucked her tongue. "If anyone needs to repent, it's those women's husbands. They spend Saturday nights here and Sundays in church. Hypocrites, all of them."

The pressure of Miss Lillian's touch increased with her rising voice.

"Ouch."

"Sorry." Miss Lillian proceeded more gently but continued her tirade. "If they must pick on someone, why not those dreadful cribs? Or better yet, that horrible pimp Mr. Fortune. There's nothing worse than a pi," she said, using the slang word for pimp. The gentle euphemisms used to describe her own affairs were never extended to the competition.

"Why is it worse for a man?" Amy asked. She doubted God made allowances for gender.

"A man can do anything he wants, that's why. He can pursue any vocation. Start any business. Every bank is willing to give him a loan." She sighed. "It's different for a woman. Our choices are limited, to say the least."

Miss Lillian's voice held a wistfulness that surprised Amy. For a moment the mask had slipped, revealing a woman who had once been deeply hurt or disillusioned. Maybe both.

"I hope you don't mind my asking, but why have you never married?"

Miss Lillian's eyebrows shot up. "Me?"

"Yes, you. You're rich and powerful and attractive." In her younger days she might even have been considered a beauty. "Seems like you could have had just about any man you set your cap for."

Miss Lillian set the tube of salve on the desk and wiped her hands on a towel. "Perhaps. But do you know how many married men cheat on their wives? There's not a man alive who can be trusted. Why would I want to put myself through that?"

"There are good men out there. Men who are honest and committed to their families." At least Amy hoped there were, though lately she'd begun to question if that was true.

Miss Lillian discounted the notion with a wave of a jeweled hand. "You can't keep a good man good. When a man marries, he says adios to the single life and hello to adultery."

"That's not true."

"Isn't it? What do you think keeps me in business?" Miss Lillian threw up her hands as if it didn't matter, but the sadness in her eyes betrayed her. "Let's just say where men are concerned, I wouldn't trust a one of them. What good is marriage without trust?" She gave Amy a scolding look. "Don't tell me a bright woman like you believes otherwise."

Amy thought of Tom Colton — a man committed to redeeming his brother's reputation and finding his killer. Would he be just as committed to a woman? Before her stay at the parlor house she would never have asked that question. But that was before she knew how lightly some honest, hardworking, and even churchgoing men took their marriage vows.

"I hope you're wrong," she said with feeling. "I hope that good Christian men really do exist." *God, please let it be true.*

"If I thought for one moment that such a man existed, I would —" Miss Lillian shook her head. "Enough of this talk." She probed Amy's shoulder. "I don't think you have any serious injuries, but I'll fetch Doc Graham if you like."

"That won't be necessary." Amy worked her arms into the robe sleeves. "Thank you."

Miss Lillian looked pleased. "I wanted to try out my shooting skills. Now I just have to put my new investigative skills to work."

"New —" Amy inhaled sharply, and a pain shot through her shoulder.

Miss Lillian picked a dime novel off her desk. "I've been doing some research on the subject. Did you know that tightrope

279

walkers have wide feet?"

Amy shook her head. "I can't say that I did."

"Said so in this book I'm reading. It's a detective story, and I've learned all kinds of interesting things about detecting. The killer left a footprint at the scene of the crime and the detective was able to determine it belonged to the tightrope walker because of the width of the foot."

Amy didn't know what to say. The last thing she needed was for Miss Lillian to go around playing detective. She had enough trouble contending with that snoop hound Checkers. On the other hand, she needed Miss Lillian on her side.

"I'm hoping to get some ideas on how to investigate Rose's murder," Miss Lillian continued.

"I'm not sure that a dime novel offers the best advice."

"Maybe not." Miss Lillian set the book down. "But we all have to start somewhere, now don't we?"

CHAPTER 25

Any hope Amy had that Miss Lillian's ledger or Rose's journal would clear Colton's name soon proved futile. She had no idea where Tom's brother was during the crimes in question, but he sure wasn't at the parlor house.

Maybe his landlady at the boardinghouse could shed some light as to his activities. Surely she would know if he'd left town for any extended length of time and what dates.

Amy closed the ledger and decided to return it to the office. On the way back to her room she practically bumped into Buttercup and her "guest."

The man needed no introduction. Even if his fine three-piece suit, black patent shoes, silk cravat, and top hat didn't give him away, Amy would have known this was Mr. Monahan, the town's richest man.

An extravagant lifestyle had done him no favors appearance-wise. His red, fleshy face revealed a fondness for alcohol, and his wide nose was seamed with purple vein threads.

Mr. Monahan tipped his hat and raked her over visually. Amy felt naked beneath his lusty gaze, and all she could think about was his young wife, no doubt sitting home alone waiting for him.

"You must be the new girl," he said with a surface charm that could probably wash off in the rain.

Keeping her emotions in check, Amy dug her fingers into the ledger's leather cover.

"Yes, I am. My name's Amy."

"I look forward to getting to know you better, Amy." Neither his voice nor expression left a question as to his meaning.

It would be a cold day in Hades before that ever happened, but she managed a casual nod. "I'd like that." About as much as she'd like keeping company with a rattlesnake. "I also like your gold watch chain. Is it new?"

His hand went to his fob. "This? No, it was originally my grandfather's." He turned to his escort. "Come along, my dear."

Buttercup led him down the hall with a forced smile. She glanced back at Amy with a look of woeful resignation before leading her "guest" into the room at the end of the hall.

So that was the infamous rich man of Goodman. He was the right height as the Gunnysack Bandit and probably the right age.

As a businessman, he likely also owned a typewriter or two, probably one of the few in town who did. She guessed the bank owned at least one and maybe the assay office. The mayor's office was also likely to have a typewriter, as were the three lawyers in town.

Of all the possibilities, Mr. Monahan topped the list of suspects. Not only did he fit the bandit's description, but he lived high on the hog, too.

Just where did the man get all his money?

On second thought, perhaps she would have to get to know the man better — if not him, then his typewriter.

Later that afternoon, Amy sat staring out her bedroom window waiting for Colton. Grimacing, she rubbed her sore shoulder. Actually, her injuries were a blessing in disguise as they gave her a good excuse to wear the matching green silk shoulder cape over her gown. Polly had helped her cover her black eye with paint, and it hardly showed.

Spotting Tom riding up to the parlor

house, she dropped the curtain in place. She didn't want to look anxious.

Forcing herself to breathe, she grabbed Rose's journal. Moving as fast as her sore body allowed, she left her room. She walked gingerly down the stairs, reaching the door before Tom rang the bell.

"Amy," he said, tugging the brim of his hat. His eyes seemed to soften at the sight of her. Or was that wishful thinking on her part?

"What happened out there?" he said, with a nod toward the debris left by the mob.

"Just some disgruntled ladies," she said.

His forehead creased. "Is everything all right?"

"Yes, everything's fine." Not wanting to discuss the matter further, she reached into her pocket. Before she could hand him Rose's journal, Coral entered the entry hall, voice first.

"Who's at the door?"

Amy shoved the journal back into her pocket. She'd hoped to send him on his way before anyone even knew he had been here, but already Coral was peering over her shoulder.

"Why, Mr. Colton," Coral cooed, all sweetness and light. "What is your pleasure?"

Cheeks flaring, Amy met his gaze. "Mr. Colton came to . . ." What? Her mind scrambled. Have his hair cut? A singing lesson? "Have his fortune told."

"Oh." Coral sounded surprised. "Well, what are you waiting for? Do let the gentleman in."

Amy stepped away from the door. Tom pulled off his hat as he entered. There was something solid and upright about him, and she needed that, needed to believe that good, honorable men really did exist, especially after her disturbing conversation with Miss Lillian.

Showering him with flirtatious smiles and batting eyelashes, Coral pushed her bare shoulder forward in a provocative pose, hand at her waist. "You don't strike me as a man who has to worry about his fortune," she said in a syrupy sweet voice.

Tom grinned. Much to Amy's disappointment, he appeared to be enjoying himself. "A man has to look ahead."

"Of course he does," Amy said, trying not to let her irritation show. "There's not much future in the past."

Coral flicked imaginary lint off his vest and gave him her most seductive smile. "I'll fetch Miss Lillian."

"That won't be necessary," Amy said. "I

have the . . . gift." She slipped her uninjured arm through the crook of Colton's elbow, and together they walked into the parlor.

He played his part without question, and Amy could have kissed him on the spot — figuratively speaking, of course. She would never actually initiate . . . Flustered by the thought, she released his arm.

Much to Amy's annoyance, Coral followed them. "What makes you think you have the gift?" she demanded.

"I'm the seventh daughter of a seventh daughter," Amy said smoothly.

Coral didn't respond, but the suspicious gleam remained in her eyes. She crossed her arms and plunked herself down on a settee.

Having no choice but to go through with the charade, Amy pointed to a chair in front of the crystal ball. "Please be seated," she instructed Tom.

"Seventh daughter?" he mouthed, his back toward Coral. He raised his eyebrows like a cat arching its back but did as directed.

She turned to draw the draperies against the afternoon sun. A pain shot down her arm as she raised it and she grimaced. Striking a safety match, she had to hold her hand to keep it from shaking as she lit the candles.

After touching the flame to both candles,

she blew out the match and ever so carefully took her seat at the table opposite him. Their knees touched, and she quickly pulled her legs in.

He watched her, head slanted and alert. "Are you all right?"

She rubbed her shoulder. "Yes. I just pulled a muscle."

His eyes brimmed with concern. "Perhaps you should see a doctor."

"I'm fine."

Hoping to divert his attention, she smoothed the black velvet cloth that covered the table. She'd watched Miss Lillian on numerous occasions and knew the ritual by heart. Maybe if she drew out the procedure long enough, Coral would grow bored and leave.

The crystal ball was five inches in diameter and stood on a wooden base. She struck a match to light the sage smudge stick.

"This is to cleanse the ball of any negative energy," she explained in a low voice.

His mouth twitched. "Sure can't have that."

She was tempted to laugh. Never could she have imagined playing fortune-teller, but since Coral was watching, she maintained a serious demeanor.

As she smudged the ball, she stared deep

into the crystal depths and tried to recall Miss Lillian's precise words as she went through the ritual.

"Relax, Mr. Colton, and focus." Miss Lillian had explained that the crystal ball picked up a client's subconscious thoughts, but all the crystal depths reflected at the moment was the soft glow of candlelight.

"I see two women in your future," she said at last, giving her voice a dreamlike quality.

"Two, uh? Well now. Which is the lucky one?"

Keeping her head lowered, she lifted her gaze to his. His mouth quirked with humor. Obviously, he was enjoying himself at her expense, and she couldn't help but tease him back.

"The one you *don't* marry."

His warm chuckle made her smile. Much to Amy's relief, Coral had finally given up the watch and left the room. Now, it was only the two of them.

"Is that it?" he asked. "Is that the extent of my fortune? I'll make some woman happy by *not* marrying her?"

She smiled. "If you want more, you're going to have to pay." With a glance toward the archway to make certain no eavesdroppers lurked, she reached into her pocket for Rose's journal.

"Here it is," she said, and his fingers brushed hers as he took it from her. The jolt of his touch made her heart skip a beat. "I hope you like reading about birds."

"Birds?"

"Rose was a bird-watcher, and she kept track of the birds she spotted, along with their habits. I don't know that there's anything useful." Certainly there was nothing to clear his brother's name.

He gave the leather book a cursory glance before slipping it into his pocket.

The marshal's accusations rang in her head: *"Dave Colton was the Gunnysack Bandit."* No matter how many times she tried putting that disturbing thought out of her mind, it kept coming back.

Rubbing her hand against the smooth fabric of her dress, she moistened her lips. "Please return it when you're finished." She had no further use for Rose's journal and wasn't even sure why she wanted it back.

"Will do." He hesitated. "Is that all?"

No, it wasn't all. *My real name is Jennifer Layne,* she wanted to say. *And I'm not who you think I am.*

"Not entirely." She hesitated. "About your brother . . ."

He stilled. "Go on."

"As you know, I saw the marshal earlier."

She forced herself to breathe, but it did little to calm her anxiety. "Marshal Flood thinks your brother might have been . . . the Gunnysack Bandit."

A muscle quivered at his jaw and a storm cloud of emotions darkened his face. "Flood doesn't know what he's talking about," he said, his voice as taut as his expression.

She wanted to believe that was true, but the evidence was beginning to suggest otherwise. "You said he'd been in trouble in the past, and no one's heard of the Gunnysack Bandit since your brother —"

"It makes no sense." He shook his head. "Why would he ask for my help protecting Rose if he was the bandit?"

She glanced down at the unblinking eye of the crystal ball and felt as if it mocked her. "I don't have an answer for that."

"And that doesn't explain who killed *him*. And we know he didn't kill Rose."

She lifted her gaze to his. "The marshal doesn't think the deaths are related."

He stood abruptly and his chair fell back. "My brother was many things," — his words were clipped and devoid of his earlier humor — "not all of them good, but he was *not* the Gunnysack Bandit." He tossed a gold coin on the table and stalked across the room.

"Wait!"

He turned, his eyes ablaze. She couldn't be sure if he was angry at her or his brother. Probably both. People often hired the Pinkerton agency to investigate a family member, then threatened to sue the company when the information was not to their liking.

"I don't want your money."

"I hired you to spy for me, and that's what you did. Keep it." He spun around without a word and left the room.

The parlor suddenly felt empty. Cold. *"Which is the lucky one?"*

She'd teased him, of course, but that was only to keep from saying that she wanted the lucky one that he wed to be her.

CHAPTER 26

Georgia didn't come down to breakfast that Thursday morning, and the rest of them ate in silence.

Amy was grateful for the quiet as it gave her time to plan her next move. She had spent the previous day checking every possible place in town that might have a typewriter. Dressed in a plain skirt and blouse, she pretended to look for a secretarial job and came up empty. Nobody was in the market to hire, and only two businesses had a typewriter — a lawyer who had yet to take the machine out of the box, and the Monahan Express Company.

It was possible that someone in town owned a typewriter at home, but unlikely. Not only were the machines expensive, but a private individual would probably have no need for one.

Miss Lillian folded her newspaper and tossed it aside in disgust. "The theft of a saddlebag gets a full column and Rose's death merited no more than two sentences."

"Doesn't surprise me none," Coral said. "Dirt is given more regard than the likes of us."

Her words were punctuated by the angry clang of silverware.

After several strained moments, Polly asked, "W–where's Georgia?"

"She's not feeling well," Buttercup said as she poured syrup over the stack of hotcakes on her plate.

Coral glared at Amy. "There's been a lot of that going around lately."

Miss Lillian set her coffee cup down. "Perhaps we should fetch Doc Graham."

Amy rose from her chair. "I'll check on her." Grateful for an excuse to escape Coral's daggered looks, she threw her napkin on the table and hurried from the room before anyone could object.

Upstairs, she tapped on Georgia's door. Receiving no answer, she turned the knob and pushed the door open. The shades were drawn against the bright morning sun and a dim gray light bathed the room.

"Georgia?"

The mound beneath the covers was as still as a log. Amy closed the door behind her and crossed the room. "Miss Lillian and the others are worried. Are you okay?"

Georgia rolled over. Amy moved closer, and even in the dimly lit room she could see the tears. She dropped to her knees by the side of the bed and stroked Georgia's cheek.

"What's wrong?" she asked. "Are you ill?"

Georgia wiped her wet cheeks with the palms of her hands. "Today's my little boy's birthday," she whimpered. "He's six years old." Fresh sobs wracked her body. "Such a big boy. I just want to . . . hold him and wish him happy birthday. Is that so wrong?"

Amy shook her head. "No, it's not wrong. It's what any mother would want."

"But not this mother." She smothered a sob. "My son doesn't deserve a mother like me."

"Don't say that, Georgia. You love your children very much, and I'm sure they love you, too."

"They love the person I used to be." Georgia let out a long, harrowing sigh. "That person no longer exists."

"I don't believe that, and you mustn't believe it either."

Georgia pulled a pillow in front of her and held it as one would hold a child. "I used to be a good girl." Her voice trembled. "Went to church every week and —" She gulped hard, but the tears continued to roll down her cheeks. "Now I don't think God even knows I exist."

"Not only does God know, but He cares." Amy laid her hand on top of Georgia's. "Talk to Him. Tell Him how you feel. He'll help you." She squeezed the small, pale hand tight. "Do it for your sake as well as your children's."

Georgia pulled her hand away. "You're a fine one to talk. You're no better off than I am."

Georgia's words stung, and Amy wanted to scream with frustration. There was so much she wanted to tell her about God's love, so much that needed to be said about God's grace, about His forgiveness and compassion. But saying it would only make her sound like a hypocrite.

"If I had children, I wouldn't be here," she said instead. If she had a family of her own, she wouldn't be here either. It was a startling thought and one she immediately banished. She loved her job; nothing else mattered to her. As long as she kept reminding herself of that, perhaps all these worrisome doubts and feelings of late would go away.

Georgia's forehead creased. "What if they were hungry? What if you had no way of feeding them? What would you do then? Let them starve?"

"No, I wouldn't do that but . . . There are people out there who can help you." Back home she would know where to send Georgia for help, but here she was a relative stranger and knew so few people. She thought for a moment, and something suddenly occurred to her.

"There's this churchwoman. Her name is Mrs. Givings, and she knows what it's like to be a mother. Go to her. She'll help you. I know she will."

"But that's the same as asking for charity." Georgia tossed the pillow away. "That's only one step away from what I'm doing now."

Amy drew Georgia's hands in her own and looked her straight in the eye. "In the Bible, charity is just another word for love."

"I don't know —"

"Think about it, Georgia. You'll be with your children. Any charity you receive will only be temporary, until you get on your feet and find employment." A glimmer of hope flared in Georgia's eyes, but for only a second. "Who would hire me? I don't have any skills."

"You can sing." Georgia's soprano voice had the same pitch and range as Allan

Pinkerton's daughter, Joan — a beautiful singer. "If Miss Lillian can give singing lessons, I dare say so can you."

Georgia's eyes widened. "That's the craziest thing I ever heard. I mean . . . I used to sing in the church choir but —"

Amy pushed a strand of hair away from Georgia's forehead. "Go and see your little boy. Make this a happy birthday for him."

Georgia shook her head. "I can't. Those are the only clothes I own." With a quick movement of her head, she indicated the open wardrobe stuffed with gowns that no respectable woman would be caught dead wearing.

"I don't want my children knowing that their mother —" She stopped amid a fresh flood of tears.

"Stay here." Amy jumped to her feet. "I'll be back."

Moments later, she ran into her room and reached into her private trunk where she kept her own clothes hidden. She pulled out a yellow gingham dress. She shook it out and held it out in front to examine. It was a little wrinkled, but the color would complement Georgia's raven hair and olive skin.

Returning to Georgia's room, Amy pulled off Georgia's covers. "Come on, get up."

"What are you doing — ?"

"Put this on." She tossed the dress at Georgia. "Hurry, before someone comes."

Georgia pulled the dress away from her face and gazed up at Amy with questioning eyes.

"It's time to get ready for your little boy's birthday."

"You mean now?"

Amy smiled. "Yes, now."

Georgia let out a soft gasp as she slid out of bed, clutching the dress. Fresh tears filled her eyes, and she tried to speak but the words remained on her trembling lips.

Amy helped her out of her silk nightgown. Without all the bother of a corset, stockings, bustle, and paint, it took only seconds to get Georgia dressed, instead of the usual two hours or more.

Georgia was thinner than Amy and stood an inch or two taller. The waist was a bit loose and the hem fell to just below her ankles, but otherwise the dress fit fine.

"Hold still," Amy said. After fastening the last of the hooks and eyes, she spun Georgia around to face the beveled glass mirror.

Georgia stared at her own reflection as if staring at a stranger. Without her customary paint, she looked younger, prettier. Her lips appeared softer, her eyes less haunted.

Amy tied the ribbon at Georgia's waist and studied her from every angle. "A dress fit for a little boy's birthday." She tapped her chin. "Let's see, what's a proper hairstyle for a proper lady?"

Georgia smiled through her tears. "Nothing too fancy."

Amy reached for the silver-handled hairbrush on the dressing table and set to work. She brushed Georgia's long, thick mane till it shone and then twisted the glossy lengths into a ladylike bun.

She finished pinning the hair in place and met Georgia's gaze in the mirror. "You look beautiful," she said, and she meant it. "Your little boy will be so proud."

Georgia's cheeks reddened as she turned one way and then the other. "I almost forgot what I looked like. Who I was . . ." She met Amy's gaze in the mirror. "I don't know how to thank you."

Amy smiled and squeezed Georgia's hand. "No need. Just give your son a big hug for me." She tossed a nod toward the door. Mr. Studebaker had started his singing lesson, and the thick walls offered little protection against the onslaught of high-pitched screeches.

"I'll see if the coast is clear."

She cracked the door open. A man she

didn't recognize ran down the hall shirtless and coatless with trousers to match. She shut the door and turned.

"What is it?" Georgia asked.

"Just one of the guests."

Georgia wrung her hands. "Are . . . are you sure this will work? What if I run into someone? What if a guest sees me like this? Miss Lillian will have a fit."

"Trust me, no one will recognize you. Anyone looking at you will see only the woman you really are. The woman God meant you to be."

CHAPTER 27

God, help me.

Tom's anguished prayer seemed to bounce from wall to wall of the empty church like a mustang trying to escape a corral. Was God even listening?

Tom's grandpappy often said that things never looked quite so hopeless when one was down on his prayer bones. Well, Tom had been on his prayer bones so long they were about to give out, and still he felt miserable. It didn't help that the stained glass window overhead depicted a picture of Cain and Abel. He understood too well the rage one brother could feel for another.

He could still hear Amy's voice as she broke the news about Dave. Could still see the sadness on her face as she repeated what the marshal had said. Faked — all of it. Nothing about her was real, no matter how much he wanted to believe otherwise. She and his brother were two of a kind. Both knew how to play upon other people's emotions. The only difference was she did it for money.

Dave the Gunnysack Bandit? No, it can't be. *God, tell me it's not true.*

A footfall echoed from behind and he rose.

The reverend stopped in his tracks. "My apologies. I didn't know anyone was here." He started to leave.

"Wait. I came to see you," Tom said.

The minister turned. "Well then . . ." He hurried down the middle aisle toward the altar. Tom couldn't help but notice the shiny black boots with the garish rose. He'd seen a pair just like them at Miss Lillian's. But surely a preacher wouldn't —

"You like them?" the reverend asked, extending a foot.

"They're something, all right," Tom said.

"Bought and worn in the line of duty," the minister said good-naturedly and offered his hand. "Name's Reverend Matthews."

"Tom Colton."

"Colton? You're not by any chance related to Dave Colton, are you?"

Surprised that the reverend knew Dave, Tom replied, "He was my brother."

"Ah, I do see a bit of a family resemblance. Sorry to hear what happened. Such a waste.

What can I do for you?"

"Did you know my brother well?"

The preacher nodded. "Well enough. Used to sit in the very back pew as if he wasn't certain he belonged here. Know what I mean?"

Tom's eyebrows rose. "Dave came to church?"

"Most every Sunday that he wasn't in the hoosegow or out of town. Then one week just before he died, I took the pulpit and looked out over the congregation and what did I see? The Colton fellow had moved down several rows toward the altar. It was the middle, right there." He pointed. "I took that as a good sign."

Something tugged at Tom's insides. If Dave came to church, that had to mean he was a changed man. He couldn't have been guilty of the things the marshal said.

The minister continued. "I talked to him after the service. He told me he'd done some things in the past he regretted. Said he asked for God's forgiveness and now wished to marry one of the parlor girls. Rose was her name, and he asked me to officiate."

"That must have put you on the spot."

"Not at all. It was my duty, of course, to ask if his future bride was a woman of faith.

He said she was. So, my answer to him was then her faith will save her."

"So you agreed to marry them?"

"I did. Dave was greatly relieved, but he was also in a hurry. He insisted that I marry them right away. I told him I needed to meet his young lady first. We agreed to meet at the church the following Friday, and he swore me to secrecy. The couple never arrived, and that's when I learned of Dave's death."

"Did my brother say why he was in such a hurry to wed? Or why it was necessary to keep it secret?"

"No, but I assumed he was anxious to get Rose away from the parlor house. Couldn't blame him there." The minister shook his head. "I was shocked when I heard the news of his death. I made several attempts to contact Rose, but she never responded. I understood from Dave that she didn't want anyone at the parlor house to know her plans, so I didn't attempt to contact her in person. I wish now that I had."

"I don't think it would have changed anything," Tom said.

"You never know."

"Did Dave say what things he'd done?"

"No, and I couldn't tell you if he had. But I can tell you this much — he deeply regretted hurting his family."

Was that true? Or was the kind reverend only trying to make him feel better?

Matthews laid a hand on Tom's shoulder. "Would you like to join me in prayer?"

Not sure that God would be any more likely to answer two prayers than one, Tom nonetheless nodded and turned toward the altar.

Moments later, he walked up the aisle of the church and paused by the middle pew. The vision of Dave sitting, head bowed, was so vivid he had to blink to make sure it wasn't real.

He left the church with a heavy heart. Had Dave fooled the reverend as he'd fooled others in the past? It was a question very much on his mind for the remainder of the day.

The following morning, Amy woke to loud voices. She turned over, punched her pillow, and tried to go back to sleep, but the voices persisted. Having grown up with brothers, she wasn't used to the feminine squabbles and petty jealousies that were now part of her daily life.

She lifted her head from the pillow and glanced at the clock. It wasn't even seven. The high-pitched chatter grew louder and sounded more serious than a simple spat over someone hogging the bath.

No longer able to hold back her curiosity, she slid out of bed and padded to the door barefoot.

Miss Lillian and the others were gathered in the hallway in front of Georgia's room.

Amy covered her mouth. Oh no, not Georgia! *Please, God, no!* She flew down the hall expecting to see Georgia's body on the floor, but instead the room — the bed — was empty.

And just that quickly a voice echoed from the past: *"Thared, Tenfer. Monster tay me."*

The vision of Cissy's empty bed on that long-ago day seemed so real, Amy slumped against the door frame. It was all she could do to catch her breath.

Polly touched her shoulder. "Are you all r–right?"

Shaking away the fog of the past, Amy nodded. "Yes . . . I . . ." Everyone stared at her, and she gave herself a mental shake. "What's the matter?" she asked. "What's all the fuss?"

Polly looked close to tears. "Georgia's g–g–g—"

Buttercup clutched the neckline of her blue satin dressing gown. "What Polly's trying to say is that Georgia's gone and didn't come home last night."

Coral made a face. "And she didn't tell anyone where she was going."

A dozen questions raced through Amy's thoughts. Had Georgia decided not to return? Had she decided to stay with her children instead? *Oh, please, God, let that be true!*

"What do you think happened to her?" Buttercup asked in the kind of hushed voice people saved for sickrooms and funerals.

"You don't s–s–suppose —" Polly fell silent, but she glanced down the hall to Rose's old room.

"I'm sure she's all right," Amy assured her. She didn't want to break Georgia's confidence, but neither did she want the others to worry.

Miss Lillian looked especially distraught. Was she concerned about Georgia's well-being? Or simply annoyed that she'd lost yet another girl in such a short time?

"Now there's just the four of us," Buttercup said. "That means we'll be . . . busy."

Coral glared at Amy. "Some of us."

Amy pretended not to notice, but it worried her. Coral suspected something, and she wasn't the kind of person to keep it to herself.

Miss Lillian wrung her hands. "Perhaps we should notify ole Tin Star."

"What's the marshal gonna do?" Coral snapped. "He hasn't done anything to find Rose's killer. We could all be murdered in our beds and no one would care."

"God cares." Amy hadn't meant to say the words aloud, but they just bubbled out of her. The silence that followed couldn't have been more brittle had she announced she had a contagious disease.

"The stories we tell ourselves," Coral muttered as she walked away.

Miss Lillian and the others left, too, scurrying away like frightened little mice.

Amy watched them flee. It was hard to know what worried them more: Georgia's absence or God's presence.

CHAPTER 28

At midnight, the street directly in front of the Monahan Express Company was relatively quiet. From a nearby saloon came the high tinny tune of a tightly wound banjo. Clapping hands and stomping feet were punctuated with bouts of raucous laughter.

Amy took careful note of her surroundings. The marshal was convinced the Gunnysack Bandit was Tom's brother, and tonight she hoped to prove him wrong. Earlier that day, she had gone to Dave's boardinghouse and pretended to be his long-lost cousin. But the proprietor, a widow in her sixties, had little to offer. She had no idea what hours Dave had kept while living there. Though the man had been dead for a little less than three months, she hardly remembered him. Amy hoped her efforts tonight would prove more successful.

Her plan was simple: break into the express office, check the keys on the typewriter or typewriters, and leave. She was by no means an expert in machines, but it shouldn't be hard to check the type bars. The most used letter in the English language, *e,* would no doubt show wear. She would be far more interested in comparing the letter *m* to the list found on Dave Colton's person. *M* for Monahan.

Directly across from the express office stood the Grande Hotel and Bath House. In front of the hotel's two-story building, a tethered horse nickered and pawed the ground. From the distance came the bark of a dog.

She pulled her gaze away from the hotel but not soon enough to stop unbidden memories from coming to the fore.

"Why do you care?"

"I don't know."

She gave herself a mental shake. What Tom thought or didn't think was no concern of hers. None!

Focusing her attention on the locked door, she pulled a hairpin from her hair. After straightening the metal wire, she jabbed one end into the keyhole. She wiggled it back and forth. Nothing. She pulled the hairpin out of the lock and reinserted it.

She had no business breaking into anyone's office. The marshal considered the case closed, and it was only a matter of time before she received orders to leave Kansas. Still, something didn't sit right. Too many unanswered questions remained for her peace of mind.

She didn't know where Monahan fit in, if indeed he did, but the more she heard about his wild spending sprees and high-stakes gambling, the more her suspicions grew. He was rich, and he was powerful, and he matched the height and agility of the Gunnysack Bandit. If that wasn't enough of a red flag, the watch chain found in Rose's room had to belong to him. It was too similar in design to the one he now wore.

True, he could have lost it at any time, perhaps even days or week before Rose's death. But then why didn't the so-called thief find it upon searching her room? What self-respecting robber would leave a valuable gold chain behind?

Blowing a strand of hair away from her face, Amy jammed the hairpin back into the keyhole for the third time.

A gas lamppost cast a yellow glow across the door, so light wasn't a problem; her aching back was. Mr. Pinkerton would have a fit if he knew one of his operatives couldn't pick a simple door lock to save her soul.

Not willing to admit defeat, she stuck her

311

tongue between her teeth and wiggled the hairpin back and forth. There had to be a tumbler in the hole somewhere. Her instructor, Mr. Welby, at the Pinkerton detective school had made picking locks seem like child's play.

A drunk staggered down the middle of the dirt road singing a ditty at the top of his lungs but paid her no heed.

Having no luck, Amy pulled the hairpin from the keyhole. Straightening, she rubbed her lower spine. Who knew that picking locks could be so physically demanding?

The pin was hopelessly bent out of shape. Dropping it into her drawstring purse, she tried to think. Why hadn't she thought to bring a piece of wire with her? Irritated at her own ineptness, she gave the door a good kick.

"Can I be of help, ma'am?"

Startled by the male voice, Amy spun around and gasped. She couldn't see his face, but there was no mistaking Tom Colton's tall, dark form.

He drew back in surprise. "Amy? Is that you?"

"Yes, it's me." Since she was bathed in gaslight, she could hardly deny it. She couldn't see his eyes but she felt his gaze.

"And the other day . . . that was you, too,

wasn't it?"

She clenched her hands by her side. "It was me. These are my non-working clothes. What are you doing here?" *Doesn't anyone in this town sleep?*

"Well I'll be a possum's uncle." Hooking his thumbs over his belt, he shook his head. "You should dress like that more often. It suits you."

His compliment made her blush. Confound it! No matter how much she fought her attraction to him, he always managed to blast through her defenses. "How did you — ?"

"I saw you from my hotel window. So what's the story?"

"There is no story. You're paying me to spy, and that's what I'm doing."

He reared back. "You're doing this for me?"

"I'm certainly not doing it for my health."

"But I thought . . . You said that the marshal suspected my brother was the Gunnysack Bandit. I just assumed you did, too." He angled his head. "I never asked you to break into anyone's office."

She gave herself a mental kick. *Think. Think!* "I just have a feeling that we're on the wrong track. Call it woman's intuition."

He glanced up at the sign over the door.

"So how does Monahan fit into the scheme of things?"

"That's what I hope to find out. You still haven't told me why you're here."

"It looks like I'm about to become a party" — he glanced at the door — "to a break-in."

He held out his hand. "Do you have a hairpin?"

Since the one she'd been using was hopelessly bent out of shape she drew a fresh one from her bun. Her hair unraveled, and his gaze seemed to follow as it tumbled to her shoulders.

Blushing, she stammered, "I–It's no good. It won't work."

He took the clasp and motioned her away from the door. "Stand back." He pretended to roll up his shirtsleeves before dropping down on his haunches.

"I told you it won't —"

"Shh. I'm working."

She glanced around. Depending on another was humiliating enough, but somehow being caught by Colton, of all people, was worse. It seemed like every time they met she was in some sort of awkward predicament that forced her to lie. And the more she lied, the worse she felt.

"There you go!" He straightened. With a

flick of the wrist, he swung the door open.

She gritted her teeth. It took him less than twenty seconds. She started forward, but he grabbed her by the arm and pulled her close.

"Not till you tell me what we're doing here. What do you hope to find?" The spicy fragrance of bay rum hair tonic tickled her nose.

She pulled away but only because she needed to keep her wits intact. "I'll explain inside. I don't want to chance being seen by anyone else."

"Fair enough." With a wave of his hand he bowed. "After you."

Throwing her shoulders back, she marched past him and into the sparsely furnished office.

On the wall over the safe was a large painting of three ships on a stormy sea. Boxes and crates were piled against one wall, presumably waiting to be delivered.

He shut the door, creating an intimacy between them that made her feel all tingly inside.

The yellow gaslight slanting through the transom window illuminated his stern expression. They squared off like two opponents waiting for the other to make the first move.

"All right. Let's hear it," he said. "What are we doing here? What's this feeling you have?" Tonight he was hatless, and a lock of hair fell across his forehead, giving him a boyish look that seemed at odds with his tall, commanding form.

She tossed her head. "*I* am here because Mr. Moneybags — I mean, Mr. Monahan — was one of Rose's guests."

"And?"

"I found a watch fob under her bed, which I believe was his."

He considered this for a moment. "Even if it's his, it proves nothing. He could have lost it at any time."

"That's true, but he does fit the general description of the Gunnysack Bandit, including his height."

"The same could be said for half the people in this town. My brother was six foot tall. So, for that matter, am I."

"Yes, but as far as I know" — she glanced down at his well-worn, dusty boots — "Mr. Monahan is the only one who owns several pairs of expensive patent leather shoes and silk suits. He also owns the best horses and carriages in the county. Have you ever wondered how he affords all that?"

Elbow resting on his arm, he tapped his chin with his finger. "So you don't think he comes by his wealth by honest means?"

"Perhaps he did at one time. The train has made such express companies almost obsolete. Why would anyone pay to have a wagon deliver goods when the train is so much quicker, cheaper, and dependable?"

"Good question."

"Thank you."

"Now I've got one for you. How did you know Monahan fits the Gunnysack Bandit's description?"

She groaned inwardly at her slip of the tongue. What was it about him that made her lower her guard and make careless mistakes?

She tried to think if his height was on the wanted posters and was certain it wasn't. "Must have been something the marshal said. Or maybe Miss Lillian's crystal ball."

He surprised her by laughing. "It seems I've been going about this all wrong. What else did her crystal ball tell you?"

"You mean other than the fact that you'll make one poor woman perfectly miserable?"

His white teeth flashed. "Yes, other than that."

"It told me to watch out for a tall, dark —" She almost said *handsome.* "Texan."

He grinned, and her heart did a flip-flop. "Good advice. Anything else?"

"That's all," she said. "Did you get anywhere with Rose's journal?"

"I was reading it just now and got distracted."

"Sorry. So what do you think?"

"I think it's for the birds. My brother might have fared better had he had a beak and two wings. What kind of woman was this Rose, anyway?"

"Watching birds might have given her hope. She believed birds flew because of perfect faith." She tilted her glance. "Just like the faith you have in your brother."

He shook his head and grimaced. "I'm a realist," he said bitterly. "And facts are facts, so you won't be seeing me grow wings anytime soon."

"Maybe not, but he was lucky to have you," she said. "Even if he didn't know it."

He hesitated. "I apologize for the way I acted. I had no right to take it out on you. None of this is your fault."

"Apology accepted." Oddly enough, without face paint and fancy clothes, she felt naked in front of him. She had nothing to hide behind. No act to fall back upon. No face-saving way to make an escape.

He stepped closer and gently nudged a strand of hair away from her face. "It means a lot to have you helping me, especially after what the marshal said."

She felt a surge of guilt. Her job — her *only* job — was tracking down the Gunnysack Bandit. Maybe the marshal was right, maybe not. Either way, she couldn't let emotions get in the way.

She stepped away from him. "We better get to work."

"Not till you tell me what we're looking for," he said.

She moved to one of the desks. "This." Pointing to the typewriter, she told him about the list the marshal found on his brother's body. "I want to see if this is the machine it was typed on."

He tilted his brow in a quizzical frown. "And you thought of this all by yourself?"

"Is that so hard to believe?" she asked, her voice edged with annoyance.

He grimaced. "I didn't mean that how it sounded. I don't know that many people would have thought of that — me included."

Regretting her thoughtless retort, she worked a sheet of paper between the paper guides and rolled it into place. As a detective, she had to work harder than any man to prove herself, and sometimes she was oversensitive.

"Sorry I snapped at you. I'm not used to breaking into buildings," she said.

He lit a match and held her gaze for a moment before moving the flickering flame next to the typewriter, his arm brushing against her shoulder. "That makes two of us."

Inhaling sharply, she fought to concentrate on the machine in front of her. It was a Sholes and Glidden typewriter with the popular QWERTY keyboard. She stroked several random keys before hitting the *e* and the *m.*

"It looks like you've done this before," he said.

"A couple of times," she said, without elaborating. She feared that after tonight she would have a hard time convincing him she was simply one of Miss Lillian's working girls.

"I never understood why the keys are all mixed up the way they are," he said, leaning his head closer to hers.

"I'll show you why." She typed a single word. "See? The word *typewriter* can be typed by using the QWERTY line alone. It was designed that way for the convenience of typewriter salesmen. They can impress customers by how quickly they type the word."

His questioning gaze came to rest on hers. "You're just full of information, aren't you?"

"My uncle works at Remington," she said. The lie fell quickly from her lips, but the guilt that followed was like a slow burn on her conscience. Pinkerton detectives tended to have a lot of phantom aunts and uncles. It was part of the job, but that didn't make her feel any better.

He blew out the match and lit another, but his gaze never left her face.

Ignoring him, she ripped the paper out of the roller and studied the type. The *e* was a bit furry, but the letter *m* was perfectly formed. "The list wasn't typed on this machine," she said, her voice thin with disappointment. She folded the paper and put it in her pocket. "Sorry."

"Not your fault." He shook the match and the flame went out. "Like I said before, you should have been a detective."

Her cheeks flared and she turned away. He halted her escape with a hand to her wrist.

"I really wanted the typewriter to match," he said, his voice husky. "I didn't want to believe —"

"Oh, Tom, I'm so sorry." She lifted her hand to his cheek and heard his intake of breath. "I don't know what to say."

"Nothing," he said. "There's nothing to say. I just wish I knew how to tell his son."

"You'll find a way," she whispered. He had been such a comfort to her the night she told him about Cissy; she had no doubt he would be just as comforting to a child.

He circled her waist with both hands, and her knees weakened. Crushing her to him, he gazed at her intently before angling his mouth against hers.

Her senses spun and waves of warm sensations rushed through her. Tossing caution to the wind, she flung her arms around his neck and, rising on tiptoes, kissed him back.

All too soon he pulled away. Confused and maybe even a little hurt, it took a moment to gain her bearings and realize he was trying to tell her something.

With a wave of his hand, he motioned toward the rattling doorknob, and she caught her breath. Finger pressed to his lips, he quietly moved to the window.

"It's a man wearing a checkered suit," he said in a hushed voice.

She groaned. The man she thought of as Mr. Checkers . . . "He's a private detective," she said quietly. "And he thinks you're a Pink."

He reared back. "Why would he think such a thing?"

She shrugged. "Probably because you act like one."

"I do?"

Not even a little bit. A detective had to blend in and not be noticed. Tom Colton's commanding presence would make him stand out among giants.

The doorknob clicked.

"I'll handle him." Colton signaled with his arm for her to hide, and she ducked behind a desk.

CHAPTER 29

Colton could no longer see her, but he had trouble pulling his gaze away from the spot where moments earlier he'd held her in his arms. If only she knew how beautiful she looked tonight without her usual face paint, and golden curls falling down her back. Still, he was shocked by what had transpired between them — yet again.

Her determination to help prove his brother's innocence, even in light of such overwhelming odds, moved him deeply, and he would always be grateful to her.

If only she wasn't . . . If only she didn't . . .

Clamping down on his thoughts, he turned his attention to the door. A squeak of a rusty hinge preceded a gush of cold air. The detective entered the office and shut the door quietly. He then struck a safety match and held it upright.

Colton stepped out of the shadows, and the man jumped back with a yelp. The match flew out of his hands and landed on the floor.

Colton casually stepped on it with his boot to make sure it was out. "Take it easy. I mean you no harm."

The man's Adam's apple bobbed up and down like a rubber ball. "I say, old chap, you almost got yourself a knuckle sandwich." He spoke in a nasally voice with a clipped British accent.

Old chap? Colton rubbed the back of his neck. "Sorry I scared you, but one of the hazards of breaking into buildings is that you never know what you'll find. Do you do it often? Break in, I mean?"

"Only when it's necessary." The detective ran a finger along his collar, and a sheen of perspiration peppered his forehead.

"That's good to hear. I'd hate to think it was a habit with you. So who are you, and what are you doing here?"

The man looked like he resented the question but, nonetheless, politely doffed his bowler. "My name is Winston Walker III, and I'm a private investigator." His British accent made him sound more pompous than he looked, and that was saying something.

"Who you working for?"

"I'm not working for anyone at the moment. I'm here on my own behalf. As you surely must know, there's a handsome reward for the capture of the Gunnysack Bandit. I aim to claim it."

"That still doesn't explain what you're doing here."

"I told Miss Lillian I was looking for someone with the initials GB for the Gunnysack Bandit. She looked into her crystal ball and said the person in question could be found at X. So I put two and two together and came up with the Monahan Express Company. Get it? Express?"

"Express starts with an *E*."

"I'm well aware of that," Walker sniffed. "But I know what poor spellers you colonists are."

"So what did the crystal ball say you'd find here?"

"Unfortunately, that would have cost me another five dollars. I decided to take a chance and look for myself."

Colton shook his head. Some private eye. He probably couldn't find a cowbell in the toe of his sock. Certainly he didn't know that the marshal considered the case closed.

"I'm afraid you're out of luck. There's nothing here. I've searched the place."

Walker frowned. "Why would I take the word of a Pinkerton operative?"

It was all Tom could do to keep from laughing. He'd met some pretty dumb detectives, but this one took the cake. "If you don't believe me, look for yourself."

Walker glanced around. "Miss Lillian assured me that the crystal ball is never wrong."

"Maybe you're the one who got it wrong. X could mean a number of things. It could mean the Gunnysack Bandit has an X in his name. Like Dixon."

"Hmm, maybe you're right." Walker sounded doubtful.

"Of course I'm right. Come on, I'll see you out before we both get caught." He took the man by the arm and firmly steered him outside, shutting the door behind them.

Walker pulled his arm away and straightened his bow tie. "You never did say what *you* were doing here, Colton."

"Same crystal ball."

"Is that so? Well, may the best sleuthhound win." He doffed his bowler and started across the street toward the hotel. "Pip-pip," he called over his shoulder.

Colton walked along the boardwalk. "Same to you," he called back. Half walking and half running, he circled around the block. By the time he returned to the express office, there was no sign of Walker.

He hastened to the door and gave it a soft rap. Nothing. He knocked again, this time harder. "Come on, come on. What's taking you so long?"

When Amy failed to answer, he felt in his vest pocket for the hairpin he'd used earlier and picked the lock. He walked inside calling her name. "Amy, it's me. Your detective friend is gone, but he might come back."

He did a quick search, but there was no sign of her. The back window was open. He flew across the room and stuck his head outside. The alleyway was empty.

He pulled in and slammed the window shut. The office still carried her faint lilac scent. It was as if she were still standing by the desk, waiting to be taken into his arms.

Dave, oh, Dave. Now look what you've done. Brought me here and . . . He shook his head and blinked away the vision of her sweet, curving smile. He didn't want to think about the rest. Couldn't.

Finding his brother's killer, that's what he was here for. That and proving the marshal was wrong — dead wrong — about Dave.

CHAPTER 30

Amy ran all the way back to the parlor house. Pausing by the front gate to catch her breath, she glanced around anxiously and squinted at every shadow. Since being attacked by the group of angry women, she took extra precautions.

The night air was cool, but her lips still burned with the memory of Tom's kiss. Somehow he had awakened a need in her that she hadn't known existed. A need to be held and kissed and . . .

Oh, God, how could this happen? Why did it happen?

If Tom knew how she'd lied to him, knew that the real reason for breaking into Monahan's had little to do with saving his brother's reputation, he'd never want to see her again. She did want to prove Dave's innocence, but not for the reasons Tom supposed.

Shamefully and maybe even selfishly, she

wanted answers to all the questions that still remained. Who killed Rose? Who killed Tom's brother? How did Monahan fit into the picture? What, if anything, did any of this have to do with the Gunnysack Bandit?

Finding answers was her lifeline. It gave her life purpose and meaning and helped her cope with her sister's mysterious disappearance. She might never know what happened to Cissy, but solving crimes offered a measure of closure — at least temporarily — until the next case and the one after that.

Shaking away her thoughts, she let herself through the gate. No horses were tethered in front — not too surprising. Since Saturday was a workday, guests seldom stayed late on a Friday night.

After Tom left the office with Mr. Checkers, she'd done a hasty search. The desk drawers revealed only the usual office supplies and a rotting apple. She found no receipts, no ledgers, nothing. Monahan either kept his records locked up in the safe or elsewhere. Finding only one typewriter was especially disappointing.

The reason she ran had nothing to do with the nosy detective and everything to do with Tom. She wanted so much — was so terribly tempted — to let him finish the kiss begun before Checkers arrived, but that would have been a mistake.

Stripped of her working-girl veneer, she was dangerously close to the real Jennifer Layne. It was getting harder to keep things from him and hold back the truth.

A rabbit hopped out of the bushes, and she jumped, causing her worrisome thoughts to scatter like little field mice.

Catching a movement out of the corner of her eye, she ducked behind a bush. It took a moment before she could pick out a black horse tethered in the vacant field next door between the trees. Odd.

Unless . . .

She crept quietly along the side of the house. Back against the brick wall, she strained her ears. Was that a voice she heard? She dropped on all fours. People look up, not down, and she had less chance of being seen close to the ground.

She peered around the corner. The dark form of a man stood outside the cellar door. He was dressed in black, which made him easy to pick out. Many criminals made the mistake of wearing solid black, a color that doesn't appear naturally in nature. Dark blue or gray was a better choice for blending in at night.

She sat up and ever so quietly pulled off her boots. Stocking feet absorbed sounds

331

better than leather soles. She felt on the ground until she found a rock to throw should she need to divert attention from herself.

Using the bushes against the house for cover, she moved slowly. The man wasn't alone. Someone was with him: a woman.

The muted baritone voice most likely belonged to Mr. Monahan, but the woman's voice was too soft to identify. She stood inside the cellar, which not only hid her identity but kept her voice muffled.

"I can't help that." The masculine voice crackled through the air like gunfire. "It's over."

Amy moved a tad closer. What's over? A twig snapped beneath her foot and she froze.

The woman said something, but the words weren't clear, only the force behind them. She and Monahan were arguing.

"I said it's over!" he snapped. As if conscious of his surroundings, he lowered his voice and Amy missed the rest.

She pushed the branches aside. With a curse, the man moved away from the trap-door. He advanced toward her, and she ducked. He stopped in front of the bush where she hid, but it was too dark to make out more than his hatless, dark form.

She froze in place and tightened her grip

on the rock, ready to throw.

The pungent, sweet smell of tobacco smoke wafted through the air and relief flooded through her. He'd stopped to light a stogie.

He moved away, and her breath escaped with a whoosh. The cool night air soothed her burning lungs. Without bothering to retrieve her shoes, she ran to the cellar trapdoor. If she hurried she might still be able to catch the woman.

At the creak of a rusty hinge, she halted her steps. Straining her ears, she waited, but when no sound came from within she started down the stairs. It was pitch black in the cellar, but operatives had been trained not to depend on sight alone.

She sniffed the air. Each resident had her own brand of perfume. Coral's had a touch of bergamot and lemon. Buttercup wore rose water, and Polly's perfume smelled of lilacs. Tonight, none of these fragrances were evident, and only the musty smell of the cellar tickled her nose.

Moving cautiously, she felt her way through the underground room with out-stretched hands. She hit her shin on a piece of furniture and paused for a moment to gain her bearings.

A soft thud made her reach for her gun.

"Who's there?"

Something slammed against the side of her head and she sank to her knees.

How long she lay unconscious on the cellar dirt floor she had no idea. It could have been minutes, maybe even hours.

Once she came out of her stupor, she remained perfectly still. Hearing no sounds, she sat up slowly. She fingered the bump above her ear and winced. She was lucky to be alive.

Something brushed against her leg and she jumped.

"Mee-ow."

Hand on her chest, she gasped with relief. "Mr. Beavers! What are you doing here?"

The cat rubbed his furry body against hers. She stroked his head before crawling around on hands and knees in an effort to locate her gun. She found it beneath the rocking chair.

Gripping the weapon, she stood. She felt lightheaded and waited for the feeling to pass before starting up the stairs.

The door to the kitchen opened to her touch. Mr. Beavers slipped past her and ran to his dish.

Holstering her gun, she felt on the counter for matches. She lit the match and held it to the kitchen clock. It was a little after 1:30 a.m. That meant that she'd been unconscious for about ten minutes — fifteen at the most. The only sound now was Mr. Beavers lapping up the last bit of cream in his dish.

Shaking away another wave of dizziness, she blew out the match and crept through the house to the stairs. All was quiet on the second floor as she tiptoed down the hall. Gaslight flickered and hissed from the wall sconces, providing more shadows than light.

Not a sound came from any of the bedrooms. She walked past each door, careful to avoid any floorboards she knew squeaked. Light fanned out from beneath the doors of two rooms. Both Coral and Buttercup were still awake.

So which one clobbered her on the head? Of equal importance, which one was in cahoots with Monahan?

Coral had been surly toward her in recent days and leery of her from the start. If she was working with Monahan, she'd have good reason to be suspicious of anyone — and on guard.

And what about Buttercup? She and Monahan had been together a few days earlier. Maybe they were plotting another heist — or worse, planning another murder.

■ ■ ■ ■

"Thared, Tenfer. Monster tay me."

It was the same old dream, but lately, it had been waking Amy up almost nightly.

It was as if someone was trying to tell her something. God? But that made no sense. Her sister's disappearance had nothing to do with the current case.

She stretched and yawned. She'd hardly slept all night, and when she wasn't dreaming about Cissy, she relived the dark, scary moments in the cellar. Just as alarming was the way the memory of Tom's kisses kept popping up.

Turning over on her side, she grimaced. She had a king-sized headache and a bump the size of a goose egg just above her right ear. Just what she needed. It was all she could do to concentrate, let alone think about the case. Still, she had to try.

Collecting clues was the easiest part of a detective's job, analyzing them correctly the hardest.

Was Tom's brother really the Gunnysack Bandit? He apparently fit the description, and it would certainly explain the items found on his body. And what part, if any, did Monahan play in the scheme of things?

Had he killed Rose, and if so, why? Or was the person who hit her over the head in the cellar the real killer?

From her open window came the sharp report of a gun, followed by another and another.

She reached beneath her pillow for her derringer. Alert now, she jumped out of bed and ran into the hall.

Coral moved cautiously toward the stairwell, holding her gun out in front. One by one, the doors of Polly's and Buttercup's rooms opened, and both women popped their heads out.

"I heard g–g–gunfire," Polly stammered.

"Me, too," Amy said. "Stay here."

Coral stared at her all funny-like. Was that surprise on Coral's face? Whoever assaulted her last night might have thought her dead. All three women were giving her odd looks. Or rather, they were staring at her plain flour-sack nightgown.

"What makes you the boss?" Coral asked.

"I know how to use a gun and you don't." Ignoring her still pounding head, Amy descended the stairs holding on to the banister. Much to her annoyance, the other three women followed on her heels.

Coffey stood behind the kitchen counter holding a rolling pin over her head. The housekeeper, Beatrice, stood behind the cook, her face drained of color.

"They come in here and that'll be the last thing they do," Coffey said, wielding the rolling pin.

"Who are 'they'?" Amy asked.

"How am I supposed to know?"

Holding the others back with her free hand, Amy approached the mudroom. More gunfire. Cautiously, she cracked open the door and peered outside. "For the love of —" She closed the door and pocketed her weapon.

"W–what is it?" Polly stammered.

Amy turned to find three guns, a rolling pin, and a broom all aimed at her.

"Put your weapons away. It's just Miss Lillian practicing her shooting."

Coffey frowned. "What she want to do that for?"

"M–m–maybe she just w–wants to feel s–safe," Polly stammered.

Buttercup giggled, and the housekeeper stood her broom in a corner.

Coffey lowered her rolling pin. "Lawdy, if we ain't got enough trouble as it iz."

Later that same morning, Amy let herself out the front door and stopped on the porch to put on her gloves.

A movement made her look up. A youth, probably in his midteens, stood on the other side of the fence. After a surreptitious glance up and down the street, he tossed a brick at the house and just missed a window.

He obviously hadn't noticed her, and his eyes widened in alarm when she leaped off the porch after him.

"Hey!" she yelled, giving chase. He was young and he was fast. He also had the advantage of running in sensible trousers rather than a long skirt and three-story hat that made the lump on her head throb.

She had just about decided to give up when a white knight came to the rescue. Actually, it was a small white terrier wanting to play.

The little dog caught the brick thrower by a trouser leg. The boy hopped around on one foot trying to shake off the dog. By the time Amy reached them, the youth was on his back yelling for help.

The dog's owner whistled, and the white ball of fluff bounced away with joyful yips.

The boy tried to get up, but Amy stopped him with a foot to his chest. "Oh, no you don't."

He lay flat on his back gazing up at her through strands of shaggy hair. Neither his bad skin nor peach fuzz took away from his boyish looks. He was probably no older than thirteen. Dressed in neatly patched overalls and a torn plaid shirt, his feet were bare, but whether by choice or necessity was hard to tell. She guessed the latter.

"What's your name?" she asked.

"Scott."

"Scott what?"

He glared up at her. "Cunningham."

She recognized the name at once. Mr. Cunningham was a frequent guest at the parlor house. Now that she knew he had a son, her temper flared. She had no patience for any of the men who frequented the parlor house, but this man did it at the expense of his family.

She removed her foot, and the boy sat up. "Why did you throw that brick?"

" 'Cuz."

" 'Cuz isn't an answer."

"I hate you." The veins stood out on his neck. "I hate all of you."

The anger in his voice made her catch her breath. "Because . . . of your father?" she asked gently.

A suspicious sheen filled his eyes, but he was either too angry or too stubborn to let the tears fall. " 'Cuz of what he's doing to Ma."

Feeling sorry for the boy, she knelt at his

side. "Breaking windows won't change anything."

"What else can I do?" He sat up and swiped the hair away from his eyes. "Huh?"

She laid a hand on the youth's bony shoulder. "Have you talked to your father?"

"He said it was none of my business what he did."

Her own father had said something similar the day she'd begged him to stop drinking. If only parents knew how such actions hurt their offspring.

She pulled her hand away. "This isn't the first time you've thrown a brick at the house, is it?"

He didn't answer. He didn't need to; his guilty expression said it all.

"Scott, I wish I could change the way things are, but some things are bigger than you and me. Some things have to be left up to God."

His eyes flashed. "Whatcha know about God?"

"You'd be surprised," she said. "I also know that breaking windows can get you in a lot of trouble. I'm sure that would cause your mother even more grief."

A shadow of worry flickered across his face. "Are you gonna report me to the marshal?"

"Not this time." She pushed herself to her feet. "But I will next time. Now go home."

The boy didn't wait for a second invitation. He jumped up and raced away as fast as his skinny legs allowed.

Weariness and a sense of hopelessness washed over her. Never had an assignment affected her on so many different levels. She felt emotionally, physically, and even spiritually drained. Why was God making it so difficult for her? Why did He keep throwing all these challenges in her path?

She wanted to help the boy, but even if by some miracle she was able to talk Miss Lillian into banning Cunningham from the parlor house, what good would that do? He would probably take his business elsewhere.

God, there has to be a way.

She straightened her hat and was just about to head to town when she realized she was standing on the corner of Madison Street. Nothing could be done for Scott, but maybe she could do a little something for Georgia.

She checked inside the cloth purse still dangling from her wrist. She could spare a few coins — enough to purchase a meal or two for Georgia's family. While in town she planned to wire headquarters for reimbursement of expenses before the case was officially closed. No doubt Robert Pinkerton would hassle her about the added expense of a hotel room, but she'd cross that bridge when she came to it.

A lively game of catch was in progress in front of Georgia's house. Georgia tossed a red rubber ball to her son and laughed when he caught it. She looked nothing like the woman of old. It wasn't just the plain gingham dress that made the difference. It was the way she moved, like a ballet dancer gliding across a stage.

"There you go!" she called cheerfully.

The little boy fumbled the ball and dropped it, and his sister chased after it. Both children had their mother's raven hair.

Georgia looked up just as Amy reached the gate, and her laughter died. A look of panic crossed her face. "Billy, Mary-Sue, inside. Now!"

Georgia's sudden change of mood seemed to confuse her children, but they obediently followed her to the porch.

"Can we play a game?" Mary-Sue asked.

"Yes, inside." She hustled both children into the house with loving pats on their little behinds.

She then hurried down the porch steps and along the walkway to the fence.

"I'm sorry," Amy said. "I shouldn't have

come." How thoughtless of her to approach the house dressed like a harlot in front of Georgia's children.

"Don't apologize. I'm glad you did."

Seeing how happy Georgia looked lifted Amy's spirits. "I just wanted to make sure you were all right."

Georgia nodded. "I'm more than all right." Her eyes shone. "I don't know how to thank you."

"No need to thank me." Amy held out her hand. "Take this."

Georgia shook her head. "Keep it. You've done enough already. Mrs. Givings has been a big help, and several church members have signed up for singing lessons."

Amy withdrew her hand. "Oh Georgia, that's wonderful news. I'm so happy for you. For your children."

Georgia hesitated. "Mrs. Givings will help you, too."

Amy inhaled. "I can't talk about this right now." She pulled away from the gate.

"Please, Amy, promise me you'll think about it."

"I've got to go," Amy said, backing away.

"God forgave me, and He'll forgive you, too," Georgia called after her. "I'll pray for you."

Amy hurried away, but she couldn't help

but smile to herself. Georgia had found her way back to God — hallelujah!

How she longed to celebrate with Georgia like a real friend would. That, of course, was out of the question. Friendships required honesty, trust, and transparency — all the things her clandestine activities prevented.

It never really bothered her before, but it bothered her now. It bothered her that she couldn't rejoice with Georgia. It bothered her even more that she couldn't act on her feelings for Tom.

Love — and yes, even friendship — if it was ever to be hers, would have to wait.

CHAPTER 31

After leaving Georgia's house, Amy found a thick envelope waiting for her at the post office. She didn't open it until reaching the privacy of her hotel room.

As usual, the letter was written in cipher. The first sentence made her sink onto the edge of the bed. *"We have determined with just cause that David Colton was the Gunnysack Bandit."* The letter went on in great detail describing the evidence against him. Not only did the banknotes found on the body prove to be part of the money stolen from the Hampton town bank, but the hotel registry also proved he was in town during the robbery.

The letter went on to declare the case officially closed. The information wasn't all that unexpected, but it was still disheartening. Tom would be devastated.

The letter ended with these worrisome words: *"Wait for further correspondence."*

As if she didn't feel bad enough already, the last sentence hit her like a punch to the stomach. After completing one assignment, she was normally dispatched to another, but not this time. It wasn't just a lack of assignment that worried her. Nothing would please the Pinkerton brothers more than to do away with the Pinkerton Female Detective Bureau altogether.

They claimed that women cost more to maintain than males, but Amy suspected a deeper, more personal reason. According to rumors, the first female detective, Kate Warne, had been Allan's mistress up to the day she died, which was probably why Robert thought women were more of a hindrance and distraction than a help.

No doubt about it, Amy's future looked questionable. But she couldn't think about that right now. She had far more pressing concerns — mainly Tom.

She tossed the file onto the desk and her Pinkerton badge fell to the floor. She picked up the tin shield and slid it underneath the file.

She then quickly changed into a dark blue skirt and eyelet shirtwaist. Free of constraining underwear, she took several deep breaths before scrubbing her face clean and brushing her hair into a sedate bun at the nape of her neck.

Feeling more like herself, she gathered the discarded garments and put them into a carpetbag. Now all she had to do was return the clothes and tell Miss Lillian she would no longer be staying at the parlor house. Her job was done.

The hall was empty when she let herself out of her room. No sooner had she turned her back to lock the door than a voice sounded behind her.

"Amy?"

Glancing over her shoulder, her gaze clashed with Tom's. She fumbled with the key and her door flew open again. She was quick, but he was quicker.

He pushed his way into the room after her and slammed the door shut. "Whose lock did you pick this time?" he demanded.

She lifted her chin. "For your information, I paid for this room."

Seeming to fill the space with his presence, he gazed at her intently. "What's going on?"

"Nothing's going on. Now if you would kindly leave." She started for the door, but he stopped her with his hand on her arm.

"Why are you staying here?"

She pulled her arm away. "I'm leaving town."

He tilted his head. "Why?"

"I decided I don't want to work for Miss Lillian any longer."

Something flickered in the depth of his eyes. "I never did think you belonged there. So what do you plan to do?"

"I — I don't know yet."

He tossed his hat on the desk and the file fell to the floor along with her Pinkerton badge. Before she could react, he bent to pick up the metal shield. Holding it in the palm of his hand, he stared at it for several seconds before lifting his head.

"What are you doing with this?"

"I —"

His gaze sharpened, and his square jaw tensed visibly. "Go on."

She hesitated. If she hadn't made a big enough mess of this whole investigation, she was about to put her career in even greater jeopardy than it already was. She just didn't have it in her to tell him yet another lie.

"I'm not who you think I am."

His eyebrows slanted in a frown. "What does that mean?"

"What it means is . . ." She moistened her lips. "My real name is Jennifer Layne, and I work for the Pinkerton National Detective Agency." Or at least she did. There was no way of telling what awaited her back at the home office now.

He reared back, a dumbfounded look on his face. "That means that you're —"

She nodded. "A Pinkerton operative. And if you say, 'But you're a woman,' I'll slug you."

To his credit, he didn't say that. He didn't say anything. He just stared at her in total disbelief.

She frowned. "Say something."

He set the badge on the desk. "I don't know what to say. So . . . all that business at Miss Lillian's was just an act?"

"Not a very good one, I'm afraid."

"I always thought that something wasn't right, but I never suspected this." He shook his head as if he still couldn't believe it.

"I was dispatched here to work on the Gunnysack Bandit case. Rose deposited stolen banknotes tied to one of his robberies into her personal account."

"That's a mighty big case for a . . . uh . . ." She challenged him to continue with an arched brow, but he wisely changed course. "How long have you worked for Pinkerton?"

"Five years. And for your information, I've been instrumental in catching some well-known criminals." She named the most infamous outlaws she'd helped put behind bars, not to impress him — okay, maybe a little — but mostly to postpone having to tell him about the Pinkerton report.

His eyebrows inched upward as she spoke, and when she finished, he let out a low whistle. "That's some record. Those outlaws would have given the Rangers a run for their money."

"Tell that to the Pinkerton brothers."

He studied her as if trying to reach into her thoughts. "I've worked with a lot of private detectives, and I can usually spot them. But you . . ." He shook his head. "Does the marshal know?" He frowned. "You haven't told him, have you?"

"I told him."

He hung his thumbs from his holster. "What did he say?"

"Pretty much what everyone says, and it all comes down to anatomy."

His eyes blazed with sudden anger. "All that business about wanting to help me . . . That was a lie."

"It wasn't a lie. I really did want to help you."

"What about the story that you're leaving town?" His face grew hard, as did his voice. "Is that a lie, too?"

"No, that's true. The agency is no longer working the case."

His gaze sharpened. "Why not?"

351

She hesitated.

"Why not?" he repeated, louder this time.

She flinched at the tone of his voice. "Your brother was in Hampton when the bank was robbed and the guard shot." Biting her lip, she looked away. "The case is officially closed."

"Is that it?" he asked, his voice cold and exact. "Is that all they have?"

She shook her head. "The banknotes found on his body" — her voice wavered — "they matched the ones stolen from the Hampton bank."

"That proves nothing. They could have been planted."

She drew in her breath. "Also, the handwriting on the note to the teller was similar to your brother's signature on the hotel register."

"Similar? Not a match?"

"A person's handwriting changes under duress. Signing a guest register is less stressful than writing a holdup note. That could account for any inconsistencies."

A muscle quivered at his jaw. "Or someone could have forged Dave's handwriting."

She'd considered that possibility, but there was no way of proving it. Allan Pinkerton believed that handwriting and even the skin furrows of the fingers would eventually identify criminals, but right now graphology was still an imperfect art.

"It's not just the handwriting." She weighed his reaction before continuing. "The agency believes Rose may have gotten the stolen notes from your brother."

"What about the rest?" he demanded, his face dark.

"The rest?"

"Somebody killed Dave. I'll bet my boots it's the same person who killed Rose."

"I've seen the report on your brother's death. There're no similarities. There's no proof that the two deaths are even related. Rose's death could have been a robbery."

"And Dave's? Was that a robbery, too? Is that why they found banknotes on his body?"

"I wish I had more answers for you, but it was never my job to investigate his death or Rose's. I was assigned to track down the Gunnysack Bandit and turn him over to the marshal. That's all."

He breathed through gritted teeth. "And all this time you let me think you were helping me."

"I didn't have a choice."

"You could have refused my offer to spy. Instead, you led me on."

If his anger wasn't hard enough to bear,

the hurt in his eyes was like a knife to her heart. "I really did want to help you."

"By using me?"

"It wasn't like that." She reached for his arm, but he pulled away. "Please, you must believe me."

"Believe you? After all the lies?" He grabbed his hat and turned to the door.

"Wait," she pleaded. "Don't go." She hated to leave things so strained between them.

He stilled, his back toward her. Did he hate her so much that he couldn't even look at her? "There's nothing more to be said."

She clasped her hands together to steady herself. "I'm not the enemy here, Tom. I was only doing my job."

He stared at her over his shoulder, his expression remote. "You should be happy, then." He reached into his pocket for Rose's journal and tossed it onto the bed. "Your job is done."

Tom stood in the hotel corridor outside her door. He tightened his hands into fists in an attempt to check his raw emotions. He always knew that Amy or Jennifer or whatever she called herself didn't belong at the parlor house. But never in a million years would he have guessed she was a Pinkerton

354

detective.

He'd met Allan Pinkerton only once, but he would never forget it. He was a tough old bird with a thick Scottish brogue. His hard-nosed tactics had gotten him and his agency in a lot of trouble through the years. So it wasn't surprising that Amy would use any means available, including trickery, to reach her goals.

Still, it pained him to discover he'd been duped by her. To find out she'd used him to prove his brother guilty.

As for Dave . . .

It wasn't the first time he'd been wrong about him, but this was the worst. If Dave really had been the Gunnysack Bandit, he wasn't just a thief, he was a killer.

Thank God his parents hadn't lived to see this day. He didn't even know how to tell his nephew. As for Grandpappy, he blamed Dave for making a mess of his life, and this latest was the final nail in that coffin.

Tom only wished he hadn't found out this way.

Logically, he understood why Amy had to keep her identity secret. That didn't make him feel any less manipulated.

The truth was it hurt to high heaven, and that made no sense. He'd trusted her, told her things about his childhood he'd never told anyone else. And all that time she was working undercover to find evidence against his brother.

What a fool he was. Not only did he fall for Dave's lies but her lies, as well. Nothing about her was real, not even the kisses she seemed so willing to return.

That last thought brought an instant, squeezing pain that shook him to the core. This thing with his brother had done a number on him, made him think things he had no business thinking. Made him wish he'd put his brother away for good when he had a chance. Had he done so, his brother might still be alive and Tom wouldn't be standing outside a hotel door like a crazy man.

CHAPTER 32

Amy stayed at the hotel that night but hardly slept. She kept hearing Tom's last harsh words in her head. And every time she closed her eyes she saw the expression on his face — not the anger, the hurt.

By morning, not only was she a bundle of nervous energy, but she was also madder than blazes. None of this was her fault. She was only doing her job. How dare he blame her for his brother's actions!

After waiting for the sun to fully rise, she stormed down the hotel hallway to room fourteen. Much to her surprise, the door was open and a Mexican maid was making the bed.

"Where is Mr. Colton?" she asked.

The maid shrugged her shoulders and said something in Spanish.

Amy left the room and scurried down the stairs to the reception desk. "Room fourteen. When did Mr. Colton check out?"

The desk clerk was an older man with stooped shoulders. "About a half hour ago."

She glanced at the clock behind the desk. The morning train was scheduled to leave in less than ten minutes. If she hurried . . .

The train was just pulling out of the station when she arrived. She ran along the wooden platform and jumped off the edge. She raced along the graveled buffer next to the tracks. Spotting him through a smoky window, she frantically waved both arms to gain his attention.

Just like that, she forgot her original intent for coming to the station. Forgot even her anger. Instead, a horrible realization took hold: she would never see him again. Never see his crooked smile. Never again hear his baritone voice or feel his amazing lips on hers.

He opened the window and stuck his head outside. "What are you doing here?" he demanded, his face dark as night. He was obviously still angry. Still hurt.

She shouted back, "I want you to know that —" The train whistle blew, drowning out her voice.

He cupped his ear. "What? What did you say?"

"I said —" The train picked up speed,

leaving her behind and out of breath. By the time she stopped running, her lungs felt ready to explode.

Gasping for air, she bent over, hands on her thighs, and watched until the train was but a dot on the horizon, leaving behind only a thread of blue smoke. "I said I love you," she whispered, and with those few words came the tears.

The following day, Amy found her next assignment waiting at the post office in a thick envelope. Normally such a dispatch would fill her with excitement and anticipation. Today she felt only depression. She read the detailed instructions through a cloud of gloom.

She was instructed to travel to Denver as a widow and strike up an acquaintance with a suspected counterfeiter who managed to foil even the Secret Service. A banknote was enclosed to cover hotel, traveling, and living expenses, plus money enough to purchase widow's weeds.

At least now she had something to do. Maybe once she settled into her new role she would forget Tom Colton. She counted on it.

Later that afternoon, she stopped at the

parlor house to say good-bye to Miss Lillian and thank her for her help.

Sitting behind her desk, Miss Lillian tried to act nonchalant, but the suspicious sheen in her eyes gave her away. "Does this mean my sleuthing days are over?"

Amy smiled. Strange as it seemed, she'd grown fond of the madam. "I'm afraid so."

"Too bad. I believe I have a real knack for it." Miss Lillian heaved a sigh, and her face seemed to sag. "What about Rose? Do you think they'll ever find her killer?"

"Unfortunately, the longer a crime goes unsolved, the less chance the perpetrator will be caught." Trails grew cold, memories faded, clues missed initially were forever lost.

Miss Lillian grimaced. "What does ole Tin Star say?"

"The marshal's convinced Rose's killer left town." He was wrong, of course. She had checked, and no local citizens had left in recent weeks, and a stranger wouldn't know about the trapdoor. That meant the killer was still in Goodman.

Miss Lillian's scarlet mouth thinned. "Who do you think killed her?"

"Most victims know their killers," Amy said. And it was probably the same person who knocked her out in the cellar. "I think

Rose knew hers."

Miss Lillian nodded. "I agree."

"I wish I could stay and work on Rose's case, but it's out of my hands." She was still haunted by Rose's death, perhaps because it happened under her very nose. She hated nothing more than loose ends, and the whole affair with the Gunnysack Bandit was rife with them.

The madam let out a sigh. "What should I tell the others? They'll want to know why you left."

"Tell them I didn't work out." Coral certainly wouldn't be sorry to see her go.

"When are you leaving?"

"On the morning train."

Miss Lillian tucked a red strand of hair behind her ear. "Would you like me to read your fortune so you know what lies ahead?"

Amy grinned. "Thank you, but I think I'll leave the future in God's hands."

"Very well. I just hope you find what you're looking for."

Amy wasn't sure she'd heard right. "What I'm looking for? Oh, you mean my next assignment."

"I'm not talking about your work." Miss Lillian gave her a long, level look. "Every night in your sleep you cry out for someone named Cissy. I hope you find her, whoever she is."

Amy didn't know what to say. She knew the nightmares had returned but had no idea she cried out in her sleep. *What is happening to me, God? Would You answer me that? And why do I feel like You're trying to tell me something?*

She boarded the train dressed in a black skirt and tailored shirtwaist with a black band around her arm. Beneath the sedate black hat, her hair was pulled back into a shiny, smooth bun. On the ring finger of her left hand, she wore a simple gold band.

The woman named Amy no longer existed. By the time she reached her destination, Jennifer Layne would be transformed into the widow Mrs. Stephen Hoyt.

According to the dossier Pinkerton sent on Ralph Cooper, not only was he a counterfeiter of the highest order, but he also had a soft spot for widows — particularly those needing assistance with investing a late husband's estate.

As if sensing her need to escape, the train picked up speed, leaving the town behind in a cloud of dark smoke. Unfortunately, the memories traveled along with her, which made the current task that much harder.

Prior to reaching Denver, she had to create a new history for herself and her dead "husband." Not only did her fictional past have to sound believable, but it must also play on Mr. Cooper's sympathies.

Creating an image in mind was easy. Her late make-believe husband was six feet tall, had dark hair, blue eyes, a square face, and crooked smile. The vision conjured just happened to be the spitting image of Tom Colton.

Sighing, she stared out the smoky window where the wide-open prairie sped by in a blur. She wiped the tears from her eyes with a gloved hand and blew her nose in her handkerchief.

Fortunately, the gray-haired man in the seat opposite didn't seem to notice her misery. He was too involved in his book.

The *clickety-clack* of the rails on the track made her head spin. *Clickety-clack . . . lickety-lack . . . flickety . . . flack.* She tried clearing her head but then thought of Tom, and just like that, the train changed its tune until it sounded like the very rails called his name. *Tomety-Tom. Tomety-Tom.*

The sound was broken only by the strident voice of the child sitting directly behind her. Not only did he talk excessively, but he kept kicking the back of her seat, too. Leaning into the aisle, she turned her head to ask him to please stop. Recognizing the young boy, she pulled back and faced the front of the train. Behind her sat the mother and child she encountered at Max's General Mercantile and Flower Shoppe.

She forced herself to calm down. No one would recognize her dressed in widow's weeds, her paint-free face pale from lack of sleep.

Still, she couldn't afford to take a chance. Children tended to be perceptive, and the little boy might very well see through her guise. The last thing she needed was to create a scene.

The boy kept talking and kicking her seat, and Jennifer's head began to pound. He asked a dozen questions in his high-pitched voice.

"Play your game, Adam," his mother said in a weary tone.

"No pay dame."

"All right, then look out the window. Look at all the cows."

The cows kept the boy entertained for all of thirty seconds. "Are ve there yet?"

"No, we have a long way to go."

The questions continued, and finally Jennifer gave up trying to concentrate on her new assignment and let herself become lulled by the rhythmic movement of the train. Her eyes drifted downward.

A male voice floated into her consciousness. "Would your little boy like a sweet?"

The boy's mother said, "How kind of you to offer. Thank you. What do you say to the nice man?"

"Tank you, monster."

Jennifer's eyes flew open. *"Monster tay me."*

The man opposite her lowered his book and said something. She stared at him, not comprehending.

He spoke again. "Are you all right, ma'am?"

This time she nodded. "Yes, thank you."

He went back to his book. Still shaken, she stared out the window. What if her sister hadn't said *monster*? What if she'd said something else?

She reached into her satchel for notebook and pencil. Hand shaking, she wrote down every word she could think of that remotely sounded like monster and circled two of them: minister and mister.

"Minister tay me."

"Mister tay me."

Next she tackled the words *tay me*. What if Cissy hadn't been trying to say *"take me"*? What if *tay me* was actually something else? After several futile attempts to find similar-sounding words, she gave up and gazed out the window with unseeing eyes. Maybe she was going about this all wrong.

She wrote down the names of people who regularly visited the family farm — at least the ones she could remember. Fifteen years had passed, so she had to think hard.

She could remember most but not all of the locals who purchased eggs, cream, or butter from her mother. She had a crush on the boy who delivered groceries, so his name quickly came to mind, but not so the names of the men who helped her father during harvest. The doctor's name was Davis, and the minister was Reverend Stafford. She listed the people known through church. Most had lived in the area all their lives.

This was crazy. Cissy had simply awakened from a bad dream. Children her age often had nightmares. The fact that she was missing the morning after was purely a coincidence.

The problem was, Allan Pinkerton didn't believe in coincidences and neither did she.

She stared at the names she'd written down. A three-year-old child wouldn't know that many people by name, only the ones she saw on a regular basis like their piano teacher, Mrs. Jeremy.

She froze. *"Monster tay me."* Cissy pronounced the letter *j* like a *t,* and she often dropped the middle consonants.

Mister Jeremy.

She stared at the name written on her paper. No, no, it couldn't be true. Mrs. Jeremy had been her piano teacher and she would never . . . *Mr.* Jeremy would never . . .

But once the thought had worked its way into her consciousness, it refused to go away. Mrs. Jeremy's husband worked at the bank. He was a friend of the family and had been instrumental in helping her father save the farm during that terrible drought. He would often drive his wife to the farm for the weekly music lessons and stay to chat and sample her mother's cooking.

He and his wife never had children of their own, and Mrs. Jeremy doted on the Layne children. It soon became clear that she favored Cissy and always brought her sweets from Mr. Dorsey's Confectioners. Even at three, Cissy could pick out simple tunes on the piano by ear. Jennifer was an adequate player, but Mrs. Jeremy insisted that Cissy had "the gift."

Jennifer never forgot the day Mrs. Jeremy announced they were moving away. Mr. Jeremy had been transferred out of state with his job.

She had been too young at the time to pay much attention to the reasons they were leaving, but the loss had seemed enormous, especially coming so soon after Cissy's disappearance. Jennifer had practically bawled her eyes out. Secretly, she always believed that the real reason they left was because Mrs. Jeremy missed Cissy.

Never once had it occurred to Jennifer that there could be another reason.

Even now, she didn't want to believe these sudden suspicions true. It was crazy.

She gazed at the passing scenery. The little boy behind her had finally fallen asleep. Without his high-pitched voice, there was nothing to divert her attention from the *clickety-clack* of the track that now sounded alarmingly like *Jer-Jer-Jeremy.*

CHAPTER 33

St. Louis, Missouri

Jennifer pulled the rented horse and buggy in front of the modest one-story clapboard house and set the brake. She pulled a piece of paper from her purse and checked the address.

It had taken only three weeks to track down her old music teacher. Fortunately, Allan Pinkerton was sympathetic to her plight and offered to help. The Pinkerton agency had operatives in practically every major city in the country and put them all on alert.

They soon received word from Detective Joseph White working on an embezzlement case in St. Louis. He checked the bank personnel files in town and discovered Mr. Jeremy had worked for the St. Louis Bank until his death nearly five years ago. His widow lived on the outskirts of St. Louis.

Jennifer studied the house. It sorely

needed paint, but the garden was perfectly maintained and filled with birdhouses and feeders. Another bird lover like Rose.

To think her beloved music teacher capable of doing anything so awful as abducting her sister was crazy. Or was it?

As a detective she knew that people were inclined to see only what they wanted to see. A wife was often the last to know that her husband was cheating. Family members often expressed shock when a loved one was arrested for robbing a bank or stage, though the signs had all been there. But if Mr. and Mrs. Jeremy really had abducted her sister, she wasn't the only one who had turned a blind eye. So had her family, so had the town.

Why now, God? Why after all this time was she led to this place, this house? Why did it feel like a gale-force wind pushing her to face the past in a way she never could or would before? Coming here on what could very well be a wild goose chase meant she had to turn down a plum assignment, but it couldn't be helped. Once the theory of Cissy's abduction took root, she could hardly think of anything else.

She tucked the address back into her purse, surprised to find her hand shaking.

It had rained for three days solid, but now

the clouds parted, revealing patches of clear blue sky. She lifted her gaze toward heaven and a stabbing pain shot through her chest. The clear azure sky was almost the same color as Tom's eyes. How she wished he were here with her now. Holding her hand. Telling her it was all right. She needed that. Needed to hear his reassuring voice.

Climbing down from the buggy, she forced herself to count to ten. Thus braced, she walked through the sagging gate and followed the crooked brick path to the house. No outlaw had ever made her feel as nervous as she felt at that moment. Doubt gnawed at her, turning her insides into a knot. She could be wrong. Then what?

She felt woefully unprepared and was acting on pure emotion. That went against everything she'd been taught: a detective never acts without information, without facts.

White's embezzling case had heated up, so he had provided only an address. She didn't even know if the Jeremys had a daughter. No detective worth his or her salt would act with so little information. Maybe someone in town or one of the neighbors could answer her questions.

Losing her nerve, she turned to leave, but the sound of a piano stopped her. Could that be Mrs. Jeremy playing? Or was it one of her students?

The quick, lilting tune of "Für Elise" brought back so many memories her knees threatened to buckle. Even now, after all these years, she could hear Mrs. Jeremy's voice. *"Sit up straight. Don't look at your hands. Count!"*

And then, *"Cissy has the gift."*

The music pulled her toward the porch as if by some strange magnetic force. Trembling, she stood in front of the weathered door, rooted in place. She had to force herself to breathe.

She should go. This was crazy! Mrs. Jeremy would no doubt want to know why she was there.

I think you stole my sister, she'd say, and Mrs. Jeremy would . . . what?

Laugh in her face. Ask her to leave. Stare at her as if she'd lost her mind.

She thought about praying but wasn't even sure what she hoped to find behind that closed door. Would finding Cissy be worse than not finding her?

It took every bit of courage she could muster to raise her hand and knock. The music stopped. Footsteps. The door flew open, revealing a pretty young woman dressed in a floral-printed frock.

"May I help you?"

Jennifer felt as if her breath had been cut off. Was this Cissy? She couldn't be sure, and that alone horrified her. How could she not know her own sister?

Trained to work under pressure, she fought to get her emotions under control. She pretended that this was a job, that she was working undercover. She mentally went down the same checklist used when sizing up a suspect.

The girl was probably in her late teens, so the age was right. Her eyes were greenish, almost turquoise, but her hair was darker than Cissy's had been and was now light brown with golden highlights. But hair tended to darken with age. Hers certainly had.

"May I help you?" the girl repeated.

"I'm sorry to disturb you." She cleared her throat and began again, this time in a stronger voice. "I'm looking for Mrs. Jeremy."

"That's my mother. I'm Charity Jeremy. Who shall I say is calling?"

Jennifer's mind scrambled. Charity? "Uh . . . Jennifer Layne." The girl showed no sign of recognition so she added, "I — I knew your mother in Illinois."

The young woman shook her head. "You

373

must be mistaken. My mother was never in Illinois."

"Who is it, child?" a crinkly voice called from somewhere inside the house.

Charity glanced over her shoulder. "Someone to see you. She said she knew you."

"Well, don't be rude. Show her in."

The girl stepped aside, and Jennifer forced her leaden feet into the house. After the bright outdoor light, it took a moment for her eyes to adjust to the dim parlor. Finally she spotted an older woman sitting in an upholstered chair. She looked nothing like the strong, robust music teacher she remembered. This woman appeared small and frail, a shadow of her former self.

Faded blue eyes peered from a well-lined face. She was dressed in a long housecoat and tendrils of white hair escaped from the confines of a frilly mobcap.

"Charity, get our guest some refreshment," she croaked. The girl left the room, and the older woman gave Jennifer her full attention.

"Are you from the church?" she asked.

"The church?"

"Reverend Whitcomb is always sending someone to pray with me. I don't know what sin he thinks I can commit confined to my chair."

"I'm not from the church." She glanced at the sheet of music on the piano: "Für Elise."

The woman followed her gaze. "Do you play?"

"Not very well."

"As you probably heard, my daughter plays beautifully. She's giving a concert next week. You should come. The proceeds support the Orphan Children's Fund."

"I don't expect to be in town that long."

The widow frowned. "What did you say your name was?"

"Jennifer. Jennifer Layne." When that got no reaction, she added, "I'm sure you remember my parents, Cynthia and Howard Layne."

The woman stared at her for a moment, and then something strange happened. She began to shrivel up as if someone had taken the stuffing out of her. But it was the panic in her eyes that confirmed Jennifer's suspicions.

"I — I don't know anyone by those names."

"You taught me to play piano." Jennifer fell silent as the full impact hit her, and it was all she could do to keep her wits about her. "It's true, isn't it? That's Cissy. That's my sister."

Mrs. Jeremy gripped the arms of her chair

and the color drained from her face. "What . . . do you want?" she croaked.

Rage unlike anything Jennifer had known exploded within. "How . . . *could* you." She was breathing so hard she could hardly get the words out. "How could you take her from us? You walked off with my sister as if she was of no more value than an umbrella!"

Mrs. Jeremy started to deny it, but Jennifer grabbed her bony wrist. Her skin felt like parchment. The woman shrank back and stared at Jennifer's raised hand.

Horrified at how close she was to striking the woman, Jennifer lowered her arm and released her. Shaken, she stammered, "How . . . how could you?"

"I . . . I don't know what you're talking about."

"Don't lie."

The woman's face crumbled and a ragged breath escaped. "Please. You must understand. I couldn't have children of my own, and your mother . . . could barely care for the ones she had. So when my husband suggested that we . . . I agreed."

Jennifer shook her head, but the nightmare persisted. "You had no right."

"We . . . we gave her a good life. You have to believe that. Better than your parents could have done. We sent her to the best schools and —"

Jennifer stared at her, incredulous. No matter how great the sin or bad the crime, people always tried to justify it. Just like Miss Lillian and her guests. Just like Coral and all the rest.

"Do you know what you did to my family? Have you any idea how we suffered?" Nothing could justify that!"

"I thought that after all this time . . . H–how did you know?"

"That night . . . Cissy cried out. She told me someone was trying to take her, but I misunderstood." The thought of Mr. Jeremy hiding in the dark while she comforted her sister filled her with horror. The worst part was her failure to figure out the clues she'd held all these years. For that she would always feel guilty.

"I'm sorry —"

Jennifer drew back. "You're sorry? That's it? That's all you can say?"

Mrs. Jeremy opened her mouth to say more, but a funny choking sound came out instead. Her eyes rolled back, and her head grew slack.

Shaking her, Jennifer called for Charity, the unfamiliar name like acid to her tongue.

The girl rushed into the room, carrying a tray. With a cry of alarm, she set the tray on the table and hurried to the old lady's side.

"It's all right, Mama, I'm here." She felt her mother's pulse, covered her with a quilt, and stroked her head like one would comfort a child.

It was obvious that she cared deeply for the woman, and each worried frown that crossed her beautiful young face was like a knife slashing into Jennifer's heart. Shivering, she ran her hands up and down her arms and swallowed the bile in her mouth.

"What's wrong with her?" she asked in a hushed voice.

"She has these spells. Sometimes she doesn't even recognize me, her own daughter." As she worked to make the old lady comfortable, she glanced at Jennifer. "You were lucky to arrive on a day when she was lucid."

Jennifer didn't know what to say, what to do. "Should I fetch a doctor?"

Charity shook her head. "There's nothing he can do for her. We just have to let her rest." She left her mother's side and poured lemonade into a glass. "The doctor said she doesn't have much time left, but I hope she lasts for my wedding."

Jennifer took the offered glass. "You're getting married?" It seemed inconceivable that her baby sister was now all grown up.

In her mind, she was still the roly-poly little girl of three who called her *Tenfer* and refused to eat peas.

Charity smiled, and an inner light brightened her face. "I haven't told anyone yet, not even Mama. The least bit of stress sends her into one of these spells."

"You think your marriage will cause her stress?"

"I know it sounds crazy, but she's always been afraid of losing me. I think it's because I'm an only child."

Jennifer sipped her lemonade. The cool, bittersweet beverage did little to soothe her dry throat. How many times had she imagined this very scene? Imagined meeting Cissy for the first time after so many years? Imagined the two of them crying and laughing. Talking about the good times, the bad . . .

"I heard you playing the piano. Beethoven."

Charity nodded and poured a glass of lemonade for herself. " 'Bagatelle in A Minor,' " she said, calling "Für Elise" by its more formal name. "I don't know why, but it's always been one of my favorites. Everyone plays it, but few play it well."

I know why, Jennifer wanted to shout. *I know why it's your favorite. It's because I played it for you when you were a little girl. You sat on my lap and placed your chubby little fingers on the yellowed keys and tried to imitate me.*

Keeping her thoughts to herself, she said, "I always had trouble with the middle part."

"It's all about the proper tempo." Charity talked about the technicalities of the piece like a true musician. "Your fingers should rotate up and . . ."

Questions churned in Jennifer's head, begging to be asked. *Do you remember me? Do you remember the stories I used to tell you? The games we used to play? Do you remember that you named your doll Elise? Or how, on that long-ago night, you woke from a deep sleep and I tried to calm your fears?*

But this wasn't the Cissy she knew. This wasn't the one whose diapers she'd changed and tears she'd wiped and hurts she'd soothed. This was a grown woman who evidently had no memory of her early childhood.

"I'm sorry, I'm boring you," Charity said.

"No, not at all," Jennifer hastened to assure her. "I'm afraid that I'm one of those who play the piece poorly. I should practice."

"I'd be happy to help you."

"Thank you, that's very kind, but I won't

be staying in St. Louis for much longer."

Charity glanced at her mother. "I should probably put her to bed."

"Yes, of course. I won't keep you." She placed her glass on the tray. "Is he a good man?" she asked. "Your fiancé? Is he a Christian?" Will he love you and cherish you and always be true? Or will he satisfy his needs in another woman's bed like so many men do?

"Oh yes," Charity said, and there was no question that she believed it with her whole heart and soul. "He's a minister and one day plans to build his own church."

Jennifer envied her sister's faith in her fiancé and prayed that it wasn't misplaced. "I wish you every happiness," she said, bringing a smile to Charity's face.

All through her teens, Jennifer thought that finding her sister would fix her family's problems — that her father would stop drinking and her mother stop mourning and her brothers stop running wild. Maybe it would have made a difference at one time, but not now. It was too late to save her parents. Her mother and father were both dead. As for her brothers, they were now married with families of their own, their wild days a distant memory.

Charity walked her to the door. "You said

you knew my mother in Illinois."

Feeling more numbed than angry, Jennifer gazed past her to the woman in the chair. Vacant eyes stared from a face as round and still as the moon.

"I . . . was mistaken. I never knew your mother at all."

Outside the world looked different, somehow. Losing her sister had been her personal north guiding her every move. Knowing that her sister was safe and happy freed her from the chains locking her into the past.

Was that God's plan all along? Was that the reason she ended up at Miss Lillian's? Not to solve the mystery of the Gunnysack Bandit but to unlock the mystery of her own past?

The ruby-throated hummingbird flitting around a red carnation seemed to think so. She would have sworn the bird nodded his shiny green head. The pastor of her church liked to say that God works in mysterious ways.

That was true, of course, but lately His ways seemed even more mysterious. She only hoped God had something more up His heavenly sleeve because she had no idea where to go from there.

After turning down the Colorado assignment in order to track down her sister, she wasn't even certain she had a job left. Then there was Tom. Weeks had passed since she'd last seen him, but her misery was no less potent today than it had been when he left. She sighed. Her life was a complete mess.

The sun hung just above the horizon like a crystal ball shooting arrows of red and yellow across the sky. The hummingbird continued to flit from blossom to blossom. With its whirring green wings and ruby throat, it looked like a rainbow in flight.

"You're getting married?" How was that possible? Her baby sister?

"I haven't told anyone yet."

Two thoughts churned in her head. They seemed totally unrelated but in some strange way connected. A sense of uneasiness came over her, but she couldn't define the source.

"I haven't told anyone yet."

The hummingbird hovered over a red blossom.

"I haven't told anyone yet."

She drove the rented horse and buggy back to town, the thought persisting. Something churned just outside her memory, but she couldn't for the life of her bring it to the forefront.

"I haven't told anyone yet."

Hummingbird.

CHAPTER 34

Texas

Jennifer tugged on the reins and muttered, "Where is it?" The wagon rolled to a stop and the dapple gray horse nickered and flicked his tail as if protesting the delay.

The man at the stables told her to follow the road and it would lead straight to the Colton ranch. *"You can't miss it."*

So far the land revealed nothing but sagebrush, dry ground, and an occasional cattle skull. If there was a ranch anywhere to be found out here, she would be inclined to eat her hat.

She mopped her damp forehead with a handkerchief. Though she'd passed mesquite trees at the start of her journey, she hadn't seen a spot of shade since. If the buzzards overhead and bright scorching sun weren't bad enough, the humid air weighed upon her like a wet blanket and her clothes stuck to her like glue.

Feeling hot and tired and more than a bit lightheaded, she reached for the canteen. The few precious drops that remained did nothing to ease her thirst, and she tossed the flask aside.

If only it hadn't taken her all this time to figure out that Rose's journal wasn't about birds. Instead, it held the clue to the identity of the Gunnysack Bandit — and it wasn't Tom's brother. Of that she was certain.

The incongruity of it amazed her. She had gone to St. Louis to find her sister and ended up solving not just one mystery but two.

Anxious to reach Tom, she picked up the reins and, with a glance at the still circling vultures, urged the horse forward. *Please, God, just let me live long enough to tell him the good news.*

Tom stood by the fence, hands over the top railing, watching the black mustang circle the corral. It was June but felt like August. Last night's rainstorm left a blanket of hot, sticky air behind.

The steed with its thundering hooves, flying mane, and fiery breath looked no less wild today than when he was first brought to the ranch three months earlier.

Twice already that morning, the animal

tried clearing the fence. The first time he fell on his side, mouth open, eyes frantic, body arching until he was finally back on all fours.

The next time he looked about to jump, the horse trainer, Clint, snapped his whip down hard on the ground, and the mustang thought better of it.

Sure-footed as a mule, Clint Saunders moved fast and talked slow. It wouldn't be so bad if he were but a man of few words. Unfortunately, he liked to talk almost as much as he liked horses. Once he got going on one of his long-winded tales, all the glazed eyes and yawning in the world couldn't stop him.

Now he sauntered over to Tom, his white hair held down by a floppy brimmed hat and tied at his neck with a piece of rawhide. "I don't know, Tom. I've tamed my share of wild horses, but this one . . ." He shook his head. "This one's off his mental reservation. Never thought I'd say this about a horse, but he's an outlaw. Reminds me of the time —"

"Let him go."

Clint pulled off his hat and wiped the sweat off his forehead with his sleeve. He pressed his hat back on, gray eyes narrowed. "Never thought I'd hear those words come outta your mouth."

"Let him go."

Tom pulled away from the fence and started for the barn. It had been more than a month since he'd returned to the ranch, and he still didn't want to believe the things said about his brother.

Even now, the thought sickened him. His brother the outlaw, his brother the killer.

The signs had all been there, but Tom hadn't wanted to believe them. He wanted to think there was a simple explanation for the stolen banknotes found in his brother's pocket and the neatly typed list of holdups. He wanted to believe what Reverend Matthews said was true, but that was only wishful thinking on his part. On the preacher's part, too, probably.

Perhaps the most damaging evidence of all was the lack of holdups since his brother's death. His brother was a criminal, and it was time to let him go.

The problem was how to break the news to his young nephew. He couldn't hold back the truth much longer.

He lengthened his stride. Since returning home, he'd brushed off his nephew's questions with vague answers. That had to change.

Like it or not, it was time to sit down with

the boy and tell him the truth about his pa. He expected honesty from his nephew and the boy deserved the same consideration in return. Maybe then they could put this whole episode behind them and start afresh. *God, don't let me fail my nephew like I failed Dave.*

What didn't make sense was the way he kept thinking of the woman he now knew had tricked him. *God, what is wrong with me? Why can't I sleep? Eat? Why does everything remind me of her, even a wild horse that stubbornly refuses to be tamed?*

To make matters worse, he imagined seeing her at that very moment as he walked toward the stables. Imagined seeing her wave, seeing those big beautiful eyes of hers that lit up a room as they lit up his heart. He blinked, but the vision stubbornly remained behind the shimmering heat. It was like looking at her through a dream. He stopped in his tracks. Or was it?

Amy? Jennifer?

Was it really her or were his eyes playing tricks again? His legs carried him forward without hesitation. This time the vision didn't fade away as it had so often in the past.

He ran to her and would have taken her in his arms had she not lashed into him.

"Tom Colton, you had no right blaming me for anything that happened. You know I couldn't reveal my real identity and . . ." On and on she went, emphasizing her displeasure with finger pokes to his chest. "You were a Texas Ranger. You have to know what it's like to work undercover." Green fire shot from her eyes. "Furthermore . . ."

At last she ran out of words, or maybe she just needed to take a breath. "Are you finished?" he asked.

"Yes," she shouted back. Then she did something completely unexpected; she fainted dead away. It was a miracle that he was able to catch her before she hit the ground.

Alarmed, he lifted her into his arms. She was hot, dangerously hot.

"Clint! Take care of the lady's horse," he called.

"Will do, Boss."

Anxious to get her out of the blistering sun, Tom carried her into the ranch house and to his bed.

Jennifer opened her eyes and moaned. Battling through the fog, she tried making sense of her surroundings. *Where am I?*

A voice sounded from a distance, but she couldn't make out the words. She blinked and gradually her vision cleared. A face . . . She inhaled. "Tom?"

"Well look a there, sleeping beauty is finally awake."

Was that really him or was she dreaming? "Where . . . where am I?"

"You're in Texas."

Texas. A whirlwind of disconnected thoughts spun in her head before the cotton disappeared completely. "What . . . happened?"

"Looks like the heat got you." He reached for a glass on the bedside table. "Here, drink this." He slid an arm under her head and raised the glass to her lips. The water tasted cool and sweet.

He pulled the glass away and set it on the table.

She tried saying "thank you," but her parched lips wouldn't cooperate.

He stood by the side of the bed, looking down on her. She couldn't tell by his expression whether he was still angry, but he sure didn't look like himself.

"So what do I call you?" he asked. "Jennifer or Amy?"

"My name is Jennifer," she said.

He repeated her name after her as if trying it on for size. "I brought your carpetbag in from your rig in case you want to change.

Your shirt's all wet from when I tried to cool you down."

She struggled to sit up.

"Take it easy." His hand on her shoulder made her heart leap even in her weakened condition. Surprised by the unexpected jolt, she swayed before falling back onto the pillow.

"Are you all right?" he asked, a shadow of alarm on his face.

She nodded. "Just a bit woozy."

He waited for her dizziness to pass before straddling a chair by her side.

She felt an overwhelming need to touch him to see if he was real, to push the wayward strand of hair from his forehead, to run a finger over the intriguing cleft on his chin. Fearing she might still be dreaming, she looked away to see if the world around them was real.

The room was small. Furnished with a single bunk, wardrobe, and chair, it had Tom's partiality for simplicity written all over it. "Your room?"

He looked around as if seeing it for the first time. Or maybe he was simply seeing it through her eyes. "Yep, it's mine. So, what brings you way out here? Other than to chew me out, I mean."

Now she remembered. She'd been so

overwhelmed at seeing him, all the frustrations, disappointments, and loneliness of the past few weeks spurted out of her like flames of fire.

"Way out here is right." A wan smile was all her parched mouth would allow, but it seemed to be enough to soften the worry lines on his face. "They told me your ranch was only a mile or two out of town."

"That's Texas miles. If you want to go by how a crow flies, it's closer to ten."

She made a face. "It felt like twenty." It was hard to know what was worse: the heat, humidity, dust, or horse-sized bugs.

She moistened her dry lips. So much had happened since she last saw him. She had so much to say, but between her parched throat and lightheadedness, she couldn't get the words out.

Feeling a sudden urgency, she struggled to get out of bed. So much to do . . .

"Whoa," he said, hands on her shoulders. "First things first. You'll never make it back to town before dark. That's for sure and certain. Better spend the night here."

She looked down at the bed, *his* bed.

As if to guess her thoughts, he added, "I'll sleep in the bunkhouse." He hesitated. "I wish I could offer you better accommodations, but I'm not used to having guests."

"Thank God for that."

It took him a moment to grasp her meaning. The corners of his mouth turned upward. It was hardly the smile she'd come to expect from him, but it was enough.

"Ah, yes. Miss Lillian and her 'guests.' "

She studied him. "Are . . . are you still angry that I lied to you about who I was?"

"You did what you had to do. I'm just glad you aren't a . . . you know."

"Sporting lady?"

He ran his hand across his chin. "So what brings you to these parts?"

You. You bring me to these parts. Aloud she said, "I have news." She cleared her voice and started again, this time louder. "The Gunnysack Bandit is still alive."

His expression grew tight as did his voice. "What are you talking about? My brother —"

"No!" She moved her hand toward him but fell short of touching him. "Your brother tried to stop him. That's what he was doing in Hampton."

He stared at her, his mouth in a straight line. "That makes no sense. The list of holdups, the banknotes —"

"Planted to make him look guilty. Just as the handwriting on the holdup note was made to look like your brother's work."

"If this is true . . ." He raked his fingers through his hair. "Then who? Why?"

"I don't have all the answers yet. What I do know is that your brother didn't do the things they said. You have to believe that."

A shadow of doubt hovered on his forehead. "How do you know all this?"

She laughed. She couldn't help herself. "You won't believe this, but it was the birds."

His forehead creased. "I better send one of the boys to fetch the doctor. The heat rattled your think box."

She shook her head. "There's nothing wrong with my thinking. I'm serious. Did it ever occur to you why Rose went to so much trouble to hide her journal beneath the floorboards? A journal about birds?"

His gaze remained on her face. "Go on."

"She was keeping track of everything that happened at the parlor house using birds as a code." As a Pinkerton detective, she'd worked with many codes, though never one using birds.

She gave him a moment to process this information before continuing. "Your brother was right; Rose figured out the identity of the Gunnysack Bandit."

"If that's true, why didn't she go to the marshal?"

"You said it yourself. Who would believe one of Miss Lillian's girls? She told your brother instead. He then decided to follow the bandit to Hampton to gather proof. That's when Buttercup heard the two of them arguing. I think Rose was against his getting involved."

The doubt began to fade from Tom's face. "But he went anyway."

She nodded. "I think he got the proof he was looking for but was unaware that the Gunnysack Bandit was onto him."

"So he made it look like Dave had robbed the bank and killed the guard."

"Exactly. Dave didn't know that his cover was blown, of course, and had no clue that the real bandit followed him back to town. I think Dave had the proof he needed to put Gunny behind bars. But after things turned violent and the guard was shot, he was worried about Rose's safety."

"So instead of going to the sheriff in Hampton, he rushed back to Goodman."

She nodded. "I think once he knew that Rose was safe he would have gone straight to Flood."

"But he never got the chance." Tom gave his head a shake, an incredulous look on his face. "And you base all this on a bunch of birds?"

"Actually, it was the hummingbird. Rose wrote that there was a hummingbird in her room."

"So?"

"The journal entry was dated December 20th."

He shrugged and splayed his hands. "And?"

"When's the last time you saw a hummingbird in December?"

He shook his head. "I'm a rancher, not a bird-watcher."

"For your information, hummingbirds fly to Mexico for the winter."

He thought for a moment. "Okay, so what was she really saying?"

"Someone was in her room, perhaps going through her things, the person she called Hummingbird. Her name for Georgia was Canary because she liked to sing. Buttercup can't pass a mirror without gazing in it, just like the magpie that lives behind the parlor house."

"Magpies look in mirrors?"

"Windows." She wasn't able to figure out the rest. Who was the loon? Who was the mockingbird? Most important of all, who was Hummingbird?

He scratched his head. "What does any of this have to do with the Gunnysack Bandit?"

"Why, he's the waxwing, of course."

"What?"

"Cedar waxwings are called bandit birds because of their black masks. If you recall, she wrote that the waxwing accosted her in the yard."

"And the waxwing is?"

"Who else but Monahan?"

He thought a moment. "I don't know. If what you say is true, how do you explain the lack of robberies since Dave's death?"

"That puzzles me, too. Maybe it's because Monahan almost got caught during the last holdup and is running scared. Think about it. If the marshal and Pinkerton agency believe the Gunnysack Bandit dead, then he has nothing to worry about. The dogs are off his trail."

He rubbed the back of his neck. "That's a pretty big if."

"Maybe," she said. "But the pieces fit." Or at least some of them did. "Don't forget, the reason I was sent to Goodman was because of stolen banknotes deposited in Rose's account." It was actually Allan Pinkerton who talked banks throughout Kansas into marking notes. He figured that eventually one of the marked notes would lead to the Gunnysack Bandit, but Dave beat him to the punch.

"Maybe the money found on your brother came from Rose." She paused for a moment. "If Monahan knew that Dave suspected him that would be motivation enough to kill him. Rose, too."

Tom sat on the bed and covered her hand with his own. "I'm much obliged for what you're doing. But something about this whole affair doesn't sit right. How did Monahan know my brother was onto him?"

"He may have spotted him in Hampton during the holdup. Maybe your brother confronted him."

He rubbed his forehead with his free hand. "It's possible. I don't know. . . ."

She gazed up at him. "Tom, I'm right about your brother. I know I am. He was not the Gunnysack Bandit."

He studied her for a moment. "What about Flood? What does he think?"

"I haven't notified ole Tin . . . the marshal. I haven't even told my bosses."

He frowned. "If you're right about Monahan, he's dangerous. He's already killed three people and could kill again."

She lifted her chin. "You don't think I know that?"

He drew his hand away. "Now, don't go getting all riled up. I'd say the same if you were a man."

She doubted it, but she didn't want to argue. "I thought you might like to be there when we clear your brother's name."

He gazed at her long and hard. "How sure are you about this?"

"Sure enough to bet your boots."

He arched a brow. "That's sure and certain, eh?"

She smiled. In truth, all she had was a theory, and that wasn't worth a plugged nickel in a court of law. It wasn't worth much as far as the agency was concerned, either. Allan Pinkerton demanded proof, not conjecture.

"So what do you say?" she asked. "Are you game?"

Game? Colton didn't want to answer that question. Didn't want to think about it. He'd been wrong too many times about his brother.

More than anything he was worried about Jennifer's safety. Yes, it bothered him that she had such a dangerous job. So shoot him. Just her size alone put her at a disadvantage. She hardly came up to his shoulders, and a good wind would probably blow her away.

He had nothing against women in the workforce, not like some men he knew who thought a women's place was in front of a cookstove. But chasing down outlaws was not a job for a woman. There had been times in the past when he'd wondered if it was even a job for a man.

She laid a hand on his arm, and if that wasn't enough, she locked him in her green-eyed gaze. "We can do this," she said, and something stirred inside him. "Will you work with me?"

What he wanted to say was no. What he wanted was to keep her in Texas where she would be safe. Knowing how she felt about her job, he'd have a better chance of talking the hide off a mule.

Was she right about Monahan? Tom didn't know. What he *did* know was that he had no intention of letting her find out alone. He just wished it didn't feel like he was about to jump into a snake pit.

Pushing his worries aside, he asked, "What's the plan?"

CHAPTER 35

Jennifer had just finished cooking breakfast when Tom's eleven-year-old nephew wandered into the kitchen. Tall for his age, he had sandy hair and big blue eyes. He looked and carried himself like his uncle.

She greeted him with a smile. "You must be Davey."

"And you're Miss Layne. Uncle Tom said you were like a lady Ranger."

"Actually, I'm a detective."

He gazed at her with eyes too old for such a young face. "I'm going to be a Texas Ranger, just like Uncle Tom was." He gave a determined nod and added, "And I'm gonna find the man who killed my pa."

Something tugged at her insides, and she felt a maternal need to protect him. She knew all too well the frustrations and heartbreak that such a quest could bring. For his sake, she hoped she was right about Monahan. She didn't want Tom's nephew devoting his young life to looking for answers as she had done with her sister.

"I'm sorry about your father."

He studied her as if measuring her sincerity. "Grandpappy said he was a bad man, but he wasn't. I know he wasn't." His intensity reminded her of the Cunningham boy whose frustration with his own father had led him to throw bricks.

"I believe you." She wanted to say more — much more — but all she had was a theory, and she didn't want to give the boy false hope. "Well, Ranger Dave, you better sit for a spell and have yourself some grub."

He didn't need a second invite. The minute she set a plate of eggs and bacon on the table in front of him, he dived in with his fork.

Tom stomped into the house, and she caught a whiff of sunbaked earth before he shut the back door against the shimmering heat. "Something sure does smell good," he said.

She greeted him with a smile. "Good morning." The mere sight of him made her heart flutter. The way he affected her was a worry. As a detective she knew the importance of letting the clues speak for themselves and not to bend them to support a theory. She thought she could remain professional, but after seeing Tom again and meeting Dave's son, she feared she could no longer be objective.

She handed him a cup of coffee.

He blew on the steaming brew and took a sip. "Hmm. Just how I like it." He set his cup on the table and ruffled Davey's hair before sitting, but his gaze remained on her.

"How'd you sleep?" he asked.

The memory of spending the night in his bed — even alone — made her blush, and she turned to the stove to hide her reddening face. "Like a log."

Fighting for composure, she arranged his breakfast on a plate and placed it in front of him.

He stared down at his food before lifting his gaze to hers. "How did you know I like my eggs scrambled and my bacon burned to perfection?"

"She's a detective," Davey said, and Tom laughed.

Grinning, she placed her own plate on the table and sat on the chair opposite him. "I also asked your friend Clint."

"I should have known." He glanced at Davey. "You better get to your chores, son, before it gets any hotter out there."

Davey stuck a piece of bacon in his mouth before jumping up. "It was nice meeting you," he called as he dashed to the door.

"Nice meeting you, too," she called back.

He grabbed a hat off a peg on the wall and ran out of the house, banging the door shut behind him.

"That's quite a boy you have there," she said.

Tom nodded. "He kind of grows on you, doesn't he?"

"Said he wants to be a Texas Ranger like you."

"He'll make a good one, that's for sure and certain."

She hesitated. "How much . . . does he know about his pa?"

Tom grimaced. "More than he should. His grandpappy isn't one to keep his thoughts to himself." He mopped his plate with a biscuit. "I didn't know you were such a good cook."

"It looks like you could use some fattening up," she said. Tom had lost weight since she last saw him. Because of his brother? That was the obvious answer, but she couldn't help but hope that there might be yet another reason.

"You cook like that and I'll be as big as the side of the barn before you know it." He pushed his empty plate away. "Much obliged."

She lowered her coffee cup. "For what?"

"For wanting to clear my brother's name — clear Davey's pa's name."

She chewed on her lower lip. Clearing Dave's name might not be all that easy. The truth was, it might even be impossible, and she felt inadequate for the task. But she'd done a lot of praying, and miracles really did happen. Finding her sister was proof of that, even though it hadn't turned out the way she'd hoped.

"Something wrong?" he asked, his voice gentle. "Why the sudden grim look? You're not having second thoughts, are you? About Monahan?"

She *was* having second thoughts — third and fourth thoughts, too — but that had nothing to do with her sudden gloom. "I found my sister."

He set the coffee cup down. "The one who disappeared? Where?"

She filled him in on all that had happened during the past few weeks. It felt good to talk about it. To talk to him.

"What did your sister say when you told her who you were?" he asked.

"I didn't tell her."

His eyebrows shot up. "Why not?"

She flattened her hands on her skirt. "What good would it have done?" The child she'd carried around in her heart all these years was now someone she didn't recognize. "She's a woman now. She's also engaged to be married. Why ruin her happiness?"

For an instant, his glance sharpened. "But that means the woman who stole her gets off scot-free."

She thought about the expression on Mrs. Jeremy's face. The fear, the horror, the haggard face that looked far older than its years. "God doesn't let anyone off scot-free."

Her lack of malice surprised her. Finding out what had happened to her sister had given her incredible pain but also hope. God had closed the door on her past and opened a door to the future. Her sister was alive and well. Her prayers had been answered. It was time to move on.

Still the tears came. She wasn't even aware of Tom leaving his chair until she was soundly locked in the comforting warmth of his arms.

"It's okay," he whispered, holding her close. "Let it out."

"I'm sorry," she said. She brushed her hand across his chest. "I got your shirt all wet."

"Well, now, will you look a there?" He

pulled out a clean handkerchief and ever so tenderly dabbed her wet cheeks. His gaze fell on her lips, but before his mouth could follow the same path, she pulled away.

Distractions, even the romantic kind, could be disastrous. She needed to keep a clear head for the task ahead. She needed to do it not just for her own sake but his, as well. Otherwise she might never prove his brother's innocence.

"How soon can we leave for Kansas?" she asked, purposely keeping her voice free of emotion.

Her sudden change of mood seemed to confound him, and his brows drew together in a frown. "Soon as you're ready," he said, and hesitated. "Your work as a detective . . . It means a lot to you." It was a statement more than a question.

"Yes, it does." She knew no other life, had no real home. Her stay at Miss Lillian's was the closest she'd come to any sort of routine or stability since leaving the farm at eighteen. It was almost impossible to spend time with her brothers and their families. It was a lonely life but ultimately satisfying — or at least it was. Now she wasn't so sure.

CHAPTER 36

After Tom and Jennifer stepped off the train in Goodman, they went straight to the marshal's office. Following their meeting with Flood, Tom headed for the hotel and Jennifer returned to Miss Lillian's to resume her role as Amy.

Forcing an outer calm that belied the knot of nerves inside, she dressed in the new green taffeta dress with the "Niagara Falls" bustle.

The tightly laced corset pinched her torso. If things went as planned, this would be the last time she'd have to put herself through such torture.

Before leaving her room, she struggled for a bracing breath. It was a Friday night in late June, and Miss Lillian expected a full house. So much depended on what happened during the next few hours, she couldn't afford to let her guard down. One misstep could ruin her carefully laid plans.

Planting a bag of banknotes at the express company was a brilliant idea, if she did say so herself. Monahan wouldn't be able to resist the temptation to steal from his own safe before the shipment was made, knowing he would never be caught.

A package traveling across the country passed through dozens if not hundreds of hands. No one would be the wiser until the package reached its destination, and anyone along the way could have stolen the money inside and replaced it with the fake notes. It's what made express companies such a popular target for corrupt employees and a nightmare for lawmen. Her only hope was that Monahan fell for the trick.

Coral, Polly, Buttercup, and Miss Lillian were already seated downstairs in the parlor when Amy entered. Candles flickered from silver holders. Summer had yet to arrive weatherwise, and a fire blazed merrily in the fireplace.

Buttercup was the first to spot her. "I didn't know you were back."

All eyes turned in Amy's direction.

Coral's expression darkened and she jumped to her feet. "What is *she* doing here?"

"I invited her to return," Miss Lillian said smoothly. She motioned to Amy. "Come and have a seat."

"I always knew she was your favorite!" Coral sputtered. Hands at her waist, she glared at Miss Lillian, her face twisted with jealousy. "You let her get away with anything."

A look of annoyance crossed Miss Lillian's face. "I don't have time for this. Now hush up. Our guests are due to arrive at any moment."

"Guests. Guests?" Coral spat out the words with contempt. "We don't have *guests*. We have johns." She pointed a threatening finger at Miss Lillian. "And you're not a hostess or even a businesswoman. You're nothing but a madam, and the only thing separating us from those horrid cribs is this house."

Angry words shot out of Coral's mouth like poison darts. "We're trash. All of us are nothing but trash!" She turned away from Miss Lillian. "Trash!"

Buttercup stood in her way. "Don't say that. It's not true —"

"Is that what your mirror told you?" Coral asked. "You vain little —"

"I'm not vain!" Buttercup shouted and in a softer voice added, "I look in the mirror to see if I'm still me."

Coral opened her mouth to speak but

instead flounced across the room, forcing Amy to fall back. A strained silence followed her departure. Buttercup held her hand over her mouth, and Polly looked close to tears. It was as if the ground had opened and spit their shameful secrets onto the parlor floor for all to see.

Miss Lillian's face seemed to crumble and her ruby lips puckered. Not even the shiny red gown or thick coat of face powder could hide the pallor of her skin.

Amy pressed her hands against her chest. *God, this can't be happening!* She needed Miss Lillian's help; so much depended on everything moving like clockwork. Now thanks to Coral, her carefully laid plans appeared to be ruined.

The door chimes rang and tension in the room grew tauter. All eyes turned to Miss Lillian.

Standing, Miss Lillian threw her shoulders back and lifted her chin. "Our guests have arrived," she announced. She may have been stripped of all pretenses, but for now the show must go on.

For the next couple of hours, all five women played their parts as if nothing had happened. Only the most discerning eye could have noticed the forced smiles and tense expressions. Coral had returned and moved about the room with her usual grace but never missed an opportunity to shoot a visual dagger at Amy.

Polly noticed the dark, hateful glances. "B–b–better watch your b–b–back," she whispered in Amy's ear.

Amy nodded, but watching her back was the least of her worries. Tonight it was all about the plan. It was a deceptively simple one: catch Monahan in the act of robbing his own express company.

The plan wasn't foolproof; its success teetered on one of the seven deadly sins, namely, greed. She chanced a glance at Monahan, who looked perfectly relaxed. As usual he was dressed in a fine tailored suit, tan trousers, brown vest, and coat. She was no expert in fabric, but Miss Lillian told her his clothes were cut from only the finest Italian silks.

Gold rings glittered on several fingers as he mouthed his Partagás cigar imported directly from Cuba. Even the smoke circling his head looked richer, fuller than the smoke from the hand-rolled cigarettes and cheaper cigars of the other guests.

He had the best that money could buy and owned half the town, maybe more. He didn't need for a thing, not a thing. Her only hope was that greed would get the best of him, and he would fall into her trap.

Still, something bothered her, though she couldn't for the life of her think what it was. For some reason she kept recalling the night he stood outside the cellar door, the night someone had knocked her unconscious.

She studied each woman in turn, hoping to see a telling look, a conspiratorial wink, a whispered exchange. One of these women had been in the cellar that night. One of them had hit her over the head, and she was willing to guess that woman had been Coral.

Miss Lillian played a lively ditty on the piano and Mr. Cunningham got up and danced a jig. This brought gales of laughter and applause from the others. Since Coral was watching her, Amy had no choice but to clap, though it sickened her. All she could think about was the man's son, Scott, and the desperation that drove the boy to throw bricks at the parlor house.

Mr. Studebaker announced he had some sort of throat trouble that prevented him from singing that night. Coral cooed with mock sympathy, which the silly man took for the real thing.

A smile plastered on her face, Amy held her fan judiciously and willed herself not to keep looking at the long clock when Mr.

Miller cornered her. The man had nothing of interest to say but insisted upon saying it, anyway.

His broad face and walrus-like mustache bore a striking resemblance to President Arthur, a man Mr. Miller soundly abhorred.

She glanced at Coral, who was engaged in what looked like an intimate conversation with Mr. Monahan. Amy would give anything to hear what the two discussed.

Polly, as usual, didn't say much for fear of stuttering, but with her pretty blond hair and deep blue eyes, she didn't need to talk. Buttercup was bookended by two men vying for her attention. She looked bored but kept glancing in the nearby mirror and fiddling with her hair. None of her admirers seemed to notice her dull eyes or disinterested expression.

Having played the second of her two-song repertoire, Miss Lillian scooted around the piano stool and gave her jeweled hands several dainty claps.

"Amy has graciously agreed to read everyone's fortune tonight. On the house," she said, careful to use the words she and Amy had rehearsed earlier. "Mr. Tully, you're first."

Mr. Tully stood and straightened his cravat. Built like a cracker barrel with skinny legs, he stabbed the floor with his cane. "There's nothing like a good fortune."

Miller gave a low-pitched snort. "Yes, but with President Arthur in charge, good fortune will be hard to come by."

Amy didn't want to have to go through the entire charade, but it would surely raise suspicion had she zeroed in on Monahan alone. Playing her part to a T, she slipped her arm through Mr. Tully's crooked elbow and led him out of the room and across the entryway to Miss Lillian's office. Having no need of his cane for mobility, he tucked it beneath his other arm.

"I'll pay you handsomely for a good fortune," he said.

She smiled. "Why, Mr. Tully, you wouldn't be trying to bribe me now, would you?"

The office had been prepared in advance. Candles were already lit and draperies drawn so as not to let in any moon or starlight. The desk was covered with a black velvet cloth and the crystal ball looked like a bubble ready to pop.

"Have a seat," she said in a quiet voice. She took her place behind the desk and peered into the shiny globe. Miss Lillian explained that the purpose of staring into a crystal ball was to reach a person's subconscious. Most people thought a fortune-teller's glass sphere foretold the future; such ignorance made some charlatans rich.

Though her insides were tied in a knot, she forced herself to take her time. "I see a woman crying. An older woman . . . with frilly curls and a mole."

Mr. Tully's gaze involuntarily landed on her chin, and she placed her finger on the exact spot.

He looked startled. "That . . . that's my wife. Why is she crying?"

"Shh." She stared into the ball and pretended to concentrate. "Oh dear."

"Go on," he said, his voice anxious.

"She's holding a gun."

He drew back. "Good heavens!"

"Someone has . . . betrayed her."

"No!"

"She doesn't think she has any reason to live. She raises the gun. . . ."

Jumping to his feet, he held out an arm like an overwrought actor in a bad play. "Tell her no!"

Amy sat back. "I'm sorry. I can't tell her anything. The vision is gone."

Face pale as a winter moon, he stammered, "D–do you suppose that she . . . ?"

"The future is in your hands, Mr. Tully. Perhaps if you talked to her . . . Let her know you would never . . . betray her."

"Yes, yes, of course." He backed toward the door. "I'll go home and tell her that right away." He swung around and exited the office, leaving his fashionable cane behind in his haste. Amy laughed. "You do that, Mr. Tully. And if you're smart, you'll stay home."

A moment later, Miss Lillian poked her head in the office. "Mr. Tully left in a hurry. Is everything all right?"

"Everything is perfect," Amy said. "Send in the next guest."

One by one, Amy read each man's fortune, careful not to rush the ritual. She told Mr. Webber what would happen if he continued ignoring his wife. No sooner had she finished the session than he hurried away to buy his wife her favorite sweets.

She "read" a bleak future for Mr. Cobble's mining company if he didn't stop overworking his employees. She "foresaw" a terrible illness if Mr. Sweeney refused to mend his ways and kept avoiding church.

For Scott's father, Mr. Cunningham, she poured it on especially thick. "I see a boy. About twelve or thirteen . . ."

"That must be my son."

Pretending not to hear him, she swayed slightly as if in a trance. "His name begins with an *S*. Samuel, Steve. Scott."

"Yes, yes," he thundered, "Scott. That's him. That's my son."

She kept her gaze focused on the crystal ball. "Oh dear. Oh my."

He gave an anxious gasp. "What do you see? Tell me!"

"I see . . . the sign of death."

His eyes widened in horror. "Whose death? Not Scott's!"

Encouraged by the man's obvious concern for his son, she continued in a low monotone. "Your family will be safe, providing you —"

"Go on, providing what?"

"Ask God's forgiveness and change your ways."

"Change my ways?" He looked mortified. "You mean stop coming here?"

"And similar places." She raised her head and looked him in the eyes. "If you don't, sir, your family's safety will be in serious jeopardy."

He stood so quickly his chair slammed against the door. "I'm much obliged to you for letting me know. I must go. My family needs me."

He quickly left the room.

"Yes!" Amy banged on the desk. Praise the Lord!

So far, the evening had been an unexpected success. For that she was grateful, but she also felt deeply humbled. Words had popped out of her mouth from seemingly nowhere. Somehow she knew exactly what to say to each man, and she could think of only one explanation; while she was hoping to trap a killer, God had worked through her to change lives.

He really did work in mysterious ways — and in a bordello, of all places. The thought filled her with unspeakable emotion.

A knock sounded, and she immediately checked her neckline to make certain the lace tucked there for modesty's sake was in place.

"Come in."

Mr. Monahan entered the room and sat, placing his palms on the desk. "So what does the future hold for me?" His oily smile and mocking tone made it clear he didn't believe in such nonsense and was just playing along for the fun of it.

She lowered her gaze to the crystal ball, surprised to find her knees shaking. *God, please help me make this work. For Tom's sake. For Davey's.*

"I see . . . gold." She raised her gaze to his. "Do you own a gold mine, Mr. Monahan?"

"Unfortunately, no." His eyes glittered as if she had just proven how ridiculous this whole business was. "At the price of gold, I wish I did."

Amy lowered her gaze to the crystal ball. "I see . . ." She held her hands to the ball without touching it. "I see a ship. No, not just one. I see three ships on a stormy sea."

She sensed Monahan stiffening but she kept her gaze focused on the ball. "I see a steel box." Not wanting to be too obvious, she avoided using the word *safe*. "It holds great riches and it will make you very happy." She let him digest that for a moment before gasping in alarm. "Oh dear. Should a ship arrive before midnight, peril awaits. After midnight, your treasure will be safe."

She relaxed as if letting the vision drain away. "It looks like your ship is about to come in, Mr. Monahan."

He stood and tossed a gold coin on the desk. "Since we live in Kansas, that would be an interesting trick."

He left the room, and she knotted her hands. Had she been too obvious? Too subtle? Most importantly, did he fall for it?

The last fortune she read was Mr. Studebaker's. "Do I have a future as a singer?" he asked, his voice still hoarse.

She kept her gaze fixated on the crystal ball. The man couldn't carry a tune in a basket, but since she wouldn't be around much longer to hear him, she saw no harm in offering encouragement. "I see many notes in your future, Mr. Studebaker." *Flat* notes.

The news seemed to please him to no end. "I knew it," he rasped. Despite his sore throat, he left the room humming.

No sooner had Studebaker left than Miss Lillian entered her office, wringing her hands. "The guests are gone!"

"Everyone?"

"Everyone!"

Amy felt a rush of cautious optimism. The news was encouraging, but it didn't necessarily mean Monahan had taken the bait.

"What did you say to make everyone leave?" Miss Lillian asked with a frown.

Amy rose. "I guess they were overwhelmed by my predictions."

Miss Lillian's lips puckered with annoyance. "Remind me not to let you play fortune-teller again. It's bad for business." She lit the lamp and covered the ball with a black cloth. "Do you think the suspect fell for it?"

Amy wished she could answer that. It was

hard to tell what went on behind Monahan's polished veneer. "We'll know soon enough."

"You better get ready." Miss Lillian picked up the crystal ball. "You don't want to keep Mr. Monahan waiting."

Amy's jaw dropped. "I never said it was him." She'd told Miss Lillian her plan but not the name of the suspect.

A smiled inched across Miss Lillian's face, the first real smile Amy had seen all night. "I've been practicing my detective skills. I figured there was a reason why you wanted to read the men's fortune in a particular order."

"I didn't want anyone to be suspicious." Amy glanced at the open door to make sure no eavesdroppers lurked in the entry hall.

"Don't look so worried. Discretion is my middle name. I know how to put two and two together and keep my mouth shut." She waved her hands. "Now go and get ready. Detective Lillian will hold down the fort."

Grateful that Miss Lillian had not let Coral's earlier outburst ruin the plan, Amy paused at the doorway. "Coral was wrong. You *are* a good businesswoman. You're just in the wrong business."

Without waiting for a response she left, but not without peering into the parlor. Coral, Polly, and Buttercup sat in waiting silence, no doubt wondering where all the guests had gone. *Detective Lillian* better have a good explanation.

Yanking the taffeta skirt up to her knees, she rushed up the stairs two at a time.

Chapter 37

Amy changed into a plain blue skirt and tailored shirtwaist. She stared at herself in the mirror. It was unusual to feel this nervous or anxious before an undercover operation, but then never had there been more at stake.

If she was wrong about Monahan or if she botched this up in some way, she could pretty much count on her career as a Pinkerton operative coming to an end.

Oddly enough, the thought wasn't quite as devastating as she expected. Finding her sister had changed her in surprising ways. She no longer felt quite as restless or driven. She wanted to catch Monahan, no question. But not because of career advancement; this time her goal was far more personal.

Nothing could bring Dave Colton back or change the past, but at least she could restore Tom's faith in him. Perhaps even more importantly, she could give a young boy a legacy of pride instead of shame.

She checked her derringer and slid it back into her leg holster. It was time and she was ready. At exactly ten minutes past ten o'clock, she opened the door and peered cautiously into the hall. Normally at this time on a Saturday night, the house bustled with activity. The silence felt odd, eerie, as if even the walls were afraid to breathe.

Here we go, God. Here we go.

The downstairs appeared deserted. So far so good. Now if Miss Lillian just remembered to leave the front door unlocked. She didn't want to waste time using the trapdoor.

She descended the stairs quietly and glanced into the parlor. Much to her relief, the room was empty. The lamps were still lit and the sickly smell of perfume hung in the air, but all that remained of the fire was red embers.

She started for the door.

"Where do you think you're going?"

Halted by Coral's voice, Amy turned. "Out for fresh air."

"Liar!" Coral descended the stairs, and even the paint piled on her dark-skinned face couldn't hide her hateful expression.

"What did you say to drive all the guests away?"

"All I did was read their fortunes."

"Don't lie to me. I knew there was something not right about you from the start."

Amy's hands balled at her sides, but she maintained a calm demeanor. She didn't have time for an argument. "I have nothing more to say, Coral."

"Well, I have plenty to say to you."

"What's going on?" Buttercup appeared at the top of the stairs. Wearing a corset and bloomers, she stood braiding her hair into a single plait. Polly peered over her shoulder.

"Nothing's going on," Amy said.

Coral advanced toward her. She was still dressed in her working clothes, and the taffeta rustled like dry leaves. "It's not the first time you left the house at night."

If Coral had been the one with Monahan at the cellar door, she was a fine one to talk.

The quick pitter-patter of footsteps preceded Miss Lillian's arrival. Her gaze bounced between Amy and Coral. "What's all the fuss?"

"Coral objects to my going outside for air," Amy said.

Coral's brown eyes flashed with dangerous lights. "What I object to is your sneaking around and pretending to be something you're not. You might fool Miss Lillian, but you can't fool me." She turned to the others. "Not only was Rose murdered the day Amy arrived, but somehow she got Georgia to leave. Then after disappearing for weeks without a word, she comes back and chases away all our guests."

The chimes of the tall clock rang out the quarter hour. Amy was anxious to get to town. She didn't want to miss seeing Monahan arrested. "I don't have time for this." She reached for the doorknob, but Coral grabbed her by the wrist.

"You're not going anywhere until I get some answers."

Amy tried pulling away, but Coral's grip tightened. "Let go of me."

Coral's nose was practically in Amy's face. "Over my dead body."

Amy glared at her. "Be careful what you wish for."

"I declare to goodness!" Miss Lillian clapped her hands. "I won't have my girls acting like a bunch of alley cats," she said, but no amount of pleading would loosen Coral's grasp.

Amy couldn't afford to wait another minute. She slipped her one free hand into her false pocket and pulled out her derringer.

Coral fell back, her face a mask of astonishment. Amy muttered an apology, though she didn't feel particularly sorry. If Coral had hit her over the head in the cellar as suspected, a gun to the face was the least the woman deserved.

Without another word, Amy left the house and ran.

Amy was out of breath by the time she reached Main Street. A painful stitch shot from under her rib cage. Rubbing her side, she glanced around. Tethered horses lined the street. Lamps blazed from hotel windows, casting a patchwork of light onto the dirt road. Male voices and laughter wafted from the saloons. A banjo played a Stephen Foster tune to the sound of stomping feet.

"Psst."

Amy swung around. Tom beckoned her from the alley next to the hotel almost directly across from the Monahan Express Company. Only his dark form was visible, but it was enough to quicken her pulse.

She ducked between the buildings where both Marshal Flood and Tom stood waiting for her. Light from the hotel windows turned the alley into a checkerboard of bright squares.

Tom pulled her to his side, and his nearness was both comforting and disturbing. "I thought you'd never get here," he said, his voice hushed.

"I had a problem getting away," she said, trying to maintain a businesslike demeanor. "Everything all set?"

Flood nodded. "We got lucky. Crenshaw worked on the safe and had the combination in his files." Crenshaw was the town blacksmith.

That *was* lucky, but not too surprising. Blacksmiths were the first people operatives turned to when needing access to a safe or vault. That's because hinges and locks often required repairs, and blacksmiths were the only ones in town who could fix them. Oddly enough, few safe owners remembered to change combinations after repairs.

"Any sign of Monahan?"

"None," the marshal replied, sounding peeved. "And the longer I stand here, the more this whole things sounds like a wild goose chase."

"Did Monahan fall for it?" Tom asked.

"I think so." She couldn't be sure. "He gave no indication, but he did leave Miss Lillian's the moment I finished reading his fortune. I thought he might make a beeline to his office."

Tom shook his head. "That would have

been foolhardy. Too many people in town. Unless I miss my guess, he'll wait till after midnight, just like you told him."

She closed her eyes to block Tom from view, but that didn't make it any easier to concentrate. She could still feel the warmth of his body and hear his every breath. Then there was the intriguing combination of leather and bay rum that played havoc with her senses.

"You okay?" he asked.

She opened her eyes and forced a smile. "I think so."

Flood made a grunting sound. "This whole thing about Monahan . . . I'm still having a hard time believing it."

The marshal's doubts added to Amy's anxiety. What if she was wrong about Monahan? About Coral? Had her feelings for Tom compromised her judgment?

She felt Tom bristle by her side. "I see something."

"It's too early," she whispered. "Maybe he decided not to wait."

She dropped down on hands and knees and peered around a corner. A figure darted along the opposite boardwalk, but even the dark shadows couldn't hide the checkered suit.

"Oh no," she groaned. "It's that private

detective." That's all they needed.

"What's he doing here?" Tom whispered.

"That's what I want to know." She left her hiding place and ever so quietly ran across the street and up the steps to the boardwalk. She found him paused in front of Harry's Gun and Bakery Shoppe, his back turned.

"Fancy meeting you here."

"Ahhhh!" Had Checkers been touched by a cattle prod, he couldn't have jumped much higher. He swung around, hand on his chest. "Blimey! You've got to stop sneaking up like that. You'll give me heart failure."

"Shh. Keep your voice down. Why are you here?"

"Haven't the foggiest idea. I simply followed you."

Amy palmed her forehead. She'd been so anxious to get to town she'd not taken the usual precautions to prevent being followed. Now, all she could do was make the best of it.

"Quick." She grabbed his arm and practically dragged him across the street to the alley.

He greeted Tom and Flood with a questioning glance and straightened his bow tie. "I demand to know what's going on."

"What makes you think you're in a position to make demands?" Flood asked.

"I'm a private investigator, that's what." He turned to Tom. "I don't know why she's here, but you're working on a case, right?"

Tom glanced at Amy. "Well —"

"I knew it!" Checkers practically jumped for joy. "And it's got something to do with Monahan, right?"

"Yes, well, we won't know till he shows up," Flood muttered.

"Shh," Tom cautioned. "Someone's coming."

Mr. Checkers sniffled. "I smell perfume." He held his finger under his nose but sneezed anyway. "Ah-choo!"

"Shh!"

"I can't help it. Perfume bothers me."

Amy peered out of the alley, and her mouth dropped open. *Please, God, let me be seeing things.* Only she wasn't. It was Miss Lillian — no question. Following close behind were Coral, Buttercup, and Polly.

"Psst. Miss Lillian. Over here!" Amy motioned with her hand.

Miss Lillian turned her head in Amy's direction and waved. "Oh, there you are."

The four women tottered daintily toward her, lifting their fancy skirts above the ankles. Miss Lillian reached the alley slightly out of breath.

"We didn't miss anything, did we?"

"Unfortunately, no," Checkers said, his voice muffled by the handkerchief held to his nose.

Amy pulled Miss Lillian into the alley where she couldn't be seen from the street. The madam looked momentarily startled but quickly recovered. The others pushed their way into the alley, forcing the marshal and Checkers to move back. The smell of perfume was almost overwhelming.

"What are you all doing here?" Amy demanded.

Coral pulled her shawl around her shoulders. "Miss Lillian told us everything."

Amy swung around to face the madam, hands at her waist. "You had no right." Her hushed voice hardly did her anger justice. "You promised."

"I had to tell them something," Miss Lillian sniffed and didn't sound the least bit sorry.

Amy groaned and curled her hands by her sides. She squeezed past the others to reach Tom's side. "Watch Coral," she whispered.

"Will do."

"I want so much for this to go right." For his sake, for young Davey's.

He squeezed her hand, but his reassuring smile failed to allay her worries. So far little had gone as planned, but Coral's presence was particularly worrisome. She could be working with Monahan, and if so, she might try warning him.

Buttercup pushed her way from the rear of the alley to Amy's side. "I can't believe you're a detective."

Checkers sneezed. "What do you mean a detective?" His gaze shot from Amy to Tom. "Don't tell me you're both Pinks."

"No, only the lady," Marshal Flood said.

Amy gritted her teeth. "Why don't we just shout it from the rooftops?"

Polly patted her on the arm. "W—we just w—want to h—help."

"It's not like we have anything else to do," Coral said, "since you chased all our *guests* away."

Miss Lillian pushed Amy aside to peer out to the street. "Oh dear. Where are they?"

"Who's they?" Tom asked.

"Why, Mrs. Givings and her friends. They were right behind us." Miss Lillian stuck her head out of the alley and waved. "Yoo-hoo. Over here."

"Shh." Amy pulled her back. "Do you want to wake the dead?"

"Sorry."

Mrs. Givings, Mrs. Compton, and Mrs. Albright came running. "There you are,"

Mrs. Givings said. "We thought we'd lost you."

"It's getting rather crowded," Checkers complained from behind his handkerchief.

"Will you look at this?" Mrs. Givings straightened her feathered hat. "There are enough people here for a revival."

Flood pushed a feather from her hat away from his face. "Yeah, well don't get any ideas."

Mrs. Givings ignored him. "Miss Lillian said you needed our prayers, and that's what we're here for." She craned her neck to address those at the back. "So are we all ready to repent?"

"Now, don't go getting on your high horse," Miss Lillian admonished. "We're not here to repent. We're working on a case."

"What do you mean, a case?" Mrs. Givings asked, sounding confused.

"We're here to nab an outlaw," Buttercup said and giggled.

Mr. Checkers groaned. "There goes my reward. It's not bad enough that I lost out on the Jesse James reward, now this!"

Mrs. Albright gave him a soothing pat on the back. "There's only one reward that counts."

Amy turned to Mrs. Givings. "I know why they're here, but what are you ladies doing out at this time of night?"

"One of our church members has a sick little girl," Mrs. Givings explained, "and we were praying for her."

Amy's breath caught. *Georgia?*

As if to read her mind Mrs. Givings leaned closer and whispered, "Her daughter's fever broke and the doctor said she'll do just fine."

"That's good news," Amy whispered back with relief.

Checkers let out a loud sneeze. Startled, Buttercup flew forward and her chest practically landed in Mrs. Givings's face.

The churchwoman cried out. "Oh dear. If this gets back to the church, only God knows what it will do to my reputation."

"Don't worry," Miss Lillian said. "You can only lose your reputation once, and after tonight, you won't have one to worry about."

"Do you have a gun?" Buttercup asked, pulling out her own.

Mrs. Givings's mouth dropped open and her eyes widened behind her spectacles.

"No guns," the marshal said. "I mean it. No guns!" He confiscated Miss Lillian's gun first and demanded that Coral, Polly, and Buttercup give up their weapons, as well.

He turned to Amy. "Pinkerton is no longer

involved in the case. That means I'm in charge. Hand over the gun or I'll put you all in jail."

Amy gritted her teeth, but she pulled out her gun and slapped it soundly into his open palm. The night just kept getting worse.

"It's okay," Tom whispered, his breath warm on her ear. "I've got you covered."

CHAPTER 38

They waited.

Midnight came and went and still they waited. The temperature dropped and tempers flared. The full moon was now directly overhead and the alley was almost as light as day.

Coral snapped at Buttercup, "You're standing on my foot."

"That's because your elbow is in my back," Buttercup complained.

Checkers had stopped sneezing, but by that point he'd broken out in hives and his eyes watered.

"Maybe you ought to leave," Miss Lillian suggested.

"And let you get the reward?" He rubbed his eyes with his handkerchief. "Not on your tintype!"

Amy had lost patience long ago. "Quiet, all of you," she rasped. So help her, if her carefully laid plans were ruined she would personally wring each and every one of their necks.

Stakeouts were a necessary part of an operative's job. She had done more than her share through the years but never under such difficult conditions.

"This is so exciting," Mrs. Givings whispered, after only thirty seconds of blessed silence. "I still think we should use this opportunity to pray."

"Only if you promise to pray for a cup of hot tea," Buttercup said.

Mrs. Givings sniffed. "I can think of a lot of things you need, and tea isn't one of them."

"Shh."

They waited.

"I wish something would happen," Miss Lillian complained after a while. "We need our beauty rest."

"I'm hungry," Buttercup moaned.

They waited.

"W—what is that noise?" Polly asked.

"Sounds like crinkling paper," Checkers said, and all heads turned toward Buttercup.

"What? It's just a peppermint candy." She popped the sweet into her mouth and tossed the paper wrapper to the ground.

Tom laid a hand on Amy's shoulder. "I see something."

"Quiet, everyone." Amy dropped to the ground and peered around the corner. She saw it, too. A shadow; someone moved stealthily along the boardwalk toward the express office. She expected Monahan to arrive on horseback, not on foot. Apparently he was taking extra precautions.

"When do we catch him?" Miss Lillian whispered.

"Shh."

For several moments, no one said a word.

Tom reached for his firearm. "I think he's inside."

Flood pulled out his Peacemaker. "No guns," he hissed.

"What do you call that?" Coral asked.

"It's called 'I'm in charge.' "

"This is so exciting," Buttercup said and tittered.

"Get off my foot," Coral said in a harsh voice.

Minutes passed.

"What's taking so long?" Miss Lillian asked.

"Robberies take time," Checkers said. "Especially if you have to break into a safe."

"Doesn't he know his own combination?" Coral asked.

Checkers looked confused. "Good point."

"I think he's coming out," Tom said.

Flood moved to the head of the crowd. "Okay, men . . . and ah . . . ladies. Stay put. I'll let you know when it's safe." Ducking low, he ran out of the alley. "Put your hands up."

A shot rang out, and the marshal doubled over like an empty purse.

Polly screamed. Mrs. Givings gasped, and Miss Lillian swayed. Shouts filled the air as men began pouring out of the Golden Hind Saloon like frenzied ants.

Monahan moved away, and Amy rushed to the marshal's side. "Get him," she called to Tom, dropping to her knees. "Get Monahan!" A dark stain marked Flood's right shoulder. She pulled a handkerchief from her sleeve and pressed it against his wound to stem the bleeding.

Flood grimaced and said something, but his voice was lost in the scuffle that suddenly exploded around them as a fight broke out. Fists flew and the pounding of flesh was followed by grunts and groans.

She searched the mass of moving bodies, hoping to find a familiar face. "We need a doctor!" she called.

Checkers barreled into one of the men headfirst, his arms windmilling. One clumsy punch from his opponent and he jackknifed to the ground. Miss Lillian jumped off the

441

boardwalk onto someone's back and pounded him with her fists.

Straining her neck, Amy searched for Tom, spotting him heading for the express office, gun drawn. A man took a flying leap and landed on Tom's back. Heart sinking, she watched the two fall to the ground.

She grabbed Flood's firearm. "Sorry, Marshal, but the one in charge is the one who didn't take a bullet." She stood and glanced at the express office but couldn't find Tom amid the chaos. Nor was Monahan anywhere in sight. Stepping around two fighting men, she scrambled up the wooden steps to the boardwalk. *Where was he?*

CHAPTER 39

Crouching low, Amy darted past Harry's Gun and Bakery Shoppe and paused at the corner. A sign overhead swayed back and forth in the soft breeze. Judging by the shouts and curses behind her, the brawl was still in full swing.

Compared to her derringer, the colt Peacemaker weighed a ton, but she kept it aimed in front of her.

A movement ahead made her stop short. Was that Monahan, or was the moonlight playing tricks on her? She jumped off the boardwalk and ran toward the church. The gate to the cemetery stood ajar.

Senses alert, she moved cautiously along the side of the church, staying close to the bushes. The iron gate creaked to her touch. The slight wind rustled the trees. Shadows flitted across the gravestones and her spirits sank. Monahan could be anywhere.

Something hard suddenly rammed against

the back of her head. "Drop the gun."

Mouth dry, she laid the Peacemaker down on the ground and turned. For a moment she thought the moonlight was playing tricks on her. "Mr. Studebaker?"

He looked almost as surprised to see her as she was to see him, but the barrel of his gun never wavered. "Amy?"

She let out a sigh of relief. He had complained earlier of a sore throat, which is why she hadn't recognized his voice at first.

"You near scared the life out of me. I thought you were —" She caught a whiff of tobacco and a horrid realization washed over her. "*You're* the waxwing!"

He reared back, startled. "What?"

"The waxwing. It's a bird with a mask." Suddenly, all the missing pieces fell into place. It was Studebaker seen that night at the cellar door, not Monahan — an easy mistake since both men were similar in height and weight and even sounded alike. Buttercup had made a similar mistake. The man she heard Rose arguing with was Studebaker, not Monahan.

"*You're* the Gunnysack Bandit!" That's what had bothered her earlier in the parlor: Monahan's cigar had a distinct odor far different from what she'd recalled from that night.

"I don't know what you're talking about." His voice grew harsher, as if his throat were lined with sand. "Do I look like I'm wearing a gunnysack? What are you doing here, anyway?"

"I'm a Pinkerton detective."

An incredulous look crossed his face. "A Pink —" he croaked and stopped to clear his throat. "But you're a —"

"A woman. I know." Outlaws could be so predictable at times. "If you're not who I think you are, put down that gun."

The gun stayed firmly in place. "You should have stuck with fortune-telling." He held up a jute sack. "You said I had a lot of notes in my future, and here they are." He grinned. "*Bank*notes."

She frowned. "How did you know about the money?"

"I heard you tell Monahan his ships were coming in. I've been in his office enough times to know about the painting on the wall."

Not only did Studebaker have a loud singing voice when his throat wasn't acting up, he apparently had big ears, as well.

"You can't get away, you know. Not this time. You're going to pay for what you've done."

An evil smile inched across his face.

"That's where you're wrong. The Gunny-sack Bandit is dead. Long may he rest in peace."

"That's what you wanted us to believe, and you almost got away with it." Had he not been so greedy and decided to rob again, he *would* have gotten away with it. "You stole enough money through the years to make you a rich man."

"Very," he croaked.

"But you were almost caught during the last robbery, and you killed a bank guard. That's when you decided that maybe your luck was about to run out. So you decided to call it quits."

"Nothing like quitting when you're ahead." His voice grew rougher but he continued. "All my life I've worked my fingers to the bone in jobs I hated. Now I get to do what *I* want to do."

"Like take singing lessons," she said. Something suddenly occurred to her. "Only it wasn't voice lessons you were after. You were looking for something. Rose's journal, no doubt." Now she knew who had searched her room. "You were also keeping your eye on the one person who knew you were the bandit."

He neither confirmed nor denied her allegations. "It seems you have me at a disadvantage."

"You're the one with the gun."

"Yes, but you know a lot about me, and I know so little about you. Did you talk to — ?"

"Rose?" she asked. "Dave Colton? Or someone else?"

He waved his gun. "No matter. They're both gone to the great by-and-by, and you're about to meet them there."

"You won't get away with it. Too many people know Monahan was robbed tonight."

"Yes, but they'll think that he did it. I made certain of that."

"Just like you made certain that Dave Colton was blamed for your crimes," she said. "Is that why you killed him?"

"I killed him because he knew too much and was about to turn me in. You can blame Rose for that. One night I had too much to drink, and I said things that made her suspicious. While I was passed out, she went through my belongings and found incriminating evidence — a map of a bank and list of robberies. She showed them to her beau. That's when he started nosing around."

"So you had to kill him. But that still left Rose."

"She wasn't a problem. I told her that if she said a word to anyone, Dave Colton's kid would never see the light of day."

Amy stared at him. Supposedly only Coffey knew about the baby prior to Rose's death. So how did Studebaker find out?

"You'd be amazed what a woman will do to protect a young one," he added.

She knew firsthand the sacrifices a woman would make to protect a child. Isn't that what she'd done in St. Louis when she'd walked away from Cissy? Protect her? Same as Georgia had done when she'd knocked on Miss Lillian's door.

He pointed his gun in the direction of the cemetery. "Move, and don't try any funny business."

Just as she started toward the iron gate, something whizzed by, missing her head by barely an inch. It struck the church wall hard and bounced back to hit Studebaker on the temple.

"Ow!"

All at once a barrage of objects flew out of nowhere. He fought them off with frantic thrusts of his arms. Dodging low, Amy grabbed his wrist and they wrestled for the gun. She kneed him where it counted, and he loosened his hold.

"Drop the gun!" Tom's voice was music to her ears.

Still smarting from the low blow, Studebaker let his gun fall to the ground. Blood trickled from his forehead where he'd been hit by flying items.

"I thought you'd never get here," she said.

Tom moved into the moonlight. "Sorry, I was what you might call occupied." He gave her a crooked grin.

The marshal hobbled up behind him, his arm in a makeshift sling. "Here." He tossed a pair of handcuffs to Tom with his one good arm. Tom snapped them around Studebaker's wrists.

Miss Lillian limped toward them followed by her girls and the three churchwomen, all in stocking feet.

"We got him!" Miss Lillian cried.

Amy handed the marshal his firearm and picked a velvet slipper off the ground. "Shoes? You threw shoes?"

The madam shrugged. "The marshal said no guns."

Mrs. Givings giggled and glanced around. "Anyone see a pair of high-button boots?"

"Over here," Mrs. Albright called from behind a bush.

Tom holstered his gun and cupped Amy's elbow in his hand. "You all right?"

She grinned up at him. "I'm fine. You?"

He rubbed his jaw. "Except for a couple of bruises, I couldn't be better." He picked up the gunnysack that Studebaker had dropped. "Look a here." He held up a packet of banknotes.

Mrs. Givings clucked her tongue. "Just think what the church could do with that much money."

Checkers limped up looking bedraggled. His suit coat was torn and his bow tie askew. "Does this mean I have to share the reward?"

Coral glared at him. "What are you talking about, reward? I don't see any of *your* shoes here."

"I'll decide who gets the reward," Flood said.

Polly walked up to the captive. "I hope you hang for what you did to Rose." She shoved him on the chest. "And even that will be too good for you."

Studebaker glowered but said nothing.

Polly stepped back and glanced at the others. "Why are you all staring at me?"

Amy squeezed her arm. "It's because you didn't stutter."

Polly's hands flew to her mouth. "I didn't, did I?"

"No, you didn't," Buttercup said, and she threw her arms around her. Even Coral gave Polly a quick pat on the back.

"I'll take it from here," Flood said. He

gave Amy a sheepish look. "If you ever get tired of working for Pinkerton, I could use someone like you."

It was probably as close to a compliment as he was likely to give, but that was okay. They caught the Gunnysack Bandit, and Tom's brother was now off the hook. That was enough for her.

"You better have the doctor look at that shoulder of yours," Miss Lillian said.

Flood nodded. "I will, just as soon as Studebaker here is behind bars." It was probably the most civil conversation he and the madam ever exchanged.

Amy helped the others find their shoes. She handed Coral a velvet slipper. "Thank you for your help."

Coral took the shoe without so much as a thank-you.

Buttercup hopped on one foot while she slipped on a satin slipper. "We were glad to help."

"That's what sisters are for," Polly said. "To help each other."

Amy felt a lump form in her throat. She never thought to call anyone *sister* again, and now suddenly she had a pack of them. God sure did have a funny sense of humor.

Moving away from the cemetery gate, the women formed a circle. Coral looked momentarily startled when Polly reached for her hand.

Smiling, Amy stepped forward to join them. Grasping Mrs. Albright's hand on one side and Miss Lillian's on the other, she closed the circle.

"Oh dear," Mrs. Albright said. "What would the church deacons say if they saw us now?"

"Don't worry," Polly said. "We're the *sole* of discretion." She laughed at her own joke.

Amy's gaze traveled around the circle with a thankful heart. The show of solidarity was not only surprising but significant.

Reaching out to one another could very well be the first step to reaching out to God. For the first time since coming to Miss Lillian's Parlor House, Amy felt hope for the women who worked there.

"Any room for a brother?" Tom asked.

The women laughed as he broke the link between Amy and Miss Lillian and took both their hands in his. For once, Miss Lillian didn't try to sell him anything.

The grasp of Tom's hand sent warm tremors up her arm. He winked at her and she smiled back.

Checkers threw up his arms. "Oh, why not?" Sniffling, he took his place between Coral and Buttercup and sneezed.

"What about you, Tin Star," Miss Lillian called. "Would you care to join us?"

"I don't need no more family. I've enough troubles of me own," Marshal Flood grumbled. Holding his Peacemaker in one hand, he tossed a nod in the direction of the jailhouse and ordered his prisoner to move.

After Flood hauled Studebaker away, Miss Lillian and Mrs. Givings left together, chatting away like two old friends. The others also drifted away, leaving Tom and Amy alone.

Unexpectedly, he put his hands at her waist and spun her about. She threw back her head and laughed, releasing all the worry and tension of the last few hours.

With a grin as wide as Texas, he lowered her to the ground, but his hands remained on her waist. "You did it."

She blushed. "We all did it."

"Just so you know, I don't think of you as a sister."

His heated gaze held her still. "And I don't think of *you* as a brother."

"I can't believe it's over," he said. "To think that Studebaker is the Gunnysack Bandit and Dave —"

"Really did turn over a new leaf." She gave him a teasing look. "I guess you could say it was a shoe-in."

He laughed. "Well, look a there." His face grew serious and his gaze locked with hers. The promise of a kiss hung between them, but just as he was about to capture her lips with his own, a horseman rode by, and he released her.

"I can't wait till you break the news to your nephew," she said to relieve the sudden tension between them.

He nodded and cleared his throat. "Now we can give his pa a proper burial in the family plot." He pulled a derringer out of his pocket. "I think this is yours."

She took it from him and slid it into her own pocket. "I — I guess I should start back. It's late."

He hesitated. "In my Ranger days, me and the boys celebrated whenever we captured a bad guy. So are you up for some coffee ice cream? I happen to know my way around the hotel kitchen."

The vision of him sneaking around the hotel kitchen in the middle of the night made her smile. "I'm always up for ice cream," she said, "but it's too soon to celebrate. Studebaker killed your brother, but he didn't kill Rose."

He frowned and drew back. "How do you know that?"

"Something he said."

His gaze sharpened. "If he didn't kill her, then who did?"

She raised up on her tiptoes and whispered in his ear, "Hummingbird."

CHAPTER 40

Jennifer sat at the old piano in Miss Lillian's parlor and the rippling tune of "Für Elise" filled the air. Her secret was out so there was no reason to pretend. Amy Gardner no longer existed.

Her fingers moving lightly up and down the keys belied the heaviness in her heart. Memories of her sister accompanied each note.

Her sister had explained that the trick to playing the piece correctly was to rotate the fingers up. That's not all her sister said.

"I haven't told anyone yet. Not even Mama."

There were many reasons why someone might want to keep news of an upcoming wedding secret. There were probably even more reasons to keep quiet about expecting a child, and Rose's baby was the one loose end that bothered her.

A footstep sounded behind her. The mirror over the piano told her who had entered the room, but she forced herself to play the piece to the end. She then scooted on the stool until her back faced the piano.

The housekeeper's feather duster stilled. "Want me to come back later?" she asked, her expression bland beneath a starched cap.

"No, that's all right, Beatrice. I've finished practicing." She watched the woman work her way around the room, flicking her feather duster this way and that, like a hummingbird darting from flower to flower.

"I suppose you heard. Mr. Studebaker is in jail."

She couldn't see Beatrice's face, but her hand stilled for an instant before she continued dusting. "So I heard."

"He confessed to everything except one thing . . . Rose's murder."

Beatrice kept dusting.

"Isn't it strange how little things can nag at a person?" Beatrice made no response so Jennifer continued. "Take for example Rose's baby. No one but Coffey knew she was with child, and she swore she told no one else. So the question is, how did Studebaker find out?"

Beatrice glanced over her shoulder but said nothing, and Jennifer continued.

"My guess is that you found her journal

one day while cleaning her room and read it."

Beatrice's eyes narrowed. "I would never do such a thing."

"Oh, but you would and you did. That's how you knew about the baby. I thought it was odd that Rose didn't write about being with child and hardly mentioned the man she hoped to marry. Then I remembered that some of the pages were missing from the journal. Pages *you* tore out."

Rose must have decided to write in code after she discovered pages of her diary missing. From that moment on, her unborn child was referred to as "Chickadee." It was actually quite a clever ruse.

"Rose's journal contained her suspicions about Studebaker, and you saw this as an opportunity. You decided to feed Studebaker information, provided he pay you. That's how he knew Colton was onto him. It's also how he knew about Rose's baby."

Beatrice kept dusting and Jennifer continued. "It worked, but not for long. After the Hampton bank fiasco, Studebaker decided to call it quits. That meant no more money for you. That's when you decided to look for Rose's diary again. You hoped to use it to blackmail Studebaker into paying you more.

"So you sneaked into Rose's room. She caught you, and you hit her over the head."

Beatrice swiped her feather duster over a tabletop.

"After killing Rose, you couldn't find the journal, at least not that night. It didn't show up until later when you were cleaning Rose's room. Miss Lillian was with you so you had no choice but to turn it over to her. What you didn't know at the time is that it wouldn't have done you any good. Rose wrote in code, and the birds represented real people. You were the hummingbird. You're also the person who hit me over the head in the cellar."

She should have known it was Beatrice by the lack of fragrance in the cellar that night. Beatrice and Coffey were the only two women in the house who didn't drench themselves with perfume — and Coffey always smelled of onions and vanilla.

"The morning after you assaulted me I saw you in the kitchen, and you looked like you'd seen a ghost. I thought it was gunfire that scared you, but it wasn't, was it? It was seeing me."

Beatrice spun around, her face an ugly mask. "You can't prove any of this."

"I don't have to. As you know, Mr. Studebaker enjoys singing, and I can't tell you how much we've enjoyed his recent song."

"Why, that no good, double-crossing —"

Realizing what she'd said, a panicked look crossed Beatrice's face. Dropping her feather duster she ran, but Tom and the marshal blocked her way. Standing next to the two men were Miss Lillian, Coral, Polly, and Buttercup. Each held a shoe over her head ready to throw.

Flood unclipped the handcuffs from his belt and snapped them around Beatrice's wrists. "I said no weapons."

Buttercup slipped her foot into her shoe. "You said no *guns.*"

Miss Lillian glared at her housekeeper and looked about to clobber her with the heel of her shoe. "I can't believe that you killed Rose."

"She killed her all right," Jennifer said. "She's the one Rose called Hummingbird."

"Not any longer." Tom gave a grim nod. "From now on she'll be known as jailbird."

"Are we done now?" Flood asked. "Or is there someone else I need to arrest?"

"I think that'll do it," Jennifer said. "For now."

Miss Lillian's expression dropped along with her shoe. "There must be someone else. Otherwise, what will I do with my new-found detective skills?"

■ ■ ■ ■

"What I don't understand," Tom said later as Jennifer sat with him in the hotel dining room sharing a dish of coffee ice cream, "is why Studebaker took singing lessons. It's obvious he can't sing. So what was he doing? Keeping an eye on Beatrice?"

"Perhaps. But I also think he was worried that Rose might have confided her suspicions to someone else," she said. "Dave was a problem and had to be stopped. Rose, too. Her death must have been a great relief to him."

"Except that still left Beatrice."

"Yes, but he must have known she killed Rose, so he had something to hold over her head."

"He could have just gotten rid of her like he did Dave," Tom said.

"Yes, but don't forget she was a housekeeper. Her death would have carried more weight than a mere harlot's and was bound to gain more attention. That's the last thing Studebaker wanted."

"And the typed note found on my brother?"

"Typed on the typewriter found in Studebaker's home."

461

Tom blew out his breath. "Thank God it's over. Now the town can rest easy."

She sighed. Funny, but it didn't feel like it was over. It felt like there was still work to be done — God's work. "I just wish —"

He studied her. "Go on."

"I wish there was something I could do to persuade my *adopted* sisters to quit what they're doing and follow the Lord." Some madams managed to retire and go on to live respectable lives, but most good-time girls fell into poverty and despair. Some even took their own lives.

Tom studied her. "People can't change unless they want to change."

She set her spoon down and dabbed her mouth with her napkin. "That's just it. I believe they *do* want to change but don't know how. It's not easy for a woman to earn an honest living. Even secretary jobs are almost always held by men."

"So what's the answer?" he asked.

"Education. But it may be too late for them. Coral and Buttercup don't even know how to read." She would never forget the joyful expressions on the women's faces the night they captured Studebaker. They even walked and talked with more confidence. Polly had mostly stopped stuttering, and on that glorious night her words had flowed like music.

Tom set his spoon down. "Times are changing. More women *are* getting educated. There's even a female ranch owner in Texas."

"A ranch owner? How do you feel about that?" People often resented women horning in on what was traditionally a man's job."

"Don't bother me none, long as her cattle don't bring in more than mine at market time."

"And women detectives?" she couldn't help but ask. "How do you feel about them?"

A faint twinkle glimmered in his eyes. "I'm willing to admit that women detectives have a few advantages over a man. For one thing, men look terrible in skirts."

She laughed. "Women are also more observant."

He quirked an eyebrow. "How so?"

She glanced around the dining room. No sign of Checkers, but the battling couple was at it again. "He forgot her birthday," she said, indicating the intense man and woman three tables away.

"How do you know?"

She smiled mysteriously. "A woman knows these things. And look over there. That drummer is unable to convince his companion to buy his product. That's because he's totally incompetent as a salesman."

Tom followed her gaze. "What makes you think that?"

"He's eating fruit pie without ice cream."

"Ah." He nodded. "A sure sign he couldn't sell water to a thirsty man."

She indicated another table with her spoon. "See that man and woman over there? I'm telling you, it won't work. Love is supposed to suppress the appetite, but she's already on her third dish of ice cream."

"What about the other couple?" he asked. "My guess is that he wants to lasso in a partner, but he's not sure if the lady wants to be roped."

"What?" Her gaze swung around the room. "Where?" Her eyes met his and she caught her breath. "You don't mean . . . You're not —"

He leaned forward and took her hand in his. "You once asked me why I cared. I didn't have the answer then, but I do now. The moment I saw Studebaker's gun pointed at you was the moment I knew how much you meant to me."

"I — I don't know what to say," she stammered.

"Then I'll make it easy for you. Say you'll

marry me, Jennifer."

Her heart squeezed tight and it was all she could do to breathe. "I don't think that's a good idea." She pulled her hand away and laid it on her lap. "So much has happened."

"Your sister?" He sat back and his eyes brimmed with concern.

"It's not just that." How could she make him understand what she was having trouble understanding herself?

Arms on the table, he leaned forward. "I'm not saying we have to marry right now, today. We can wait till next week if you like."

He was joking, of course, but she wasn't in the mood to laugh. Better to just say it and get it out there. "I can't marry you," she whispered hoarsely. "Not today. Not next week. Not anytime."

Her words hung between them for several painful moments before he spoke. "That's it? That's all you have to say?"

She swallowed the lump in her throat. "You said you were a simple man."

"That's before I fell in love. Now things are more complicated."

She sat back. *Love!* He said love. Why did he have to say that? She pressed her hands together on her lap and tried to calm her rampaging emotions.

"Marrying you would mean . . ."

"Giving up your job, I know." He held her gaze. "I'll be honest with you. The ranch is a pretty poor substitute for the Pinkerton National Detective Agency. The only outlaws we have are the four-legged kind. Adventure is delivering a foal in the middle of the night and 'seeing the world' is what we call riding into town. The only thing I can give you is love. That's all this cowboy's got."

Her heart lurched madly at the word *love,* and she wanted so much to say yes. Yes, she would marry him. Yes, she would give anything for the privilege of being his wife. But the words stuck in her throat.

He regarded her quizzically. "I thought you might have feelings for me, too."

"Oh Tom, I do, I do."

The muscle at his jaw tightened. "But your job means more."

"It's not my job," she said miserably. If only it were that simple. "It's not that important to me anymore." Hard to believe but true. After finding Cissy, she no longer felt compelled to keep searching. Or maybe she was just tired of chasing around the country after criminals.

"Is it Davey?" He knitted his brow. "I have no right to ask you to raise another man's son, but I thought you liked him."

"I *do* like him. He's not the problem." During the short time she'd known him, the boy managed to carve out a place in her heart.

"Then it must be me," he persisted.

"No, Tom, it's me." Her voice broke as she tried to piece together her fractured thoughts. "Staying at Miss Lillian's taught me some things about myself. I now know how important fidelity is to me. I don't think I could ever again trust a man, any man, to be faithful." She lowered her lashes. "I would always wonder if . . ."

"Go on."

She lifted her gaze to his. "If you were cheating on me . . . If our marriage was built on lies and deceit, I don't know how I could live with that."

He looked at her long and hard. "What you're saying is you don't trust me."

"Not just you, Tom. Any man. Miss Lillian said you can't keep a good man good."

"And you believed her?"

"I saw it with my own eyes." Everything bad her father and brothers did she blamed on Cissy's disappearance, and that included her father's unfaithfulness to her mother. Not only did people try to justify their own bad behavior but also the bad behavior of others.

She was trembling now but forced herself to continue. "Parlor house guests included family men — husbands and fathers. Churchgoers. So-called pillars of the community."

"I would never cheat on you," he said, and the sincerity in his voice almost unraveled her resolve.

"You say that now. But what about five or ten years down the road? Will you still be faithful then?"

"If you can't trust me, then trust my faith in God." His low, deep voice shimmered with intensity. "I would never do anything to you that would go against God or His commandments."

She wanted to believe him. If only she hadn't glanced at the battling couple across the way. The woman had forgiven her man yet again, but the way he looked at the pretty girl at the next table indicated the couple's troubles were far from over. With this thought came unsettling memories.

A woman slapping her on the face. *"That's for my Charlie!"*

The pain that caused a young boy to toss a brick through the parlor house window.

"You can't keep a good man good."

She turned her gaze back to Tom. "I want to trust you, Tom, I do." Each spoken word felt like a rock that had to be pushed out. "But I don't think I have it in me to trust any man." They were the hardest words she'd ever spoken but perhaps the most necessary.

She expected an argument: something, anything. None came, and they ate the rest of the ice cream in tense silence.

"Say something," she said at last.

"What do you want me to say?" he asked, his voice clipped.

"How about 'I'll always be faithful to you no matter what'?"

"Would you believe me?" He tilted his head with a beseeching look. "Would you?"

"I don't know. Maybe." Tears sprang to her eyes. "No."

He grimaced as if suddenly stabbed. "That's what I thought." He signaled the waiter for the check. His eyes met hers, and the remoteness in their blue depths nearly broke her heart.

"I'm sorry," she said, her voice hoarse.

"Not as sorry as I am."

CHAPTER 41

Jennifer paced her hotel room. The walls felt like they were closing in. If something didn't happen soon she would scream. It had been a week — seven long days! — since she sent a telegram to Pinkerton requesting another assignment and still no word.

William Pinkerton wasn't happy when she turned down her last job to find her sister, and he made no bones about it. Nor did catching the Gunnysack Bandit earn her any favors with him. The agency was officially off the case and received neither money nor credit for the outlaw's capture.

The uncertainty of her job accounted for only part of her misery. She had to be out of her mind to turn down Tom's proposal. What was wrong with her? His being unfaithful in the future couldn't possibly be any more painful than the loneliness she experienced now. The worst part was his acceptance.

He could have tried to change her mind, fought for her, even. But no, he'd simply left town without saying good-bye. He said he loved her, but what kind of love gives up that easily?

She was right to turn him down. If only it didn't hurt so much . . .

A tap sounded at the door, and her heart thudded. Tom? She threw the door open and it was all she could do not to let her disappointment well up in tears. It was Scott Cunningham, the boy who had thrown a brick through Miss Lillian's window, but he obviously didn't recognize her.

"A telegram for Miss Gardner," he said.

"I'm Miss Gardner." The use of her assumed name told her immediately it was from Pinkerton headquarters. She took the telegram from him and reached into her pocket for a coin. "How's your father?" Miss Lillian had said she hadn't seen hide or hair of Mr. Cunningham or any of the men since the night Jennifer read their fortunes. For some odd reason, the madam didn't seem all that upset about the sudden drop in business.

If Scott was surprised by the question, he didn't show it. "He's okay. He and Ma are away on a trip. When they come back, me

471

and him are going fishing," he said with none of his previous anger.

She smiled and handed him the coin. "Hope you catch some big ones."

She closed the door and ripped open the telegram. She was being dispatched to Boston to shadow a man suspected of committing a series of bank robberies.

Normally, starting a new assignment filled her with excitement, but today she felt nothing, only numbness. She didn't need a crystal ball to see that the future that once held so much promise now looked bleak.

Relieved at having something to do — a plan, a goal — she lifted her carpetbag onto the bed and began stuffing it with her few belongings. If she hurried she could still catch the late train out of Goodman.

She was halfway through her packing when it hit her: she didn't want to go to Boston. She didn't want to track down yet another criminal. The thought of donning another disguise and pretending to be someone she wasn't sickened her. She wanted to be the woman reflected in Tom's eyes. That woman was real and honest and true, the woman God meant her to be.

She didn't know what she would do, but one thing was clear: her searching days were over.

A loud knock startled her. Puzzled, she opened the door a crack. "Miss Lillian!"

The madam pushed her way into the room, glanced at the carpetbag, and reeled about in a cloud of red taffeta. The feathers on her hat shook like the feathers of an indignant hen. "Thank goodness you haven't left town yet."

"I was just getting ready to."

"You can't go yet. Not until you do something about Mr. Colton."

A stabbing pain ripped through her at the sound of Tom's name. "What are you talking about? He's gone. He left town."

"Then who is that sitting in my parlor?"

"What?"

"Been sitting there day and night for five days. Said you ran him off and he's not leaving until you come to your senses."

Jennifer stared at her, not sure she'd heard right. "I . . . I don't know what to say."

"Well you better figure it out because I'm at my rope's end. I can't get anything done with him there. You put a handsome man like that in a house full of hens and feathers are bound to fly."

Jennifer blinked. "You're not saying that Coral and the others are —"

"You can't blame them for trying." Miss Lillian lifted a knowing eyebrow. "You love him, and don't go saying you don't. It's written all over your face."

"Guess that's what I get for not wearing face paint."

Miss Lillian made a gesture with her hand. "Trust me, there's not enough paint in the world to hide the look on your face when I mentioned his name. So why are you being so muleheaded?"

Jennifer threw up her hands. "He didn't even fight for me. He just took off without a word."

"Didn't you hear what I just said? He's been fighting for you for five days with no end in sight." Miss Lillian regarded her like a wayward schoolgirl. "You'd be a fool to let him go."

Jennifer ran her hands up and down her arms. "You once said you couldn't keep a good man good."

Miss Lillian looked her straight in the eye, and her expression softened. "Is that what this is all about?"

Jennifer nodded. "After living at the parlor house, I don't know if I have it in me to trust a man. Any man."

"You can't trust just *any* man." Miss Lillian gave her head a vigorous nod. "But you can trust Tom Colton. Mark my words."

■ ■ ■ ■

Jennifer walked into the parlor, and it was just as Miss Lillian had described. Tom sat on a settee, arms folded. Not even his wrinkled clothes and whiskered chin robbed him of his good looks. Her heart leaped at the sight of him.

"Tom, what are you doing here? What's going on?"

He pushed his hat back and leveled her with his gaze. "You said you couldn't trust me, so I put myself in temptation's way to prove that either I'm the dumbest person alive or the most faithful. Take your pick."

"I vote for dumb," Coral said, glowering at Jennifer.

Buttercup pushed Coral away. "Just because he didn't fall for your advances doesn't mean he's dumb." Hand on her chest, she gave a wistful smile. "He loves her."

Coral rolled her eyes and her mouth puckered in disgust. "Like I said, dumb."

Jennifer gazed at Tom and couldn't believe what he'd done. "You've been here for five days?"

"And nights," Miss Lillian added.

Tom gave a sheepish look. "I didn't know

how else to prove that you're the only woman for me. The only woman I'll ever love and ever hope to be with."

Jennifer's eyes filled with tears. "I — I don't know what to say."

Miss Lillian threw her hands up. "Well, you better figure it out or I'm going to have to start charging him rent."

All eyes turned to Jennifer.

And a cry of pure joy broke from her lips. "Yes!"

All gazes swung back to Tom. "Yes? Does that mean — ?"

"It means yes! Yes, I want to marry you." She closed the distance between them. "It means yes, I want to be your wife." Somehow she ended up on his lap, her arms around his neck. "It means yes, I love you."

Polly and Buttercup clapped and Miss Lillian held out her hand. "That will be five dollars, please."

"For what?" Tom asked.

She pointed to the sign on the wall. "Showing affection is not allowed in the parlor."

Tom reached into his pocket and placed two five-dollar bills in Miss Lillian's outstretched hand. "Why so much?" she asked, looking pleased.

For answer, Tom pulled Jennifer close and

kissed her soundly, firmly, and oh-so-thoroughly on the lips.

EPILOGUE

The sound of hammering greeted Jennifer as she approached the parlor house on foot. A ladder leaned against the porch roof and a new sign hung from the eaves reading MISS LILLIAN'S PRIVATE DETECTIVE AGENCY AND FINE BOOTS.

She couldn't believe her eyes. What in the world . . . ?

The door to the house flew open and Miss Lillian stepped onto the porch and waved. "How do you like it?"

"I'm dumbfounded." Amy hardly recognized Miss Lillian in the sedate gray skirt and white tailored shirtwaist. Her hair was still a ghastly red, but today it was confined in a ladylike bun that even Mrs. Givings and her friends would approve.

Jennifer let herself through the gate and started along the path. "Does this mean you're no longer running a guesthouse?"

"That's exactly what it means," Miss Lillian said. "I decided to take my share of the reward money and start a new business in memory of Rose."

The news made Jennifer want to jump with joy. "I'm sure that would have made her very happy."

"Yes, and sleuthhounding looks to be more profitable. I've already got several clients. Unlike your former boss, I don't have any trouble accepting jobs from suspicious wives." Miss Lillian lowered her voice. "I have a feeling that with me and my detectives on the case we're going to start seeing a lot of good men in Goodman."

"Maybe there'll even be one for you," Jennifer teased.

"I doubt that, but I suppose anything's possible. Speaking of which, you're not going to believe this, but Monahan just hired me as his official fortune-teller."

"Monahan did that? But he doesn't even believe in fortune-telling." Jennifer still felt bad for suspecting him of being the Gunnysack Bandit. She now knew that he came by his wealth through prudent investments and a fortunate marriage.

"He does now. After you told him about the storm at sea, he sent a wire canceling a shipment of goods his wife ordered special for their new house. It was a good thing, too, on account of the hurricane."

Jennifer shook her head in disbelief. "There was a hurricane?"

"Yes, and the ship sank."

Jennifer couldn't believe her ears. "Incredible!"

The front door sprang open and Mrs. Givings stepped out of the house, followed by Buttercup and Polly.

The day just kept getting stranger. Jennifer leaned toward Miss Lillian and whispered, "What is Mrs. Givings doing here?"

"She's now working for me," Miss Lillian whispered back.

Jennifer drew back. "Are you telling me that Mrs. Givings —"

"Detective Givings," the churchwoman said and giggled like a schoolgirl. "Investigating is so much more exciting than quilting."

Polly was all smiles as she turned to show off her new attire. "I never thought I could be a real d–detective." In her tailored blue high-collared dress she looked as proper as a schoolmarm. Her scrubbed, shiny face no longer looked sad, and with only an occasional stutter, she sounded more confident.

Buttercup nodded and beamed. Her navy-blue frock downplayed her weight and a light seemed to shine from within. "Detective *Betty-Lou* at your service." She smiled and added, "No mirror needed."

"Oh Buttercup. I mean Betty-Lou." Jennifer threw her arms around her. Instead of the usual heavy perfume, today Betty-Lou smelled as fresh as a spring garden.

Jennifer released her. "What about Coral?"

Betty-Lou exchanged a glance with Polly. "I'm afraid Coral isn't ready to change her ways."

Jennifer lifted her gaze to the second floor and a curtain moved in one of the windows. "God's not ready to give up on her yet, and neither am I. Promise me that none of you will either."

"We'll save her yet," Mrs. Givings assured her. "Don't you worry none, you hear?"

Just then Tom drove up in a rented horse and buggy. "Better hurry," he called. "We don't want to miss the train."

After Jennifer embraced each woman in turn, Miss Lillian walked her to the gate. "You caught yourself a good one, there," she said. "Even though you never did master the fine art of walking."

Jennifer laughed. "I have a feeling I'll be doing more riding on the ranch than walking."

Miss Lillian patted her on the arm. "I

don't guess I can talk you into staying. Business is booming, and I could use a couple more good detectives."

"Thank you for the offer, but from now on I'm devoting myself to being a wife and mother." She gave Miss Lillian another hug before joining Tom in the buggy.

She took one last look at the old house as they pulled away. Everyone waved and wished them Godspeed. "Hurry back!"

"We will." Odd as it seemed, Jennifer felt like she was leaving home.

Tom laid a hand on her lap. "Why so serious all of a sudden?"

"I was just thinking how I came here to find an outlaw and ended up finding a whole new life instead." She snuggled close to him and laid her head on his shoulder. "God sure does work in mysterious ways." He also showed up in the most unlikely places.

Something shiny caught her eye. "Are those new boots?" She leaned over for a better look. "Is that a rose?" She couldn't believe it. "You let Miss Lillian talk you into buying new boots?"

"Three pairs," he said.

"What!"

He flashed a sheepish grin. "I'm good, honey, but not *that* good. Five days of listening to Miss Lillian's sales pitches made hay out of this cowboy's resistance."

She threw back her head and laughed. "I'm just surprised she didn't talk you into singing lessons."

"Eh."

"What? Oh no, don't tell me."

For answer he opened his mouth and serenaded her all the way to the train station.

DISCUSSION QUESTIONS

If every man was as true to his country as
he is to his wife — God help the USA.
— Needlepoint in a San Francisco brothel,
1891*

1. Jennifer/Amy didn't expect to find God
   in a bordello. Can you think of a time in
   your life where you found God where you
   least expected?
2. Posing as a woman of easy virtue was the
   hardest job Jennifer ever encountered. Not
   only was she forced to dress in a way that
   went against her Christian beliefs, she also
   had to keep quiet about God. How do you
   think this challenged or strengthened her
   faith?
3. Jennifer's disguise made her feel like she
   was an outsider and not welcome in polite
   society or even the church. Have you ever
   felt alone and isolated? How is the best
   way to reach out to someone who might

feel like this?

4. Denial is a powerful coping mechanism. Rather than face the fact that she was a brothel owner, Miss Lillian surrounded herself with various legitimate enterprises and insisted she was in the hospitality business. Denial can help us cope with distressing situations, but it can also keep us from receiving God's healing grace. What are some of the ways that we can recognize and deal with denial in ourselves and others?

5. Jennifer believed that everyone had a personal north stemming from a childhood trauma or early memory. Her personal north was the night her sister vanished. Buttercup's personal north was the day she was robbed of her innocence. What are the dangers of letting earthly matters become our compass? What are some of the ways that we can make God our one true north?

6. Who was your favorite character and why?

7. Tom wanted to believe that his brother had changed. Do you believe it's possible for a person to change? Why or why not?

8. Which character underwent the biggest transformation during the course of the book?

9. Do you think Coral has it in her to

change? What do you think it will take?

10. Jennifer spent years searching for her sister. It's why she became a detective. In what ways do you think this quest kept her from finding true love? How do you think the story would have ended had Jennifer not found Cissy?

11. In what ways did staying at Miss Lillian's help Jennifer unlock the mystery of her sister's disappearance?

12. Did you agree with Jennifer's choice not to tell her sister the truth about the past? Why or why not?

13. In what ways did God work through Jennifer to change Miss Lillian and her girls?

14. Birds hold a valuable key to the mystery, but they are also a metaphor for faith. As one character puts it, God gave birds the gift of flight because they have perfect faith. What are some of the things we can do to perfect our own faith and move closer to the Lord?

15. A writer finds inspiration in the most unexpected places. Upon watching a group of young children of all nationalities hold hands in unity and joy, I wanted to re-create the scene in my book. When the women clasped hands, the walls separating them from God and each other

came tumbling down — a "Jericho" moment. Name a Jericho moment in your life.

*The needlepoint quote was published in
Pistol-Packin' Madams by Chris Enss.

DEAR READERS,

After reading about the first known female detective, Kate Warne, the idea for my Undercover Ladies series popped into my head.

Kate worked for the Pinkerton National Detective Agency from 1856 to her death in 1868. Since women were not allowed to join the police department until 1890, the firm's founder Allan Pinkerton was well ahead of his time in hiring her. Originally, he thought she was applying for a secretary job, but she convinced him to hire her as a detective.

Quick to see the advantage of female detectives, he put her in charge of the Pinkerton Female Detective Bureau. Formed in 1860, the purpose of the female division was to "worm out secrets" by means unavailable to male detectives. She also managed the Pinkerton Washington department during the war.

Little is known about Kate's early life. She

was supposedly a widow when Allan Pinkerton hired her, which may or may not be true. Her job was often to elicit sympathy and therefore confessions from the criminal element, and widowhood might have been part of her charade.

No known photos exist of her, but Allan described her as a "brown-haired woman, graceful of movement and self-possessed."

A master of disguise, Kate could change her accent as readily as she could change her appearance, and her "Southern belle" disguise helped save president-elect Abraham Lincoln's life.

After verifying a plot to assassinate him, Kate wrapped Lincoln in a shawl and passed him off as her invalid brother, thus assuring his safety as he traveled by train to Washington, DC. Kate never slept the whole time Lincoln was in her charge. This may or may not have been the inspiration behind the Pinkerton logo: *We never sleep.*

Since the Great Chicago Fire of 1871 wiped out Pinkerton records, little is known about those early days. What *is* known is that Kate caused trouble between Allan and his son Robert. The two argued over Kate's expenses, which Robert thought were excessive. He didn't think it right for the company to pay for his father's "sordid affair."

There's no question that Allan cared deeply for Kate, but biographers are split on whether there actually *was* an affair. What's not in question is Kate's reputation as an excellent detective; her trailblazing efforts helped the Pinkerton Detective Agency rise to fame.

I hope you enjoyed reading Jennifer and Tom's story. The next book in the series, *Undercover Bride,* is a mail-order bride story with a twist. You can also find me on Facebook, Twitter, Pinterest, and Goodreads.

Until next time,
Margaret

ABOUT THE AUTHOR

Bestselling author **Margaret Brownley** has penned more than thirty novels. Her books have won numerous awards, including Readers' Choice and Award of Excellence. She's a former Romance Writers of America RITA finalist and has written for a TV soap. Happily married to her real-life hero, Margaret and her husband have three grown children and live in Southern California.

www.margaret-brownley.com